B.

D1154406

A SONG
IN
YOUR HEART

Pamela Evans

HEADLINE

First published in 1998
by HEADLINE BOOK PUBLISHING

10 9 8 7 6 5 4 3 2 1

British Library Cataloguing in Publication Data

Evans, Pamela
  A song in your heart
  1. London (England) – Fiction 2. Domestic fiction
  I. Title
  823.9'14[F]

  ISBN 0 7472 1892 7

Typeset by Avon Dataset Ltd, Bidford-on-Avon, Warks

Printed and bound in Great Britain by
Mackays of Chatham PLC, Chatham, Kent

HEADLINE BOOK PUBLISHING
A division of Hodder Headline PLC
338 Euston Road
London NW1 3BH

A SONG
IN
YOUR HEART

Chapter One

In the private functions room of a back-street pub in Fulham one Saturday in January 1957, a wedding reception was in progress. It was a small, low-budget affair, just a few close friends and relatives gathered together to celebrate the occasion.

'The ham's nice and tasty, love,' remarked the father of the bride, Hal Miller, to his wife Winnie, who was sitting beside him at a large communal table.

'Not bad for the price, I suppose,' she said, glad of a few words with her husband while their guests were chattering among themselves. 'The mashed potato's lumpy, though.'

'Mine's all right,' reassured Hal, a tall, amiable man with a ruddy complexion and dark, greying hair. His most notable feature was his unflappable nature, which was useful to him in his work as a bookings clerk at Paddington station.

'This is vastly different to the wedding I had in mind for our eldest daughter,' said Winnie, a dumpy woman whose anxious disposition tended to overshadow her warm heart. A pillar of respectability, she was staid in appearance, her mousy-brown hair set in tight symmetrical waves around a shiny, plump face which bore no trace of cosmetic embellishment. Still wearing her outdoor clothes because the room was draughty, she was dressed in her best tweed coat and a new red hat purchased especially for the occasion.

'It's only natural for you to want a posh wedding for both our daughters. Most mothers do,' Hal said, turning to her, his hand touching her arm in a comforting gesture, his warm brown eyes meeting her worried grey ones. 'But you've done ever so well to get this do organised at such short notice.'

'You think so?'

'Yeah, I really do,' he said, with strong emphasis because his wife's confidence was more fragile than her manner sometimes indicated.

'I suppose you get what you pay for – and lumpy potato is part of the deal when you do it on the cheap,' she said.

'Look, love, eating out is a treat for all of us here; no one is gonna worry about a few lumps in the mashed potato.'

'I hope not.'

'Just stop worrying and try to enjoy yourself,' he said, patting her hand.

1

'It isn't just the cheap wedding, Hal,' Winnie continued darkly. 'It's the tackiness that goes with it . . . the stigma.'

'He *has* married her, so there'll be nothing like that.'

'There'll be gossip,' she said sagely. 'Always is when someone gets married in a hurry.'

'If there is it'll all be forgotten by the time the baby's born, 'cause they'll be an old married couple by then.'

'There is that,' Winnie said, but she couldn't restrain a wistful sigh.

My daughter is worth more than a shabby do like this, she thought, casting her eye around the dismal room with its fusty miasma of stale beer, old cigarette smoke and boiled cabbage. The wallpaper was muddy-maroon with raised cream flowers turned beige with age, and the bumpy brown lino looked as though it had been there since the year dot. Gill should have got married in style, with church bells and bridesmaids and a reception in a big hall with dancing and a band. She would have, too – had it not been for Arnie Briscoe.

A pretty girl in her eighteenth year with an office job and music qualifications, Gill could have done well for herself. But what sort of future did she have to look forward to now? What kind of life would she have with an unskilled factory worker currently doing his national service in the army – a man who hadn't even had the decency to put an engagement ring on her finger before taking the sort of liberties that led to a cheapjack wedding with all the usual trappings abandoned for the sake of speed?

Mashing the offending potato determindly with her fork, it occurred to Winnie that she could count the times on one hand that she'd eaten out – apart from an occasional doughnut with a cup of tea in Lyon's when she was shopping. It was only over these last few years, since Britain had finally recovered from the war and a new wave of affluence had given the working classes the money and confidence to broaden their horizons, that people of their class had been able to afford meals in cafés and restaurants on a regular basis.

Winnie and Hal preferred to stay at home of an evening, though, especially now that they were the proud owners of a television set. They couldn't afford to go out very often anyway, not on what Hal earned; and Winnie hadn't been out to work in all her twenty-odd years of marriage. It had never been an option either of them even considered, because they had grown up in an age when a wife automatically stayed at home to look after the family. Even during the war years, when Hal had been away in the army and married women were forced out to work by law, as the mother of young children Winnie had been exempt.

Although she was usually shy and inhibited, Winnie's primal instincts overruled timidity when it came to defending her family; and unfortunately, in the resultant masking of her natural shyness, she had adopted a formidable air which often created a false impression.

'I could cheerfully throttle that Arnie Briscoe for what he's done to our Gill,' she said to Hal under her breath.

'Shush, Win,' he admonished in a hushed voice. 'That sort of talk isn't gonna help anybody, especially today.'

'But a third-rate wedding like this for Gill . . . She should have had a white dress and time to collect a bottom drawer.'

'I agree with you, but this is the way it's worked out and there's nothing we can do about it,' Hal wisely pointed out. 'We've done all our shoutin' and hollerin' – the recriminations are over. They're married now.'

'More's the pity,' said Winnie, who had actually been stalwart these last few weeks despite her bitter disappointment.

'Arnie isn't so bad,' said Hal, who usually managed to see the best in people. He'd been devastated when the news of Gill's pregnancy had first broken, of course, and had given Arnie a thorough trouncing – but he had now accepted the situation and decided to make the best of things.

'She could have done a lot better, though.'

'Maybe she could. But he's her husband now and we have to accept him as one of the family.'

'I know that.' Winnie sliced a piece of ham without enthusiasm. 'But they're both so young, and he doesn't have any prospects . . .'

'They'll manage.'

'Just managing isn't good enough for our daughter,' Winnie said.

'Give Arnie a chance, he might surprise us all.'

'I can't see that happening.' She paused. 'I never thought Gill would let us down, you know.'

'Nor me. But these things happen,' Hal said, careful not to speak loud enough to be overheard. 'And she's obviously dotty about the bloke.'

'Totally besotted with him,' declared Winnie, her voice rising with feeling. 'She'll do anything he tells her.'

'Keep your voice down.'

'No one's listening to us,' she said, casting a swift glance around at the babbling guests. 'They're all too busy yapping.'

'You can't be too careful at a do like this,' Hal warned. 'We don't want any arguments breaking out and spoiling Gill's day.'

'What is there to spoil at a do like this?' Winnie said glumly.

'Give yourself *some* credit, Win. We've put on the best reception we could possibly afford – and you're the one who's done all the work, getting everything arranged at such short notice.'

'I didn't have any choice, did I, as you're at work all day.'

Despite the way she was speaking, Hal knew his wife had been an absolute diamond. Once she'd got over the initial shock she'd comforted Gill, thrown herself into the wedding arrangements, offered the couple a home with the family in Maisie Road, and robbed her precious post office savings – a small nest-egg built painstakingly from years of careful housekeeping – for Gill's wedding outfit. Although Winnie's manner was often abrasive – poor Arnie had been on the receiving end of it on more than one occasion since Gill's condition had become known – beneath his wife's redoubtable presence beat a heart of gold.

'But look around you, love,' Hal said. 'They're all having a smashing time – especially Gill. And all thanks to you.'

Winnie glanced towards the head of the table where the newly-weds were laughing together, completely engrossed in each other. 'Yeah, I suppose you're right.' She shrugged. 'You can only do your best with what you have, can't you? If they'd got engaged in the normal way and given us time to save up we'd have given her the works.'

'Course we would and Gill knows that. She's as happy as a queen with what we've put on for her today. It might not be the wedding of her dreams but it'll still be a day for her to remember.'

Looking at her daughter, Winnie swallowed hard on a lump in her throat. Gill looked so young and vulnerable, her small face turned eagerly towards her new husband, dark hair worn short with a floppy, uneven fringe. It was true what people said about her: she did have a look of Audrey Hepburn, with those huge brown eyes and heavy brows dominating her slender face. Winnie had to admit that she looked radiantly happy too, her cheeks brightly suffused against her fashionable scarlet suit. The much-maligned pillbox hat she'd worn dutifully to the register office had been removed; it seemed hats weren't popular with young women of Gill's generation.

'They're just like a couple o' kids playing at weddings,' murmured Winnie, blinking back the tears. 'I hope to God they've got the stamina to cope with reality, because they'll have plenty of that when the baby arrives.'

'Let's worry about that when the time comes, shall we?' said Hal, turning his attention back to his meal and lapsing into thought. Winnie was a dear, but she was like a dog with a bone over this wedding. Personally, Hal thought Gill and Arnie had what it took to make their marriage work. Admittedly Arnie wasn't the husband they'd have chosen for their daughter – and Hal had been as much against his going out with Gill as Winnie was at the beginning – but he wasn't a bad lad. He'd been through a yobbish stage a few years ago, swaggering around the streets in teddy boy clothes with marauding gangs of louts, but that had just been youthful exuberance and he seemed over it now – partly due to the army, in Hal's opinion. And anyone who could perform on a football field like Arnie Briscoe couldn't be all bad.

'You enjoying yourself, Hal?' asked a voice from across the table that was only just audible above the conversational hubbub.

'Not half,' he replied to Arnie's mother Phoebe, a tall, busty blonde in a bright blue suit that matched her sparkling eyes. 'Are you?'

'I'm having a smashing time, thanks,' she said, smiling and glancing towards Winnie. 'You and Win have done us proud.'

Sitting next to Phoebe was her younger son, John, a lanky eleven-year-old with the same compelling brown eyes and curly hair as his older brother. The Millers and the Briscoes had lived in Maisie Road for many years. But although they had known *of* each other for all that time, they had never exchanged more than a passing greeting – until a couple of years ago, when Gill had started going out with Arnie.

From what Hal gathered from local gossip, it hadn't been easy for Phoebe, bringing up two boys on her own these last ten years since her husband had died. She'd done a variety of jobs to put food on the table, apparently: charring, factory work, and she now worked on the sweet counter in Woolworth's.

And after all she'd done for Arnie, he'd brought shame on her by getting a neighbour's daughter into trouble. Not that Phoebe seemed ashamed; that wasn't her way. Unlike Hal's dear Winnie, Phoebe was a relaxed sort of person able to take things in her stride. From the little he knew of her, she was the gregarious type who liked nothing better than a party. She had a bit of a reputation with the men, as a matter of fact.

'Winnie must take all the credit,' he said to Phoebe. 'She organised everything.'

A roar of laughter erupted nearby, and Phoebe put her hand behind her ear to indicate that she couldn't hear. 'Later,' she mouthed.

Hal nodded, and Phoebe became immediately engrossed in conversation with a friend of Arnie's sitting next to her.

'What was all that about?' asked Winnie, who had been out of earshot.

'She was just being friendly.'

'That's her speciality . . . being friendly,' she said with strong disapproval. Because Phoebe's unwavering confidence made her feel inferior, Winnie was inclined to be uncharitable towards her as a sort of defence mechanism. To a reserved soul like herself, Phoebe's self-assurance didn't fall far short of arrogance. 'It's where Arnie gets it from. It's no wonder that boy is degenerate.'

'Now that isn't fair, Win,' Hal said, gently reproachful but determinedly firm.

'Oh, do me a favour,' she replied. 'Everyone in Maisie Road knows what she's like. If snowmen hung around for long enough she'd try to get off with 'em.'

At that moment fifteen-year-old Carol Miller, who was sitting on her mother's other side out of earshot of her parents' conversation, gave Winnie a nudge.

'What's for afters, Mum?' she asked.

'Sherry trifle.' Winnie looked at Carol's plate. 'But you've not finished your dinner.'

'Don't want any more. The ham's fatty and the potatoes are lumpy.'

'That's a waste of good food,' tutted Winnie, still inclined to practise the habit she'd picked up during the long years of rationing.

'Too bad, 'cause I'm not eating it,' was Carol's petulant reply.

'Leave it then, dear,' sighed Winnie, who was ashamed to admit that she often gave in to her younger daughter out of sheer exhaustion. Unlike her sunny-natured older sister, Carol had always been a difficult child. She could bend people to her will by wearing them down to a point where they would agree to anything. She was also very sensitive and needed lots of attention. Her demanding nature had been exacerbated by the onset of adolescence, with its biological changes and heightened self-awareness, and now her head was full of romance and she always seemed to be lusting after some boy or other. She was extremely affectionate; sometimes it seemed to Winnie as though she had too much love for anyone to cope with. Having recently left school, she had a job as a filing clerk in the offices of a local shoe-polish factory.

Winnie's thoughts drifted back to the wedding arrangements – and she gave due credit to Phoebe, who had offered to contribute towards the cost of the reception because of the special circumstances. But Winnie wasn't having that! What, and have people say the Millers couldn't afford to do the traditional thing and pay for their own daughter's wedding reception? Not bloomin' likely!

In the end they had agreed for Phoebe to pay for the photographs outside the register office, and to provide a spray of flowers for Gill and the buttonholes. As a wedding present Phoebe had booked the couple into a small hotel on the outskirts of the West End for tonight.

Although Winnie thought the gift somewhat frivolous in the light of the couple's impending responsibilities, she was secretly rather relieved. The thought of the newly-weds spending their first night as a married couple at home with her and Hal in Maisie Road was acutely embarrassing to her – even though Gill's condition made it obvious that there would be no bashfulness behind their bedroom door.

'Dead romantic, innit?' said Carol with an elaborate sigh.

'What is?' asked her mother, turning to look at her daughter who didn't resemble her sister in physical appearance at all. Carol wasn't exactly pretty, but she was growing into an attractive young woman with an exceptionally well developed figure for her age. In contrast to Gill's dark colouring, Carol had light-brown hair and a pale, freckled complexion. Her almond-shaped, hazel eyes lost something because they were always simmering with discontent.

'Gill and Arnie, o' course.'

Her mother shot her a warning look, terrified that Carol might see her sister as a role model. Winnie couldn't face the prospect of having to go through all this again with her second daughter. 'There's nothing

6

romantic about having to get married, my girl,' she said.

'Getting married is romantic however it happens,' Carol stated categorically.

'It's more romantic to wait and have all the trimmings, though: the white dress and bridesmaids.' She threw Carol a look. 'Surely you wouldn't want to miss out on all of that.'

'Maybe not. But Gill and Arnie are happy together even though they didn't have any of that,' she said, looking at the couple and emitting another sigh. 'Ooh, Arnie really sends me. He's even more gorgeous than Elvis Presley.'

Winnie cast a studious eye over her new son-in-law who, admittedly, did cut rather a dash in the livery of the Middlesex Regiment, which he was wearing because Gill had wanted him to get married in uniform. Yes, she supposed his clean-cut looks would have a certain attraction for young women. Having played football since he was so high, he looked fit and athletic, and he had a smooth complexion and greenish-brown eyes that sparkled with warmth and devilment. His curly, chestnut-coloured hair was cut very short, army-style, and his smile could be quite devastating. But what use was a melting smile to the mother of his child with no home of her own?

'She's so lucky having Arnie as a husband,' continued Carol, who thought her sister's recent scandal was the most thrilling thing that had happened in ages. It had certainly livened things up at home. And such fuel for her lively young imagination too! Carol and her girlfriends had had great fun speculating on when and where the deed had actually taken place. The girl felt quite weak with excitement at the thought of what had been going on. 'I wish I was the one who had just got married.'

'Good heavens above!' reproached her mother. 'You're far too young.'

'Gill isn't that much older than I am.'

'She's nearly three years older,' declared Winnie, keeping her voice low as the waitress cleared their dinner plates. 'Anyway, Gill's still too young to get married. She wouldn't have done so if the circumstances had been different.'

'Well I still think it's romantic whatever you say.'

Romantic, my eye, thought Winnie. Drudgery, poverty and council accommodation – that about summed up her view of what life had in store for Mrs Arnie Briscoe. Winnie thanked God the pregnancy had come to light when it had. A few days later and Arnie wouldn't have been around to do the decent thing – for he'd been posted to Germany and was leaving on Monday with his regiment. He was likely to be abroad for months, certainly until after the baby was born.

Although Gill was quite naturally dreading his departure, it was a positive blessing to Winnie. At least she would be spared having a relative stranger living in her house – until after he was demobbed, anyway. Heaven only knew how long it would be before they could

7

afford a place of their own. They certainly couldn't set up home on Arnie's army pay, and his own mother didn't have room for them in her poky little flat in the pre-war block on the corner of Maisie Road.

Winnie wondered how their marriage would stand up to the trials and tribulations of everyday living when he came out of the army, especially with the added demands of a baby to cope with. It certainly didn't have the ingredients for durability, being merely an arrangement of necessity. Still, whatever happened in the future, the wedding would have served a purpose in preventing her first grandchild from being born a bastard.

Who would have thought one of her girls would have landed in trouble? She thought she'd protected herself against every mother's nightmare by giving her daughters a strict and moral upbringing, hammering decent values into them for all she was worth. Hal had left that sort of thing to her, since it was generally accepted that bringing up the children was a woman's job.

But then who would have thought Gill would have got mixed up with someone like Arnie? Until he'd come into her life she'd been a serious-minded sort of girl, diligent in her work as a clerk in an accountant's office and passionate about her musical hobby. Having shown an interest in the family piano at a very young age, Winnie and Hal had made their budget stretch to piano lessons for her, and she'd rewarded them by showing real talent and dedication.

Before she'd got friendly with Arnie most of her spare time had been spent at the piano. Practising had never been anathema to Gill; she'd passed exams with flying colours and competed regularly at music festivals. Winnie and Hal had been so proud.

Then she'd caught the eye of Arnie Briscoe and become a different person almost overnight. Her piano was forgotten in her eagerness to go with him to dance halls and coffee bars. Her taste in music changed from inoffensive ballads and sober classical pieces to crude and deafening rock 'n' roll.

Her style of dress had altered too. She now spent all her spare money on stiletto-heeled shoes with winkle-picker points, and tight skirts, or exaggeratedly full skirts with stiff petticoats and flat pumps. And as if all that wasn't bad enough, Arnie had bought her a portable record player for a birthday present, and the disgraceful Elvis Presley could be heard bellowing out some tuneless drivel about his blue suede shoes.

The amicable relationship that Winnie and Hal had always had with their daughter became fraught with arguments. There was constant tension in the house. But nothing could persuade Gill to give Arnie up. Times had changed since Winnie and Hal were young; these days youngsters were far more assertive towards their parents than they had ever dared to be.

Their disapproval only drove Gill more determinedly into Arnie's arms. There had been one dreadful scene when Winnie, in desperation, had simply forbidden her to see him again. She'd never seen her daughter so angry. Through tight lips Gill had announced that she would leave home rather than give him up.

'Just 'cause he dresses like a teddy boy doesn't make him bad,' Gill had said. 'They don't all go out smashing up cinemas and dance halls, you know. He just likes wearing the gear, that's all, and dancing to rock 'n' roll music . . . and so do I.'

After that Winnie and Hal had kept a diplomatic silence, hoping the affair would run its course and die the death. After all, he would be going away to do his national service soon – surely, they reasoned, that would put an end to it.

But it hadn't. They'd written to each other almost every day and spent every second together when he came home on leave.

God only knows where it will end, thought Winnie now, as the crockery was finally cleared away and the waitresses began serving dessert.

'I'd like to thank you all for coming to share our special day with us,' said Arnie, who was on his feet making a speech. He paused for a moment with a wicked look in his eye. 'Even though it was rather short notice . . .'

Oh, really, has he no shame? thought Winnie furiously, as the company erupted into laughter. How dare he embarrass Gill in such a cheap and vulgar way? But Gill was laughing, which spoke volumes about the power he had over her. Hal was chuckling too. Winnie gave him a sharp dig in the ribs with her elbow and scowled at him when he turned towards her.

'He's only bringing something out into the open that everyone knows about anyway, Win,' he whispered, unheard by the others beneath the gales of mirth. 'He means well.'

'He shouldn't talk like that.'

'Don't take everything so seriously, love,' he said quietly as Arnie began speaking again.

'We're all friends here, so I want to be honest with you . . .' Arnie glanced at his wife and then fixed his gaze on Winnie, in the hope of getting his heartfelt message across to her and easing her mind about this marriage. 'I'll admit that this isn't the way Gill and I planned to get married, and it's sooner than we expected. But I want you all to know that we would have got married sooner or later anyway, and we're both really happy that it's happened now.' He turned and smiled lovingly at Gill, then looked back towards the company again. 'I consider myself to be a very lucky man. This is the happiest day of my life.'

A communal sigh rippled through the females in the room, interspersed with some loud and saucy badinage from the men. Arnie could feel his mother-in-law's eyes piercing into him. She'd sent plenty of hostile vibes in his direction since he'd been seeing Gill, and had given him a real roasting when they'd told her and Hal about the baby. It was a predictable reaction and he didn't blame her. But knowing she didn't approve of him as a son-in-law made him feel uncomfortable, and he dealt with it in the best way he knew: by ignoring it and being friendly towards her, despite her coolness to him.

Thank God he was spared having to live with his in-laws – for a while, at least. Having to face his mother-in-law's disapproving stare over his corn flakes every morning didn't bear thinking about.

The very first priority on his agenda when he got demobbed was to find them a place of their own.

But that was a long way off and, although he loved Gill to bits and didn't want to leave her, he couldn't help anticipating his trip abroad with a certain amount of excitement. He was young and hungry for adventure. Since he'd been forced into the army for two years, he was glad to be given the opportunity to see some of the world at the government's expense.

It was traditional among the blokes to complain about national service, and Arnie went along with the herd in this respect. But once the torturous basic training had ended he'd begun to enjoy his service. He was luckier than most: his skill on the football field had not only got him a job as a PT instructor, it had also earned him a place in the regiment team. As well as being given time off work for football training, he also travelled all over the country to play in matches. It was a damned sight pleasanter than working at a machine all day as he'd done in civvy street.

'I'd like to thank my mother for all she's done for me all my life, and for her support this last few weeks,' he said now, looking at his mother who beamed at him in acknowledgment.

He turned again to Winnie and Hal. 'I'd also like to thank my mother- and father in-law for all their help . . . and for giving us this smashing party today.'

A cheer went up among the guests, and Arnie raised his hands for silence.

'And most of all I'd like to thank them for letting me marry their beautiful daughter.'

That's a good one, since we didn't have any choice in the matter, thought Winnie, meeting his eyes and, much to her annoyance, finding that hers were brimming with tears.

'I must assure them that I shall look after her and do my very best to make her happy.'

'You'd better do an' all, mate,' shouted Hal jokingly.

With a broad grin, Arnie assured him again before sitting down to rousing cheers from the assembled company and a hesitant smile from Winnie.

He was convincing, she'd say that much for him. She rummaged in her pocket for a handkerchief. It was no wonder Gill had fallen for him – he couldn't half turn on the charm.

Despite not having all the trimmings, this was the happiest day of Gill's life. A white wedding would have been lovely of course, if things had been different, but the important thing was marrying Arnie. The rest didn't really matter to her. She was so happy and proud to be his wife.

'Well done,' she said as he sat down.

'Was it okay?'

'It was great.'

'Phew. I'm glad it's over,' he said. 'It was a bit nerve-wracking.'

'Fancy coming right out with the reason for the wedding, though.'

'It was a sudden impulse,' he said, looking at her with a serious expression. 'As it's common knowledge among the guests even though everyone's keeping shtum about it, I thought I'd let them know that we really wanted to get married and haven't done it just because of the baby.' He paused, looking doubtful. 'I hope I haven't upset you.'

'No, course you haven't,' she said, touched by his eagerness to declare his feelings for her in public.

'I don't think your mum was any too pleased, though.'

'You know how reserved Mum is,' she said. 'Her bark's worse than her bite.'

'I didn't want to offend her 'cause she's been good to us,' he said.

'Yes, she has.'

'I was trying to reassure her about my feelings for you as much as anything.'

'I know.'

Through the mists of joy, Gill was aware of her mother's disappointment in her, even though she'd been wonderfully supportive. But the knowledge did little more than cast a slight shadow over Gill's mood because her happiness was so intense.

This didn't mean that Gill didn't feel bad about letting her parents down. She was permanently suspended between guilt and rapture. But, in all honesty, she couldn't regret marrying Arnie and carrying his child when it was all she wanted from her life, which had blossomed since he'd been a part of it.

She looked across at her mother and smiled affectionately. Winnie smiled back, a brave effort that twisted Gill's heart. Her mother looked older suddenly, somehow frailer and less stern than usual.

Tears swelled beneath Gill's lids as she realised that nothing would be the same again between her mother and herself. Her wedding day was a new beginning, but it also marked the end of an era.

Imbued with emotion, her thoughts lingered on all the good things her parents had done for her. As well as providing her with a loving family life, they had made sacrifices so that she could have piano lessons. And she had repaid them by bringing shame on the family.

But for all that she wouldn't change a thing. She was young and inexperienced, but she knew that she and Arnie were right for each other.

'It's your dad's turn now,' said Arnie, jolting her out of her reverie to see her father rising to propose a toast to the happy couple. Her eyes filled with fresh tears as he spoke from the heart, wishing them well in their life together. He'd been the only man in her life until she'd met Arnie, and she had failed him.

Does your own happiness always come at the expense of someone else's? she wondered.

Hal's toast to the newly-weds marked the end of the formalities and people began to get up from the table and mingle. As the host, Hal got everyone a drink from the bar and the atmosphere soon became thick with smoke and alcohol fumes, the volume of noise and laughter rising as the drinks flowed.

With a gin and tonic in her hand, Phoebe went over to Winnie. 'Well, it's all going with a swing,' she said, smiling. 'You did a good job organising it.'

'There were no major catastrophes anyway,' said Winnie.

Phoebe inhaled on her cigarette, looking at Winnie thoughtfully. 'Except the biggest catastrophe of them all in your book . . . the fact that your daughter has married my son, eh?' she said with a wry grin.

Winnie's stomach knotted with nerves but she felt compelled to stand up for herself. 'How would you feel if it was your daughter who'd got into trouble?' she asked.

'I can't answer that, since I don't have any daughters,' said Phoebe candidly. 'But I can't see that it's any worse than seeing a son get married before he's ready.'

'It's a different thing altogether for a woman,' said Winnie through dry lips.

'Different, but potentially as damaging to a man's future,' said Phoebe, in a tone that bore no malice and was merely her considered opinion.

'I don't see how.'

'Arnie's only nineteen. He's much too young to be tied down with a wife and kiddie to support. He needs freedom to develop, to work out what he wants to do with his life.'

'He should have thought of that—'

'I couldn't agree more, dear, but young people are fresh to what life has to offer and it makes them impulsive,' Phoebe said in an even tone. 'They don't always stop to think.'

'Arnie obviously didn't.'

'Arnie wasn't a solo player,' was Phoebe's answer to that. 'And

I haven't heard young Gill saying anything about rape.'

Phoebe sipped her drink, watching Winnie as her mouth opened then closed again, scarlet patches staining her cheeks, her mouth set in a grim line. Phoebe felt rather sorry for her. She always seemed to have the worries of the world on her shoulders.

'Look, Winnie dear,' she said with genuine friendliness, because she was a very even-tempered person who spoke her mind but rarely fell out with anyone, 'the kids have got married and we have to accept it whether we like it or not. How *we* feel about it isn't important, and certainly isn't gonna make a scrap of difference to the outcome of their marriage. So all we can do is let Gill and Arnie get on with it in their own way and stop worrying about them.'

Before Winnie had a chance to reply, Gill appeared at her side. 'Glad to see that you two are getting to know each other,' she said.

'We thought we ought to make the effort now that we're practically related, isn't that right?' said Phoebe with a meaningful look in Winnie's direction.

'Yeah, that's right,' said Winnie, because she knew it would please Gill.

Phoebe turned back to Gill. 'So, what time is Arnie going back to camp tomorrow?' she asked.

'In the afternoon.'

'How about coming to our place for Sunday dinner then . . . when you get back from the hotel? It's the last time I'll be seeing my son for quite a while.' She turned to Winnie. 'As long as that won't put you out, love.'

'Not at all,' said Winnie politely. 'We can have what's left of the joint on Monday.'

'We'd love to come then,' said Gill, smiling at her new mother-in-law.

'That's settled then.' Phoebe wriggled her shoulders and grinned to indicate her pleasure in the arrangement. 'Have I told you how pleased I am to have you join our family?'

'Several times,' said Gill, who liked Phoebe very much.

'I'll say it again just for good measure,' she said, hugging her new daughter-in-law. 'Welcome to the Briscoe family.'

'Glad to have joined.'

Aware that her mother was excluded from this uninhibited display of warmth and friendliness, Gill turned to Winnie. 'Thanks for everything you've done for us, Mum.' She hugged her tight. 'You've been really great, and we appreciate it.'

'That's all right, love,' said Winnie, warmed and softened by these few words of appreciation. 'It was the least I could do.'

'Well, I think I'll go and do some socialising before the party comes to an end,' said Phoebe, and sauntered off.

13

Watching her swinging her hips as she walked, Winnie felt a stab of envy for someone of whom she had never approved. It wasn't Phoebe's way of life she envied. Working on the counter in Woolworth's because she didn't have a husband to support her must be purgatory – and she was as common as muck with her heavy make-up and bleached hair.

But her vivacious personality and exuberant attitude to life seemed highly desirable to Winnie at that moment. She knew she could never be like that herself because it wasn't in her nature – and most of the time she didn't want to be – but at that precise moment she would have given anything for a small measure of Phoebe Briscoe's casual confidence and indomitable spirit.

Although Gill and Arnie had become accustomed to partings since he'd been in the army, they had never got any easier for Gill. And the one she faced the following afternoon cut deeper than any before because he was going abroad. There would be no weekend passes to look forward to from Germany, she thought gloomily as they left his mother's flat and made their way past the grey Victorian terraces that made up the majority of Maisie Road, heading for Fulham Broadway station.

It was a bitterly cold afternoon, with a sharp wind and dark, threatening clouds rolling above the grey slate rooftops; the tiny front gardens were bleak at this time of year. Arnie was wearing his army greatcoat, while Gill shivered inside a camel-coloured duffle-coat over black tapered trousers. His kitbag was strapped to his shoulders and her hand was tucked into his arm. She was savouring having him near, their last minutes together ticking away as steadily as the beating of her heart.

'It's been the most wonderful weekend of my life,' she said as they progressed into North End Road, which was bathed in the quiet of a Sunday afternoon, the shops closed, the street empty of market barrows until tomorrow, the wind blowing dust and litter across the road.

Dusk was already falling, and lights were beginning to appear in the windows of the homes in the residential side streets, some of which had changed since Gill was a child and the bomb-sites were built over. Lots of the slum areas in the borough had been cleared too, many of them replaced by municipal housing developments.

'Yeah, it was really smashing,' Arnie said, looking lovingly at her face, her cheeks glowing with the cold, her dark fringe flopping out of her hood on to her forehead. 'Especially last night. Cor, I won't forget that in a hurry.'

'I'll never forget it,' she declared earnestly, thinking back.

The hotel was more of a guest house really, but it was spotlessly clean and the food was delicious. One of the things Gill had enjoyed most about it, though, was the feeling of anonymity, people coming and going unnoticed, which was such a novelty to Gill and Arnie.

Throughout the whole of their love affair they had wanted nothing more than to be alone, and had expended a great deal of effort to this end, usually to be thwarted by family or neighbours or friends. Just one of the drawbacks of finding romance so close to home, Gill supposed. But at the hotel, with its dark, antiquated residents' lounge, creaky old lift and freezing starched sheets, no one had taken any notice of them at all. Immediately after dinner last night they'd gone to their room and stayed there until breakfast without raising so much as a flicker of interest. It had been bliss!

Now they were back down to earth with a bump. Arnie had said goodbye to the folks, and it would be a long time before any of them saw him again.

'I'll miss you,' Gill said.

'I'll miss you too.'

'I'll write often,' she said.

'Me too.'

'Oh, Arnie, I can't believe we're actually married,' she said, just the thought of it making her heart race. 'Can you?'

He halted in his step and slipped his arms around her, looking into her eyes. 'Ooh, yeah, I can believe it all right – and it's really great.' He gave her a wicked grin. 'I'm a bit choked about not being around to take advantage of the fact that it's legal, though.'

'Is that all you think about?'

'Men of my age think of nothing else,' he replied, teasing her. 'It's expected of us.'

She gave him a playful punch on the shoulder and said, 'As long as it's only in relation to me.'

'Of course.'

'I should hope so too.'

They walked on in silence for a while, each lost in their own thoughts.

'Do you realise that this is the last time we'll be together as just a couple?' she said. 'When you come home next time we'll be a family.'

'Yeah,' he said, his tone becoming serious. 'That's gonna take some getting used to.'

'It'll be different.'

'Me a dad. Wow!'

'You'll be great.'

'I'll certainly do my best.'

At the station, they stood huddled together in the draughty foyer, away from the crowds hurrying to and from the platform. Brimming with emotion, Gill was both dreading the parting and wanting it to be over.

'I'll be counting the days till you come home,' she said.

'Me too,' he said. 'I shall cross them off on my calendar.'

'You can keep your sexy eyes off the fräuleins out there in Germany

15

too,' she chided playfully. 'I don't want you getting off with any German girl.'

'As if I would.'

'You'd better not.'

'What about you?'

'Me?'

'Yes, you,' he confirmed with forced laughter. 'How do I know you're not gonna take a fancy to some other bloke while I'm away?'

'Oh, yeah. As a married woman with a baby on the way I'm gonna have bags of opportunity to play around,' she said with irony.

It was all just meaningless chatter to ease the pain of parting.

'Love you loads,' he said, kissing her deeply on the lips.

'Love you too,' she said.

And after one last feverish embrace he was gone, making his way across the foyer with long, purposeful strides – a tall, athletic figure, his kitbag shifting slightly from side to side as he walked.

Gill waited until he was out of sight then walked slowly out into the cold street, now fully dark and lit by the yellow glow from the streetlights which she saw through a blur of tears.

It was a punishing wrench, but she had a feeling of elation and confidence in the future too. With Arnie's wedding ring on her finger and his baby growing inside her, she felt invincible. Nothing could defeat the wife of Arnie Briscoe!

Chapter Two

Time passed slowly for Gill after Arnie's departure, as she waited out the long months until his return. But the feeling of inner strength remained with her, despite the constant ache of missing him, and his letters were a great source of comfort. She also began to look forward more eagerly to the birth of her baby as the time drew nearer.

It was as though she was in a curious kind of limbo. Although she felt married in her heart, from the point of view of everyday life it was as though she was still single, living with the family and staying on at work – which she planned to do for as long as she was able.

The pattern of her life almost reverted to the pre-Arnie days: calm and uneventful. Most evenings were spent at home, though she occasionally met up with girlfriends in a coffee bar for a gossip, and sometimes went to the cinema with her sister. With time on her hands, her interest in the piano returned, until eventually she became too enormous to sit comfortably on the stool and reach the keys and pedals.

'Wow,' exclaimed Carol, one warm summer's evening when the birth was several days overdue and Gill was trying to keep cool by lying on her bed. Even the tent-like proportions of her maternity nightdress could barely contain her bloated form. 'How can anyone be that huge?'

'It's all too easy, believe me,' said Gill with a wry grin.

'Not if you don't have a boyfriend,' said Carol wistfully.

'Give it time, kid,' said Gill. 'You're not even sixteen yet. Your turn will come soon enough. And in the mean time have some fun. Being pregnant isn't exactly a laugh a minute.'

'I'm longing to get married and have a baby,' Carol said.

'Well, it's too early for you yet, so you'll just have to make do with a niece or nephew,' said Gill, who sometimes thought her sister was unnaturally impatient for such things.

'I wish it would hurry up and get born,' said Carol.

'You and me both, sis,' sighed Gill, who was finding the heat exhausting in her inflated condition and was eager for the inevitable to begin. She placed her hands on her extended stomach and addressed the huge bump. 'It's time you showed yourself, kiddo. We're all getting fed up with waiting.'

The baby obviously had a respect for authority, because Gill's waters broke later that night and she was taken into the maternity ward of

17

Hammersmith hospital, where she entered into a very long and difficult labour.

'I'll murder Arnie when I see him,' she was heard to utter at one point of intense agony. 'For putting me through this.'

But she soon forgot the pain, when Craig Arnold Briscoe finally made his appearance and she stared with wonder at his beautiful little face with its high forehead, plump cheeks and squarish jaw that was so unmistakably Arnie.

'Oh, Craig. Your daddy is gonna be so proud of you,' she said with tears of joy running down her cheeks. 'But I do wish he was here to share this fantastic moment with me!'

Craig was a few weeks old when Arnie came home on leave bursting with health and even more handsome than Gill remembered. His tough image was forgotten in the emotion of the moment, and he wept openly when he first saw his son. Gill felt highly charged too. Seeing them together for the first time was a deeply moving experience.

Their son was six months old when Arnie finally returned to England for his demob and he and Gill were able to begin their life together properly. Although Gill had never doubted that he would settle down to marriage and fatherhood, because of his youth and the circumstances of their marriage there were plenty of people just waiting for him to let her down and go off the rails.

Happily for her, Arnie surprised them all by being a devoted husband and father. Established back at his old job at the engineering factory, he rushed home from work every evening in time to see Craig before he went to bed. He cuddled him, comforted him and even disregarded his macho inhibitions and took him to the park in his pram at weekends. He was simply longing for the boy to learn to walk so that he could teach him to kick a ball.

'The thought of coming home to you and Craig keeps me sane in that bloomin' factory all day,' he confessed to Gill one night when they were getting ready to go to bed.

'Don't you like it there now then?' she asked in surprise, because he'd always seemed happy enough with the job before the army.

'Like it!' he exclaimed as though astonished by such a curious notion. 'I hate it! Putting rivets into lumps of metal for hours on end every day is driving me stark raving mad!'

'It never seemed to bother you before you went away,' she remarked in a low voice so as not to wake Craig who was asleep in his cot.

'It didn't seem so bad then, probably because I didn't know any different,' he said gloomily, getting into bed and leaning back against the pillows with his hands linked behind his head.

She was brushing her hair at the dressing table, looking at him in the mirror. 'Sounds to me as though the army has unsettled you,' she said.

'It's bound to, innit?' he said. 'I mean, you're living a completely different sort of life for two years.'

'But everyone hates national service and can't wait for it to be over.'

'Most of 'em do hate it – but at least you get a change of scenery.'

'Mm, there is that.'

'I had it cushy compared to most of the lads 'cause of the football,' he explained. 'I reckon my game must have improved no end 'cause I got so much practice playing for the regiment.'

'And plenty of time off for training,' she reminded him chattily.

'Yeah. It wasn't so much the time off that I liked, because I didn't mind the job I was doing,' he said. 'It was being involved with the game so much more than I am in civvy street that I enjoyed so much.'

'Really?'

'Mm. And even apart from the actual football, when you play for the regiment you're always in demand,' he explained. 'It made me feel as though I counted for something, you know? Now I'm a nobody again and I miss the buzz.'

'But you play on a regular basis for the Town Park Shooters,' she pointed out, referring to a local amateur team.

'Only on Sunday mornings, if they've managed to get a game fixed up,' he said. 'In the army there were plenty of matches and regular training. I felt like a professional.'

'So you're thinking of signing on as a regular soldier just to get more soccer, are you?' she said jokingly, getting into bed and snuggling up beside him.

'Not likely.'

'I'd have something to say if you were,' she said.

'It's just that the day at the factory seems so long and boring now compared to what I've been doing this last couple o' years.'

'Can't you look for another job?' she suggested. 'There's plenty of work about.'

'There's no point. Factory work will be just as deadly boring anywhere,' he said, 'and it's the only sort of work I know.'

'You taught PT in the army,' she said. 'Can't you do something along those lines?'

'No chance. I was just an army PT instructor, that doesn't qualify me to do anything similar in civvy street.'

'Surely there must be something else you can do though,' Gill said with concern. 'Something a bit more interesting for you.'

'There probably is, but I'd have to take a drop in wages – at first, anyway – and I can't afford to do that now that I have responsibilities.'

'I'm sure we could manage.'

'No, Gill. The money's good where I am, and we need every penny for when we get our own place, for furniture and stuff.'

'True. But I don't like the idea of your doing work that makes you miserable.'

'I don't have a choice, babe.'

'Of course you do,' she insisted. 'I think you should look for another job. Even if the money is less, we'll get by.'

'It's a nice thought, but it wouldn't be practical.'

'Perhaps I could make up the difference,' she suggested with rising enthusiasm. 'I could get a part-time job.'

'And what about the baby?'

'Maybe I could ask Mum to look after him for a few hours a day.'

'Oh no,' he said emphatically. 'I'm not having that.'

'Why not?'

'Your place is at home with Craig, and it's my job to provide for you.'

'But I'd like to do something to help. I'd rather go out to work than have you doing a job you hate,' she told him. 'Just until you get yourself sorted.'

'You're a real diamond, do you know that?' he said, slipping an arm round her so that she was nestling into the crook of his neck. 'I shouldn't have said anything to you about the job. It's worried you, and there's no need for that.'

'I'm your wife, Arnie,' she said. 'I should know about these things.'

'I'll get used to the factory again in time. Don't worry,' he said, sounding positive to reassure her. 'So don't let's waste any more precious time talking about it.'

'Ooh, I love it when you're masterful,' she giggled, wriggling closer to him.

'I can be as masterful as you like,' he said, laughing softly.

Listening to the low sound of talk and laughter in the room next door, Hal said, 'Those two are as happy as anything, aren't they?'

'Yeah, they do seem to be getting on well at the moment,' agreed Winnie, who was putting curlers into her hair in front of the dressing table mirror. Reckless optimism wasn't in her nature. Being too certain of things was the surest way she knew of coming a cropper. 'But it's still early days; the novelty of his being back hasn't had time to wear off yet.'

'I think Arnie has settled down very well though,' said Hal, who was already in bed. 'It can't have been easy for him to adjust to family life after two years in the army, especially as he didn't have a chance to get used to being married before he went away.'

'Mm.'

'Living here with us can't help matters, either.'

'No it can't and I don't like it any more than he does,' she said. 'I mean, it isn't as if we really know him, is it?'

'We know him well enough,' said Hal. 'Arnie's all right.'

'Just because he can boot a football around a field, he can do no wrong in your eyes.'

'It isn't just his football. I think he's a genuinely good bloke . . . and he thinks the world of Gill and Craig.'

'Yes, that does seem to be the case,' Winnie was forced to agree.

'They need to be in their own place though,' Hal remarked.

'Definitely!'

'Perhaps the council will come up with something for them soon.'

'It won't be for a while yet, I shouldn't think,' Winnie said, her down-to-earth nature coming to the fore again. 'The housing waiting list in this area is a mile long.'

'True.'

'Anyway, they need time to get some cash together so that they can furnish the place when it does come through.'

'He's earns reasonably good money at the factory, I think.'

'Not enough to put much by with a wife and kiddie to keep.'

'Probably not.'

'They've only themselves to blame,' Winnie said, her tone becoming brusque as she thought again how different things could have been for her daughter. 'If they'd shown a bit of restraint they'd have had time to save up and get something behind them before they started a family.'

'A lot of young people seem to be buying their own places these days,' Hal remarked casually. 'Not like our generation of renters.'

'Gill and Arnie will still be living here with us when Craig's grown up if they wait until they've got the deposit on a place of their own,' she said.

'Still, they're happy – that's the main thing,' he said.

'I hope to God it lasts.'

'Let's look on the bright side, shall we?' said Hal in a conclusive manner as Winnie tied a pink hairnet over her curlers, took off her red woollen dressing gown and climbed into bed.

In the other bedroom, Carol was also listening to the low murmur coming from her sister's room. Being of a generation who thought the over-twenty-fives were a sub-culture, never mind ancient relics like her parents, she didn't share their concern for the practicalities of Gill and Arnie's life together. All she could think about was the romantic side of things. And unlike her parents she didn't want them to move into a home of their own, because she enjoyed having them here. The place would be like a morgue without other young people to take the edge off her mum's and dad's old fashioned ways. She was fond of little Craig, liked having Gill on hand to chat to, and thought Arnie was the sexiest thing she had ever clapped eyes on.

I hope they stay here for ever, she thought, turning over on to her side and settling down to sleep. Imagining that Arnie was lying beside her, she shivered with pleasure and snuggled deeper under the covers.

The match was in the final minutes and the score was still a draw. Arnie tore down the field towards the goal, took possession of the ball from a long pass, dribbled it past two defenders and took a shot at goal. It was in! He'd done it! He'd scored the winning goal just seconds before the final whistle. Cor, what a blinder!

He threw his arms in the air victoriously as the shrill sound of the referee's whistle filled the air. Arnie's team-mates were all over him, slapping his back and hugging him. It might only be amateur football in the Sunday league, but that didn't lessen the importance of the game to the players.

It was impossible for Arnie to describe to anyone, even his beloved Gill, how he felt when he was in action on a soccer pitch. Only then did he feel fully alive, his senses finely tuned, adrenalin pumping in top gear. Nothing else on earth gave him the same feeling of release and excitement. The thought of a weekend game kept him going during the loathsome week at the factory. Such was the tedium of the job, he even found himself dreading the end of the football season.

'That goal definitely calls for a pint, mate,' said one of his team-mates as they walked off the field towards the changing hut.

The sharp March wind whipped through their shirts but they were all glowing from the exercise and didn't even notice. It was a deceptively chilly day, glimpses of watery sunshine appearing intermittently through grey and white scudding clouds, the cold, earthy tang of the muddy pitch filling the air.

'Not half,' said someone else.

There was nothing Arnie enjoyed more than the camaraderie of a drink with his pals in the pub after the game. But he'd be well and truly in the dog-house with his mother-in-law if he arrived home late for Sunday dinner with the smell of beer on his breath. He'd discovered that to his peril on a previous occasion.

'You *are* coming for a drink,' said one of the chaps when Arnie didn't reply.

'No, I don't think so – not today,' he said regretfully.

'Under the wife's thumb, eh?' joshed another of the men.

'Do leave off, mate – this is Arnie Briscoe you're talking to,' he objected with typical laddish bravado.

'Why can't you come for a quick one, then?' challenged his pal.

'It isn't my wife who's the problem,' he explained. 'Gill's as sweet as a nut.'

'Who, then?'

'Her mother. She sets dinner for one o'clock sharp on a Sunday and

22

she likes us all to be there. It's half past twelve now; by the time I get changed and cleaned up—'

'Dear oh dear, I wouldn't stand for that,' interrupted one of the married men with feeling. 'It's bad enough having the wife giving you earache if you're late home, let alone the mother-in-law an' all.'

'When you live with your in-laws you have to abide by their rules,' said Arnie.

'You wanna put your foot down, mate,' suggested the man.

'I can't do that,' said Arnie, standing his ground bravely.

'Why not?'

'It's their house, innit?' he pointed out. 'It's only right that I should fit in with their way of doing things.'

'Well, I wouldn't let a mother-in-law of mine dictate to me,' said the other man.

'She isn't so bad,' defended Arnie.

'Sounds like a right old dragon to me.'

'She's a good sort in her own way,' said Arnie, 'even though she can frighten the balls off you if you get the wrong side of her.'

'She needs putting in her place though,' said his mate.

'Not really,' said Arnie. 'She's been good to me and the wife. No point in upsetting her if it can be avoided.'

'Well, I wouldn't put up with it . . .'

As they approached the changing hut, the conversation was interrupted by the appearance of a stranger who drew Arnie to one side as the others walked on.

'Can I have a word?' asked the man, who was fortyish and wearing a light tan suede coat with a fur collar over a black polo-necked sweater.

'Sure,' replied Arnie, eyeing him with curiosity.

'Frank Fisher of Thames United Football Club,' said the man, extending his hand.

'Oh really?' Arnie shook his hand, both excited and intrigued. Thames United was a professional club – only in the third division, but it was in the FA league. 'So, what can I do for you, mate?'

Frank shivered against the wind. 'It's colder watching the game than playing, and my toes are nearly dropping off,' he said. 'It'll be a lot more comfortable to talk in the pub.'

'I was going straight home as a matter of fact,' said Arnie, Winnie still in mind.

'I think you'll find it worth your while to take time to listen to what I have to say,' said Frank with a half smile. 'And I'd rather say it somewhere warm. I don't have such resilience as you players and I'm freezin' to death out here.'

'Hang on while I get changed then,' said Arnie, and he hurried towards the wooden hut.

* * *

'I'm sure Arnie will be home in a minute, Mum,' said Gill, looking at the clock anxiously. It was nearly half past one and her mother was getting more upset by the second. 'He must have got held up somewhere.'

'No prizes for guessing where,' snorted Winnie. 'Sunday morning football is just an excuse to go to the pub, if you ask me.'

'That isn't fair,' denied Gill, instinctively defensive of her husband even though she was livid with him. She had no objection to his going for a pint with the lads after the game, as long as he didn't upset her mother by being late home. He knew how strict she was about lunch on Sundays and he'd promised Gill he would be back on time today. Admittedly her mother was irritatingly inflexible on this issue, but as she did the cooking she was entitled to make the rules. 'You know how important the game is to Arnie.'

'Gill's right, Mum,' put in Carol, who wouldn't hear a word against her hero. 'He'll only be talking to his mates and there's no harm in that.'

'The food'll be burned to a cinder,' said the perplexed Winnie, whose Sunday roast really was worth hurrying home for.

The three women were in the kitchen, a long narrow room painted blue and white with a grey mottled gas cooker and a walk-in larder. In a sunny spot by the window, Craig was sitting in his high-chair banging about with a spoon.

'Why don't we make a start without Arnie?' suggested Gill, who felt guilty on her husband's behalf. 'I'll serve his on to a plate and put it in the oven for him.'

'You know I like us all to sit down together on a Sunday,' said Winnie, who geniuinely believed that Sunday lunch eaten together helped to keep the family spirit alive. She also disliked the muddle caused by people eating at different times.

The baby squirmed in his chair and began to sound fretful.

'I'll have to feed Craig anyway,' said Gill, lifting him out and holding him in her arms. 'I'll move his high-chair into the other room.'

Hal appeared from the living room, where he'd been reading the Sunday paper and where the table was already laid for lunch.

'Shall we start our dinner?' he said. 'Arnie will be home in a minute.'

'I suppose we'd better,' said Winnie, going over to the oven. 'He'll probably not appear until the pubs close.'

They adjourned to the living room, a multi-purpose chamber which was surprisingly cosy considering the amount of furniture that was packed into it – a dining table and chairs and a sideboard at one end, with easy chairs and a sofa placed around the television set in the corner.

Hal had just finished carving the meat and they were helping themselves to vegetables when Arnie breezed in exuding good humour and smelling of best bitter. Gill was spooning mashed roast lamb with veg and gravy into Craig's mouth.

24

'Well, well, so you've decided to come home at last then, have you?' said Winnie acidly. 'I'm surprised you didn't wait until they chucked you out, having stayed this long.'

'And have your delicious Sunday roast get dried up, Ma-in-law?' he said with one of his most winning smiles. 'I'm not that daft.'

'You know we eat sharp at one o'clock on a Sunday,' she said.

'Yeah, I do, and I'm really sorry,' he said, but he didn't look particularly contrite on account of his luminous smile. He moved around the table to Gill, who was determinedly ignoring her errant husband and concentrating on the baby, who was dribbling the food out of his mouth as fast as she was putting it in and finding the whole exercise a huge joke.

'Don't I get a kiss, then, babe?' said Arnie, bending over his wife and putting his face close to her head from behind.

'You're joking,' she said without even turning to look at him. 'I'm strictly off limits to people who break promises.'

'Ooh, dear. I'm well and truly in the bad books then,' he said.

'You certainly are, mate,' said Hal.

'So don't make things worse by messing about,' reproached Winnie, who couldn't help warming to his comical exuberance, despite herself. 'Sit down and help yourself before everything gets cold.'

'Craig isn't cross with me. Are you, son?' he said, making a funny face at the baby who chuckled loudly.

'Don't distract him when I'm trying to get him to eat his dinner,' admonished Gill, adding to her sister who had erupted into giggles, 'And don't you make things worse by encouraging my thoughtless husband.'

Carol was shaking with silent laughter. Arnie winked at his kid sister-in-law and turned his attention back to his wife.

'I'll feed Craig if you like.'

Gill turned to him, sighing eloquently. 'No, Arnie,' she said in a firm tone. 'You just sit down and have your dinner and stop upsetting everybody.'

'Leave the lad alone,' said Hal. 'He'll sit down when he's ready.'

'Typical male mateyness,' observed Winnie, pouring mint sauce over her meat. 'They stick together like glue.'

'It's just plain childish,' pronounced Gill in a worldly-wise manner that belied her youth.

'You're learning fast,' said Winnie.

'If I can get a word in,' said Arnie with a twinkle in his eye as he took his place at the table next to Gill with Craig between them in the high-chair, 'I've got something to tell you . . . and I think I'll be forgiven for being late when you know what it is.'

'I doubt it,' sniffed his mother-in-law.

'You scored the winning goal,' guessed Hal, slicing some more

25

meat off the joint and putting it on a plate for Arnie.

'I did as it happens . . . but that isn't it.'

'It'll take more than a goal to get you out of trouble anyway,' said Winnie.

Gill shot Arnie a look. 'Let's hear it then,' she said. 'And it had better be good.'

Arnie treated his wife to one of his most melting smiles. 'Well, after the match I was approached by a bloke and taken to the pub—'

'Taken by force,' Gill interrupted with playful sarcasm. She had already forgiven him. She could never stay angry with him for long. 'You were completely overpowered.'

'When I realised it could be in my interest – and yours – to go with him, yes, I was overpowered, by curiosity.'

'So, who was he?' asked Gill.

'Frank Fisher, a talent scout for Thames United Football Club.'

They all stopped eating and stared at him, waiting.

'He's seen me play on several occasions, apparently, and he wants me to go for a trial at the club,' he said excitedly.

'A *trial.*' Gill was impressed.

'Yep. And if his bosses like what they see, I'll be offered a contract with the club.'

'You mean you'll play football professionally,' gasped Gill.

'Well, I don't think they're gonna employ me to answer the telephone,' he grinned.

There was a hushed silence as the family digested this amazing news.

'Oh, Arnie, that's wonderful,' said Gill, leaning over and kissing him. 'I'm so proud of you.'

'Hey, steady on, I haven't even been for the trial yet,' he said, but his confidence was high and he couldn't hide it.

'You'll pass with flying colours, no doubt about it.'

'It's tremendous news,' said Hal with a broad smile. 'Well done.'

The excitable Carol leapt up and danced around the room.

'Wow! I'm gonna have a professional footballer for a brother-in-law.' She hugged Arnie from behind. 'Cor, wait till I tell my friends. They'll be green with envy.'

Arnie looked at Winnie. 'Well? Am I forgiven for being late?'

'Trust you to come up with something unbelievable to get yourself off the hook,' she said, but she was smiling and her eyes were warm. 'But – yes, okay, I'll let you off this time.' She cleared her throat because it was difficult for her to show her feelings. 'And well done, son.'

'Thanks.'

'But don't build your hopes up too high before the trial,' she added, running true to form.

'Don't worry,' he assured her, 'I've got my feet planted firmly on the ground.'

'Good. Now . . . do you think we can get on with our dinner before it gets stone cold?'

Immediately after lunch Arnie went across to the flats on the corner to pass on the good news to his mother and brother. Later that afternoon, when Winnie and Hal were snoozing in their armchairs and Carol had gone to the pictures with her girlfriends, Gill and Arnie wrapped up in warm clothes and set off for a walk to Bishop's Park with Craig in the pram.

It was still cold and breezy as they passed Fulham Football Club and entered the park, occasional bursts of sunshine glinting on the blue-painted paddling pool, dry and deserted at this time of year. The trees were swaying in the wind, which was blowing so fiercely through the shrubs and flowerbeds that some early daffodils had been flattened to the ground.

'You must be thrilled to bits to get this chance of a lifetime,' Gill said as they walked through the riverside park, which was actually the outer gardens of Fulham Palace and had been opened to the public as a park at the end of the last century.

'It's a dream come true,' he said excitedly.

'I can imagine.'

'I always hoped to get spotted as a schoolboy 'cause I played in so many matches, but when it never happened I thought I'd missed the boat,' he said. 'But I'm still only twenty; I've a good few playing years ahead of me.'

'It's wonderful for you.'

He halted in his step and turned to her with a serious expression on his face. 'Not just wonderful for me, babe,' he corrected, looking into her eyes. 'If I get that contract things will be a whole lot different for both of us.' He looked at the baby who was sitting up dressed in a bright blue siren suit with white fur trimming on the hood. 'And you, little fella.'

Craig was more interested in some young boys kicking a ball about nearby. Arnie tickled his chin and was rewarded with a fat chuckle. They continued on to the riverside path, the Thames dark and choppy in the wind.

'They're only a third division club, but the money they'll pay me is three times what I can earn in the factory,' he continued as they walked on.

'Is it really?' she said.

'Yeah. Frank Fisher was quite definite about that,' he confirmed. 'I won't get the sort of dough that first division players earn, but it'll do us nicely. The council can stuff their waiting list if I get this job, 'cause we'll be able to get a mortgage on a place of our own.'

'Oh, Arnie, how thrilling.'

27

'And the best part will be not having to go into that ruddy factory any more.'

'It'll be brilliant,' she enthused.

'It isn't the money as such that's important to me,' he said.

'No?'

'No,' he said thoughtfully. 'It's being able to earn my living doing something I love to do and know I'm good at.'

'I can understand that.'

'And I'll be able to give you and Craig a nice life.'

'We have that already.'

'A more comfortable one, then.' He slipped his arm around her. 'You and Craig are everything to me, you know?'

'I know.'

'A beautiful wife, a fine son, and a dream job in the offing,' he said, tightening his arm around her. 'I must be the luckiest bloke alive.'

'I hope you always feel that way.'

'I will . . . don't you worry about that.' He moved away from her slightly, raised his fists in triumph and danced a jig that made Gill laugh and produced one of Craig's throaty giggles.

'You're crazy,' she laughed.

'Yeah, crazy with new hope, because we're on the up, Gill – you, me and Craig,' he said.

'You really think so?'

'Yeah. I can feel it in my bones,' he said, his eyes shining. 'The future is gonna be brilliant for all of us.'

Gill's happiness was piercingly sweet at that moment. But she must have inherited a little of her mother's realism, because a warning voice nagged at the back of her mind, telling her it was too good to last.

Chapter Three

It was a warm summer's evening – Gill's twenty-first birthday – and Gill and Arnie were having a family dinner to celebrate the occasion. Gifts had been graciously received, the wine was flowing, the main course was over and the host and hostess were in their kitchen preparing to serve dessert. Arnie, however, was distracted from the task in hand.

'You look lovely,' he said, running an admiring eye over his wife, who was wearing a close-fitting black dress which was perfect on her slim figure, the effect enhanced by her luxuriant dark hair, which was longer now and backcombed over the crown to give it fullness and height. Her wrist was expensively adorned with the gold watch Arnie had given her as a birthday present.

'Flatterer,' she said, grinning at him.

'I'm only saying what's true.'

'Thank you, darling.' She lifted her arm to have another look at her watch. 'It's beautiful. I shall treasure it.'

'Glad you're pleased, babe. I enjoyed getting it for you,' Arnie said, slipping his arms around her from the back as she turned to get the cream from the fridge. 'Ooh, I could eat you.'

'You'll just have to make do with food as we have company,' she said in frivolous mood.

'They won't miss us for ten minutes if we nip upstairs,' he said jokingly.

'That's an antisocial suggestion,' she said, turning towards him and pushing him away in a firm but playful manner.

'Quite the opposite, I thought,' he said with a wicked grin.

'You're insatiable!' It was a light-hearted admonishment.

'If I am it's your fault,' he replied, stroking her bottom. 'You shouldn't be so gorgeous.'

'Behave yourself when we've got guests.'

'It isn't easy with you looking like that.'

'Glad you like the dress.'

'I like what's underneath more,' he said, wrapping her in his warm, strong arms.

'Later,' she said, drawing back, feeling weak and heady. 'And in the mean time you can make yourself useful and take the trifle into the other room.'

'You're cruel.'

'Our guests are waiting, Arnie . . .'

'Spoil-sport.'

'Shut up and take the pudding in.'

As he walked towards the door carrying an emormous glass bowl containing the product of Gill's labours, she had a sudden thought.

'Oh, by the way, this seems like a good time to tell them the news.'

'No, not tonight.'

'But it's the perfect opportunity, while we are all together.'

'This is your night, Gill,' he told her solemnly. 'You're the birthday girl and I want you to have all the attention.'

'Don't be so silly,' she said, but she was touched by his thoughtfulness. 'I'm as thrilled about your news as you are and I'm absolutely dying for them all to know about it.'

'They'll be told in due course,' he said, and headed for the dining room where their guests were seated around a large table near the French doors opening on to a lawned garden bordered with summer flowers in full bloom.

When Gill appeared behind him, Phoebe said waggishly, 'We thought you'd gone out somewhere to buy the pudding.'

'Sorry we were so long,' Gill said, her flushed cheeks and ruffled hair leaving no one in any doubt as to the reason for the delay. 'We were just adding a few finishing touches.'

'And I was a guest at Princess Margaret's wedding,' laughed Phoebe, who was looking brashly glamorous in a low-cut crimson dress in crêpe-de-Chine with satin edging.

'I bet they've been snogging,' said Carol, now an attractive eighteen-year-old with long hair, a shapely figure and heavily made-up eyes.

'Ugh,' expressed fourteen-year-old John Briscoe with boyish disgust. 'Not again. They're always kissing and cuddling.'

'What's wrong with a man showing his feelings for his wife?' asked Arnie.

'It's soppy,' said John.

'It's nice,' said Carol.

'The trifle looks delicious, Gill,' said Winnie, swiftly changing the subject for fear that this sort of talk might lead to smut. 'The meal must have taken you hours to prepare.'

'Not really – and I enjoyed doing it,' said Gill warmly.

'I intended to take you all out to a restaurant to save Gill the trouble,' said Arnie, 'but she wouldn't hear of it.'

'I wanted to have you all here on the actual day of my birthday,' she told them. 'There'll be quite a crowd at the birthday party Arnie's organised for me at the community hall on Saturday. This is a more personal way of celebrating. I'm sorry Craig couldn't stay awake long enough to join us, though.'

'Never mind, dear,' said Phoebe. 'It was thoughtful of you to invite us, and you've really done us proud.' She looked round the table. 'Isn't that right, everyone?'

During the enthusiastic roar of agreement, Gill's thoughts drifted back over the last two years or so since Arnie had become a professional footballer. It had been a very happy time for them both and they were more in love than ever. His dramatic increase in salary had enabled them to get a mortgage on this house in Danny Gardens, which was about fifteen minutes' walk from Maisie Road in a neighbourhood which, while essentially working class, was slightly more refined.

The property itself was unexceptional, an old style semi-detached with high ceilings and sash windows. What made it so special was the sense of homeliness Gill and Arnie had created, renovating it together with loving care. She had known it was the right house for them the minute she'd set eyes on it, despite the fact that it had needed a lot of work.

It comprised three bedrooms, a living and dining room downstairs, with a pleasant sunny room off the hall which they used as a playroom for Craig. Gill's parents had insisted that she have the old family piano, since she was the only one of them who ever used it, and it now stood in their living room where she played as often as she could find the time.

Because the house had been a creaking shell of a place, without a trace of Formica or fitted units, they had picked it up dirt cheap and subsequently invested time, money and effort into modernising it to their own taste. The result was light and airy walls in pretty pastel shades, abundant mirrors, deep pile carpets and sleek, contemporary furnishings and fittings.

Their standard of living was by no means excessive, but it had improved considerably since Arnie had worked at the factory. They could afford to run a car now and have decent clothes and outings.

Recalled to the present by the fact that all eyes were upon her, Gill said, 'Thanks, folks. I'm glad you're enjoying yourselves.'

The conversation became general. They touched on the recent death of the controversial Labour politician Aneurin Bevan, who was best known for inaugurating Britain's National Health Service. Carol, to whom politicians collectively were an unknown species, was more interested in talking about a horror film called *Psycho* that was currently causing a sensation in cinemas across the country.

'Talk about scary,' she said dramatically. 'There was this scene in a motel shower. God, I was nearly wetting myself!'

'We'll have to go and see that, Arnie,' suggested Gill lightly. 'You can hold me tight so that I won't be scared.'

'It's the sort of film you need to see with a strong man to hold your hand,' said Carol. 'I went with a girlfriend, worst luck.'

'I wouldn't mind going to see that,' said John. 'I've heard a lot about it.'

'It'll give you nightmares, by the sound of it,' said his mother.

'Leave off, Mum,' he said with youthful affront. 'I'm not a kid.'

'You're not an adult either.'

'Almost.'

'You're not quite there yet, son.'

'I wanna see the film, though.'

'You won't be able to get in unless you're with an adult, and these days you wouldn't be seen dead at the pictures with your mother.'

'And have my mates think I'm a mummy's boy?' he protested. 'Not likely!'

'The film isn't suitable for you anyway, so you can forget about it,' said Phoebe, who could be stern and authoritative when necessary, despite her easygoing nature.

'But M-u-um,' he protested with a pained expression.

For some inexplicable reason, Phoebe found herself awash with loneliness at that moment. She'd never really adjusted to being on her own after Bill died. Oh, she'd coped well enough over the years; she'd learned to be practical and independent, and most of the time she was happy with her lot. She wasn't short of company – she still had John living at home, and not many days passed when Arnie didn't call round to see her. He often slipped her a few quid too, now that he wasn't pushed for cash. It wasn't loneliness for people, as such, that she was struggling with now. It was more a longing for someone of her own – a soulmate with whom she could share her life.

There had been occasional boyfriends over the years – which wasn't surprising since she was widowed at only twenty-eight. She enjoyed male company, liked the special chemistry which reminded her that she was an individual as well as a working mother of two. But none of the relationships had ever got past the starting post – firstly because her sons had always come first with her, and secondly because she never seemed to meet the kind of man who had permanence in mind.

It wasn't easy for women of a certain age to meet men of any sort, let alone the type who wanted to settle down. A man could go out to a pub or a club without raising an eyebrow, but if a woman did the same thing she was branded as 'easy'. Phoebe knew that this was how she was thought of by some people anyway, but she didn't really mind. Better to be talked about than ignored, in her opinion. She was forty-one now – a bit late in the day to meet anyone. But she'd get by on her own; she'd managed this far.

She was jolted back to the present by Winnie, who was saying, 'I can't say that *Psycho* is a film I fancy going to see.'

'We've not been to the pictures for years anyway,' said Hal, pouring

32

cream over his portion of trifle. 'People don't go so often now that they have the telly to watch at home.'

'That's why so many cinemas are closing down or becoming bingo halls,' said Winnie.

'I hope they don't all disappear,' said Phoebe. 'I'm rather partial to a night out at the flicks.'

They drifted on to other things, everyone talking at once, the conversation interspersed with gales of laughter. Mentally standing back from the company for a moment, listening to the friendly chatter, enjoying the scent of roses drifting in from the garden, Gill felt an inner glow. She loved having the people she cared about gathered together in her home, even though her mother and Phoebe only just managed to tolerate each other. The fact that it was her birthday added lustre to the occasion and she felt quite sentimental.

Over coffee, she decided it was time to make the announcement. 'Listen, everyone,' she said, standing up purposefully, 'Arnie and I have something important to tell you. And, no, I'm not having another baby – not at the moment, anyway.'

'Gill,' admonished Arnie, 'I thought we agreed not to say anything tonight.'

'You said we weren't going to,' she reminded him, 'I didn't agree.'

'Don't keep us in suspense then,' said Phoebe. 'If you're not pregnant, what is the big news?'

Gill looked at Arnie, who nodded for her to continue. 'Arnie's been offered a contract with Borough Football Club for next season,' she said, swelling with pride.

There was a brief hiatus while everyone digested this news. Borough FC was a first-division London club.

'Wow!' said John.

'Oh, Arnie, well done, son,' said his mother, getting up and going over to him to smack a kiss on his cheek, her eyes glistening with tears. 'You really are going up in the world.'

When the effusive congratulations had died down, Hal said, 'So it'll be tuppence to talk to you from now on, then?'

'Do me a favour,' was Arnie's swift response. 'You know I'm not like that.'

'You're really doing well, though, son,' said Phoebe.

'I'm not complainin'.'

'Are you gonna be famous from now on?' Carol wanted to know.

'Don't be daft.'

'He's already been on the telly,' Gill proudly reminded her sister. Clips of the matches Arnie played in were occasionally shown on sports programmes. 'What more do you want?'

'But if you blink you miss him,' said Carol. 'I wanna see him on there properly, being interviewed or something.'

'You'll wait for ever if you wait for that,' said Arnie.

'Not necessarily,' said Phoebe.

'You're all making far too much of it,' declared Arnie, making a face. 'All I'm doing is changing clubs. It's no big deal.'

'I'd say that being offered the chance to play for Borough Football Club is a very big deal indeed,' said Hal.

'Yeah, don't be so modest, Arnie,' rebuked his mother laughingly.

'Will you be getting a big flash car?' asked John excitedly. 'I hope you get something that goes like a rocket.'

'You'll be moving to a posh house, I suppose,' said Winnie.

Arnie stood up suddenly and raised his hands for silence. 'Right! Let's get this thing into proportion once and for all,' he said in a firm tone. 'I'm joining Borough Football Club, which is an upward career move for me, and I'm well chuffed about it. And, yes, I will be earning quite a lot more money, which means we'll be able to manage a few more luxuries. But we won't be changing the way we live. We're not planning on moving house or anything dramatic like that. I'll still be the same old Arnie. So, let's have no more daft talk of posh houses and flash cars.'

'All right, keep your hair on, son,' said his mother.

'Yeah, stop spoiling it,' said Gill, smiling at her husband. 'This is the most exciting thing that's ever happened to this family.'

'Carol won't be long, Dougie,' said Winnie one day, about a year later, to the young man who had come to call for her daughter and was perched nervously on the edge of the sofa in the living room. Hal was reading the paper and Winnie was knitting a sweater for Craig for the winter even though it was still only midsummer. 'She's probably just putting the finishing touches to her make-up.'

'Yeah, I expect that's what's keeping her, Mrs Miller,' said Dougie Rivers politely. A regular caller at the Millers' house lately, he was an inoffensive twenty-one-year-old with a shock of fair hair and blue eyes, which currently had a worried look about them because he felt uncomfortable when he was on his own with his girlfriend's parents.

'Where are you thinking of going this evening?' enquired Winnie, who didn't think it could be anywhere special judging by the casual way he was dressed in tight jeans and a leather jacket. But there was no telling with young people these days because they were so much less conventional in their dress than they used to be.

'We might go ten pin bowling if Carol fancies it,' he said, 'or the pictures. Depends what Carol wants to do.'

'That'll be nice.'

Winnie was knitting furiously, which usually helped when she was finding a conversation difficult – and this one was impossible. She cleared her throat loudly to get her husband's attention, then appealed to him with her eyes.

'Oh . . . er, I understand from Carol that your father is a sales representative, Dougie,' Hal said, taking the hint at last.

'That's right,' the lad said. 'He works for a firm of printers.'

'That must be interestin' for him, being out and about all the time,' Hal prompted, desperate to fill the awkward silence.

'I suppose it must be, Mr Miller,' said Dougie, glancing desperately towards the door in the hope that Carol would appear and rescue him from this agonising situation.

'You didn't fancy following in his footsteps then?' asked Hal.

'No.'

'You're in menswear, aren't you?'

'Yeah. I work in a gents outfitters in Hammersmith.'

'Oh.'

'I went back to my old job when I came out of the army.'

'Does it have decent prospects?' asked Winnie.

'Yeah. I'm hoping to be a manager of one of the branches eventually.'

'As long as you're happy in the job, that's the main thing,' said Hal, trying to put the poor lad at his ease because he'd noticed a strawberry flush suffusing his face and neck.

'You're right, Mr Miller,' said Dougie, wondering just how much longer Carol was going to be.

'If you like the job and there's a future in it, you can't go wrong, can you?' said Winnie, who couldn't help viewing every boyfriend of Carol's as a prospective husband.

'No, Mrs Miller, you can't,' was Dougie's dutiful reply.

Winnie was thinking that her daughter would be wise to hang on to this one. He seemed like a steady, decent type and he had a job with prospects. Carol's boyfriends never seemed to stay around for long, though. Winnie wasn't sure why, but she thought the girl's demanding nature might have something to do with it. Still, there was plenty of time – she was only nineteen.

Thinking in terms of the present, Winnie hoped Carol wasn't going to keep him waiting much longer because *Emergency Ward Ten* would be on the television in a minute and she didn't want to miss it.

As luck would have it, at that very moment the living room door opened and Carol swept in, wearing a skinny rib top with a short skirt.

'Sorry to have been so long, Dougie,' she said smiling sweetly at him.

'S'all right,' he said, standing up and looking relieved.

'Let's go then, shall we?'

'Sure.' He almost bounded to the door in his eagerness to get away.

'Enjoy yourselves,' said Hal.

'Don't be too late now,' said Winnie.

'No, Mum,' sighed Carol with more than a hint of irritation.

As the front door closed behind them, Winnie said to Hal, 'He seems a nice enough boy.'

'Yeah, not bad at all.'

'Seems very keen on Carol,' she added.

Hal nodded and turned his attention back to the newspaper.

Winnie got up to turn on the television set and glanced out of the window to see the couple walking down the street. Carol was hanging on to Dougie's arm and smiling up at him adoringly. Winnie hoped she wasn't being too eager. She did tend to get a bit clingy with boyfriends.

It would be quite a relief to see Carol settled with a nice fellow. Being so sensitive, she had had her heart broken several times already. But Dougie seemed genuinely fond of her and, if Winnie was any judge, he was going to be around for some time – permanently, she hoped – giving Carol all the things her sister had missed: the engagement ring, the church wedding . . .

With her eldest daughter in mind, Winnie reflected pleasurably on the fact that her doubts about Gill's marriage to Arnie had proved to be groundless. Gill was happy and settled with a good life, free from financial worries.

Arnie had gone from strength to strength since he'd got into that first division team a year ago. In fact he was quite a celebrity these days. His name regularly cropped up on the sports pages of the newspapers and he was often mentioned by sports commentators on TV. A regular stream of fan letters was sent to him at the club, too, by all accounts.

He provided well for his wife and child. They had been abroad on holiday recently, the first members of the Miller or Briscoe families ever to do so. He'd even bought Gill her own little car. For all that Winnie was a no-nonsense sort of person, she had to admit to enjoying being related to someone with a touch of fame about them.

Nowadays people wanted to talk to her in the street because of her famous son-in-law. He was a hero in Fulham and his name meant something to football fans all over the country. After her earlier fears, Winnie now had no worries at all about Gill . . .

'I'm not going to bed till Daddy gets home,' pronounced four-year-old Craig in stubborn mood one Monday evening in the autumn, pressing into the back of the sofa as though to make himself invisible.

'Come on, love, don't give me a hard time,' said Gill patiently.

'Not going to bed.'

'You are, young man.'

His cheeks were flushed from the warmth of the room, his huge brown eyes heavy with tiredness and puffy from crying with disappointment because his father hadn't arrived home yet.

'Now do as you're told . . . please.'

'You said I could stay up till Daddy gets home,' said the boy, who was freshly bathed and wearing a bright blue dressing gown over his striped pyjamas, his brown curly hair shining in the subtle glow from the wall lights. 'Daddy said I could too.'

'I know we did, darling, but Daddy is much later than I expected and it's way past your bedtime,' Gill said.

'Why can't I stay up?' he whined.

'Because you have to be up early in the morning to go to nursery school.'

'Not going to bed,' he said again with petulance, desperately tired but fighting sleep to the bitter end because he so much wanted to see his adored father.

'Be a good boy and come upstairs,' she persisted, clinging to her much tried patience. 'I'll read you a story.'

'Want Daddy to read me a story.'

Gill looked at her watch and her heart felt like lead. Arnie had said he'd be home at about five o'clock at the latest. It was now seven-thirty. Money and success of the kind he'd enjoyed since he'd been playing in the first division had changed him. Although Gill had kept it from the rest of the family, he was no longer the devoted, home-loving husband he used to be. These days he preferred London's night-spots to his own home.

But it wasn't like him to be this late without letting her know, especially as he knew Craig would be waiting up for him. How long could a charity lunch go on for, for heaven's sake?

Realising that Craig was about to doze off, she sat down and lifted him on to her lap where he fell asleep almost immediately. After she'd carried him upstairs to bed and settled him for the night, she came back downstairs and tried to watch some television but was too tense to concentrate, fearing Arnie had had an accident. Her heart was beating in tune with her riotous imagination as she pictured him in a hospital bed or the mortuary.

At ten o'clock he arrived home in a taxi and swaggered into the house without a care.

'I've been worried to death,' she said.

'Why?'

'Because you're five hours late.'

'I wasn't aware that I had to clock in in my own home.'

'I thought something had happened to you.'

'Cor blimey, woman, I can't tell you to the exact minute when I'll be home,' he said condescendingly. 'You know what these things are like.'

'But where have you been all this time?' she asked, hurt by his off-hand manner.

'You know where I've been,' he snapped, frowning darkly at her. 'At the Hyde Park Hotel for a charity lunch.'

'That started just after midday,' she said spiritedly. 'It's gone ten o'clock now.'

He flopped down into an armchair and loosened his tie. He wasn't drunk, but he'd obviously had plenty to drink. His colour was high and his skin gleaming with a fine layer of perspiration.

'So, I got held up.'

'For all those hours?'

'Oh, leave it out, will you, Gill?' he said irritably. 'The last thing I want is an inquisition. I'm shattered.'

'You're shattered!' she said, her dark eyes flashing. 'You've been out enjoying yourself—'

'The lunch was work,' he corrected.

'Oh, yeah, wading through a six-course meal at a posh West End hotel with the wine and champagne flowing must be real hard graft,' she said, driven to sacrasm by the fear of losing him.

He was becoming ever more deeply immersed in his own glamorous world and increasingly distant from her. As much as she hated to think ill of him, there was no denying the fact that he had become extremely arrogant lately.

'You know damned well what I mean,' he said aggressively.

'Do I?' she said, smarting inside from his coldness.

'It was a professional engagement,' he said with seething impatience. 'I didn't particularly want to go. But I went because my being there helps to sell tickets, which helps the charity and is good PR for me. You know I have to do a certain amount of that sort of thing now that I'm a name, because it puts me in a position to help raise funds. As well as doing my bit for charity, it's good for the club. Anyway, it's expected of me.'

'I understand all that, Arnie,' she said in a softer tone, because she loved him desperately, 'but I was worried about you . . . and Craig was disappointed. I had a job getting him to bed because you promised him he could wait up to see you.'

He slapped his brow with his hand, showing the first signs of remorse. 'Craig, o'course,' he said, his manner becoming immediately conciliatory. 'I forgot I'd told him he could wait up to see me. God, I'm really sorry about that, babe.'

'I should damned well hope you are,' she said. 'Let me down if you must, but not a four-year-old child. You could have phoned to let me know you were going to be late.'

'I could have, but I didn't,' he said, irascible again. 'I've said I'm sorry, so will you please shut up about it?'

'Don't try to make me feel as though I'm in the wrong,' she said evenly, standing her ground despite the fact that she was aching inside and on the verge of tears. 'We all know you're a big man now, the famous soccer star who gets his picture in the paper and fan letters in the mail. But that doesn't give you the right to disregard other people's feelings, especially your son's.'

'Oh, I've had just about enough of this! I'm going to bed,' he said furiously, and got up and marched to the door.

She ran after him and pulled at his arm. 'Oh, no, you're not gonna just walk away from this one,' she said, her temper rising. 'I'm entitled to an explanation.'

'For God's sake,' he said, swinging round and glaring at her. 'All I've done is come home a bit late. It isn't a criminal offence.'

He was even more attractive in this slightly dishevelled state. His tie was loose, suit jacket undone, white shirt emphasising his light tan, the combined result of their summer holiday in Spain and his being out in the fresh air so much in the course of his work.

With his close proximity came a strong whiff of something that turned her heart to stone. She put her face close to the lapel of his suit and sniffed.

'You've been with a woman,' she said, buffeted by the shock. 'I can smell her perfume.'

'Don't be ridiculous,' he snapped. 'It's my aftershave.'

'Please don't take me for a fool, Arnie.' The thought of him being with another woman was physically painful to her. 'I think I know the difference between Chanel and Old Spice.' She moved away, looking into his face. 'How could you, Arnie? How could you?'

'I haven't been with a woman,' he denied hotly.

'Don't make thing worse by lying to me,' she said, her voice shaking, tears welling up. 'I can smell her on you.'

Worried now, he moved towards her but she shrank back.

'Don't touch me,' she said, her voice dull with pain. 'I don't want you anywhere near me.'

'Oh, for goodness sake,' he said, grabbing hold of her and looking into her face, eager to pacify her now that he knew he was in deep trouble. 'It isn't what you think.'

'Isn't that what all adulterers say when they get found out?'

'I'm not an adulterer.'

She struggled to pull away but he held her firmly by the arms. 'Just calm down and let me tell you what happened.'

'I'm not sure I want to hear it,' she said, her voice breaking.

'Please don't cry,' he begged, letting her go, full of regret now. 'Just give me a chance to tell you what happened, why I was late home and why I smell of perfume.'

'Go on then,' she said wearily, sitting down in an armchair, looking at him.

'I've been to a nightclub in the West End,' he explained.

'And . . . ?'

'I danced with a woman there,' he explained. 'And I mean *just* danced . . . The perfume you can smell must be hers.'

'You must have been dancing pretty damned close,' said Gill, a feeling of hysteria welling up inside her. She had known her marriage was in trouble for some time, and this seemed to confirm it. Arnie had always been an attractive man, but success and fame were an aphrodisiac to some women. She'd seen the way they looked at him at the glamorous social functions they attended nowadays. He could have anyone. Beautiful, classy women – models and showbiz lovelies. There was no shortage of temptation.

'Maybe we were, I can't remember,' he said. 'I'd had a good few drinks. It was all just a bit of a laugh. But nothing else happened, I swear to you. All we did was dance.'

'Who was she?'

'Dunno, just somebody on a night out with some friends,' he told her. 'The blokes dared me to ask her to dance.'

'God, it's pathetic,' she said, but she believed him, and it was a relief.

'It was just a bit o' fun.'

'You were in some sleazy nightclub,' she said, shaking her head and leaning forward, 'when you were supposed to be at home with me and Craig. No wonder you didn't want to tell me where you'd been.'

'It wasn't sleazy. It was quite classy as a matter of fact.'

'But you shouldn't have been there, should you? Not when you'd promised to be home,' she said. 'God knows, you have enough leeway. I'm not the sort of wife to keep you in chains. I don't stop you doing what you want to do, especially now that you're getting invitations to social functions which don't include me. But when you promise your son that you'll be here for him, then that's where you should be.'

Sighing deeply, Arnie sat down opposite her, leaning forward slightly. 'Look, I had every intention of coming home after the lunch—'

'So why are we having this conversation?' Gill interrupted, her voice thick with emotion. 'While I was trying to pacify our son because you weren't here, and imagining you'd been taken ill or had an accident or something, you were smooching around the dancefloor with some dolly bird.'

'Look, the lunch went on until well into the afternoon,' he said. 'There was this chap sitting next to me, a businessman called George Flowers who owns Flowers nightclub . . . absolutely rolling in money. He's a bit of a comedian, actually, had me in fits. I was glad of his company, because some of the others were a bit dry. Anyway, he suggested a few of us go on to his club afterwards, just to wind down.'

'And you had to go because he suggested it, of course . . .'

'I wanted to go,' he told her straight. 'The lunch had put me in a sociable mood and it seemed like a good idea at the time.'

'All you had to do was pick up the telephone, Arnie . . .'

'I honestly didn't intend to stay long,' he told her. 'I don't know what happened to the time. The club wasn't open when we got there so we had the place to ourselves. Then suddenly it was evening and the place was full of punters.'

'And there was dancing and you entered into the spirit of the thing?'

'Exactly.'

'Apart from anything else, you're not supposed to be overdoing the booze,' she reminded him. 'You agreed to that when you signed the contract.'

'It'll take more than a few drinks to upset my game,' he blustered.

'I shouldn't be too sure of that,' she said. 'It'll take its toll if you do it too often.'

'That's my business,' he roared, his temper flaring again. 'I don't need my wife to tell me how to conduct myself.'

'You're getting too big for your boots, that's your trouble,' she said, rising.

'Rubbish!'

'Being a football star doesn't make you God Almighty.'

'All of this because I danced with some woman,' he said scornfully.

'That isn't how it is and don't be so damned patronising,' she said. 'All of this is because you broke a promise to your son . . . and to me.'

'All right, so I let my hair down and forgot to ring you.' He lowered his eyes. 'I'm sorry.'

Suddenly Gill was very tired. 'Okay, Arnie,' she said, deciding that enough had been said on the subject. She walked across the room to the door feeling weak and shaky, as though she'd just had a near miss in the car, relieved to have come through it but very much aware that it could happen again. 'Let's forget all about it. I'm going to bed.'

'Okay.'

'Goodnight.'

'I'll be up in minute, babe,' he said, watching her go then leaning back and closing his eyes.

She was right, of course, he should have come home straight after the lunch. But it was hard to leave when your presence was so much in demand, people wanting to talk to you and buy you drinks.

He hadn't exactly been lying to Gill about having only danced with the woman at the club; but he had given her an edited version of what had happened. He hadn't danced with the woman because of a dare. She had been sending out signals and he'd responded. What man could resist the come-on from a Marilyn Monroe lookalike with endless legs and a bosom that would unsettle the most married of men? Dancing with her had been a tormenting pleasure, if you could call what they'd been doing on the dancefloor dancing. It was no wonder he'd come home smelling of her perfume.

When she'd invited him back to her place, however, the warning bells had been so deafening he'd managed to drag himself away. As tempting as the alternative was, and as much as he enjoyed being fancied, he didn't want those sort of complications because he was a happily married man.

Looking back over his life, he could see that he'd never played the field like most young men, had not got it out of his system. He'd only been seventeen when he and Gill had started courting, and there had been no one else for him since. But although he didn't want any other woman, he did enjoy the glamour and excitement of being out on the town, being fancied by women and envied by men.

Unfortunately, a bachelor lifestyle isn't conducive to a happy marriage, he thought, getting up and following his wife upstairs to bed.

Chapter Four

The next morning Gill behaved with determined normality, even though she'd barely slept and was still smarting from last night's altercation. She'd made her opinion clear; there was no point in inflaming the situation by letting the argument drag on.

Arnie was in repentant mood when he came down to the kitchen for breakfast.

'Sorry about last night, babe,' he said, sitting down at the table, looking disturbingly macho in a black dressing gown.

'I told you to forget it,' she said evenly, helping Craig to spread honey on his toast.

'Yeah, I know you did, but in the light of day I can see that I was right out of order.'

'Apology accepted,' she said, relieved that he seemed so keen to put things right.

'You turned your back on me when I came to bed last night,' he said with a hint of reproval.

'You didn't expect me to do otherwise, did you?' she said.

'I s'pose not, but I didn't like it.'

'Serves you right,' she said. 'But it's past history now . . . over and done with.'

'You're a diamond,' he said affectionately, reaching for her hand.

'And you've more flannel than an elephant's nightshirt.'

Having made his peace with her, he emptied some corn flakes into his bowl, poured milk over them and turned his attention to Craig.

'You going to nursery school this morning, buster?' he asked.

Craig nodded, munching his toast.

'What will you be doing there?'

'Driving the car.'

'Oh? Don't you usually do painting and drawing pictures?'

'Yeah, but I like driving the car best,' the boy explained, licking honey from his fingers.

'They've got a pedal car and all the boys fight over it,' explained Gill.

'And the gels,' added Craig.

'Ah, I see.' Arnie smiled and looked at his wife, enquiring chattily, 'So, what are you doing this morning?'

43

'When I've dropped Craig off at school I'm going to Hammersmith . . . to the music shop.'

'For anything special?' he asked in a pleasant, conversational manner.

'Yeah. I'm gonna give myself a treat and get the music of that lovely new song that's just come out called "Moon River",' she said.

'I like that one too,' said Arnie.

'Now that we have the record, I can't wait to play it on the piano.'

'It'll be a piece o'cake compared to some of the stuff you tackle.' Arnie admired his wife's musical ability and was often quite awestruck when she played difficult classical pieces. He wasn't gifted that way himself, but enjoyed the musical atmosphere Gill created in the house.

'It shouldn't be too much of a challenge,' she agreed. 'But it's fun to play light pop tunes now and again for a change.'

'I'll look forward to hearing it.'

Gill frowned. 'Which reminds me – I mustn't forget to give the piano repairer a ring,' she said. 'I've got a couple of duff keys. The strings have gone.'

'Again?' he said in surprise. 'It isn't long since he was last here.'

'It's an old piano.' She drank her tea. 'Fortunately he never keeps me waiting for long and he's good at the job. He's reckoned to be the best tuner this side of the river.'

Arnie fell silent, seeming thoughtful while he ate his cereal.

'Are you coming straight home after you've been to the music shop – or going shopping?' he asked after a while.

'I've only a few odds and ends to get from the shops, so I thought I'd pop over to Maisie Road and spend some time with my mum until I collect Craig at lunchtime,' she said, diligent in her filial duty. 'I haven't seen her for a few days.' She paused, wondering why he'd asked. 'Why? Did you want me to get you something from the shops?'

'No.'

'Why the interest then?'

'No reason,' he said lightly. 'I was just making conversation.' He gulped his tea and got up from the table, in a hurry suddenly.

'Why the rush?' she asked.

'I have to get ready for work.'

'Already?' said Gill in surprise. 'Is training earlier today?'

Seeming preoccupied, he didn't reply but hurried to the door.

'Arnie?'

'Yeah?' he said, turning.

'Why are you going to the training ground so early?' she asked.

'Oh . . . um,' he began with suspicious hesitance, 'the boss wants us all there early . . . some sort of a pep talk before training, I expect. He was miffed about last Saturday's result. He doesn't like his team to lose two weeks running and wants to make sure it doesn't happen again this week.'

'Oh, I see.'

A short time later he reappeared wearing a casual jacket over his jeans and carrying his team holdall. He gave his wife and son a preoccupied kiss and hurried out of the door like someone with urgent matters on his mind.

'Well, your daddy is certainly in a hurry this morning,' Gill said to Craig, puzzled by the swiftness of Arnie's departure.

Gill was surprised to find that her mother wasn't at home later that same morning, because Tuesday was Winnie's day for cleaning the upstairs of her house and she wasn't given to breaking her domestic routine. Gill still had a key, and had let herself in to find the place empty.

Going upstairs to find the vacuum cleaner in the middle of the landing and dusters on the small landing table, she was further puzzled. Her mother would never go out leaving a cleaning job half-done unless something really urgent had cropped up. Perhaps she'd run out of cleaning materials – which probably would be a matter of some urgency to her, Gill thought. But that explanation didn't carry much weight, because Winnie was far too well organised to run out of anything. So where the devil was she?

Gill made herself a cup of coffee and sat at the kitchen table to wait for her mother's return. To help pass the time she glanced at the newspaper, which carried reports of the massive Ban the Bomb demonstration that had taken place in Trafalgar Square on Sunday, at which over eight hundred people had been arrested, some of them prominent musicians and actors. It was an emotive issue that stirred passion in the most unexpected people.

Gill had just finished her coffee when her mother appeared, flushed from the crisp autumn weather and breathless from hurrying.

'There you are,' said Gill. 'I wondered where you'd got to.'

'Did you? Why?'

'Because you don't usually go out on a Tuesday morning.'

'I don't usually, no,' Winnie agreed, offering no explanation.

'So, where have you been then?'

'Er . . . I had to pop down to the market.'

Gill gave her a shrewd look, noticing the absence of a shopping bag. 'What for?' she asked.

'Oh, just a few bits and pieces.' She tutted and removed her headscarf. 'But why am I being interrogated?'

'Just interested, that's all.' Gill paused thoughtfully. 'If you went to the market, where's the shopping?'

'Changed my mind when I got there, didn't I?' she was rather too quick to explain. 'Decided I didn't need any veg until tomorrow after all.'

45

'It isn't like you go out and leave a job half-done, Mum,' Gill said. 'You were in the middle of doing the bedrooms.'

Winnie shot her daughter a disapproving look. 'Since when do I have to account for my actions to you?' she asked sternly, but there was something phoney about her manner somehow.

'You don't.'

'Good.'

'Is anything wrong?'

'Wrong? What could be wrong?' she said briskly, removing her coat and filling the new electric kettle that Arnie had recently treated her to.

'You seem a bit . . . well, preoccupied about something.'

'You're imagining things,' Winnie said, plugging the kettle in and turning it on.

'That's all right, then.' Gill remained unconvinced. 'I'll have another cup of coffee if you're making some.'

'Didn't you ought to be getting off home?' Winnie suggested, going over to the larder and taking out a tin of Nescafé.

Gill looked at her enquiringly. 'No. Why should I?'

For some unknown reason, Winnie's face turned bright pink. 'I dunno . . . to put your shopping away and do a few chores before you collect Craig from nursery school,' she said. 'Isn't that what you usually do?'

'Yes . . . but not this morning, because I've come round here to see you,' she said. 'I thought you'd be pleased.'

'I am, o' course, but . . .' Again there was uncertainty in her manner. 'I have to get on with the cleaning as soon as I've finished my coffee.'

'Are you trying to get rid of me or something, Mum?'

'Of course I'm not, but I can't chat for long because I've a lot of housework to do,' said Winnie, pouring boiling water into two coffee cups.

'You usually enjoy a chat,' stated Gill, puzzled.

'I know I do, but it's been one of those mornings.' She handed Gill a cup of coffee and sat down at the table opposite her. 'So, we'll make this a short break and then both get on with what we have to do, shall we?'

'Okay,' said Gill, but she couldn't help feeling worried by her mother's peculiar attitude.

Driving home in the golden autumn morning, the hazy sunshine filtering through trees ablaze with colour, Gill was thinking about her mother's odd behaviour. That tale about her going to the market and changing her mind about buying anything didn't tally with her efficient nature. She had definitely been hiding something. An unseen hand drove into Gill's chest as she thought that perhaps the subterfuge had been to conceal a trip to the doctors about some ominous symptoms her mother had been keeping to herself. Oh, well, she'll tell me when she's ready, she thought, turning into Danny Gardens and parking her green Morris Minor outside the house.

Stepping into the hall, with its polished wood floor and vase of fresh chrysanthemums on a small round table beneath a gilt-edged mirror, Gill felt the soothing atmosphere of home wash over her, calming her nerves, which were still jangling from the effects of last night's quarrel as well as her mother's worrying behaviour this morning.

Hanging up her coat in the hall cupboard, she went straight into the kitchen to put the few sundry items of shopping away, stifling the urge to get cracking with her new piece of music until she'd given the kitchen floor a once-over with the mop.

Chores completed, she went into the living room and over to the piano, looking at the music as she went. Sitting down on the stool, about to open the lid, she blinked hard. Stared again. What was going on? The old piano, with the scratch-marks and circles left by years of teacups and tumblers, had gone. In its place was a beautiful new Steinway, its polished black surface gleaming in the sunlight that streamed through the window.

The framed photographs she'd always had standing on the top of the old piano had been transferred to this new model. Propped up against their wedding photograph in the centre was a scribbled note in Arnie's handwriting.

'Sorry about last night. Hope this will help you to forgive me.'

'Oh, Arnie, you fool, you wonderful extravagant fool!' she cried to the room, tears streaming down her cheeks as she opened the lid and stroked the keys that were many shades lighter than the yellowed ones she was used to.

The sound of the telephone ringing in the hall interrupted her thoughts. She knew who the caller was even before she picked up the receiver.

'It's beautiful, Arnie,' she said, her voice ragged with emotion. 'Thank you so much. But you shouldn't have . . .'

'Am I forgiven?'

'You were forgiven anyway,' she said softly through copious tears. 'You didn't need to spend all that money . . .'

'It was about time I fixed you up with a decent joanna anyway,' he said. 'The other one had just about had its day. I bought the new one on a sudden impulse. When you mentioned you needed the repair man again, I thought it was the ideal opportunity.'

'It must have cost you a fortune.'

'You're worth it,' he said. 'And I can afford it, thanks to the job.'

'How did you manage to arrange it so quickly?' she asked.

'I was at the music shop in Hammersmith when they opened this morning, having called on your mother on the way to give her the key to our house so she could let the delivery men in,' he explained.

'No wonder you went off in such a hurry this morning.'

'Yeah. Once I'd had the idea I couldn't wait to set it in motion.'

'I'm surprised you managed to get it delivered that quickly.'

'You'll be surprised how fast people can move if you flash enough dough under their nose.'

'That's why Mum wasn't in,' she said almost to herself. 'She was here seeing the piano in when I got to her place.'

'That's right.'

'And I suppose that's why she wanted me to come home right away ... because of the suprise that was waiting for me here,' she said, relieved that the mystery was solved.

'Yeah.'

'Oh, Arnie, you're a lovely man.'

'Can I have that in writing?'

'You don't need it.'

She could hear someone calling him in the background. 'Look, I'll have to go, babe,' he said. 'We're in the middle of a training session. I managed to slip inside to the phone.'

'Okay. I'll see you later.'

'Oh, by the way, Gill, the old piano is going back to your mum and dad's place, but I've arranged for it to have an overhaul at the shop first.'

'Really?'

'Yeah. Your mum couldn't bear the idea of it going out of the family altogether.'

The thought of the old piano being back in her parents' living room made her feel sentimental, and she felt fresh tears forming. It was like hearing that an old friend was safe and well.

'I'm glad,' she said thickly. 'But thanks for the new one. It was a lovely surprise.'

'It was a pleasure.'

'Love you.'

'Love you too.'

Replacing the receiver she wandered back into the living room, an epitome of style and comfort with its cream walls, soft red carpet and pale orange velvet curtains. She sat down on the piano stool and put her new music in the stand, her joy and gratitude almost painful in its intensity.

But nagging away at her glorious sense of well-being was a speck of discomfort she couldn't quite identify. There was something about this excessively generous gesture of Arnie's that made her feel uneasy.

She pushed it from her mind and put her fingers on the keys.

One Saturday evening in March of the following year, Carol and Dougie were lovingly ensconced on the sofa in Gill and Arnie's living room, having come to visit for the evening. *Perry Mason* was on the television but no one was watching it because they were idly chatting.

'Why aren't you two young things out enjoying yourself on a Saturday night?' enquired Arnie lightly.

'We *are* out enjoying ourselves,' replied Carol.

'You know what I mean,' said Arnie. 'A young couple like yourselves, with no ties, should be out letting your hair down at a dance or a disco or something.'

'We like staying at home with you and Gill,' said Carol, snuggling closer to Dougie, to whom she had recently got engaged. 'Don't we, Dougie?'

'Yeah,' he said, but he didn't sound wildly enthusiastic.

'As long as we're together we don't mind where we are, do we, Dougie?'

Carol's tone made Gill's skin crawl because it was so embarrassingly possessive. Her sister's cloying attitude towards her fiancé was getting worse, and Gill was worried about the effect it might be having on Dougie.

'That's right,' agreed Dougie dutifully.

'Saturday night in front of the telly is for married couples with kids like me and Gill,' opined Arnie. 'You two ought to make the most of your freedom while you can and go out and paint the town red at the weekend.'

'We're saving up to get married,' Carol informed him loftily, taking Dougie's hand in both of hers and caressing it. 'We're not interested in going out to dances and discos.'

'If we'd known you were coming, Gill and I would have arranged to have a night out and left you two baby-sitting,' said Arnie.

'I'll make some coffee,' said Gill.

'I'd rather have a pint,' said Arnie, throwing Dougie a meaningful look. 'Fancy coming down the local for a quick one while the girls are chatting, mate?' He turned to Gill. 'You don't mind, do you, love?'

'Course not,' said Gill, who was used to Arnie's going out and knew he would go whether she objected or not.

'Dougie doesn't want to go out, do you?' said Carol, frowning at her fiancé.

'Well . . . er, I wouldn't mind,' he said, looking sheepish. 'Just for half an hour or so . . . It'll be a break from indoors.'

Carol stared at him with a thunderous expression. 'We're supposed to be spending the evening together,' she snorted.

'They won't be gone long,' Gill intervened, hoping to defuse the rising tension.

Glaring at Dougie, Carol said through clenched teeth, 'You do what you like. Don't mind me.'

'There's no need to get the hump, Carol,' admonished Arnie in the forthright manner that comes with long-term acquaintance. 'Surely you don't begrudge him half an hour out of the house with his future brother-in-law?'

She shot Arnie a contemptuous look. He went over to where she was sitting and looked down at her persuasively.

'I'll have him back here in half an hour – an hour at the very most, love, I promise,' he said, winking at her. 'So how about giving your big brother-in-law a smile?'

'Just go, for goodness sake,' she said, but she did manage a watery smile because she still had a soft spot for Arnie.

'Fancy a biscuit, Carol?' Gill invited after the men had gone and she had made coffee. 'The chocolate ones are yummy.'

'No thanks,' said Carol sulkily.

'Oh, come on, sis, cheer up,' said Gill. 'Dougie isn't doing any harm.'

'I haven't said he is,' she said, her hazel eyes full of pique. 'It's just that he's meant to be spending the evening with me.'

'Why come round here to visit us if you want him to yourself then?' Gill said. 'Why not go dancing or for a drink or to the pictures or something, as Arnie suggested?'

'I've told you. We're supposed to be saving up to get married,' she said.

'Is it a good idea not to have any fun, though?' queried Gill.

'You don't have to go out to have fun, you know,' Carol said huffily. 'We don't need expensive entertainment to keep us amused.'

'Even so . . .'

'We're trying to get enough money together for the deposit on a house . . . and there's the furniture and things to pay for as well,' she said crossly. 'We'll never have enough if we spend it all on going out.'

Gill sipped her coffee, looking at Carol over the rim of the cup and seeing a smart, moderately attractive young woman of twenty dressed in a black polo-necked sweater and red short skirt, her hair heavily backcombed into an exaggerated bouffant. Because Gill loved her sister and cared about what happened to her, she felt duty-bound to come right out and say something that was not going to make her popular.

'You must be doing quite well with your savings as you're staying in so much,' said Gill, leading up to her point gradually. 'Going out now and again won't make that much difference.'

'It will.'

'But you don't want your relationship with Dougie to go stale because of too much togetherness, though. Do you?'

Carol gave her sister a sharp look. 'Meaning?'

Gill braced herself to say what she felt she ought to. 'Meaning that if you're going to make a scene like the one this evening every time

50

Dougie wants to leave your side for a spot of socialising, he'll start to feel trapped.'

'Huh! You're a fine one to give advice on how to keep a man,' retorted Carol indignantly.

'What do you mean by that?'

'Don't play dumb,' said Carol, who was trembling with anger, 'everyone knows that Arnie is giving you a really hard time, that he's always out boozing and womanising. I'm amazed he was at home tonight when we called, as a matter of fact.'

'So he likes a good time and he can afford to have one,' said Gill, agonised by the thoughts this attack had evoked. 'It doesn't mean anything.'

'You've got no hold on him now,' said Carol. 'He does just as he likes.'

'How do you know all this?'

'Arnie boasts about it to the other blokes,' she explained. 'He'll be bending Doug's ear about it at this very moment, I should think. Telling him about the glitzy clubs he goes to in the West End, and how the most beautiful women in London want to go to bed with him.'

'Shut up, Carol—'

'Your marriage is heading for the rocks and you know it,' Carol said.

'And you won't get married at all if you don't give Dougie some space.'

'You're just jealous 'cause you can't hang on to Arnie.'

Gill winced. 'The state of my marriage has nothing to do with my opinion of the situation between you and Dougie,' she said, managing to stay in control as she had had to do so many times in the past when dealing with Carol's emotional over-reactions. 'But it makes me cringe to see you being so clinging with him. I've been wanting to say something for a long time.'

'I dunno who you think you are,' said Carol, her eyes shining with tears.

'Oh, Carol . . . please—'

'You've always poked your nose into my business and tried to run my life.'

'I have not,' said Gill. 'If I feel compelled to say something now it's only because I care about you and don't want you to get hurt.'

'Yeah, well,' muttered Carol, her volatile temper evaporating as suddenly as it had flared up. 'You don't have to worry, because Dougie loves me and he wouldn't do anything to hurt me.'

'Yes, I believe he does loves you,' said Gill. 'But I do think you ought to give him more freedom.' She paused, looking grim. 'But, as you say, I'm a fine one to talk.'

Carol was immediately contrite at her sister's admission of a problem. 'I'm sorry for what I said about you and Arnie,' she said, her eyes

51

brimming with tears. 'I was in a temper. I didn't mean it.'

'Don't worry about it.'

'You're not upset.'

'Not with you.'

'Sure?'

'Yeah.'

'Good.' Carol paused. 'Do I really go over the top with Dougie?' she asked, seeming very young and vulnerable suddenly.

'Well, just a bit,' said Gill with the hesitant candour of someone who genuinely cares.

'It's 'cause I love him and I can't wait to get married,' Carol said with an air of innocent enthusiasm that twisted Gill's heart. 'I want a home of my own and babies . . . everything you have.'

'It'll come,' said Gill. 'Just take it easy on yourself . . . and Dougie.'

'I'll try.'

'Good girl.'

'I really didn't mean to say that about your marriage,' said Carol. 'Arnie's great. I'm sure the two of you will work things out.'

'I hope so,' said Gill.

But life with Arnie was becoming increasingly impossible, and she just didn't know what to do about it.

Chapter Five

Gill was sitting on a bench in Bishop's Park one Sunday afternoon a few weeks later, watching Arnie and Craig kicking a ball about on the grass. She was thinking how much like his father Craig was getting – the same colouring, the greenish-brown eyes, the thick brown curly hair, similar mannerisms. He was even beginning to walk with the same swaggering gait as his father, even though he was only just coming up to five years old.

She didn't mind being slightly set apart from them by their maleness. It was the natural thing, and it gave her a sense of family. The fact that father and son were bonding was important to her because she thought it was vital for Craig as he grew up.

'Come on, son, shoot to me,' Arnie was instructing him.

'Okay, Dad.'

'Give it all you've got . . . That's it, boy. Oh, well done!'

Dressed in a football strip in Arnie's club colours, Craig leapt in the air then turned towards his mother for her approval, raising his arms proudly, his hair blowing about in the light breeze.

'Well done, love,' she called.

'He's coming on a treat,' Arnie shouted to her. 'He'll be playing in a team in no time.'

Gill smiled and nodded. Looking around the park on this sunny April afternoon – at the children shouting and calling to each other in the playground area, the youths joshing near the lake, the families out walking by the river – she was filled with a sense of isolation. Ostensibly she and Arnie and Craig were an ordinary happy family. In reality, she and Arnie were drifting ever further apart.

They had been so good together in the early years; she'd thought it would last for ever. But incidents like the one that had caused Arnie to buy her a new piano as a peace offering had become commonplace. He was hardly ever home in the evenings now because he preferred to be out clubbing in the West End. Carol had been right when she'd said Gill's marriage was heading for the rocks. She could feel it slipping away from her, and there was nothing she could do to keep them together because Arnie no longer seemed to care about their relationship.

Maybe the smart thing would be to grit her teeth and let him get on with it, in the hope that it was just a passing phase. But she was too

53

emotionally involved for clever tactics. It wasn't just the fact that he was always out; his attitude towards her when he was at home was painful too. Although he was rarely impatient with Craig, he made it blatantly obvious that Gill irritated the hell out of him. It was as though having a wife hampered the social life he had come to value so highly, and he resented it.

Their life together swung between bitter enmity and sporadic bouts of remorse and reconcilliation, during which he swore that he hadn't been unfaithful to her. At these times there was tenderness and passion. He said he still loved her despite everything, but most of the time it didn't feel like that to her. This definitely wasn't the same man she had married. Ever since Arnie had tasted the West End night-life his marriage had been a burden to him.

Perhaps they had married too young. Maybe all this was happening because he hadn't got it out of his system earlier. The money and attention he now received so much of was enough to turn the head of any ordinary working-class boy; she made allowances for that. But she wasn't ready to give up on him, even though she sometimes didn't feel able to take another day wedded to the monster Arnie had become.

One of the worst things was not being able to rely on him or anticipate his reactions, as she once had . . . And she had absolutely no idea how he was going to react to the news she had been putting off telling him!

One afternoon about a month later Arnie was summoned to the manager's office at Borough Football Club.

'You wanted to see me, boss?' he said breezily, expecting to receive some sort of commendation because that was what he had come to expect.

'That's right, son,' said Jack Benson, who was seated at his desk. A big man with greying hair and sharp, dark eyes, he waved a large hand towards a chair opposite. A famous player in his day, Jack had made a name for himself in football management and was well known for his ability to be ruthless if it was necessary for the good of the club. 'Sit down.'

Arnie did as he was told. 'So, what's it all about then, boss?' he asked cheerfully.

Jack stroked his chin, his eyes resting unwaveringly on Arnie. 'I've been hearing things about you . . .'

'All good, I hope.'

'All bad – and I don't like it,' Jack said, his tone becoming hard. 'I don't like it one little bit.'

'Oh?' Arnie was taken aback. 'What am I supposed to have done?'

'Don't get clever with me, boy!' roared Jack, who was also known for his booming voice. 'You know bloody well what I'm talking about.'

'Do I?'

'Yes, mate, you do! Birds, booze and nightclubs until all hours.'

'Oh, that.'

'Yes, that,' confirmed Jack. 'It isn't the way for a professional footballer to behave. Not one of my players, anyway. When you signed up with this club you agreed not to do anything that might affect your game or the reputation of the club.'

'I dunno who's been saying all this,' mumbled Arnie defensively. 'A bloke's entitled to a night out now and again . . .'

'From what I've heard it's a bloody sight more than just a night out now and again.'

'Who's been running to you with tales?'

'Don't be so childish, man. Nobody's been running to me with tales,' Jack said.

'How—'

'I make it my business to find out what my players get up to on *and* off the pitch, and you've made no secret of what you do in your spare time,' Jack cut in. 'Quite the opposite, in fact. You seem to like people knowing that you're out clubbing until the small hours with models and showgirls and any other bit o' spare you can pick up. You're always shooting your mouth off about the fact that you practically live at Flowers night-club. You must have known I'd get to know about it sooner or later.'

'I didn't think, boss . . .'

'That's your trouble. You've forgotten how to use your loaf.'

'This is no big thing,' said Arnie dismissively. 'Okay, I admit I like to live a little. What's so terrible about that?'

'Nothing – if you don't mind losing your job and your wife,' Jack said bluntly.

'Oh, come on,' objected Arnie. 'That's a bit over the top, innit?'

Jack remained calm, doodling with a pen on his blotter. 'When I first saw you play I was excited,' he said without looking up. 'Because I knew I was looking at real talent. That's why we gave you a contract, and why the club pays you a lot of money.' He looked up and fixed Arnie with a steely glare. 'When you first came to this club you were a genuine bloke, dedicated to your game and to the club.'

'I still am,' pronounced Arnie.

'That's a matter of opinion.'

'That isn't fair,' objected Arnie. 'Have I ever missed a training session?'

'Not yet, but that'll start to happen before long if you carry on as you have been.'

'Never! I'm a dedicated player.'

'You're dedicated to Arnie Briscoe, superstar. Not Borough Football Club,' said Jack brutally.

'That isn't true.'

'I think it is.'

'No!' Arnie shook his head, his cheeks scarlet.

'You've let the money and the fame go to your head,' said Jack.

Arnie said nothing, just stared at the floor.

'I've been there, mate,' said Jack frankly. 'Admittedly football didn't have the glamorous image in my day as it does now, because we didn't have the television to give us fame, and the game didn't have the sort of money that television has brought into it these days. We didn't earn as much as your generation of players, but we had our share of fans and adulation. Oh, yeah, we had kids queueing up for our autograph and women wanting to sleep with us – 'cause being famous is sexy. The only trouble is, when people treat you like God's gift you begin to believe it yourself. I know just what it feels like.'

'I can't help enjoying it. I'm only human.'

'Enjoying it is one thing, letting it change you is quite another.'

'Yeah, I know,' said Arnie gloomily.

'I suppose your marriage is in trouble over this,' Jack said.

'Well, the wife isn't exactly overjoyed with things at the moment.'

'You can't blame her for taking a dim view if you've been putting it about.'

'I haven't been putting it about,' Arnie denied emphatically.

'No?' Jack challenged, brows raised.

'No.' Arnie was adamant. 'I've flirted a bit – that's all.'

'Whether you have or you haven't actually done the deed is beside the point,' said Jack in a worldly-wise manner. 'Your wife will think you have. Women always do. You're young, it's natural for a young man to chase women. Wives don't understand this because they're different to us—'

'I'll say they're different.'

'Anyway, your marriage isn't my business,' Jack continued briskly. 'But your game is – and if you carry on as you are you're gonna find yourself out in the cold before very long.'

'I scored twice on Saturday,' Arnie was quick to remind him.

'I'm not disputing the fact that you can play football, Arnie,' said Jack. 'But I *am* saying that you can't burn the candle at both ends and get away with it for ever. Your game will suffer if you carry on as you are now.' His manner became uncompromising. 'No one is indispensable, not even you. A professional footballer has a short enough playing life. Don't shorten yours even more by behaving like an idiot.'

'Are you threatening me?'

'No, I'm just warning you,' said Jack. 'And hoping that you'll take notice of what I've said.'

'Oh.'

'Now bugger off and think about it and let me get on with my work.'

* * *

56

At about eleven o'clock that same night, feeling sick at heart, Gill scraped Arnie's congealed dinner off the plate and on to newspaper and put it into the bin. God only knows how much food she'd wasted in this way over the last couple of years. She was a fool to keep food for him at all when it was nearly always thrown away. But she'd been hopeful tonight, because this afternoon he'd phoned her from the club to say that he would definitely be home early.

Although she still loved him, she was at the end of her tether. It was all very well to keep trying to make their marriage work, but what sort of a life was it for any of them the way things were? Arnie was rarely home, and Gill's nerves were always on edge because of the way he was carrying on – which, in turn, must have been having an effect on their son.

She washed the plate and went upstairs to check on Craig, who had fallen asleep at last. It had taken her ages to pacify him because his daddy hadn't come home – yet again – after telling him on the telephone that he would be there in time to see him before he went to bed.

Back downstairs she sat down to wait for Arnie. She had given up waiting up for him long ago, but tonight was different. Tonight she had had enough, and she was going to tell him so.

He came in at about half past eleven.

'You waited up, then,' he said, mooching into the living room to find her sitting on the sofa.

'I was expecting you hours ago,' she told him stiffly.

'Yeah, sorry about that,' he said casually. 'I got chatting and forgot the time.'

'You're really not being fair, you know, Arnie,' she said.

'Oh, for God's sake, don't you start nagging again.' Arnie was still upset about the meeting with Jack Benson and had been drowning his sorrows in the pub. 'I've had a terrible day.'

She stood up and faced him with her arms folded in front of her. 'And I've had a terrible two years while you've thoughtlessly destroyed our marriage with your complete lack of consideration,' she said. 'Frankly, Arnie, I've had enough.'

'Oh, so you're threatening me now, are you?' he taunted, guilt making him aggressive.

'Not threatening,' she said through dry lips, 'but I am saying that I'm not prepared to carry on like this any longer, sitting here every night on my own while you're out living it up, sleeping with any dolly bird who takes your fancy for all I know.'

'I haven't slept with anyone,' he said – and it was true, though he'd had a few near misses.

'I'd like to believe that—'

'You can believe what you damned well like,' he said nastily. 'If you don't trust me you can do the other thing – I couldn't care less.'

'Don't tell me you don't chase women at Flowers.'

'You've got it the wrong way round, babe,' he said with an air of blatant conceit. 'It's the women who chase me.'

'And you sit back and think of me, I suppose,' she said.

'No, I dance with 'em, chat 'em up,' he said. 'It's all just a game.'

'A dangerous game for a married man to be playing—'

'Oh, stop moaning, woman. You do all right for yourself,' he stated. 'I provide well for you and Craig. You've got a lovely home, your own car, and I make sure you're never short of money in your purse.'

'I'm not denying any of that,' she said. 'But I'd rather be penniless and have you by my side.'

'I am by your side—'

'No you're not,' she said. 'Even when you are here, you're somewhere else in your mind.'

'Rubbish.'

'I want my husband back, Arnie,' she said. 'I want a proper family life again.'

'Bloody hell. First I've got Jack Benson on my back, now you,' he said, his voice rising along with his temper. 'What is it with you people? Why can't you let a bloke alone?'

'You've changed.'

'Of course I've changed,' he snapped. 'I've got money in my pocket now, I couldn't afford to go out enjoying myself before.'

'I don't want to stop you going out, Arnie – but every night . . . and coming home at all hours. It really isn't on.'

'Look, Gill. I don't want to stay at home gawping at the telly like some old geezer,' he said. 'I like going out on the town, I like the atmosphere of Flowers and other night-clubs. I want to come and go as I please. I'm only twenty-four, for Pete's sake! I'm just not ready to sit at home and do the pipe and slippers routine.'

'I wasn't suggesting you should sit at home every night,' she told him. 'But I do think you should behave a bit more like a responsible husband and father.'

'I'll do what I like, when I like, and you can't do a damned thing about it,' he heard himself say.

'In that case you can take your things and go,' she heard herself say.

'Go! Me? Don't be ridiculous.'

'Get out, go on!' she shouted, beside herself now with pain and exasperation, her words tumbling out almost of their own volition. 'And leave Craig and me in peace.'

'If anyone's gonna go, it'll be you,' he said, saying things he didn't mean in the heat of the moment. 'It's my house.'

'Okay, if you feel comfortable about forcing your wife and child out of their home, then I'll go,' she stated boldly.

'Good.'

'I'll take Craig and leave first thing in the morning.'

'Don't worry, you can have the bloody house.' He couldn't believe he had actually told her to leave their home. *His own wife.* What was happening to him? 'I don't wanna stay here for another minute with a nag of a wife like you.' He stormed from the room, shouting back from the front door, 'I'll be back to collect my things tomorrow . . . or sometime soon.'

Shaking so much that her teeth were chattering, Gill heard the front door slam. Frantic, she rushed out into the street after him. He was already in his car.

'Arnie, wait, we need to talk.'

'Not likely.'

'That's right, run away from your responsibilities like you always do!' she shouted through the car window as he started up the engine and revved hard. She was in far too much of a state to worry about her voice echoing in the night and disturbing the neighbours as she tried to make herself heard. 'And just to bring you up to date: before very long you'll have another responsibility to run away from. I'm pregnant.'

And without knowing if he'd heard her or not, she turned and ran back inside, sobbing uncontrollably as she heard him drive away at high speed.

Arnie didn't have any particular destination in mind. He was a trembling mass of emotions – anger, frustration, pain and remorse, which he vaguely realised were the combined products of guilt – as he sped out of London, screeching to a halt at each set of red lights, glad when there were fewer of them as he distanced himself from town.

Having his foot pressed hard on the accelerator gave him a welcome rush of adrenalin that he needed to help him release some of his pent-up aggression.

The trouble with guilt is that it tears you apart inside. Arnie was angry – with himself for wanting things he shouldn't want, and with the woman he loved for restricting him. He knew that Gill was right. He knew Jack Benson was right. But he didn't want to admit it, because to do so would put a stop to his current way of life.

The bright lights had become like a drug to him. He got high on the excitement of a night-club, the glamour of being among beautiful women and well-dressed men, being one of the 'in crowd'. He loved the scented air that greeted you in an evocative cloud when you walked into Flowers club: the smell of expensive cigars and even more expensive perfume.

George Flowers made a great fuss of him, had introduced him to important people, made him feel special. That was what it was all about: being in demand and feeling like a somebody.

Although he would never admit it to the lads, Arnie hadn't actually been unfaithful to Gill. He'd come pretty close to it a few times, but had never actually gone through with it. Sex wasn't really what it was about; it was more of an ego thing. Being strongly fancied by women who wouldn't have given him a second glance a few years ago, and being able to call the shots, was heady stuff.

But was all this worth losing Gill for? Gill and Craig, whom he loved so dearly? Oh yes, he might be confused about a lot of things, but he wasn't confused about that. No matter what he'd said or how badly he'd behaved, he had never fallen out of love with Gill. He had merely become disenchanted with the lifestyle of a married man.

It was true what they said: you can't have your cake and eat it. So what was he doing driving towards Heathrow at this time of night while his wife was worried sick at home? Something had to go, and he didn't want it to be Gill.

At the next roundabout, he turned back.

Homeward bound, he received a strong mental image of Gill shouting at him through the car window as he'd driven away. He'd only caught snippets of what she'd been saying because of the noise of the engine and his preoccupation with his own thoughts. What he had heard hadn't registered properly.

Something she'd said was bothering him, but he couldn't quite piece it together. He began to replay the incident in his mind, over and over again. She'd been saying something about another responsibility. That was it . . . another responsibility for him to run away from. My God, she must have been telling him she was pregnant!

He pushed hard on the accelerator in his urgency to get home and put things right. There wasn't too much traffic about at this late hour, and soon his foot was pressed right to the floorboards. The driving conditions were ideal, being a clear dry night with a bright moon.

Like a man possessed, he forced the needle ever higher on the speedometer, all respect for the law disregarded as the car moved through the night ever faster on the almost deserted dual carriageway.

All the signs were there to indicate that he was approaching the Hogarth roundabout, but he paid little attention. All he could think of was getting home to Gill to tell her that he loved her and was sorry for the appalling way he'd been behaving lately.

He didn't need to stop or even slow down as he approached the roundabout. He was Arnie Briscoe – in control and invincible!

The car hit the roundabout head on, throwing Arnie forward with such force that he was pushed half-way through the windscreen, where he was suspended as the car bounced sideways off the concrete barrier.

It rolled over into the middle of the road with the crump of metal and the splintering of glass. With the final bump, Arnie was thrown to the

60

ground with a horrific crunch, where he lay perfectly still, oblivious to everything, a silent figure in the road beside a heap of mangled metal. Blood began to trickle from his mouth.

Chapter Six

'Why don't you go and have a lie down in the relative's room, love?' suggested Phoebe to Gill. 'I'll stay here with Arnie.'

'I daren't leave him . . . just in case he comes round . . . or—'

'Don't even think about the alternative,' Phoebe cut in, her voice quivering emotionally despite her indomitable spirit. 'My Arnie's a fighter. It'll take something worse than this to finish him off.'

Looking at the unconscious figure attached to tubes and wires, both legs and one arm set in plaster, Gill wondered what could be worse than this. He was unnervingly still, only a fraction of his face visible through the bandaging.

'It doesn't seem like Arnie lying there, does it?' she murmured.

' 'Cause you can't see him through all the bandages?'

'I meant more that he isn't the sort of person you can imagine lying in a hospital bed,' said Gill through parched lips.

'That's true,' said Phoebe. 'He's usually so noisy and full of beans.'

'I don't suppose he's ever been so quiet for this long in his life before.'

'That's a fact,' said Phoebe.

Observing her mother-in-law across Arnie's bed, and seeing the ashen tinge of her skin and the eyes raw from weeping, Gill said, 'You look absolutely shattered.'

'So do you.'

'Yeah, I am.'

'At least I've been for a bit of a rest, even though I couldn't sleep,' said Phoebe. 'I think you should do the same. Even half an hour's break will freshen you up.'

'I'll stay here for a while longer,' said Gill, though she was light-headed with tiredness, her muscles aching with tension.

'Okay. I'll go and see if I can get us some coffee then,' said Phoebe, yawning heavily as she plodded to the door of the small side-ward that was used for emergency cases.

'That would be a life saver,' said Gill. 'I'm gasping.'

It was the morning after the accident, and Gill and Phoebe had been at the hospital all night. Because of the seriousness of Arnie's condition, they had been allocated a room for personal use.

Thinking back to last night, Gill recalled how she'd rushed to answer the doorbell full of hope, thinking it was Arnie come back to make up with her. Instead she'd been faced with everyone's most dreaded

63

scenario: two policeman standing on the doorstep. They had been very kind and helpful, had even gone to Maisie Road to get her mother to stay with Craig while she went to the hospital. Gill had collected Phoebe on the way.

Now she was afraid to take her eyes off her husband in case he slipped away. The doctors said he had a slim chance of recovery, but it was touch and go because he had internal injuries as well as many broken bones. They didn't know yet if there was any brain damage.

It was a miracle he had survived the crash at all, apparently. The police had ascertained from the state of the car and the skid marks on the road that he'd been way over the speed limit when he'd hit the roundabout. If he did pull through he would probably face a charge of dangerous driving.

The parlous state of their marriage had paled into insignificance against the possibility of Arnie dying. His survival was the only thing that mattered to Gill now.

'Don't die, Arnie,' she whispered, taking his still, cool hand in hers, her tired eyes filling with tears. 'Please don't die.'

Because Arnie's condition was critical, people could visit at any time. Not surprisingly, there was a stream of visitors throughout the day. Winnie came while Craig was at school, Arnie's brother John took time off from the factory where he worked to pay a visit, Carol came in her lunch hour, and some of Arnie's team-mates visited with the manager, Jack Benson. And Arnie remained oblivious throughout.

By late afternoon Gill was dead on her feet and forced to take a break when she could no longer function properly. The clinically clean room they had been given was small and basically furnished with two single beds and a washbasin. It was permeated with the antiseptic smell of the wards, which made Gill feel nauseous.

She flopped down on the bed fully dressed. Yet, although she was bone-tired, sleep eluded her. Her nerves were painfully taut, her mind racing . . . If only Arnie had been driving his car at a safe speed he probably wouldn't be on the critical list now, she couldn't help thinking as she finally dozed off.

Waking suddenly and completely disorientated, she flew into a panic the instant she remembered where she was. Jerking upright, she dragged herself out of bed, realising as she did so that she had been woken by a sharp pain across her middle.

Sitting on the edge of the bed, clutching her stomach and rubbing her back, her heart thudded as the alarming implications of the pain registered. Sweating with fear, she hurried back to the ward, established that there was no change in Arnie's condition, told Phoebe she would be back in a minute, then rushed into the ladies' toilet. Emerging soon after, ashen-faced and trembling, she found a nurse.

'I think I'm having a miscarriage,' she said, her face screwed up in agony.

'Are you and Arnie trying to make Hammersmith hospital into your family home or somethin'?' Phoebe forced herself to be cheerful when she visited her daughter-in-law in the gynaecology ward the next day. 'Both of you being in here as patients at the same time is a real turn up for the books.'

'It is, isn't it?' said Gill flatly.

'Handy for visiting, though.'

'There is that.' Gill managed a watery smile.

'I'm ever so sorry you lost your baby, love.' Phoebe's mood became serious. She took one of Gill's hands in both of hers and gave it a comforting squeeze. 'You're getting it from all sides at the moment, aren't you, duck?'

'It seems like it.'

'I had no idea you were pregnant.'

'Neither did anyone else.'

'It isn't like you to keep something as important as that to yourself.'

'I was going to tell you all, but you know how it is . . . if you make it generally known too early, the pregnancy seems to go on for ever.' Her skin was paper-white and her dark eyes bloodshot and swollen from weeping. 'I needn't have worried, as it happened, need I?'

Phoebe shook her head slowly, her eyes glistening with tears. 'Does Arnie know?' she asked grimly.

'I'm not sure. I did try to tell him just before he drove off in the car, but I don't know if he heard what I was saying.'

'Oh, I see.' Phoebe paused. 'I suppose it must have been the shock of the accident that caused the miscarriage.'

'There isn't much doubt about that, according to the doctor.'

'Well, I shall have a thing or two to say to that son o' mine when he does come round,' said Phoebe, who determinedly refused to believe that Arnie wouldn't recover. 'He shouldn't have been driving like a lunatic.'

'We'd had a row. He was in a foul temper,' Gill explained. 'Anyway, you know Arnie – he's a law unto himself.'

'This'll teach him to drive more carefully, though.'

'Maybe.' Gill sighed. 'No change in his condition, then?'

'No.'

'Is anyone with him?'

'Don't worry. John's sitting with him till I get back.'

'That's good. I don't like to think of him lying there on his own, even though he doesn't know a thing about it. I'll be able to sit with him again soon.'

'The doctor was saying that each day he survives makes the chance of recovery more likely,' said Phoebe.

'That's really good news,' Gill said, but she was too numb to feel anything much beyond the loss of her baby. Being pregnant had been a symbol of hope in her crumbling marriage. Her beloved son and the thought of a new baby had given her a reason for continuing as Arnie had grown ever more distant. What made the miscarriage even harder to take was knowing that it need never have happened. If Arnie hadn't stormed out in a temper and been driving so carelessly, he wouldn't be fighting for his life now and their baby would still be growing in her womb. It seemed wrong to blame him for anything at all, but she had wanted that baby *so* much.

'Look, love, I know how much you must be hurting, and I know it's what everyone says at a time like this because they don't know what else to say . . .' Phoebe was speaking with deep compassion. 'But you're still young, you can try again.'

Gill shook her head slowly, her dark eyes dull with pain.

'You mean . . . ?'

'When they gave me the routine D and C after I'd lost the baby, they found some damage to my womb,' she explained, tears burning beneath her eyelids. 'I can't have any more children.'

'Oh, Gill, love . . .' Phoebe moved closer and put her arms around her. 'I'm so very very sorry.'

At that moment some visitors headed down the ward towards them. Winnie and Hal with Craig, followed by Carol and Dougie.

'What's up?' asked Winnie, instantly perceiving that her daughter was on the verge of tears. 'Has something happened? Has he taken a turn for the worse?'

'Don't panic. Arnie's condition is just the same,' said Phoebe. 'But I think the one person in the world Gill needs right now is her mum.' She turned to the others. 'Come on, you lot. Let's go and see Arnie and leave mother and daughter alone together for a few minutes.'

Experiencing a rush of gratitude to Phoebe for her sensitivity, Gill flung her arms around her mother, the tears finally falling.

At first it was nothing more than a slight flickering of his eyelids. Then he opened his eyes for just a few seconds before sinking back into unconsciousness.

Arnie's slow recovery began a few days later. Gradually and painfully, he was awake for longer periods and on the mend.

Although Gill was very low in health and spirits, she managed to fake a cheery manner for her husband. He was in a great deal of physical pain despite being heavily dosed with pain-killers. He had enough problems; she didn't want to add to them by telling him about hers.

When he was taken off the critical list she had to adhere to normal visiting times, but she was always there with a smile and a positive outlook. Arnie had no idea of the mental torture his wife was suffering as she tried to come to terms with the loss of her baby and the fact that she couldn't have any more.

On Wednesdays, visiting was allowed in the afternoon as well as the evening. Gill was often his only visitor then, because most people were at work. One such afternoon, a few weeks after he'd regained consciousness, Gill arrived at his bedside loaded with goodies.

'So, how are you feeling today?' she asked, leaning over to kiss him.

'Fed up with being stuck in here, babe,' he told her.

His attitude towards her was more like it had been in the early days, before fame and fortune had taken its toll. The argument that had preceded his accident had been forgotten. One of the first things he'd done when he'd regained consciousness was make his peace with her about that. And because she wanted to stay married to him she'd been happy to forgive him and put the past behind them.

'Yeah, I expect you are – but there's no point in them discharging you too soon.'

'It's so boring.'

'Better to be bored than dead. You're lucky to be alive,' she said, emptying the grapes she'd brought out of the brown paper bag into a bowl on his locker, and putting a bag of his favourite toffees down beside them. 'So just remind yourself of that and be patient.'

'Easier said than done.'

'I know.'

'I want be up and about again.'

'All in good time.' She unwrapped a toffee and popped it into his mouth. One of his arms and both legs were still in plaster, but the bandages around his head had been removed.

'It isn't easy for someone as active as me to lay about all day,' he said, the toffee bulging at the side of his mouth. 'I'm dying to get back to playing football again.'

Gill's heart lurched. 'You've been very badly injured, you know, Arnie,' she said cautiously.

'I know it'll be a while before I'm actually on the field again, even after I get out of here,' he said, 'but it's the thought of getting back to the game that's keeping me going. That and coming home to you and Craig, o' course.'

'Mm,' she muttered non-committally.

'How's Craig?' he asked.

'Fine. He's full of the school sports day at the moment,' she said. 'He's entered for some of the races.'

'Ah bless him,' said Arnie, his expression softening at the thought of his son, who had started primary school after Easter and was in his first term.

'He has to get through the heats first though, or he won't be competing on the big day.'

'He'll do it,' said Arnie. 'He's a natural sportsman, that boy.'

'I hope you're right. God knows how I'll console him if he doesn't make it,' she said. 'He's set his heart on it.'

'He takes after me. I used to be just the same at his age.'

They chatted about Craig some more. Arnie ate a few grapes as they talked.

'Have some, Gill,' he said after a while.

'No. I bought them for you.'

'I know, but I want you to have some too,' he said. 'They'll do you good. You're eating for two now, remember?'

He'd told her a few days before that he'd realised what she'd been saying to him as he drove off, just before the accident. He had gone on to say how delighted he was at the idea of becoming a father for the second time – and she'd spared him the truth because he'd been so ill and in such terrible pain. She and her parents and Phoebe had previously agreed that she should wait until he was stronger before she told him about the miscarriage.

Now, though, she knew that time had come.

'I'm not eating for two, Arnie,' she said, her throat so dry and constricted that she could hardly utter the words.

'Not three is it?' he said jokingly. 'You're not having twins?'

'I'm not having a baby at all, Arnie,' she told him.

He looked at her with light-hearted puzzlement, as though he thought she was teasing. 'Not having a baby?'

She shook her head.

'You mean I imagined that you told me you were pregnant that night through the car window?' His expression darkened. 'Well, honestly, Gill. Why the hell didn't you tell me the truth instead of going along with me about it?'

'You didn't imagine it, Arnie,' she explained. 'I was more than three months pregnant. I lost the baby while you were unconscious.'

'What!'

'I didn't tell you the truth because I didn't think you were up to it.'

His face worked, the grape in his hand dropping to the bed and rolling on to the floor.

'Bloody 'ell, Gill.' He had turned very pale. 'That must have been a terrible blow for you on top of everything else.'

'Yes, it was.'

'Are you okay?'

'It was a huge disappointment, of course,' she said with feigned calmness. 'But, yes, I'm all right.'

'What caused it, do you know?'

She couldn't bring herself to reply.

'It was the shock of the accident, wasn't it?' he said, shooting her a look. 'That was what caused you to lose our baby.'

'No one can ever be really sure,' she said to spare him. 'These things happen.'

'It was my fault,' he said, looking stricken. 'If I hadn't had the accident, which was caused by my reckless driving—'

'Don't torture yourself,' she cut in, taking his hand. 'It just wasn't meant to be, that's all there is to it.'

'Oh, God!'

'We've an awful lot to be thankful for,' she said soothingly. 'You're alive and getting better, and we have Craig . . .'

'That doesn't alter the fact that you lost our baby through my fault and I wasn't there for you,' he said. 'You had to go through something as awful as that on your own.'

She put her arms around him and held him close. No matter how badly he'd behaved in the past, she was still in love with him. How could she tell him the extent of the damage she had suffered to her womb because of the miscarriage? He was feeling guilty enough already; it would be too cruel to throw something else at him now. It could wait until he came out of hospital.

'It's all over now,' she said. 'We have to look to the future.'

'Yeah.' He sighed deeply. 'I suppose that's all we can do.'

'It'll be lovely to have you home with us again,' she said to cheer him.

'I'm counting the days,' he said, brightening at the thought of going home.

'I bet you are.'

'I just can't wait to get back to work,' he said, a hint of the old sparkle shining in his eyes. 'It'll be so good to get those football boots on again.'

His total lack of doubt about returning to his career made her feel duty-bound to introduce a note of reality.

'Have you given any thought to what you'll do if you can't play football professionally again?' she asked.

'No.'

'Don't you think you should?'

'There's no need, because I'm determined to get back on the field.'

'But—'

'People have been more badly smashed up than I am and still got back into the game,' he told her adamantly.

'Arnie . . .'

'There's no question about it, Gill,' he said. 'It's simply a matter of determination.'

Gill was all in favour of the power of positive thinking, but it did have its limitations, especially when so many bones had been broken.

But Arnie obviously wasn't ready to accept this salient fact – not for the moment, anyway.

Peter Attwood was putting away a delivery of sheet music when Gill called at the music shop in Hammersmith a few days later while Craig was at school.

'Hi, Peter.'

'Hi, Gill.'

'I've come for a browse through the music,' she said, glancing around at the selection of pianos, guitars and other musical instruments on display.

'Anything in particular?' Peter was about thirty. An arty type with a look of faded boyishness about him, he had clear grey eyes, a prominent nose and fair hair that was long and wild. A good-natured man, casually dressed in a T-shirt and jeans, he always reminded Gill of a folk singer.

She had only got on to first-name terms with him from being a regular customer at the shop, and she knew nothing about him except that he played the guitar in his spare time. He'd been working here for about six months and seemed to be in charge, assisted by a trendy young girl called Wendy who was far more interested in selling records than musical instruments.

'Something that will appeal to children – but not nursery rhymes,' she explained. 'I've already got a good selection of those, as well as a lot of the pretty classical pieces kids play when they're learning. I saved all mine.'

'Do you give piano lessons?' he asked, pausing in what he was doing and looking at her.

'Oh, no,' she said. 'I just play for my own amusement.'

'It's worth learning an instrument so that you can do that.'

'It certainly gives me a lot of pleasure,' she said. 'I'd like my young son to learn eventually, but I don't want to force him – and I don't think he'll do it willingly because he's more interested in going out to play football.'

'Sounds pretty typical,' said Peter. 'Most kids are more interested in playing records than instruments these days, anyway.'

'He's a bit too young for that yet; he's only five,' she explained. 'It's for his fifth birthday party I want the music, actually. I thought a sing-song around the piano might keep them amused if things get out of hand when we've exhausted all the other entertainments.'

'More "That Doggie in the Window" than Chopin's *Polonaise* then.'

'Definitely,' she said. ' "That Doggie in the Window" is a very good suggestion for the party, actually. Do you have it in stock?'

Nodding, Peter turned to the racks of sheet music at the back of the counter, pulled out the requested item and handed it to her.

'Smashing,' she said, getting her purse out of her handbag.

'Do you know anyone around here who gives piano lessons?' he asked.

'There's someone in Wallis Street,' said Gill thoughtfully.

'She doesn't do it any more apparently.'

'Really? I didn't know she'd given it up.'

'She got fed up with all the kids coming after school when she wanted to get the tea ready,' he explained.

'That is one of the drawbacks of the job.'

'What about the person who taught you?' asked Peter.

'She retired a few years ago,' said Gill. 'I know of people out of the area who give lessons, though.'

'No good, I'm afraid,' he said. 'The person who asked me, a customer here, wants someone local to teach her daughter. The girl's dead keen at the moment, apparently. Her mother wants to strike while the iron's hot.'

'Before she goes off the idea.'

'Exactly. She doesn't want her to have to travel out of the area, though.'

'Very wise.'

'I told her I'd ask around,' he said. 'I'll put a notice in the window too. There must be some qualified person needing to earn some extra cash.'

This struck a chord with Gill. She had the necessary qualifications to give private lessons. Although money wasn't a problem at the moment because the club was still paying Arnie, they wouldn't continue to do so indefinitely if he couldn't go back to work for a while – or if the worst happened and he couldn't go back to football at all.

It could take a long time for Arnie to find another means of earning a living within his capabilities. There was also the possibility of his receiving a hefty fine for dangerous driving. The few shillings she'd make from one pupil wouldn't make much difference, but at least she would be doing something to help.

And apart from the money, she liked the idea of doing something useful with her skills. At present she had time on her hands too, with Arnie being in hospital. Teaching could prove to be awkward when he came home, of course, with the television being in the same room as the piano, but that was a minor problem that could be easily solved with a little co-operation from the family.

'I wouldn't mind taking on the job myself, actually,' said Gill. 'I am qualified.'

'Oh, that would be great.' Peter smiled and handed her a pen and a piece of paper. 'Can I tell her to give you a ring?'

'You certainly can,' Gill said as she wrote down her telephone number, feeling quite excited at the idea of a new project.

* * *

The doctor in charge of Arnie's case called Gill into his office one day when she was on her way out after visiting.

'We'll be discharging your husband soon, Mrs Briscoe,' he said. He was a small, neat man with thinning hair and a moustache.

'That *is* good news,' she said with a warm smile. 'We guessed it wouldn't be long.'

'The thing is,' he said, obviously troubled, 'I don't think Mr Briscoe realises just how difficult life is going to be for him when he is back at home.'

'Oh?'

'Things are going to be very different to how they were before the accident,' he said, leaning back and putting his two forefingers under his chin meditatively.

'How different, exactly?'

'I'm afraid that you're going to have to be very patient with him until he adjusts to the situation,' he said, evading the question.

'My husband won't ever play football again, will he?' she said. 'That's what you're trying to say.'

He tapped his chin with his pointed fingers thoughtfully. 'Miracles can happen, of course.'

'But you don't think one will happen in Arnie's case?'

'I think it's most unlikely. He'll definitely not play as a professional again.'

'Oh, God!' Although she had been trying to prepare herself and Arnie for this, it was still a crushing blow. 'Is there no chance?'

'Because his right leg was broken in so many places it is slightly shorter than the left one, as you know,' he explained. 'The limp he has been left with will be permanent. He won't be able to walk very fast, let alone run.'

Gill sighed, running her hand through her hair in agitation.

'Originally we thought we might be able to correct the imbalance, but we now know that isn't going to be possible,' he continued.

'Does Arnie know this?'

'He has been told, but I don't know if he's heard what we've been saying,' he said, frowning at her. 'We've given him the facts and told him to think in terms of alternative employment, but he doesn't seem willing to accept this.'

'No, he wouldn't.'

'He seems to think that if he's determined enough to get back into football, he can make it happen,' said the doctor. 'I don't know if determination will be enough for his employers at the football club, though.'

'I suspected this might be the case, and I've been trying to persuade him to view the situation realistically for some time,' she told him. 'But football is his life. He can't even bear to contemplate going on without

72

it. Even when he wasn't playing as a professional he played regularly for an amateur team. For someone like Arnie it's going to be really hard.'

'He'll just have to get used to being a spectator,' said the doctor.

'Yes.' Gill brushed her brow with the back of her hand, her thoughts racing. 'It isn't going to be easy for him to go back to working in an engineering factory after playing soccer for a living.'

The doctor's brow became even more deeply furrowed. 'He won't be up to such heavy work as that, Mrs Briscoe,' he informed her quickly.

'But that's all he knows, apart from football,' she said.

'In that case he'll have to retrain to do something else altogether,' he said. 'There's plenty of employment about.'

'Yes, I realise that, but persuading him to consider something else is going to be difficult,' she said.

'Worse things happen than having to change one's occupation,' he said in the way of someone who sees pain and disaster on a regular basis. 'At least he's alive and not brain-damaged.'

'Indeed.'

'Anyway, I'm sure you'll work it out between you.' The doctor stood up to indicate that the interview was over.

'I'm sure we will,' Gill said with false confidence.

Chapter Seven

Bracing herself for a scene, Gill went into the living room. Arnie was sitting in an armchair with his feet on the pouffe, staring blankly at a children's television programme.

'Mary will be here for her piano lesson in a minute,' she said.

'So what?' he replied, but he knew exactly what she meant.

'So . . . would you be a dear and go into the other room for half an hour?'

'No.'

'Can you turn the television off then, please?' she requested.

'No.'

'But I can't teach against that racket,' she pointed out. 'It'll be much too distracting for Mary.'

'Tough.'

'Please, Arnie . . .'

'Oh, for God's sake!' he blasted. 'Isn't a man entitled to some peace in his own house?'

'It'll only be for half an hour,' she said patiently. 'And I'm sure you're not really interested in *Small Time*.'

'That isn't the point.'

'Craig's in the kitchen having his tea,' she told him hopefully. 'Why don't you go and keep him company?'

He threw her a glare, his eyes dark with resentment. 'As if I don't have enough to put up with, being in constant pain and not having a job,' he said, steeped in self pity. 'Now I have to get out of my armchair and have the noise of the bloody piano banging through the house, setting my nerves on edge and giving me a headache.'

'We could try to squeeze the piano into the dining room in time for future lessons, to save disturbing you,' Gill suggested.

'Don't be stupid,' Arnie said rudely. 'We won't be able to move with the piano in there.'

'I suppose not,' she was forced to agree. She felt so tense that her jaws ached from clenching her teeth and her shoulders were stiff.

It was the autumn. Arnie had been home from hospital for three months – three months of hell for them both. He sat around the house all day sinking ever deeper into despair, angry with the world in general because he no longer had a future as a professional footballer.

Gill's compassion and patience were being stretched to the limit,

75

especially as Arnie made no effort to look for a job – mainly, she suspected, because he had lost confidence in himself. She truly believed that gainful employment was the cure to his depression, but whenever she suggested he look for work he flew into a rage and accused her of being heartless.

'I'm sorry my teaching upsets you so much, love, but it's too late now to cancel today's lesson,' she said with determined tolerance. 'Mary will already be on her way here.'

With seething irritation Arnie got up, slowly and laboriously because of the lingering pain from his injuries, the effort of his movements exaggerated to gain sympathy. 'You can tell her mother not to bring her again,' he ordered. 'I'm not having my life disrupted every Wednesday afternoon.'

Her heart was pounding. She knew she must stand up to him.

'I'm not going to do that,' she told him.

His frown grew darker. 'You are, you know.'

'No I'm not . . . for two reasons,' she said. 'Firstly, because I've made a commitment to Mary—'

'Someone else will have to teach her,' he interrupted. 'You're not the only person in London qualified to teach the piano.'

'And secondly,' she continued determinedly, 'because we need the money.'

'Rubbish,' he said dismissively. 'Our mortgage repayments are low because we bought the house so cheap. Anyway, we've still got some of the cash I saved when I was earning big money.'

'That won't last long now that the football club have stopped paying you,' she wisely pointed out. 'Especially as we had to pay your fine for dangerous driving.'

'That's right, have a go at me about it,' he said, immediately on the defensive.

'I wasn't—'

'Yes you were,' he said maliciously. 'You're always getting at me.'

'Not intentionally.'

'I'll get a job when something I know I can do comes along, and not before,' he stated firmly, as though she had accused him of something.

She took a deep breath and silently counted to ten. 'I'm not getting at you, Arnie, honestly,' she said. 'I realise how difficult life must be for you at the moment. I'm just trying to be realistic about money.'

'We're not exactly on the bread-line,' he said aggressively.

'No, but—'

'It isn't as though I don't bring money into the house,' he cut in gruffly. 'There's my disability allowance.'

'Yes, and it's a great help,' she said, 'but it won't be enough when our savings run out.'

'The little bit you earn from teaching isn't enough to make any difference.'

'It's a contribution.'

'Not much of one.'

'Well, I'm going to continue to do it, because I feel I must do anything I can to help with things as they are at the moment,' she said firmly. 'Anyway, I enjoy it.'

'You're lucky to have something you really enjoy,' he said miserably.

'Yes, I am – very lucky,' she said, and she meant it. Music was a joy and companion, especially now that Arnie was so difficult to live with. Her piano soothed her nerves and provided an escape from the constant pressure of his black moods. 'I'm really sorry you lost what you love to do.'

'Me an' all.'

The doorbell rang.

'So, are you going to co-operate with me on the question of Mary's lesson?' Gill asked.

'I don't have much choice do I?' he growled, and limped painfully towards the kitchen while Gill went to answer the door.

She greeted her pupil, who was accompanied by her mother. The latter was about to depart as Gill ushered Mary inside, when she turned back.

'Oh, before I forget, Mrs Briscoe,' she said, 'a friend of mine is looking for a piano teacher for her daughter. I've told her how good you are with Mary and she asked me to ask you if you might consider taking her daughter on too.'

Another pupil would double the trouble I have from Arnie, was Gill's first thought.

'She's the same age as Mary,' the woman continued when Gill didn't reply. 'And she's very bright and keen to learn.'

But it would also double her earnings, and they were going to need every penny if Arnie didn't pull himself together and get a job soon.

'Yes,' she said decisively. 'Can you tell your friend to give me a ring and we'll get something arranged?'

Despite all the problems this was going to cause, Gill was thrilled to have her teaching skills recommended.

'Wotcha, Arnie,' greeted Phoebe one afternoon a few weeks later when she happened to meet her son in North End Road market. 'What are you doing around here?'

'Just mooching about to pass the time away,' he said. 'You not at work today?'

'I've got a day off, love.' She looked at her shopping bag. 'I've just been to the butchers for a couple o' pork chops for tea. Though I dunno why I bother as far as John is concerned – he rushes in from work, gets changed and goes out again without noticing what he's eating. I could put fried doormat on the table and he'd scoff it. Teenagers, eh? Who'd have 'em?'

'Is he still knocking around with Head-Butter Harris and his crowd?' Arnie enquired, referring to a friend of his brother's who was well known for using his head as a battering ram on anyone who upset him.

'Yeah, unfortunately.'

'That gang o' losers are bad news.'

'You're telling me, but John thinks they're the next best thing to the Beatles.'

'He should steer clear of 'em.'

'I know, but what can I do about it?' Phoebe said worriedly. 'He's sixteen and working and paying his way at home. I can't tell him who to go out with, and neither can you.'

'No, I suppose not,' agreed Arnie. 'But I don't like it. He'll end up in trouble if he carries on hanging out with them.'

They moved out of the way of the tangled crowds. People were queuing at a nearby fruit and veg stall which was bright with oranges and shiny green apples, and a colourful autumn display of carrots, swedes and parsnips just asking to be made into stew. They continued their conversation outside the bakers, near a stall selling army surplus clothing.

'Anyway, how are you, son?' asked Phoebe.

'Surviving,' Arnie replied glumly.

'Cor, you've got a face like a bunch o' leeks,' she said. 'Cheer up, for Gawd's sake.'

'What is there to cheer up about?' he asked gloomily. 'I've got no job, and I've been chucked out of my armchair again 'cause Gill's teaching some snotty-nosed kid the piano.'

'The fresh air will do you good on a lovely afternoon like this,' Phoebe told him. Indeed it was glorious autumn weather, with hazy sunshine and a sharp chill in the air which was fragrant with the scent of bonfires.

'Bloody nuisance,' Arnie grumbled. 'The house is being turned into a music school.'

'Gill's doing her best to help out, love,' Phoebe admonished. 'Anyway, she's only got about four or five pupils, hasn't she?'

'At the moment, yeah. But it won't end there, will it?' he said. 'Not now that she's building a reputation for herself. And she doesn't seem willing to turn anyone away.'

'You should be proud of her for having the gumption to earn a few bob, not complain about it,' said Phoebe. 'Anyway, if you weren't moping around the house all day you wouldn't be inconvenienced by the piano lessons.'

'Don't you start,' he snapped. 'I know I ought to be providing for my family—'

'Course you should.' Phoebe thought a spot of brutal candour might shake her son out of the doldrums.

'And it's that easy, I suppose – when half the bones in my body have been broken.'

'They're mended now, son.'

'After a fashion.'

'You've had a very bad time, Arnie, but you're better now,' his mother said gravely. 'Okay, so you still have a certain amount of pain, you walk with a limp and you can't do the sort of work you're used to. But you're not incapable. And it isn't good for you to sit about the house all day feeling sorry for yourself. I'm sure you'd find some suitable work if only you'd look.'

'Oh, yeah, they're crying out for smashed-up ex-footballers.'

Phoebe was about to tick him off for being sarcastic when the utter despair she saw in his eyes touched her heart.

'It was the only thing I was any good at, Mum,' he said.

'I know how much your football career meant to you, son,' she said, swallowing hard on the lump in her throat, 'but you can learn to be good at something else . . .'

'You can't know what it's like to lose something so important.'

'Look, why don't you come home with me for a cuppa?' she suggested kindly. 'A chat with your mum might help.'

Looking into her face, Arnie wanted to weep with love. There was pure kindness in those vivid blue eyes, feathered with lines now, her plump cheeks brightened by rouge and the nip in the air, her bleached hair short and backcombed into a bouffant. He wanted to bare his soul to her, and to luxuriate in the warmth and comfort of her unconditional love. The child in him cried out for her to take away the black depression that shadowed his life and controlled his actions, making him mean to his wife even though he hated himself for it.

How wonderful to be a boy again, to have his mother talk him out of the clinging guilt over his reckless driving. An action that had killed the child Gill had been carrying and robbed him of his career and confidence, leaving him incapable of providing for his family and even more weighed down by conscience.

His mother was right. He probably could find a job, and every day he intended to start looking. He studied the newspaper, the advertisements for storemen and light labourers; he even occasionally got as far as the door of the labour exchange. But he couldn't bring himself to go inside because he felt worthless and unfit to take up any sort of employment. As each day passed with an increasing sense of failure, his confidence diminished further.

'You coming then, love?' asked Phoebe, recalling him to the present.

The temptation to go with her was strong . . . but he was pathetic enough already, without turning to his mother. He knew he must find

79

the strength for himself, to defeat the self-pity of which he was so ashamed but unable to dispel.

'No, I'd better be getting back home,' he said. 'We'll do it another day.'

'Just as you like, son,' Phoebe said amicably.

'Tata, Mum,' he said, kissing her cheek. 'See you soon.'

'See you, son. Give my love to Gill.'

'Will do.'

Watching him walk away with his dragging limp, she felt his pain as her own. Her son was obviously a very troubled man. As an adult he must work these problems out for himself, she knew that; but her maternal instincts made her want to go after him and cuddle him, make him feel better, as she had done when he was a boy.

One evening in January of the following year, after Craig had gone to bed, and Gill and Arnie were relaxing by the fire in the living room, Gill said, 'I think it would be a good idea for me to take on more pupils and build up a proper teaching business.'

'Oh, nice,' Arnie said with bitter irony. 'And I'm supposed to sit in the dining room or kitchen for hours on end while you do it, I suppose.'

'No. If I were to do this as a proper business we'd have to make some changes,' she said. 'We could turn the playroom into a music room and give Craig the spare bedroom for his toys. The playroom would make an ideal room for teaching, being downstairs and near the front door. Pupils could come and go without invading our privacy as much as they do at the moment.'

'But the piano is a part of the furniture in here,' he said, looking fondly at it.

'I wouldn't use this piano,' she said, glancing towards the shiny black Steinway and feeling a pang of regret at what she was planning to do. 'I'd use my old piano from Mum and Dad's.'

'Have two pianos, you mean?'

'No, sell this one and use the old one for the lessons,' she said. 'All it needs is a good tuning and it'll be perfectly adequate. I tried it out the other day when I was round at Mum's.'

Arnie looked grim. 'You want to sell the piano I gave you as a present?' he said, sounding very hurt.

'Of course I don't *want* to sell it,' Gill assured. 'But we have to be practical, Arnie. We need the money.'

'We're not that desperate.'

'We're heading that way,' she said. 'Now that all our savings have gone things are going to get really dodgy. The fact is, we simply can't afford such an expensive luxury as a beautiful piano when I can use the other one as a working tool and for my own pleasure.'

'I do bring in my disability allowance, you know,' he reminded her, trying as usual to justify himself.

'Stop defending yourself, love,' she said with feeling. 'There's no need. You've provided for us well over the years. Now it's my turn to do something to bring in some cash until you find a job that's suitable for you.'

'I still don't see the necessity,' Arnie said. The idea of his wife being the breadwinner was abhorrent to him.

'If we don't address the problem now we'll start to run up debts,' she said. 'I don't want to have to tell Craig he can't have new football boots or the things the other kids are having, when I know I have it in my power to help us keep a reasonable standard of living. If I do well, we might even be able to afford to run a car again.'

Arnie grunted.

'Selling the piano will give us some capital while I build up my teaching business,' Gill went on. 'I've been turning people away because having pupils in the living room is too disruptive to our family life. If we make the playroom into a music room, you and Craig won't be inconvenienced at all and I can give lessons on Saturdays too. It'll take some of the pressure off you if I'm earning more money, give you time to find a job you feel happy with.'

Although he could see the wisdom of her plan, it heightened Arnie's sense of inadequacy. But there was a new radiance about his wife that made his heart turn over. However low he had sunk, and however badly he behaved towards her, she still meant everything to him.

'You really want to do this don't you, Gill?' he said.

'Yes, I do.'

'I suppose we'd better get it organised then,' he said, smiling properly at her for the first time in ages.

'Oh, that's great.' She went over to him and wrapped her arms around him in a spontaneous burst of affection. 'I do love you.'

'I love you too,' he said, kissing her.

Such tender moments between them were rare these days. But when they did happen, Gill knew that no matter how bad things had got between them, they did have something special.

'Can I have some more apple pie please, Gran?' asked Craig one Sunday in March.

'Course you can, love. Pass your plate to me.' Winnie took his plate and glanced around the table at which her family were having Sunday dinner. 'Anyone else for seconds?'

'I wouldn't mind a bit more please,' said Dougie, handing her his plate.

'He never can resist your apple pie, Mum. Can you, Dougie?' said Carol.

81

'I'm hooked, I admit it,' he laughed.

'You can blame Winnie's pastry for my paunch,' said Hal.

'Well, Carol, now you know how to keep Dougie happy after you're married,' said Gill, grinning. 'Get Mum's recipe and give him apple pie and custard for Sunday afters.'

'And while we're on the subject of your getting married,' Arnie teased, 'isn't it about time you tied the knot?'

'It's funny you should say that . . .' said Carol meaningfully, smiling coyly and nudging her fiancé.

All eyes were on the couple.

'You've set the date at last?' Gill asked.

'Yeah. We've decided on a September wedding,' Carol beamed. 'So you've all got plenty of time to get fixed up with your new outfits.' She turned to Gill excitedly. 'I'd like you to be my matron of honour and Craig to be my pageboy.'

'We'd be honoured,' said Gill.

The atmospere became charged with excitement as the family discussed the forthcoming nuptials. Winnie wondered how different this wedding would be to Gill's sorry affair. Carol and Dougie had been engaged for a year, which had given her and Hal time to save up, hoping to give their daughter a proper send-off. Winnie was really looking forward to making all the arrangements, having been unable to provide all the trimmings for her eldest daughter.

'So, your days of freedom are numbered then, mate,' joked Arnie. 'Well, it happens to the best of us in the end.'

'Enough of that sort of talk,' said Gill, giving her husband a playful slap on the arm. 'It works two ways. Carol is giving up her freedom too.'

'And I just can't wait,' she said, squeezing her fiancé's arm lovingly. 'I'll be happy to be enslaved to Dougie.'

Oh, if only she wouldn't be so obviously besotted, Gill thought, burning with vicarious embarrassment. Despite her warnings, Carol still smothered the poor boy with cloying lovey-doveyness. Her eagerness to get him to the altar worried Gill, especially as she sometimes detected a pained look in Dougie's eyes.

'What more can any man want from a wife?' laughed Arnie.

As her concern for Carol passed off, Gill felt warm inside at this happy family occasion. It was a treat to see Arnie so relaxed. Although she often found it hard to like him these days, she still loved him desperately and wanted the best for him. But she knew this affable mood wouldn't last. He was still a very tortured man.

Mary Mitchell was sitting very upright at the piano as she came to the end of *Fur Elise*, which was one of the pieces in her exam repertoire. When she'd finished, she turned to her teacher expectantly.

'That's coming on very well, Mary,' Gill said encouragingly. 'There's still a few weeks to go till the exam and you're almost ready. Keep practising, and don't forget to go over the scales.' She looked at her watch. 'That's all for this week. I'll see you again at the same time next week.'

The child slipped off the piano stool and gathered her music. 'Thank you, Mrs Briscoe.' Mary was a thin, sensitive child with dark eyes and brown hair tied back in a pony tail.

'You're welcome.'

Outside in the hall, a nine-year-old boy called Matthew Tucker was sitting on a chair waiting for his lesson, alongside Mary's mother who had come to take her daughter home. Gill and Mrs Mitchell exchanged a few words before Gill saw them out and ushered Matthew into the music room.

It was June, and she now had twenty weekly pupils and a waiting list. This was a particularly busy time for her, as she was preparing entrants for the thrice-yearly exams which would take place here, in the presence of an official examiner from one of the London Colleges of Music.

She was enjoying the work more than she'd imagined possible. It was a good feeling to be part of a child's musical development, working closely with them and watching their technique improve. Some pupils were really hard work, though, especially those who took lessons only because they had been persuaded to do it by their parents. When Gill came across a child with no aptitude for music and even less interest – rather than someone who was just a bit lazy about practising – she told their parents she would rather not continue, preferring to spend her time on someone with a genuine wish to learn.

Determined that her family life would be disrupted as little as possible by her new career, she made a point of being organised. She got up early to keep on top of the household chores, prepared meals in advance, and made sure that the teaching didn't encroach upon any time she wanted to spend with Craig and Arnie.

Arnie didn't actively stand in her way now that she worked in a separate room. But neither did he take much of an interest. It was almost as though he was pretending it wasn't happening. She knew he thought he was failing her because she was making a substantial contribution to their family budget. No matter how often she told him that she enjoyed the work and would want to do it even if they didn't need the money, he still castigated himself. There were brief spells of harmony between them, but tension was always simmering just below the surface.

Although she wanted to help him more than anything in the world, she knew this was something he must solve himself. She still thought the answer lay in employment, which would give him back his self-respect. But while she could gently suggest that he might try harder to

83

get a job, to come on too strong about it could be even more damaging to his self-esteem.

Whereas her teaching took the pressure off him financially, it was stressful to him because of the guilt he insisted on carrying. But it was a crucial outlet for Gill; it made her less susceptible to Arnie's bad temper because she was busy teaching for several hours every day.

'Right then, Matthew,' she said to her next pupil, who was one of her most reluctant and not an exam candidate. 'I'd like to hear you play the scale of C major, please.'

A fat boy with a moon face and a mop of ginger hair and freckles, Matthew Tucker was daydreaming and didn't reply.

'Matthew?'

'Yes?'

'C major, please.'

He gave an eloquent sigh, put his fingers to the keys and produced a noise so punishing Gill had to ask him to stop.

'You don't enjoy your piano lessons, do you, Matthew?'

He turned scarlet and chewed his bottom lip nervously.

'You can be honest with me, I won't bite you,' she said.

'Well . . . it's just that I'm no good at it, Miss,' he said, adding bravely, 'and I don't want to be either.'

'You have no interest at all, do you?'

He turned to her slowly, lowering his eyes shamefully.

'It's nothing to be ashamed of, you know,' she told him.

'Isn't it?' he said, sounding surprised.

'Of course not.'

His face lit up, as though she had physically lifted a burden from him. 'I thought . . .'

'Well you thought wrong,' she said. 'We can't all enjoy the same things. I expect you have other hobbies you're good at.'

'I'm good at drawing and painting,' he said.

'There you are, then.'

'But Mummy says I'll regret it later on if I don't learn to play now. My cousin is brilliant at the piano. He wins medals for it.'

That explains a lot, thought Gill, but she said, 'I'll have a word with your mother about your finishing lessons.'

'Cor, thanks, Mrs Briscoe,' he enthused, smiling properly for the first time since Gill had known him. It was like looking at a different boy.

'Are you saying that you don't want to continue teaching Matthew?' said the boy's mother, a matronly woman with an expensive but frumpish look about her.

'It isn't a question of my not wanting to,' explained Gill. 'It's just that it's a waste of my time.'

'Hardly, since I'm paying you.'

They were in the music room, Matthew now waiting outside in the hall. The late-afternoon sunshine shafted through the window, striking the corner of Gill's desk which was piled high with music theory papers to mark and other general paperwork.

'I'm not in business to force punishment on children who have no interest in the piano and who, therefore, are never likely to get to grips with it,' she explained.

'It's merely a question of perseverence,' insisted Mrs Tucker.

'But learning the piano is agony for Matthew,' Gill informed her.

'I didn't like mathematics when I was at school, but I had to do it,' was Mrs Tucker's answer to that. 'That's life. We all have to do things we don't care for. It helps in the process of character building.'

'Some things must be endured for success in later life, I agree,' said Gill. 'But music is a different thing altogether.'

'It takes a lot of effort, the same as anything else.'

'It also requires a certain amount of aptitude,' said Gill. 'I don't believe in forcing the piano on anyone. Children have quite enough compulsory subjects to learn at school.'

'He'll thank me later on.'

'It's far more likely that he'll never go near a piano again once he's of an age to please himself.'

'I shall get another teacher for him,' snorted Mrs Tucker.

'That's entirely up to you,' said Gill, irritated by the woman's lack of consideration, the blatant snobbery that made her want to indulge in one-upmanship through her child.

'It certainly is,' Mrs Tucker said and swept out of the room.

Standing at the front door, watching her march down the path dragging Matthew by the hand, Gill knew she had done the right thing in refusing to continue. But she pitied poor Matthew, who might not have such an understanding piano teacher next time.

'Do I *have* to be a pageboy at Auntie Carol's wedding on Saturday?' asked Craig one Sunday lunchtime in the autumn of that same year.

'Yes you do,' declared Gill with an air of finality.

'But M-u-m, all my friends will laugh at me,' he wailed.

'None of your friends will see you,' Gill reminded him.

'There'll be other kids around, though, won't there?' he complained. 'I mean, I'm gonna have to go outside in that stupid outfit.'

'I thought it looked quite smart,' said Arnie helpfully.

'It's very smart,' said Gill, looking at Arnie. 'He looks smashing in it.'

'I look like a pansy.'

'Don't be silly,' said Gill.

'Never mind, son,' said Arnie. 'You won't have to keep it on for long. As soon as the photographs have been taken you can get changed into your ordinary clothes.'

'Can't Auntie Carol get someone else to do it?' he whined.

'Certainly not,' said Gill firmly. 'You can't let her down now. She wants you as her pageboy and you should be honoured to be asked. Anyway, you might enjoy it when the time comes.'

'I won't.'

'I should forget all about it until Saturday if I were you,' Arnie said. 'And in the mean time, how about going over the park for a kick-about this afternoon?' Although he could no longer play football as such, he could still throw and stop shots for Craig.

The boy brightened considerably. 'Cor, yeah! That would be smashing, Dad,' he enthused.

'I fancy a walk too,' said Gill. 'So I'll come along with you.'

They set off, Craig running ahead and bouncing the ball, looking colourful in a Fair Isle sweater and blue trousers. It was a fine September afternoon, the low sun shining from a steely blue sky and gleaming on the privet hedges hung with spider's webs, the grey streets looking even dustier in the glare.

'God knows how we're gonna get him into his wedding clothes on Saturday,' said Gill as they strolled into Bishop's Park and walked beneath the luxuriant trees, the neat paths banked on either side with fallen leaves. 'Velvet and satin isn't exactly his thing.'

'I'll threaten to confiscate his football if he plays up,' said Arnie.

'If anything will do it, that will,' she said with a chuckle, enjoying the rare moment of togetherness.

'He's growing fast,' Arnie remarked.

'Yeah. Six years old,' she said. 'It hardly seems possible.'

'It certainly doesn't,' he agreed heartily. 'Makes you realise that it's time he had a brother or sister.'

Gill went cold. Arnie had been too wrapped up in himself since the accident to think about increasing their family, and because he'd had such personal problems she hadn't had the heart to tell him that this was no longer possible. Now she knew she must.

Steeling herself for his reaction, she said, 'I can't have any more children, Arnie.'

He halted in his step and turned to her. 'No more kids?' he said, looking puzzled.

'When I had the miscarriage my womb was damaged,' she explained.

'Huh! Nice of you to tell me,' he said with withering sarcasm.

'I should have, I know,' she said, 'but you had so much else to cope with, I didn't want to dish out more bad news . . . and it's not as though we've been considering trying for another baby since the miscarriage.'

'Even so, I should have been told.'

'I'm sorry. I didn't want to—'

'Make me feel more guilty,' he finished for her bitterly. 'Because it's my fault . . . because of the accident . . .'

'No, that isn't the reason,' she said. 'I saw no point in telling you something I knew would upset you when it wasn't necessary.'

'Spare me the pity.'

'I was waiting for the right opportunity.'

'Oh, God,' he said. 'Will the long-term effects of that bloody accident never stop coming?'

'It isn't the end of the world, Arnie,' she pointed out.

'Feels like it.'

'We have Craig.'

'My fault,' he muttered as though he hadn't heard her.

Sometimes Gill had had moments of desolation on this subject herself; occasionally she had experienced rage when she considered the fact that it need never have happened. But it wasn't going to help Arnie or her marriage for her to tell him this. 'Try not to brood on it, love,' she said.

'How can I not?'

'I've managed to accept it,' she said. 'You must do the same.'

'Yeah, I know,' he said, but she knew he didn't mean it.

Craig was bouncing the ball excitedly and shouting to his father, so Arnie limped across the grass to join him. Gill walked over to a wooden bench near the gently undulating river, tinted green in places by the sun. The quiet presence of the Thames was achingly sad to Gill at that moment, as she sat down and watched father and son enjoying each other's company. Despite the happy scene before her, she knew another brief period of marital bliss had been shattered.

Gill and Craig travelled together in the wedding car to the church on Saturday. Arnie was one of the ushers, so had gone on ahead. The weather was fine, and Craig looked a picture in his red velvet jacket with black satin trousers and a white shirt with a lace ruffle, his face scrubbed and rosy, curly hair combed neatly into place. Although she knew he would never admit it, Gill suspected that he was rather enjoying the attention now that the show had actually begun. She was wearing a pale peach satin dress and carrying a posy of freesias.

Arnie and the other ushers were outside the church when they arrived. 'The bridegroom hasn't arrived yet,' Arnie said in a low voice as he helped Gill out of the car into the sunshine.

'The best man?'

'Neither of 'em.'

'Oh, dear.'

'Probably held up in traffic,' suggested Arnie.

'I hope he isn't going to keep Carol waiting,' said Gill as they went into the cool, dim church and stood at the back to wait. 'He won't live to enjoy his honeymoon if he does.'

'He'll be here in a minute,' said Arnie, going back outside.

She straightened Craig's collar and patted his hair proudly, feeling the buzz of excited apprehension rippling through the pews as the guests waited for the main protagonists to arrive. Heads turned and people smiled in approval as they caught a glimpse of the matron of honour and pageboy in their wedding finery.

The expectant hush soon became a murmur of concern, however, when events didn't progress as expected.

Gill went to the church door and peered outside to see Arnie waving the bridal car on, indicating to the driver to go around the block again. And still they waited. She had a sudden chilling memory of the trapped look she had sometimes seen in Dougie's eyes when he and Carol were together.

My God. He isn't going to come, she thought with horror.

She was right. A few moments later the best man arrived with the awful news that Dougie wasn't coming. They were to tell Carol that he was very sorry but he just couldn't go through with it!

'Bloody 'ell,' said Arnie. 'What are we gonna do now?'

Chapter Eight

The stunned congregation trailed out of the church murmuring among themselves, the bride having been taken home without even getting out of the car. As it was too late to cancel the wedding reception at a local hotel, Winnie suggested the guests should go to it anyway.

'No point in wasting all that food and drink,' Hal told them, taking control because Winnie had gone home to look after Carol. 'You were all expecting a party, so a party you'll have.'

Dougie's relatives were too embarrassed to stay, but most of the guests on Carol's side went along to the hotel, their mood respectfully subdued. Arnie and Hal looked after things there while Gill and Winnie tried to console the heartbroken Carol.

'How could he have done it to me?' she wailed, lying on her bed in her dressing gown, her face tear-stained and streaked with mascara, her carefully chosen wedding dress in a heap on the floor where she insisted it stayed. 'I really believed that he loved me.'

'This doesn't necessarily mean that he doesn't,' said Gill.

'He's got a damned funny way of showing it if he does,' snorted Winnie, tactless in her rage.

'All right, Mum, don't rub it in,' sobbed Carol.

'It's marriage he's rejected, Carol – not you personally,' Gill said in an effort to revive her sister's shattered confidence. 'He'll have got cold feet about the responsibility. Some men are really frightened of that.'

'He certainly chose his time to back out,' declared Winnie angrily. 'I'll murder the bugger if I ever set eyes on him again.'

'You won't have to if I get to him first,' said Gill.

She could have told her sister that she'd seen this coming and had tried to warn her. But it would only add to her pain, so was best left unsaid. All she could do to help Carol was to be there with moral support and friendship. Sadly, though, there seemed to be nothing anyone could do to ease her pain, and Gill felt frustrated by her own powerlessness.

As Christmas approached and the world mourned President Kennedy's assassination in November, Arnie sunk to a low personal ebb and took to drowning his sorrows of an evening in the pub with his mates. While Gill was all in favour of his having some male companionship, he made too much of a habit of it, and soon the cost of his drinking became an expense they couldn't afford.

But if she dared to comment on it he lost his temper and accused her of penny-pinching. The situation between them was becoming intolerable, and she couldn't see things improving unless he regained his self-respect. Unfortunately there was only one way to do that and he wouldn't make any effort towards it at all . . .

One morning in early December when she happened to be in Fulham Broadway, she saw something that gave her an idea. An empty shop was being refitted, and on the window was a notice announcing the forthcoming opening of a branch of Bex Sports. This was a reputable firm of sportsgear retailers with branches in various areas of London. Gill had often used their Hammersmith shop for stuff that Craig needed.

The proprietor of the company was a well-known West London entrepreneur called Len Bex who was a retired professional footballer. Gill didn't know him personally, but she'd heard a lot about him, as most Fulham residents had. He was a hard nut with a soft centre, apparently. If you crossed him you'd be made to regret it, but if you earned his trust there was nothing he wouldn't do for you.

Seeing some shopfitters working inside, she went in and asked how she might contact Mr Bex.

'He's usually at the Hammersmith shop,' said one of the men. 'The main Bex Sports office is over the top of it.'

'Thanks very much,' she said, and left with a spring to her step.

'So, what can I do for you, ducks?' asked Len Bex, a robust man of about fifty with a solid jaw, shrewd brown eyes, and a nose shaped like the jagged edge of a broken bottle. He had a shock of white hair and thick, riotous eyebrows of the same colour. Though his harsh features gave him a look of toughness, he exuded charisma by the bucketful. His mode of dress was smart if somewhat flamboyant: he was wearing a silver-grey continental suit, a shocking-pink shirt and a multi-coloured tie.

Gill had not given her reasons for wanting to see him to the person she'd spoken to when she'd telephoned for an appointment. She'd simply said it was a personal matter, and was now in his office over the shop in Hammersmith, talking to him across his desk.

'I think you and I might be able to help each other,' she said.

'Oh?'

'I'm Arnie Briscoe's wife,' she explained. 'He used to play for Borough FC.'

'I remember Arnie,' he said in a warm tone. 'I used to be a great fan of his.'

'You weren't alone in that.'

'I heard about his accident,' he said, looking concerned. 'He's a great loss to the game.'

'The game is a great loss to him, too.'

90

'How is he now?'

'Not too bad.'

'What's he doing these days?'

'Nothing very much,' she said. 'Being forced to come out of the game at such an early stage really knocked the stuffing out of him and he hasn't found anything suitable in the way of a job yet.'

Len shook his head slowly and sighed. 'It's a bugger when that happens to you,' he said, sucking in his breath loudly. 'I know that only too well.'

'Really?'

'Oh, yes. I had to retire from the game early because of injury too. It took me quite a while to get back on my feet. It's a hard thing to come to terms with.'

'The thing is, Mr Bex,' Gill said, emboldened by her belief in what she was about to suggest. 'I've noticed that you're opening a shop in Fulham in the new year, and I think Arnie would be an asset to you as a member of staff.'

'You do?'

'Yes I do,' she said without hesitation. 'He knows everything there is to know about football gear and he's still enough of a name in sporting circles to attract punters into your shop.'

Bex leaned forward, his chin resting on his linked hands, observing her thoughtfully. 'I quite believe it, my dear,' he said. 'But if Arnie wants a job, why doesn't he come to see me himself?'

'Because he doesn't see himself as an asset to anyone,' she explained, 'so there's no chance of his applying for a job with you or anyone else for that matter. He thinks he has nothing to offer now that he can't play football. It wouldn't even occur to him that he could be useful to you, and he'd be furious if he knew I'd come to see you with the idea of your offering him a job.'

'Mm . . . I see.'

'He doesn't have any experience of the retail trade, but he has a good all-round knowledge of sport so he could converse intelligently with the customers,' she went on. 'And he'd soon get the hang of working behind a counter.'

'Would he be up to shop-work physically, though?' Len enquired. 'He'd be on his feet for a lot of the day.'

'I'm sure he'd be fine,' she said. 'It's just heavy work he can't cope with now.'

He stroked his chin, mulling it over.

'I'm not asking for charity,' Gill was quick to point out. 'I really do believe that if you were to give Arnie a chance, you wouldn't regret it.'

Len knew what she said made sense. Players of Arnie Briscoe's calibre were long remembered. He'd been a hero in his day and would be an attraction to the punters for years to come. He knew he couldn't afford to be sentimental when it came to business – he'd worked too hard for what he had to lose any of it by being soft – but giving Arnie Briscoe a chance could prove to be a really smart move.

'If you don't have any vacancies at the moment, maybe you could bear him in mind for later,' Gill was saying persuasively.

'Wait here a minute, ducks,' Len said. He left the room, returning a moment later with the woman who had been in the shop when Gill arrived and had shown her up to the office. He introduced her as his wife, Mary.

Shaking her hand, Gill saw a woman of about the same age as Len, with shortish white hair and warm brown eyes. She was plump and pink-cheeked and had a homely look about her, being plainly dressed in a navy blue jumper and grey pleated skirt. Her appearance was in total contrast to that of her flashy husband, but somehow they seemed exactly right together.

'I've been helping out in the shop,' Mary explained, sitting down at the other desk in the room. 'I quite enjoy a break from the office now and again. It helps to keep me in touch with the grass roots of the business.'

'Mary and I run the firm together,' explained Len. 'And I never make an important decision without talking it over with her first.'

Instinctively liking the other woman, Gill said, 'I see.'

'This young lady is married to Arnie Briscoe, love,' Len told his wife.

'What – the Arnie Brisco who used to play for Borough FC?' Mary asked in a soft, slightly husky voice.

'That's the one,' said Gill, proud of the instant recognition of her husband's name.

'Mrs Briscoe has come to put a proposition to us,' said Len, and he went on to tell his wife about Gill's suggestion.

'Sounds like a good idea to me,' said Mary, 'and we do need staff for the Fulham shop.'

'It would have to be for a trial period, though,' said Len.

'Of course,' said Gill.

'But tell me . . .' said Len, peering at her. 'If Arnie isn't going to come to see me about a job, and he mustn't know that you've been here, how am I going to take him on?'

'Hmmmm . . . You do have a point there,' Gill admitted.

But Mary had an idea. 'You could just happen to come across Arnie somewhere, Len . . . in the pub he uses, for instance,' she suggested, turning to her husband. 'You could say you recognise him from his playing days and get talking to him the way men do in pubs. When he says he isn't working, you can offer him a job as though the idea has only just occurred to you.'

Len gave his wife a crooked smile and Gill perceived real devotion between them. 'My wife is the brains of our operation,' he said, looking at Gill.

'I can see,' she smiled.

'So . . . tell me which pub your husband uses and when I'm likely to find him there.'

'The Big Bell in Fulham, and he's there most evenings, unfortunately,' she said.

'Right. I'll make a point of being there one night soon then,' he said.

'Thanks ever so much,' Gill beamed. 'This could be just what Arnie needs to put him back on his feet.'

'He's a very lucky man to have a wife who cares enough about him to go to all this trouble for him,' said Mary.

'Whatever you do, don't let him know I approached you on his behalf,' she said to Len urgently. 'He won't even consider the job if he finds out I had a hand in it. He's fiercely proud.'

'Don't worry, my dear, we'll keep shtum,' Len promised.

'We won't breathe a word,' added Mary.

For the first time in ages there was a happy atmosphere in the Briscoe household in the run-up to Christmas. Arnie was in such good spirits; it was incredible the difference the offer of a job had made to him.

'Len Bex wants me to work in the new shop he's opening in Fulham Broadway in the new year,' he'd said excitedly, having told Gill all about his 'chance' meeting with the well-known entrepreneur in the Big Bell. 'But they can use me at the Hammersmith branch right away, with it being so busy just before Christmas. So I'm going there to help out and learn the job.'

'Sounds right up your street.'

'I do fancy working there, I must admit,' he confessed. 'I'd never have thought of it if he hadn't approached me. But he really seems to want me on the staff.'

'I should think so too, Arnie . . . You'll be good for his business with your wide knowledge of sport,' she said innocently.

'He's a really nice bloke,' remarked Arnie. 'We hit it off right away. We've a lot in common, both being ex-footballers.'

'I'm so pleased things are looking up for you,' she said.

There were times when subterfuge was permissible, she told herself, and this was definitely one of them.

December was hectic for Gill, with the piano exams to organise as well as the family's Christmas preparations. There was always a feeling of excitement in the house on exam days with candidates coming and going, usually accompanied by parents. Gill used her living room as a waiting room because there tended to be a build-up of people and the hall wasn't big enough. To make a special occasion of it, she filled vases with fresh flowers and dressed in something smart – as did most of the candidates, since looking one's best is a great confidence booster. The atmosphere was charged with nervous expectation, and Gill made sure she was on hand with praise and encouragement.

Once the exams were over she threw herself into the Christmas preparations, enjoying it all the more with the return of Arnie's good humour. They went to her parents' for Christmas day and invited the Millers and the Briscoes to their place on Boxing Day.

After a traditional Boxing Day lunch of cold turkey and pickles, they lounged around chatting and eating sweets. When Arnie decided to take Craig to the park for some exercise and fresh air, Carol and John joined them.

'Carol still seems a bit down in the dumps,' remarked Phoebe after they'd gone.

'She'll get over it,' said Winnie, whose pride wouldn't allow her to admit to Phoebe how worried she was about Carol.

'It's bound to take time for the poor girl to get over a thing like that,' said Phoebe kindly.

'Mm.' Winnie nodded.

Gill was also worried about her sister. She never went out now except to work, and spent most of the time at home alone in her room. Gill had never known her to be so quiet and withdrawn. She had given her an open invitation to visit any time, but Carol had not been near Gill's place since that heartbreaking fiasco in the autumn. To help take her mind off things Gill had suggested that they go to see a show one evening together, or to the cinema while Arnie looked after Craig, but Carol didn't seem to want to do anything.

'It's still early days,' she said now to ease her mother's mind. 'Three months isn't long when you think of what she's been through.'

'True,' said Phoebe.

Curiously, Carol seemed to have undergone a transformation by the time they got back from the park. She was smiling and full of beans.

'What did you do to Carol when you were out to get her smiling?' Gill asked Arnie after tea when they were both in the kitchen.

'Nothing that I know of,' he said.

'Well, something seems to have cheered her up.'

'As far as I know, nothing out of the ordinary happened,' he said. 'I teased her a bit as I always have done. We all had a kick-about, if you can call what I do with a ball these days kicking. But that's about it.'

'Oh, well, not for us to reason why . . .'

'Perhaps the fresh air and exercise helped her to forget her troubles,' Arnie suggested.

'Could be. Let's just enjoy it and hope it lasts . . . for the rest of the day anyway,' Gill said, guessing that Carol's change of mood wouldn't be permanent.

Going into the other room, Carol's problems were pushed to the back of Gill's mind by a heated argument that had blown up between Phoebe and John Briscoe. They were standing in the middle of the room shouting at each other while Gill's parents and her sister sat on the sofa looking embarrassed, especially Winnie. Craig was watching the quarrel with a mixture of fear and fascination.

'It's plain ignorant, to walk out of your brother's house when you've been invited for the day,' Phoebe was saying to her youngest son.

'Give over nagging, will you, Mum?' John said. 'We came for the day and it's evening now. I'm meeting me mates.'

'Don't worry about us if you want to go out with your friends, John,' said Gill reasonably. 'We don't mind.'

'We do mind,' objected Arnie. 'Don't encourage him in his bad manners, Gill.'

'Be fair, Arnie. We all wanted to be out with our friends when we were his age,' she said. 'Not stuck at home with the family.'

'We didn't have mates like Head-Butter Harris and his crowd though, did we?' said Arnie.

'Butter's all right,' John defended. 'He's a good laugh.'

'Harris is trouble.' Arnie glared at his brother, at the leather jacket and tight jeans, the hair cut into a Beatle fringe. 'And if you hang about with him and his mates for long enough you'll be in trouble too.'

'You know nothing about them,' John defended hotly.

'Everybody in Fulham knows about Head-Butter Harris,' said Arnie. 'He spent more time in the juvenile courts than he did at school.'

John let out an expressive sigh. 'I don't pick holes in your mates, so don't criticise mine,' he said angrily.

'You've no cause to criticise mine 'cause I don't go around with scum,' said Arnie.

'Oh, I've had enough of this,' said John huffily. 'I'm going out.' And he marched out of the house leaving a resonant silence behind him.

'The young bugger,' said Arnie, making as though to go after him.

'Leave him,' said Phoebe commandingly. 'The more we disapprove of his mates the more determined he'll be not to give 'em up.' She turned to Gill. 'I'm sorry he was so rude, love, after all your hard work and hospitality.'

'Don't worry about it.'

'That boy is a real pain lately.'

'He'll grow out of it,' said Gill.

'If he had something to interest him besides those yobs he goes about with, I'd feel more hopeful about him,' said Phoebe glumly. 'But he hates his job at the soup factory and he's got no hobbies. He hasn't even taken an interest in football since he got in with Harris.'

'I think I'll have to try to get him a job at Bex Sports once I'm established there myself,' said Arnie. 'So that I can keep an eye on him.'

'I wish someone would straighten him out,' said Phoebe. 'He's driving me round the bend.'

'Arnie will get it sorted, don't worry,' said Gill, realising that there were other people here to be entertained. 'And in the mean time let's all have a drink and enjoy the rest of the evening.'

'Yes, let's do that,' said Phoebe.

— Gill and Carol emerged from Earl's Court station one Saturday in the spring, having spent the morning shopping in the West End. It was a fine day with blue skies and pale sunshine, a deceptively fresh breeze whipping around corners and flapping through the shop awnings.

'Well, are you pleased with your new clothes?' asked Gill, who'd finally persuaded her sister to go out on this shopping spree.

'S'pose so,' said Carol flatly as they headed along North End Road to their parents' house. Winnie, who was looking after Craig while Gill was out because Arnie was at work on a Saturday, was making lunch for them all. Lessons had finished for the Easter holidays which meant that Gill had a free Saturday.

'Don't overdo the enthusiasm,' Gill said with irony.

'Well . . . where will I go to wear them?'

'Out enjoying yourself, I hope,' said Gill.

'Who with?' was Carol's answer to that. 'I gave up all my friends for Dougie. They're all married or got steady boyfriends anyway, now.'

Gill could see the problem. But she felt as though she had achieved a minor success in getting Carol to buy some new clothes. At least she'd brightened up a little. 'You need a new man,' she said.

'Unattached ones don't exactly grow on trees, you know.'

'No . . . but they do go to dances and discos in the hope of meeting someone.'

'I wouldn't go to something like that on my own,' said Carol, horrified.

'I suppose not,' said Gill. 'I'd go with you myself to keep you company but I don't think Arnie would approve.'

'You're so lucky,' said Carol enviously. 'You've got everything . . . a husband, a home, a child.'

'And so will you have one day.'

'I don't think I'll ever meet anyone,' moaned Carol.

'You're only twenty-two, for heaven's sake,' said Gill.

'But everybody else is fixed up,' Carol wailed, 'and I'm never likely to meet anyone at work.'

'Someone will come along,' said Gill. 'Just give it time.'

'It's so lonely not having anyone of your own,' said Carol. 'You don't know what it's like, Gill. You never have. You didn't have time to because you started going out with Arnie at such a young age.'

If she only knew how lonely you can be within a relationship, Gill thought, but she simply said, 'I understand what you're saying. But perhaps you should stop thinking about it so much. Mr Right will come along when you least expect it.'

'I thought Mr Right was Dougie.'

'Dougie's past history.'

'I know.'

The market was in full flow and they had to elbow their way through the vociferous crowds thronging the pavements, queueing at stalls, standing in groups chatting, some just idly browsing through the goods on offer. Gill stopped at a fruit stall to buy some apples and oranges.

'Arnie's a really big fruit eater,' she remarked casually. 'He reckons it's the key to good health.'

'Must be why he always looks so fit.'

'Maybe.'

'I think he looks great.'

'You've always had a soft spot for him, haven't you?' said Gill lightly. 'Ever since you were a schoolgirl.'

'Yes I have,' Carol replied, though what she'd been feeling for Arnie lately was more than just a girlish soft spot. Her sister would have a fit if she knew what passed through Carol's mind about Arnie sometimes, especially since Boxing Day in the park with him and the others, when she'd first glimpsed an end to the depression left by Dougie's rejection. Nothing had happened between herself and Arnie, but realising how much she wanted it to had made her feel better somehow. At least it proved that Dougie hadn't done any permanent damage and that everything was still in good working order . . .

Arnie was busy serving a customer late that same Saturday afternoon when Len came into the shop and went straight through to the manager's office.

'Are you hoping to get into the school team one day, son?' said Arnie to his customer, a young boy who was here with his father buying a pair of football boots.

'Yeah.' The lad looked at Arnie with blatant admiration. 'I bet you played for your school, didn't you?'

'I did, as a matter of fact.'

'What was it like playing as a professional?' asked the boy as Arnie laced the boots for him.

'Magic,' he said. 'Sheer magic.'

'Did you ever play in a Cup Final?'

'No, I never did make that,' said Arnie with a note of regret – but not the self-pity that had once been so prevalent in his attitude. He finished tying the boots. 'You can stand up and see what they feel like now.'

The boy walked up and down to check the fit of the boots. 'They feel great,' he said.

'Good.' Arnie turned to the boy's father while the lad sat down to remove the boots. 'It's a bit late in the season for new boots, isn't it?'

'The kids where we live play soccer all year round.'

'We used to too. Cricket was never really in the running.'

The boy handed Arnie the boots to be boxed and Arnie went behind the counter to complete the transaction with the boy's father, answering a series of questions about his life as a soccer star as he did so.

Other customers came into the shop and were eager to hear what Arnie had to say, remembering how famous he'd once been. Despite all the chatter, however, Arnie continued serving, managing to balance entertainment with efficiency.

Considering the fact that it was almost the end of the football season there was still quite a demand for boots and replica strips of the professional teams, but the sales in cricket gear were also beginning to gather momentum. Over the next half-hour or so Arnie did a brisk trade in cricket bats, billiard cues and golf balls, glad he'd always taken an all-round interest in sport because it enabled him to converse with the customers whatever their chosen pursuit.

He was in his element in this job. The shop had taken over from the football field as his territory, a place where he felt important and in demand. Apart from the manager, Arnie was the only full-time assistant, but they had several part-timers and a schoolboy who came in on a Saturday. If they were especially busy Mary Bex would leave her desk in the office to lend a hand.

Len was still talking shop to Jack, the manager, in his office. Glancing though the glass partition into the shop, Len watched Arnie working, impressed with what he saw.

'He seems to be shaping up very well,' he remarked.

'He's a ruddy marvel,' said Jack, following his employer's gaze. 'He could sell football boots to legless seamen, that one.'

'Yes, he does have a way about him,' Len agreed. 'Do you reckon people come into the shop just to chat to him?'

'I'm sure they do,' said Jack. 'But they never go out empty-handed, Arnie sees to that. He's full of chat, but he's a real slogger. He can talk and work at the same time.'

'So I've noticed.' Len looked at his watch. 'Well, it'll soon be time to shut up shop. How about my buying you all a drink when you've cashed up? As it's the end of the week and the shop is doing so well.'

'Sorry boss, I've gotta rush off,' said the manager. 'The wife and I are going out for a meal tonight and she'll have my guts for garters if I'm late home. But I'm sure the others would love to go with you.'

Arnie was the only member of staff who wasn't in a particular hurry, as it happened, and he welcomed the chance of a social half-hour with his employer, whose company he found he enjoyed.

Inevitably, however, they talked shop.

'Why don't we have an end-of-season sale of football gear?' Arnie suggested, leaning on the bar with a pint.

'The way you shift the stock, we won't need to,' said Len, holding a glass of whisky and puffing on a cigar.

'It'll slow down soon, though, when all the organised games finish – until the new season,' Arnie pointed out.

'True.'

'Don't worry, though, boss – I'm becoming an expert on cricket . . . tennis an' all,' he said with a wicked laugh.

His employer chuckled too. Arnie was a man after his own heart.

'You've got a good head for business, Arnie, and you're a natural with the customers,' said Len. 'Mary and I are pleased with the way you've taken to the job.'

'Thanks, mate. I'm glad about that,' said Arnie, grinning. 'I'm dead chuffed about the way it's turned out an' all. Cor, if I'd known I was gonna have a talent for the sportsgear trade I'd have come to see you about a job long ago.'

Len drew deeply on his cigar, feeling relaxed and happy. 'You wouldn't have been thinking straight when you first came out of the game,' he said. 'It makes you feel too sick at heart to want to do anything for a while.'

'You're telling me.'

'I was just the same when my football career came to a sudden end.' He sipped his whisky, relaxing even more, rather too much as it happened. 'As I said to your missus when she came to see me, it's a hard thing to have to come to terms with.'

'People don't understand unless they've actually been through it.'

'Course not,' said Len. 'How can they?'

Arnie looked suddenly baffled.

'What was that you just said?' he asked. 'Did you say my wife came to see you?'

'That's right.'

'Oh?'

'Good job she did as it turned out, innit?' said Len.

Arnie didn't reply. Only on seeing his thunderous expression did Len remember his promise to Gill.

'Oh, blimey,' he said, making a face. 'I was supposed to keep shtum about that. Still, as you're doing so well, I don't suppose it matters now.'

'My wife put you up to it, didn't she?' said Arnie through tight lips. 'My wife came to see you and asked you to give me a job.'

'Calm down,' Len urged. 'It wasn't like that at all.'

'We didn't meet by chance in here that night you offered me the job, did we?' said Arnie, looking stricken. 'Did we?' he persisted when Len remained silent.

'Well, not exactly, but—'

'The whole thing was a set up, to give poor old useless Arnie a leg-up.'

'That wasn't the way it was at all,' Len declared ardently.

'That's exactly the way it was,' said Arnie coldly. 'Now, if you'll excuse me, I have to go.'

And he marched out of the pub.

'How dare you belittle me!' Arnie roared, storming into the kitchen where Gill was busy preparing the evening meal. Craig was out at a friend's so they were alone in the house. 'I could kill you for what you've done, you interfering cow.'

She looked round at him, startled, her hands encased in oven gloves. 'What *are* you talking about?'

'You went to see Len to beg him to give me a job,' he blasted.

'No I didn't,' she said, shaking her head vigorously.

'Don't lie to me,' he said, grabbing hold of her arm in his fury. 'I know you went to see him. He admitted it.'

'All right. I did go to see him, but I didn't beg him to give you a job.'

'It's a bloody conspiracy,' Arnie growled. 'He told me you asked him not to say anything about it. Luckily for me he forgot his promise after he'd had a drink, or I might never have found out the truth about the job.'

'It's true, I did ask him to keep quiet about my visit, but I certainly didn't beg him to give you a job.'

'Oh, not much,' Arnie said, beside himself with shame and fury. 'He told me it was all a set-up, him and me meeting in the pub that night, organised by you . . . you scheming bitch.'

Gill looked at him, knowing he was feeling wretched. His eyes were ice-cold, lips set in a grim line.

'The only way you would have accepted the position was if he approached you and offered you the job on a plate.'

'Bitch.'

'If you'll calm down, I'll tell you exactly what happened,' she said firmly. 'Now let go of my arm, please. You're hurting me.'

He released her, looking at his hand in puzzlement as though he hadn't realised he'd been holding her so roughly. 'Let's hear it then,' he said.

'I went to see Len Bex because I noticed that he was opening a new shop and I genuinely believed you would be an asset to him,' she explained.

He clutched his head with his hands dramatically, closing his eyes. 'Oh, God, I can hardly bear to think about it,' he said, his voice trembling with rage. 'My wife begging someone to give me a job. It makes me want to crawl into a hole and die.'

'How many more times must I tell you? I did *not* beg him to give you a job,' she said wearily. 'I told him I thought you would be valuable to his business – and I was right, wasn't I?'

'He would never have offered me a job if you hadn't gone to see him, though, would he?' he queried miserably.

'How could he when he didn't even know you were available?' she pointed out. 'He'd heard of you from your playing days, but he wasn't to know that you weren't fixed up with work. All I did was bring the two of you together, and it's worked out very well for you both. You're enjoying the job and his business is reaping the benefit. So what does it matter how it all came about?'

'I don't need a woman to go out job-hunting for me,' he said.

'You weren't doing anything about getting a job yourself, though, were you?'

'I would have.'

'The longer you left it the harder it would have got.'

'You had no right—'

Suddenly Gill had reached the end of her patience. She was tired of pandering to his fragile ego, treading on eggshells around him and making allowances for his moods. All the heartache and worry he had caused her this last two turbulent years culminated in a blistering surge of rage. 'Now you just listen to me for a minute!' she ordered, her voice high and brittle. 'Okay, so you think I had no right to do something I truly believed would help my husband. But you had no right to put me through nearly two years of misery because you lost your football career.'

'You couldn't possibly imagine what it was like for me when that happened.'

'And you couldn't imagine what it's been like for me,' she said, hating him at that moment for causing her such pain. 'Living with someone so drenched in self-pity as you were, on my back the whole time, criticising everything I did and making no effort to drag yourself out of the doldrums. You were even perverse enough to make it difficult for me to bring in some extra cash through teaching when we desperately needed it. And all because I hadn't lost my ability to use my talent and you had.'

'That's right, turn the knife—'

'I had to do *something* to help you back on your feet, Arnie,' she told him. 'I couldn't just sit back and watch you become a vegetable with no purpose in life when you still had so much to offer. That's why I went to see Len Bex.'

'How do you think I feel now – knowing that I wasn't taken on on my own merit?'

101

'You *were* taken on on your own merit,' she insisted loudly. 'All I did was make Len Bex aware that you were around.'

'Huh!'

'If you've any sense at all, you'll be proud of yourself for making such a success of the job,' she said. 'They wouldn't keep you on if you weren't good at it.'

'I can't stay there now.'

Gill sighed in exasperation. 'Oh no, don't tell me you're going to pack it in,' she said.

'I'll have to.'

'*Why?*'

' 'Cause I feel such a bloody fool, that's why,' he snarled.

Now it was her turn to clutch her head. 'Oh, give us a break, Arnie, please,' she entreated. 'Don't you think I've had enough to put up with since your accident—'

'That's right, drag it all up again,' he interrupted through clenched teeth, his eyes dark with hatred because every time he looked at her he remembered how much he hated himself for failing her. 'You don't have to remind me that it's my fault you lost the baby and my fault you can't have any more.'

She felt his words like a blow to the heart. She'd had no idea he was still brooding about that, still blaming himself. 'That wasn't what I meant.'

'You said—'

'I was referring to your bad temper and lack of co-operation, which have made my life hell,' she cut in. 'Despite what you may think, you are not the only person in the world.'

'And don't I know it?'

'You're prepared to give up a job you need and enjoy just because of vanity?'

'Vanity?'

'Yes – vanity,' she said loudly and with strong emphasis. 'That's *exactly* what it is. You're so damned vain, you won't even stay in a job you're good at because somebody else gave you a helping hand.'

'You don't understand . . .'

She turned away and continued with the task in hand because she was sick of trying to communicate with him. She took a packet of frozen peas from the ice compartment of the fridge and emptied them into a saucepan of boiling water. 'You do what you feel you must about the job, Arnie,' she said, her voice quieter now.

'I will, don't worry.'

'I'm sure.' She paused for a moment. 'Craig will be home at any minute. His pal's father is bringing him back in his car,' she continued evenly. 'I don't want this quarrel to continue in front of him.'

'Give me credit for having some sense.'

'If you want to cut off your nose to spite your face and give up your job, then I can't stop you,' she went on determinedly. 'But do be aware of what you're giving up. It might be a very long time before you find another job you like as much.'

'Oh, give over nagging, woman,' he said and marched from the room.

Gill's hand was trembling as she stirred the gravy in a saucepan. Somewhere along the way she and Arnie had lost something precious. Was it that too many of the bad things of the past still stood between them – guilt on his part, and resentment on hers? Or was it just that he had worn her out with his demanding and difficult ways? Maybe it was simply that first love hadn't stood the test of time.

Was I wrong to interfere on the question of his employment? she asked herself, and couldn't in all honesty accept that she was. But she did accept the undeniable fact that there was something seriously wrong with her marriage, something she didn't seem able to put right. Her latest efforts had backfired on her. So what else could she do?

Chapter Nine

'You and your big mouth,' said Mary Bex reprovingly. It was Monday morning, and she and her husband sat at their desks, reeling from the shock of Arnie's resignation, which was to take immediate effect. Storming into the Hammersmith office to give in his notice, he'd told them he would rather lose a week's pay than spend another minute in their employ now that he knew the truth.

'What on earth possessed you to tell him when we both promised we wouldn't?' Mary asked.

'I didn't intend to say anything.' Len looked suitably shamefaced. 'It just slipped out when I was feeling relaxed.'

'When the whisky had loosened your tongue, more like . . .'

'Maybe that's what it was,' he freely admitted, lighting a cigarette. 'Anyway, I feel bad about it whatever.'

'I should hope you do,' she said. 'I could murder you.'

'What's done is done. There's no point in your going on at me about it.'

'True.' She put on her spectacles and flicked through a pile of invoices, but her mind wasn't on her work. 'I bet his wife has had a rotten weekend. He's bound to have given her a bad time.'

'I don't know why he's so upset about it,' said Len, tutting and shaking his head. 'I mean . . . what does it matter how he came by the job in the first place – as long as he's doing well now?'

'Male pride is a powerful thing.'

'It must be in his case.'

'He's obviously lacking in confidence, even though he's so chatty and full of himself,' Mary said. 'Some men can't bear to think that they might have a woman to thank for something other than having their supper on the table when they get home from work.'

'You banging the drum for women's rights?' Len said, drawing on his cigarette.

'No, just stating facts.'

'Not with me in mind, I hope.'

'Of course not,' she said with emphasis. She and Len were a team; he freely admitted her contribution to the business and made no secret of it to other people.

'Just kidding.' He paused, thinking about Arnie. 'Okay, so he's had his pride dented. Surely that's no reason to give up a job he enjoys.'

'He obviously thinks it is.'

'Silly young hothead.'

'You were just the same at his age . . . and you were impossible to live with for ages after you came out of football.'

'I've never understood why you put up with me,' he said, teasing her.

'For your money.'

'I didn't have any.'

'It must have been your body then,' she joshed. 'It certainly wasn't your refined manners.'

'Cheeky bitch.' Len paused, becoming sentimental as he was inclined to do when thinking about his marriage. 'We've come a long way since those early days, haven't we?'

'We certainly have. Nearly thirty years married, and six sports shops to our credit,' she said. 'Not bad for someone who had his football career cut short.'

'I couldn't have done any of it without you,' he said in a sober tone. 'And I couldn't manage without you now.'

'Oh, I daresay you'd muddle along if you had to.' She leaned back, clasping her hands behind her head and staring meditatively into space. 'But more importantly for the moment, what are you going to do about Arnie?'

'He's a bloody nuisance, causing us all this trouble.'

'I agree with you,' Mary said, 'but he's also the best thing that's happened to this business in a long time.'

'Mm.'

'So what are you going to do about it?'

'What do you think I'm gonna do?' he said, meeting her eyes.

'That's my Len,' she said, winking and treating him to one of her warmest smiles. 'And don't be too long about it either, because they're short-staffed at the Fulham branch without him.'

'I guessed I'd find you in here,' said Len.

Arnie was standing at the bar of the Big Bell drinking a pint. Observing the other man gloomily, he said, 'What are you having?'

'It's my shout,' insisted Len, puffing on a cigar. 'You can't afford to flash your money about now that you're out of a job.'

'That's my business,' said Arnie, reaching into his pocket.

'Shut up and do as you're told,' commanded Len. 'I've had about as much as I can take of your nonsense for one day.'

'Why don't you push off back to Putney then?' said Arnie rudely. 'This is my local. I didn't ask you to come round here looking for me.'

Len threw him a hard look. 'That's quite true. But since I *have* taken the trouble to come over from Putney, you'll listen to what I have to say.' He spoke with such authority that Arnie didn't argue, but followed him meekly over to a table in the corner carrying the drinks.

106

'Right, I won't beat about the bush,' said Len, swallowing some whisky. 'I think you're behaving like a spoilt brat and I don't like it.'

A shrug of the shoulders was Arnie's reply.

'Not only have you let me down, you've let your wife down an' all.'

'There's no law that I know of against giving up a job,' Arnie said sullenly.

'Oh, don't be so damned childish.' Len looked grim. 'Your wife didn't come to me begging for a job for you. In fact, the way she put it, I was the one who should consider myself lucky to have the chance to take you on. And what she said made sense. Having you behind the counter in my shop is a winning formula.'

Arnie said nothing.

Len leant back slightly and stared at the other man. 'Okay, let's look at this another way. Just supposing your missus had come to me on bended knee pleading with me to give you a job. What difference would it have made to the fact that you're doing well and enjoying the work?'

'It's in here, mate,' said Arnie, pointing to his chest. 'Right inside.'

'Oh, yeah, very dramatic,' said Len scornfully. 'But it doesn't impress me.'

'That's up to you.'

'Personally I think you should be grateful that your wife bothered to do something to help you. In fact, you're damned lucky she's still with you at all if this is the way you treat her.'

Drinking his beer, Arnie remained silent.

'You don't deserve her, mate,' Len continued. 'And it'd be your own fault if she buggered off and left you. She's too good for you.'

'You're not telling me anything I don't already know,' said Arnie, his voice quivering with emotion suddenly. 'It's a recognised fact that Gill's too good for me.'

'It's up to you to make yourself good enough for her then, innit?' said Len.

'Gill's in a class of her own,' said Arnie in a deeply serious tone. 'She always was a cut above, even when we were kids living in the same street. She never raked the streets like me and the others. She stayed indoors practising the piano while the rest of us were getting up to all sorts o' mischief in Maisie Road. Now she's a successful piano teacher and I'm a broken-up football player.' And I keep hurting her, a voice screamed inside his head. I can't stop hurting her and it's destroying us both. I can hardly bear to look at her because of what I'm doing to her.

'Ease up on the self-pity, for Gawd's sake, Arnie,' said Len. 'You'll have me crying into my whisky in a minute.'

'Sorry.'

'I should think you ought to be sorry an' all,' said Len. 'You've got a lovely wife who takes the trouble to do something to help you, and you repay her by throwing it back in her face. And if that isn't bad enough, you've got the brass neck to mope about feeling sorry for yourself.'

Knowing that what Len said was true made Arnie feel even worse, so he blotted out the truth and defended himself by attack. 'She shouldn't have—'

'She was only thinking of you,' Len interrupted in exasperation. 'Anyway, only someone without any responsibilities can afford to be sensitive about that sort of thing. You've got a wife and kid to support; you need to be working to provide for 'em.'

'I'll go back on to benefit until I find another job,' he said.

'And what are you gonna do with yourself until you find a job you fancy, eh?' Len demanded. 'Sit on your arse all day while your wife works to put jam on the bread for you all?'

Arnie lowered his eyes shamefully. 'No, I'll go out looking until I find something suitable,' he said. 'A job that I'll apply for myself.'

Len lapsed into silence, sipping his whisky thoughtfully. 'How long is it since your accident?'

'Two years.'

'Don't you think that's more than long enough to be feeling sorry for yourself?' Len asked.

'Yes it is, and I'm not.'

'Phew, not much!'

'Oh, you think what you like,' snapped Arnie. 'I couldn't care less.'

'I always admired you as a player, and when I met you in person I took an instant liking to you,' Len carried on regardless. 'I thought you and I were two of a kind. I thought you were the sort of person I wanted to have working for me. Bright, tough, full of good ideas . . . I also thought you could be trusted. It just goes to show how wrong you can be about someone, doesn't it?'

'I've never had my hand in the till,' exclaimed Arnie with affront.

'I know that.'

'You implied I'm not to be trusted.'

'There's more to trust than dishonesty,' Len told him.

'Oh yeah?'

'Don't act thick,' said Len. 'I'm talking about commitment to the job, reliability and respect for your employer.'

'I do respect you—'

'You say you respect me yet you're willing to leave me short-staffed with no one to cover for you until I can find a replacement,' he said angrily. 'And not even willing to work your week's notice. You call that respect?'

There was nothing Arnie could say to that. He had dug a hole for himself and he didn't know how to claw his way out. Everything Len had said was true, and Arnie felt deeply ashamed. But pride wouldn't allow him to do what Len wanted.

'Anyway, if this is the way you conduct yourself the firm is better off without you.' Len finished his drink and stood up to go. 'No one's indispensable, mate. I'll have no trouble finding a replacement for you.' He stubbed his cigar out in the ashtray. 'You'd be wise to keep that in mind before your wife realises the same thing.' And without another word, Len marched across the bar and left the pub.

After only a few moments' deliberation, Arnie got up and went after him.

That same evening, just after Craig had gone to bed, Gill received an unexpected visitor.

'I've called round to see how you're bearing up,' said Mary Bex as Gill showed her into the living room and invited her to sit down. 'In the light of what's happened with Arnie.'

'That's very kind of you, Mrs Bex,' said Gill, warming to her.

'Mary, please.'

'I'm all right, Mary,' she said with a wistfulness in her tone.

'Are you sure?'

'Well, naturally I'm fed up about the way it's turned out for Arnie . . .'

'I should think you are. I could have murdered that husband of mine for spilling the beans.' Mary was wearing a plain navy-blue suit and white blouse which was smart in a matronly sort of way.

'I was mad with Len too, at first,' said Gill. 'But now all my anger is aimed towards Arnie. I mean it's so irresponsible to give up a job he likes for such a silly reason.'

'Is Arnie at the Big Bell now?'

Gill nodded.

'Good. Because Len has gone there looking for him to try to talk some sense into him,' said Mary in her gentle voice. 'We aren't prepared to let him go without a fight.'

'Ooh good,' said Gill, feeling a surge of new hope. 'It would be such a relief if Len could persuade him to change his mind.'

'If anyone can do it, Len can.'

Gill invited Mary to stay for coffee and she said she'd love to. Within minutes they were chatting like old friends.

'I suppose things will be difficult for you if Len can't talk him into staying on,' said Mary, sipping her coffee.

'We'll manage like we did before he got the job,' said Gill. 'There isn't much left over for treats, but we'll get by. Fortunately I enjoy my work, so being the breadwinner is no hardship to me.'

'It must be annoying for you, though, knowing that Arnie could make life easier.'

'His frame of mind worries me far more than the financial side of things,' said Gill. 'He's so bitter about my working, even though he knows we need the money.'

'Men, eh?' said Mary.

Gill threw her a look. 'Not Len?' she said in a questioning tone.

'Steady as a rock now,' said Mary, 'but we had our bad times when we were younger.'

'Really?'

'Not half. Len was cut up about having to come out of the game too. Impossible to live with for quite a long time – so I know what it's like for you. But once he set up in business he never looked back. He started off selling sportsgear in the markets.'

'The two of you seem to be very close,' remarked Gill.

'We are. We've been together for nearly thirty years,' she stated. 'We've never had any children, so we only have each other. You might say the business is our baby.'

'Does it ever get a bit much – working and living together?' Gill enquired.

'No, not really,' Mary said. 'We have our off days, of course, like everyone else. I'm not in the office full-time anyway. I'm one of these old-fashioned people who enjoys being a housewife; I like to have some time at home. I can usually manage to get done what I have to in the office and still have some time to myself. Unless we're short-staffed and I have to help behind the counter.'

'Sounds as though you've got yourself very well organised.'

'I'm happy with the way things are,' she said, smiling. 'But what about you? I understand you're a piano teacher.'

'That's right.'

'It must be lovely to be able to do something like that.'

'I'm glad of it, I must admit,' Gill said. 'I don't know what I'd do without my piano.'

'I'd love to be able to play.'

'Well . . . it's never too late to learn.'

'I'm a bit too long in the tooth now.'

'Not at all,' said Gill.

'You teach adults?'

'I don't actually have any on my books, but all ages are welcome.'

'Maybe one of these days, after I retire . . .' Mary said, smiling. 'Life is a bit too hectic at the moment for me to take anything else on.'

'I can imagine,' said Gill. 'Running a home and a business doesn't leave much time for other things, does it?'

'It isn't only those two things,' said Mary. 'Both Len and I have our own separate outside interests. He's involved with several associations who organise various kinds of social events to raise money for charity.'

'Which means a busy social life for you?'

'Yes, we do go to quite a few dinners and so on,' she said.

'And what about your outside interests?' queried Gill.

'I'm closely involved with the Friends of St Theresa's.'

110

'St Theresa's,' said Gill, trying to place the name. 'Isn't that the children's home down Walham Green way? The one run by nuns?'

'That's right.'

'I've seen crocodiles of girls walking with the nuns around there.'

'Yes. The older girls go outside to the local school,' Mary explained. 'The little ones are taught inside the home.'

'What does being involved actually entail?' enquired Gill with interest.

'I'm chairman of the Friends of St Theresa's committee,' Mary explained. 'We work closely with the nuns, organising social events and trips out for the girls.'

'What a lovely idea.'

'Yes, I think it's a worthwhile cause. The children are very well looked after at the home, though the nuns are quite strict. But these girls miss out on so many things that other children take for granted.'

'I can imagine.'

'Our aim is to give them something special to look forward to outside of the institution,' Mary went on. 'We can't give them what they want most of all – family life – but we can arrange for them to have a few of the treats other kids have as a matter of course. Seaside outings, cinema trips, that sort of thing. We organised a trip to the ice-skating rink the other week and they thought that was great fun.'

'I bet they did,' said Gill, intrigued.

'It all takes money, of course, so we are endlessly fund-raising.' Mary smiled her warm smile. 'People must dread meeting me in the street for fear I'll try to flog them raffle tickets or get them to take part in some kind of fund-raising event. You're quite safe tonight, though, 'cause I don't actually have anything to sell.'

'I wouldn't have minded,' said Gill.

'The days of the old-fashioned orphanage with grim dormitories and very little to eat have gone in this affluent society,' said Mary. 'But the girls need more than just food and drink and education. The nuns can't provide everything.'

'Of course not,' said Gill thoughtfully, a germ of an idea beginning to form.

They chatted for ages until Mary said she had to go.

'I've really enjoyed your company, my dear,' she said as she was shown to the door. 'We must get together again sometime soon . . .' She paused and looked at Gill. 'Whatever the outcome of Len and Arnie's meeting tonight.'

'Yes, I'd like that,' said Gill, knowing she had made a new friend.

'What do you think of the idea of Bex Sports sponsoring a local amateur football team?' Arnie suggested that same evening after offering profuse apologies to Len, who had reinstated him. The two men were buddies again.

'We have sponsored local teams before from time to time,' said Len.

'I was thinking in terms of a boy's team, though.'

'What exactly did you have in mind in the way of sponsorship?'

'Supply the team strips, have a list of the match fixtures in our window, that sort of thing,' Arnie said with enthusiasm. 'We could also try to get the local paper to cover their matches. It would be good for them and good for us.'

'Hmmm.' Len pondered the idea.

'Okay, so it'll cost the firm a bit to kit the team out. But the word will soon get round about what we're doing. And where will the parents go for their cricket stuff in summer and tennis gear and anything else they need?'

'To us.'

'Exactly.'

'It's a good idea,' said Len. 'You get it organised and the firm will cover the cost.'

'You're giving me the okay without speaking to Mrs Bex?' said Arnie in surprise.

'You're getting to know me a bit too well, son,' Len smiled.

'Not really – but I do know how important her opinion is to you.'

'We're a team.'

'She's a great lady,' said Arnie. 'Everybody likes her.'

'She's a soft touch with the staff, that's why they're so fond of her,' said Len jokingly. 'But seriously, I know she'll go along with this idea, so you can go ahead. I'll mention it to her as soon as I get home.'

'You'll square it with the manager so he'll be in the picture?'

'I certainly will, but this will be your baby, Arnie, your responsibility,' Len said. 'The business will put up the money, but it's up to you to do all the work.'

'No problem.'

'Good.'

This latest scheme of Arnie's convinced Len that he'd done the right thing in hanging on to him.

'I'll get it organised for the new season,' said Arnie.

Len moved the conversation on to something else that was on his mind. 'The Fulham shop is getting so busy, we could do with another full-time assistant,' he said thoughtfully. 'You don't happen to know of anyone who might be interested, do you?'

'I do, as it happens.'

'Really?'

'Yeah. My younger brother,' Arnie said. 'If anyone needs a new challenge in his life it's John. He's working in a factory and he hates it. I could keep my eye on him and teach him the job.'

'Would he be interested in our type of work, though?' Len enquired. 'Because that's my main concern when taking someone new on. Lack of experience can easily be rectified. But enthusiasm for the job is essential.'

Arnie wasn't sure how to answer this. John had used to be keen and knowledgeable about sport, especially football – before Head-Butter Harris and his crowd got such a hold on him. Now the gang seemed to dominate him completely. Lately, though, Arnie had got the impression that the novelty of hanging out with thugs was wearing thin with John, even though he had shown no real signs of breaking away from them. He denied it, of course, but Arnie suspected that this was the case. Maybe a new job was just what John needed to put him back on the right track. Arnie was certain that John's salvation lay in a new sense of purpose of some sort.

'I'm not absolutely sure, but I'll talk to him about it,' he said.

'Tell him to come into the office at Hammersmith to see me for a chat if he's interested in a job,' said Len.

'I'll do that.'

Arnie had a horrible suspicion that he would live to regret introducing his brother to Bex Sports. But he felt duty-bound to do it anyway, in John's best interests.

With Arnie settled back into the job, life fell into a pattern for Gill that summer. Craig had his seventh birthday and continued to take after his father, both in appearance and personality. He became increasingly football-mad with every day that passed. Arnie said he was a natural, and got him into a local team for the under-nines.

Beatlemania continued to sweep across Britain and abroad, as the group's popularity spread throughout the world. Gill thought their music was great and had fun playing their songs on the piano. She even encouraged pupils whose interest was flagging to play catchy Beatles numbers in the hope of reviving their interest. Even Craig loved Beatles music – but not enough to inspire him to piano lessons. The house was filled with music of all kinds, from classical to pop, from piano to record player.

Gill saw quite a lot of Carol, who still didn't have a man in her life and grew ever more despairing about it. She often talked about getting a flat of her own, but Gill doubted if she'd do more than talk about it because she was too comfortable living at home with Mum and Dad.

For all that Gill was fond of her sister, she couldn't deny the fact that Carol was becoming even more self-centred. Her desperation for love and marriage was still an obsession with her too, and was a constant worry for Gill and her parents.

Now that Arnie was working and more settled in himself, Gill hoped their marriage might regain its former unity. But although he seemed to get closer to Craig, he grew more distant from her. They acted out a normal relationship, and on the surface everything was fine, but there was an underlying coldness between them now. They were always just a whisper away from an argument which might flare up at the slightest thing.

They didn't talk about it, but they both knew that something was wrong. It stood between them, an unspoken mutual understanding they daren't confront, for fear it would lead to a parting of the ways if brought out into the open.

So they sidestepped the issue, going through the motions of married life from day to day, loving Craig but not each other – or that was what it felt like to Gill.

John Briscoe started work at Bex Sports in the early summer.

'The Briscoes are getting into your business in numbers now,' Gill remarked lightly to Mary one afternoon. The two friends were having tea outside on the tiny paved terrace in the sunshine. The small back garden, which was lawned and secluded by high walls and mature shrubs, was currently overrun by exuberant little boys as Craig and his friends made the most of the summer holidays.

'They certainly are.' Mary looked across at Craig, who was using the swing frame as a goal into which his friends were kicking the ball. 'Will Craig follow in his father's footsteps, do you think?'

'As a member of your staff?'

'As a footballer.'

'Not as a professional if I've got anything to do with it,' Gill said adamantly. 'I shall do everything I can to discourage it.'

'Really?'

'Oh, yes. Football messed up Arnie's life; I don't want it to do the same to Craig. Play for fun and recreation by all means. But not as a professional . . . up in the clouds one minute and down in the dumps the next.'

'It isn't like that for everyone,' Mary wisely pointed out. 'Some professionals have a steady career.'

'Even if it goes the full term, it's short by normal standards,' said Gill.

'Yes, but there's always the possibility of going into management later on.'

'For a few, yes,' agreed Gill. 'But still I'd rather Craig got qualified for something safer. There are many more chances for youngsters these days than there were when I was growing up.'

'It's a bit early to think about it seriously yet, anyway.' Mary had sensed she'd hit on a raw nerve and deemed it wise not to continue with that topic.

'Yes, it is.' Gill paused. 'Changing the subject, I've had something on my mind ever since you told me about your work for St Theresa's.'

'Really?' Mary shaded her eyes from the sun and looked at her friend.

'I've been thinking about offering free piano lessons to any of the St Theresa's girls who might be interested.'

'What a good idea.'

'Will the nuns approve?'

'I should think they'd welcome you with open arms.' She paused thoughtfully. 'You'd have to go there to teach, though, because the girls aren't allowed out unaccompanied and the nuns wouldn't have time to bring them to you.'

'I'd already thought of that, and it isn't a problem. I take it they've got a piano.'

Mary nodded, smiling.

'We'd have to work the details out,' said Gill. 'But I was thinking in terms of going there on Saturday mornings for a couple of hours. Craig usually goes to my mum's place at that time. If we think in terms of two hours, that's four pupils. There probably won't be a huge demand because lots of kids are put off by the idea of practising.'

'Sounds fine to me.'

'Can I leave you to mention it to whoever is in charge?'

'Sure. I'll call in there on my way home.'

'Providing we get some interest, I'd like to start lessons at the beginning of the new term,' said Gill excitedly.

Going through the gates of St Theresa's was like entering another world. The building, which was hidden from the road by high walls and mature trees, had been built in the early 1900s and was a huge, grey place with attic windows and wide stone steps sweeping up to double front doors.

Inside the entrance hall, heading for the mother superior's office to finalise the details of her forthcoming lessons, Gill was struck by the strong spiritual aura: there were religious statues and paintings everywhere; the whole place gleamed with cleanliness, and the sweet scent of polish from the glossy wooden floors pervaded everything. Gill's footsteps seemed to echo intrusively into the hushed atmosphere.

The mother superior was an elderly woman with kindly blue eyes and pale skin, scrubbed and shiny next to her starched wimple, which looked paper-white against her black habit. When the arrangements for the lessons were complete, she handed Gill over to a middle-aged nun called Sister Maud who took Gill on a tour of the orphanage.

As they walked through the building away from the awesome quiet of the entrance hall, the atmosphere changed startlingly. Hoardes of girls piled noisily into the playground for their morning break. Gill was shown the dormitories, which were basic and spotless with wooden floors that the girls themselves kept shiny, she was told. As well as classrooms, the main building comprised an assembly hall, a refectory, a chapel, and a recreation room with a table-tennis table, a large cupboard containing indoor games, small tables and chairs, and a piano tucked away in the corner.

Set slightly apart from the main building were a group of newly built houses, each basically furnished but comfortable, and each containing, to Gill's amazement, a television set and a table laid out for tea.

'These are our pride and joy,' said Sister Maud, a softly spoken woman with an Irish accent.

'The children live here, in ordinary houses?' Gill asked in surprise.

'Only some of them.'

'Even so . . .'

'There are ten girls in each unit, with two nuns in charge,' she explained. 'We're hoping that all the children will live this way eventually. The plan is for the old dormitory system to be replaced by home units. But it will be some time before the whole project is complete.'

'What a wonderful idea.'

'Indeed. It gives the girls more of a sense of identity and family,' she said.

'They eat here too?'

'They go over to the refectory for main meals, but we have facilities for drinks and light snacks here,' Sister Maud explained. 'It makes it more homely for them in the evenings.'

'I'd no idea there had been such advances,' said Gill. 'One tends to think of children's homes as rather austere places.'

'Things have improved since the old days before the war,' the nun said. 'But we are still very strong on discipline here. We have to be, with so many girls to look after.'

'I can imagine.'

'Anyway,' she said as they moved on, skirting the noisy playground on their way back to the main gates, 'I've arranged for you to have the use of the recreation room from ten to twelve on a Saturday morning for your lessons. The other girls will be told to keep to the other end of the room.'

'Thank you.'

'Thank *you*, Mrs Briscoe; it's a fine chance for our girls,' she said. 'Sister Bernadette plays the piano in assembly and takes the music lessons for the little ones in the school here, but she doesn't have a spare minute to give individual piano lessons.'

'I wonder if there'll be many volunteers,' remarked Gill. 'The idea of piano lessons seems dull to some children, I know.'

'I think there'll be a lot more girls coming forward than you've time for,' said the sister. 'I shall allocate the places strictly on a first-come-first-served basis. There's sure to be some who are keen to start and will then drop out as soon as the novelty wears off.'

* * *

116

In the event there were more takers than Gill could fit in, so a waiting list was duly introduced.

'There's one volunteer who won't last beyond the first couple of lessons,' said Sister Maud when Gill arrived at St Theresa's for the first session in September.

'Really?'

'Yes. Young Cherry Betts . . . She's a child of the devil,' said the nun.

'Oh dear.'

'She's the naughtiest girl we have, and she'll give you a whole lot of trouble if I'm not very much mistaken.'

'Why would she bother to volunteer for lessons if all she wants to do is cause trouble?'

'For the sheer devilment of giving you a hard time, I should imagine,' said the nun shrewdly. 'Someone new to torment is a challenge to that one.'

'I see.'

'If hers hadn't been the first name on the list I'd have turned her down flat,' said Sister Maud. 'But I like to be fair.'

'What does she actually do that's so terrible?' Gill wanted to know.

The other woman shook her head and spoke to Gill in a conspiratorial whisper. 'She's rude, rebellious, disobedient . . . She's even run away on more than one occasion. She's caused more trouble than all the rest put together.'

'Is she . . . I mean, does she have trouble keeping up with the others?'

'Quite the opposite,' said the nun. 'She's one of the brightest girls of her age group. But she seems determined to make life as hard for herself as she possibly can . . . and for the rest of us too, in the process.'

'What happened to her parents?'

Sister Maud drew a shuddering breath. 'Her father walked out on his wife and child,' she explained. 'And her mother couldn't cope. She put Cherry into our care eight years ago when the child was two years old. The mother never kept in touch . . . not so much as a postcard.'

'That poor child,' said Gill.

'Yes, it's sad indeed. I only hope you can find it in your heart to be as sympathetic towards her after you've given her a lesson,' said the nun.

'I'll do my best.'

'You'll have to be very firm with her, Mrs Briscoe,' the nun advised. 'Don't take any nonsense from her at all. If she smells so much as a hint of weakness, she'll run rings around you.'

'I'll remember that,' said Gill, wondering what she had let herself in for.

Cherry Betts was a plain child with straight auburn hair and huge blue eyes. She was bean-pole thin and this was emphasised by a baggy grey jumper and shapeless grey skirt. Gill immediately felt the impact of the anger and defiance that exuded from every pore.

'Why did you put your name down for piano lessons?' she asked as the girl sat down on the piano stool, the eloquence of her sigh leaving Gill in no doubt that she was bored.

'I've as much right as anyone else,' she said, immediately on the defensive. 'Sister said the first names on the list get the lessons.'

'But if you don't want to learn, what's the point in coming for lessons?' Gill enquired, sitting down beside her and putting a music primer on the stand.

'Who said I don't wanna learn?' said Cherry abrasively.

'Well you don't seem very pleased about it,' said Gill.

'What am I supposed to do, dance a jig or somethin'?'

'Don't be so rude.'

Cherry flushed scarlet – which was strange for a girl with no conscience, Gill thought. 'The nuns have told you things about me, haven't they?' she said accusingly.

Gill remained silent.

'They've got it in for me. Always have done. I hate the lot of 'em.'

'Let's just get on with the lesson and stop wasting time, shall we?' said Gill firmly, guessing that this pupil wouldn't stay the course, yet liking her for some unaccountable reason. 'And I'll tell you at the end of half an hour if it's going to be worth your while continuing.'

'What do you mean by that?' Cherry asked sharply. 'Why wouldn't it be worth my while?'

'Some people don't have any aptitude to learn the piano at all,' Gill explained evenly. 'And I can usually tell within half an hour.'

'I ain't thick.'

'I'm not suggesting you are. Now, can we please get on with the lesson?' said Gill patiently. 'There are other people waiting.'

'Okay, I ain't stopping you.'

Much to Gill's surprise, there was a stillness about Cherry as she listened intently to her explanation of where the keys were on the piano and how they corresponded with the notes on the music. In a first lesson she didn't expect to do more than impart the fundamentals and get a pupil to play a few notes with separate hands. But Cherry was exceptionally quick to learn, and managed 'Three Blind Mice' right through without a mistake. Gill was thrilled, especially as the girl seemed to be enjoying it.

'That's very good,' said Gill.

'I told you I ain't thick.'

'Yes, you did.'

'They're stupid tunes we have to play, though, aren't they? Bloomin' nursery rhymes for little kids,' said Cherry with scorn.

'You'll soon progress to other, more interesting music,' said Gill.

118

Quite suddenly Cherry's mood changed. Gill was startled to see her banging her fists up and down on the keys, making a terrible racket, her face contorted with anger. Nevertheless she let her continue, perceiving a rage inside this child that needed an outlet.

When the noise finally abated and the girl sat still, silent and spent, she turned to Gill with tears glistening in her eyes, her face ashen with two spots of colour standing out on her cheeks. 'That's what I really think of your poxy piano lessons,' she said thickly, her face tight and grim. 'I didn't want to do them anyway.' She got up from the stool and stared at Gill as though waiting to be dismissed.

'I'm sorry you feel like that,' Gill said, looking at her gravely.

'Why?'

'Because I think you could be good if you were to persevere.'

'I don't care.'

'Okay. As you're obviously not interested, I'll cross you off my list.'

'Good.'

Gill was disappointed. She had seen genuine musical potential in this troubled little girl. Cherry was truly exasperating, but Gill suspected there was more to her than her difficult behaviour.

Guessing, however, that any attempt on her part to encourage Cherry to continue with lessons would produce a negative reaction while she was in this mood, she turned back to the piano and flicked the music book back to the beginning ready for the next pupil. 'Can you tell the next one to come in on your way out, please, Cherry?' she said.

Cherry walked to the door, her plimsolls squeaking on the polished wooden floor. She stopped suddenly and turned back to Gill. 'It isn't that I don't wanna learn, exactly,' she said.

'You could have fooled me,' said Gill, swinging round to face her. 'You've made every effort to convince me otherwise.'

'I mean, if you really think I could be any good . . .'

'I don't like time-wasters, Cherry,' Gill told her, remembering the nun's warning and staying firm.

'I've blown my chances of piano lessons then?' she said.

'Stop messing me about,' said Gill with authority. 'You either want to learn or you don't: it's as simple as that.'

'I do wanna learn.'

Gill looked at her doubtfully, half expecting her mood to alter again. She found herself actually wanting to teach her. 'If you're really serious about wanting to learn, I'll teach you . . .' she said.

'I do want to.'

'But I'm not prepared to tolerate the bad manners you have shown me here today,' she said in a strong voice.

'I won't do it again.'

'One wrong word and I'll give your place to the next one on the waiting list,' she told her. 'Is that clear?'

Cherry nodded. 'I'm sorry, miss,' she said, looking genuinely contrite.

'Why do it, Cherry – why behave so badly?' asked Gill.

'Dunno,' she said, shrugging her bony little shoulders.

'You really don't know?'

'No I don't,' she confessed glumly. 'Something just comes over me . . . I get in a temper and I've done somethin' bad before I can stop meself.'

She looked so forlorn and lonely, Gill wanted to hug her. The urge to get closer to Cherry was strong. But she didn't want to upset the nuns by making too much of one particular pupil, especially on her first day.

'Well, if you behave like that again you're out. Is that clear?'

'Yes, miss.'

Looking at her watch, Gill said, 'There's still five minutes to go of your time – so how about another go at "Three Blind Mice"?'

The little girl gave Gill a smile which altered her whole appearance, her eyes lighting up, a dimple appearing in her right cheek. 'That would be smashing,' she said, and walked back to the piano to sit down next to Gill.

Chapter Ten

One Saturday afternoon in January of the following year, the staff and customers at the Fulham branch of Bex Sports were discussing the recent demise of Sir Winston Churchill, who had been buried that day.

'It's very sad,' remarked a woman who was buying a pair of football socks for her son with the assistance of Arnie. 'But the great man had a good innings.'

'Not half,' Arnie agreed, putting the socks into a bag. 'I wouldn't mind living to be ninety myself.' He picked up his pen to write the sales invoice. 'I wouldn't fancy the idea of having people file past me as I lay in my coffin, though. I'd sooner be out o' sight once I'm dead.'

'Don't worry, Arnie,' smiled Mary Bex, who was standing in at the shop today because everyone except the Briscoe brothers had gone down with flu. 'There's no chance of your body laying in state.'

'Oh, I dunno so much about that,' joked John, who was serving a boy with a goalkeeper's jersey in the colours of Tottenham Hotspur. 'We could put his coffin on the turf at Borough Football Club so that all the old codgers can come and pay their last respects.'

'Watch it, bruv,' admonished Arnie, grinning. 'Any more of your cheek and I'll be ordering your coffin prematurely.'

Laughter rippled through the shop. Many of the customers were regulars and enjoyed the cheerful banter between the Briscoe brothers.

Mary, who was working her way through a queue at the other counter and had just been to the stock room in search of soccer boots, came over to Arnie. 'Are there any more football boots anywhere?' she asked.

'Only what's there,' he said, glancing towards a pile of boxed boots behind the counter, 'and in the stock room.'

'Mm. That's what I was afraid of,' Mary said, frowning.

Having explained to the customer that they didn't have what he wanted, Mary served those people who were waiting then went to the small staff room at the back of the shop to make some tea, leaving the Briscoe brothers holding the fort.

They worked well together, and she and Len were pleased to have them on the staff. John had been a bit surly at first, but once he'd settled down and got to grips with the job he'd proved to be an excellent counter hand. Like his brother, he had a natural way with the customers. They made an entertaining double act and were a definite asset to the business.

'The tea's made, boys,' she called into the shop to them. 'You can take it in turns to come in for your break.'

Arnie joined her as soon as he'd finished serving his customer, leaving John in the shop alone.

'Why is the stock of football boots so low?' Mary enquired as she and Arnie sat down with their tea.

'We've had a run on them.'

'But more should have been ordered in plenty of time – especially at the height of the season,' she said. This was a matter of some concern; Mary was a shrewd businesswoman. 'I've lost several sales today because we didn't have what the customer wanted.'

'It's annoying, isn't it?'

'It's more than just annoying, Arnie,' she said. 'It's bad for business and it shouldn't happen.'

'Nothing to do with me,' he swiftly pointed out. 'Jack's in charge of stock control. He does all the ordering.'

'Yes, I realise that.'

'He might have more on order,' said Arnie, 'I'm not sure.'

'I'll find out and get things moving,' Mary said. 'I shall also tell Len to have a few words with Jack when he gets back from sick leave. We can't carry on like this, losing business just because of sloppy stock control.'

Personally Arnie thought the manager needed a rocket up his arse to get him moving, but he had no intention of being disloyal to his colleague by saying so. He liked Jack as a person but didn't rate him as a manager at all. Unbeknown to the Bexes, Arnie was always reminding Jack to do things and covering up for him because certain jobs hadn't been done. It was irritating, especially as Arnie was convinced that this shop could do even better with more efficient management.

They talked about business for a while longer, then Mary asked, 'How's Gill?'

'She's fine.'

'And how is the budding musical genius from St Theresa's?' she asked.

Arnie looked blank.

'The little girl who's doing so well with her piano lessons,' explained Mary.

Still no reaction.

'Hasn't Gill told you about her?'

He shook his head.

'Really,' said Mary in surprise. 'I thought she would have mentioned her because she's so pleased with the way Cherry's coming along. She's always been a very difficult child up until now, but she's a changed girl since she started lessons with Gill.'

'That's good,' Arnie said flatly.

'She must have found her forte, I suppose.' Mary giggled to ease the sudden tension. 'Oh dear, what a dreadful pun.'

'Yeah,' he grinned.

'Anyway, the nuns are delighted with what Gill's doing for Cherry.'

'Good for Gill,' he said with an edge to his voice that worried Mary. She liked and trusted Arnie as a colleague, and considered Gill to be a dear friend. And if she wasn't very much mistaken they were having serious problems with their marriage. It was a pity, because they were both such lovely people and obviously made for each other, despite their current difficulties.

'She was full of it when I last saw her,' Mary continued. 'She seems to have become very fond of young Cherry.'

'She doesn't say much about her work to me,' Arnie said, his conscience troubling him for not taking as much interest as he might. 'Probably because I'm tone deaf.'

'Most married couples find it helpful to talk about their work, I should think,' said Mary casually, sipping her tea and nibbling a biscuit. 'But not you two, by the sound of it.'

'Not to any extent, no,' he said. He didn't add that he and Gill never talked about anything these days. All they did was bicker and snipe at each other, except when they were putting on an act for Craig's benefit. They seemed to drift further apart with each passing day, and he wasn't able to put things right because his feelings towards his wife were in such turmoil.

'Seems a shame.'

'We just never seem to get around to it,' he fibbed. 'You know how it is – you start watching the telly in the evening and it's bedtime before you know it.'

'That's the trouble with television,' Mary said. 'It destroys the art of conversation.'

It was more than just the art of conversation that had been destroyed between Arnie and his wife. Every time he looked at her he was reminded of the bad things he'd done to her, which inflamed the guilt that had festered and grown over the years rather than diminished with the passing of time. The accident, the miscarriage and its consequences, the loss of confidence that had prevented him from providing for his family and made him so hateful – none of these things would have happened if he'd not let success go to his head. The events were all in the past, but his feelings about them remained as strong as ever.

Perversely, his own sense of self-loathing made him want to hurt *her*. And when he'd done that with a few cutting words and a cold attitude, he hated himself even more. Because deep in his heart he still loved her. No matter how hard he tried to be different, it just didn't happen. The whole situation was driving him crazy, which was why he spent so much time out of the house – if he wasn't at home, he couldn't hurt her.

The little girl from the home was probably a surrogate daughter to Gill, he thought bitterly.

Personally he didn't regret not being able to increase their family, because he was content with Craig. But he sensed that one child wasn't enough for Gill, whatever she said to the contrary. She always used to talk about wanting a daughter – years ago, when that was still possible.

'So they reckon,' he said now to Mary. 'But few of us want to be without it, do we? Not if we're really honest.'

'That's very true, Arnie,' she said. 'It's become part of the culture.'

Mary had perceived a definite change of mood in Arnie since she'd mentioned his wife. Despite their cheery manner, both Gill and Arnie Briscoe were falling apart inside and there seemed to be nothing anyone else could do about it.

Mary finished her tea and stood up with a purposeful air. 'Right, I'll go and cover for John so that he can have his break,' she said.

'Okay, I'll just finish my tea and I'll be back on duty.'

As Mary re-entered the shop, the customer John had just finished serving was leaving with his purchases. In the split second before John realised that she was there, Mary saw something that turned her to stone and put all thoughts of Gill and Arnie's marriage out of her mind.

Arnie stormed into Phoebe's flat that evening looking for his brother, whom he found sitting at the table in the living room with his mother, tucking into sausages and chips for tea.

'You thieving toe-rag,' Arnie fumed, dragging his brother from his chair so roughly that John's knife and fork clattered to the floor.

'Here, what's going on?' Phoebe demanded, abandoning her meal and standing up with an anxious look on her face.

'Yeah, what's got into you?' asked John breathlessly.

'You've had your sticky little fingers in the till at the shop,' said Arnie grimly. 'That's what's the matter.'

'Oh, no, John,' said Phoebe with a sob in her voice. She was scrupulously honest herself and had always tried to raise her sons to be the same.

'No I haven't,' John denied.

'You bloody well have, you young tea-leaf,' said Arnie, holding him by the arms and shaking him. 'So don't lie to me.'

'Calm down, for Gawd sake, Arnie,' said his mother, who didn't want to believe these allegations. 'If John says he hasn't done it, then he hasn't.'

'I'm sorry that you're having to hear this, Mum.' Arnie let go of John and looked at his mother. 'But I've just come from the shop. Len came over to the branch just before closing time and asked me to stay on because he had something to tell me.' He looked at his brother, his eyes full of fury and disappointment. 'He wanted me to know before he fired you because it was me who recommended you for the job. You're getting your cards first thing Monday morning, mate. Mary Bex saw you pocket the money you took from a cash sale instead of putting it through the till. She actually *saw* you do it, so don't bother to deny it.'

John was whey-faced and silent, staring at the floor.

Arnie sunk down heavily into an armchair, a grim expression on his face. 'This isn't the first time, is it?'

Silence.

'You've been milking the cash sales, haven't you?' said Arnie with a heavy sigh.

John didn't reply.

'Haven't you?' said Arnie, leaping up and staring at his brother.

The younger man nodded shamefully.

'How long?'

'Dunno . . . a few months maybe,' he said, looking utterly miserable.

'But why, for God's sake?' Arnie started pacing the room. 'Why do a thing like that? Why jeopardise a job you enjoy by stealing from a fair employer like Len? I mean, it isn't as though he doesn't pay us a decent wage.'

No reply.

'Len's a good bloke. He doesn't deserve this.'

Still John remained silent.

'Greed. Pure and simple!' Arnie roared. 'You'd put a good job at risk just so you can keep up with those thugs you hang around with.'

'That isn't why I did it.'

'Why did you do it, then?' asked Arnie. 'You just tell me that.'

'I can't.'

'You can't, I see,' Arnie said with withering sarcasm. 'Oh, that's wonderful, that is. My brother betrays my trust by nicking from the boss, and he can't even tell me why.'

The green tones in John's eyes looked vivid against his ashen skin as he stared at his brother. Suddenly perceiving terror lurking there, a possible explanation occurred to Arnie.

'Is someone leaning on you?' he asked in a softer tone.

'Course not,' said John, his denial too fast and emphatic to ring true.

'Did Harris and his mates put you up to it?' demanded Arnie.

'No.'

'I don't believe you.'

'That's up to you.'

Arnie changed tack, becoming more understanding. 'Look, Bruv, if those louts forced you to do it, then tell me and I'll get them sorted,' he said. 'And Len might give you another chance . . .'

'You can't get 'em sorted.'

'So they *are* behind this?'

John stared at the floor.

'You must tell Arnie the truth, son,' Phoebe urged. 'So that we can get this thing cleared up once and for all.'

'You can't get it cleared up,' John insisted in a shaky voice.

'Oh no?' Arnie's tone was challenging.

'You don't know what Harris and his gang are like.'

'They've threatened to beat you up if you don't steal money for them – is that it?' asked Arnie.

'You think I'm scared of a beatin' from that bunch o' losers?' said John with affront. 'I ain't that feeble.'

'They've threatened to do something if you don't steal from the shop for them, though, haven't they?' said Arnie.

John's silence was answer enough.

'Is it me . . . or Gill or Craig?' Arnie demanded. 'Have they threatened to harm us if you don't do as they say?'

John shook his head, his eyes moving away from Arnie.

'Mum!' Arnie gasped in horror. 'They've threatened to do Mum over?'

Sinking weakly into a chair, John nodded. 'I thought Harris and his mates were great at first, a really good laugh. But I got bored with 'em after a while . . . sick of hanging about the streets looking for mischief. So I stopped seeing 'em and they didn't like that one little bit. They would wait for me when I went out and give me a good smacking. I had quite a few of those, but I still didn't go back with 'em. Eventually they lost interest and left me alone.'

'So why this, now?' asked Arnie.

'They got to know that I was working in a shop with access to money and they started leaning on me really heavily,' he explained. 'They said they'd beat Mum up good and proper if I didn't do what they said. They would have, too . . .'

'Oh, John, you damned fool,' said Arnie. 'Why didn't you come to me?'

'Because you'd have gone after 'em and got yourself hurt,' he explained. 'There's too many of them; you wouldn't stand a chance. They're evil, I tell you. They'll kill me if they find out I've told anyone. And Mum won't be safe.'

'I'd like to see 'em try to harm any member of this family,' said Arnie determinedly. 'We'll get Head-Butter Harris and his mates sorted, don't you worry about that, Bruv. But before we do anything else at all, we are going to see Len and Mary Bex to tell them what's been going on.'

'Now?' John asked worriedly.

'Yes, now,' Arnie told him. 'It can't wait till the morning. We'll go over to their house in Putney. I know where it is.'

126

'They probably won't be in,' John said, hoping to talk his brother out of it.

'We'll take a chance on that. I know Len well enough to know that whatever he's doing he'll want to hear what we have to say.'

'I can't face 'em.' John bit his lip.

'You're going to have to face 'em, whether you like it or not,' said Arnie. 'And you're going to do it *right now*.'

'All right, all right,' said John and went to get his coat.

On Phoebe's day off the following week, she caught the bus to Hammersmith and went to see Len and Mary Bex at their office.

'I just had to come and thank you in person, and tell you how grateful I am to you both for all you've done for my boy,' she said after introductions had been made. 'It's ever so good of you to give him another chance. He's been a damned fool.'

'He certainly has, Mrs Briscoe,' agreed Len.

'Everyone calls me Phoebe.'

'Then we'll do the same, Phoebe,' Len said, glancing towards his wife, who nodded.

'Thanks anyway for what you've done; it means a lot to me.'

'We decided to give young John another chance because we think that what he's done was stupid rather than criminal, and he does seem genuinely sorry.'

'He is, I promise you.'

'If he'd taken so much as a penny piece from here for himself, I'd have had him in court before his feet could touch the ground – and if he ever does anything like that again, that's what I will do no matter what the reason,' Len said in an adamant tone. 'I've made that very clear to him.'

'So I've heard.'

'But I think he's basically honest, if not very careful when it comes to choosing his friends.'

'You don't have to tell me that,' Phoebe said, smiling and looking very striking in a red coat with a black furry collar, her blonde hair beehived on top and taken back into a french pleat at the back. The passing years had been kind to her, and her trim figure belied her forty-six years. 'Arnie and I have been worried to death about John ever since he got in with that Harris and his crowd. Of course, we didn't realise he'd tried to break away from them.'

'When we found out what was behind his pilfering, it put a different light on the matter,' said Len. He paused, and a hard look came into his eyes. 'He has to pay the money back, though.'

'And quite right too.'

'We've worked out roughly how much he's taken and we're going to deduct something from his wages every week until it's paid off,' said

Mary. 'I know he doesn't actually have the money, but we have to recoup our losses. The louts certainly don't have any of it left. All gone on drugs, I shouldn't wonder. We're hoping it'll teach John never to get involved in anything like that again.'

'It's only right and proper that he should pay the money back, and it's very good of you to be so understanding,' said Phoebe, flashing a warm smile from one to the other. 'It's a load off my mind to have John away from that rough crowd, I can tell you.'

'I'm sure it must be,' said Mary. 'It's all behind him now.'

'Yeah, thank Gawd.' Phoebe paused and directed her gaze to Len. 'I understand that you've taken care of Harris and his gang,' she said, meeting his eyes and feeling dazzled by his overwhelming physical presence. It was as though he alone filled the room.

'I certainly have, my dear. They won't be bothering John again,' he replied.

'They're a wicked lot,' said Phoebe. 'I hope you didn't get hurt.'

'I didn't go anywhere near them,' Len explained. 'My brawling days are long over. But I've plenty of contacts around here. I only had to pick up the phone and the matter was dealt with sharpish.'

'You didn't arrange to have 'em killed, I hope,' Phoebe said worriedly.

Len threw back his head and laughed, a deep booming sound that touched something deep inside Phoebe.

'Even if I felt they deserved it, I'm a businessman not a gangster,' he said, still smiling. 'You can relax. All I did was arrange to have 'em roughed up and sufficiently shaken to make sure they keep away from young John in future.'

'I think it's taught him a lesson,' said Phoebe. 'In being more careful in the company he keeps, if nothing else.'

'Let's hope so,' said Len, observing her with approval. She was good-looking in a brash kind of way – the sort of woman he might have fancied if he hadn't been happily married.

'Fancy a cup of tea?' Mary asked. 'We're just about to have one.'

'That's very kind of you,' said Phoebe. 'I'd love one.'

When Mary had left the room to make the tea, Phoebe said, 'I hope I'm not holding you up.'

'We'd soon tell you if you were, don't worry,' Len said. 'We'd have been taking a break about now anyway. I'm going over to the Acton branch when I've had a cuppa, while Mary gets on with the wages.'

'She does the office work then?'

He nodded. 'She works on the counter an' all if necessary. We both do. You have to be versatile when it's your own business.'

'I suppose you do.'

'You not working?'

'Yeah. I work in Woolworth's, but it's my day off today,' she said.

'Do you like it there?'

'Yeah, it's okay,' she said. 'I've done worse jobs.'

'Such as . . . ?' Len asked with interest.

'Factory work, cleaning shops and offices at four o'clock in the morning, charring in people's houses to make a few bob. Not to mention my share of war work. I had to do whatever I could find with two boys to bring up on my own.'

'You've done a good job with those two.'

'Thank you,' she said without false modesty. 'I like to think so.'

'So . . . Woolworth's suits you then?' he asked chattily.

'It gets a bit boring sometimes on the counter, but most of the time it's all right,' she said. 'I like dealing with people.'

'Must be where your boys get it from,' Len said. He had noticed in Phoebe the same casual confidence he'd seen in Arnie and John – especially Arnie.

'Could be,' she said. 'You've got to like people to do shop-work. The public can be infuriating at times when you're the wrong side of the counter, as you well know.'

'I'll say.'

'Some people get all high and mighty because your job is to serve them,' she said. 'A lot of the girls I work with get quite upset about it, but I don't have much trouble.'

'We'll have to bear you in mind next time we're looking for an assistant in one of our shops then, won't we?' Len said lightly.

'Oh, I dunno about that,' she said, surprised by his remark. 'I'm quite happy where I am.'

'A change is as good as a rest, so they say,' Len persisted, grinning and cocking his head.

'I have heard it said.'

'I bet you know a lot about football, as the mother of a one-time professional player.'

'Not half.' She threw him a shrewd look. 'But you're not seriously offering me a job, are you?'

'Not at this moment, but I might be in the future when a vacancy comes up,' he said, because even without seeing her in action, he knew Phoebe was right for Bex Sports.

She was flattered. 'We'll talk about that another time, then,' she said.

'Sure.'

'You'd have more Briscoes than Bexes if I were to join the firm,' she laughed.

They were both chuckling when Mary came in with a tray of tea and biscuits. Len told her what they'd been talking about.

'It'd be company for me to have a woman on the staff,' said Mary. 'It's always the men who apply for the jobs in our shops, which means I'm completely outnumbered.'

'Maybe I'll help to even things up one of these days,' Phoebe said casually.

'I do hope so,' said Mary with genuine enthusiasm. There was something about Phoebe Briscoe that made her want to see more of her. She was so warm and hearty you knew instinctively that she'd be popular with the customers.

When she'd finished her tea, Phoebe left the shop and walked along King Street to the bus stop, thinking what a smashing couple the Bexes were. Mary was a real dear. It was no wonder Gill was so friendly with her. And as for him . . . well, he was what Phoebe called a *real man*. He would probably be described as ugly by some people, with his broken nose and granite jaw, but his charisma sent shivers up her spine. And when those piercing brown eyes had rested on her she'd felt like a girl again, hungry for all the physical pleasures of love.

Even though Phoebe had had occasional boyfriends since she'd been widowed, it was years since a man had aroused her that way. Silly cow, she admonished herself, catching sight of her reflection in a shop window and seeing a woman long past her prime – the man is happily married to a lovely woman, so there's no point in your getting any ideas.

Anyone is entitled to their fantasies, though, she thought, and she had a faraway look in her eyes as she got on to the bus.

'That was very good indeed, Cherry,' Gill said as the girl came to the end of a short classical piece that was one of the pieces she was to perform in her forthcoming exam. 'You play to that standard on the day and you'll earn yourself a distinction, just like you did in the theory exam.'

'Can I start on the music for the next grade if I pass this one?'

'Certainly. As long as the nuns agree to your continuing with lessons, I'll have the music here ready for you at the beginning of next term,' said Gill.

'I can't wait.'

Gill had no doubt that Cherry would sail through the practical exam, as she had the theory, which she had taken in a local hall with all the other candidates from the area. Gill didn't expect Cherry's performance to be spoiled by nerves as happened to so many pupils during a practical exam. This child didn't have a nerve in her body when it came to performing to an audience. In fact, she became so absorbed in the music that she hardly seemed aware other people were present.

After that difficult first meeting last autumn, Gill had found her to be a delight. She still had her moods like any other growing child, and there were times when Gill had to tick her off for being saucy. But for the most part she was a joy to teach because she was so keen and had such a natural aptitude for it.

Music had given her a new lease of life, according to the nuns, who were finding her much easier to deal with. She was still cheeky to them at times – that was undoubtedly inherent in her nature – but apparently she spent every spare moment she could at the recreation room piano. She often did a practice session before school in the mornings when there was no one else around.

Whether or not Cherry would retain this level of enthusiasm in the autumn, when she changed schools and went outside of St Theresa's for her education, Gill couldn't be absolutely sure. If she was selected for the grammer school, as the nuns expected she would be, she would have homework to cope with. There would be new friends and pastimes to distract her attention whichever senior school she attended. But Gill doubted that Cherry would lose her interest in music altogether, because she was a born musician.

'Can I do that piece again, please, miss?' she asked now.

Gill looked at her watch. It was past time, but Cherry was the last pupil. 'Only if you go through the whole exam paper, including the scales and arpeggios.'

Cherry did a mock groan, then played the pieces with accuracy and feeling. It was a pleasure to listen to her.

'You'll do,' said Gill, smiling. 'Now I really must go. I have to collect my son from my mother's and take him to a football match he's playing in.'

'How old is he?'

'Nearly eight.'

'Are you teaching him to play the piano?'

'No.'

'Why?'

'He doesn't want to learn.'

'Can't you make him?' she asked with youthful innocence.

'I could do, I suppose,' said Gill. 'But I don't believe in using force – not when it comes to music, anyway.'

'Sister Maud says that doing things you don't like makes you a better person,' said Cherry.

'I'm sure she's right,' agreed Gill. 'But I think there are enough hated tasks in Craig's life to keep him on the right track. I'm sure it isn't necessary to add music to them.'

'What sort of things?'

'All the usual ones ... lessons he finds difficult like arithmetic, running errands for me when he wants to play, going to bed at a reasonable hour, eating his greens—'

'Oh, those.'

'You see, Cherry, I believe you have to have a feel for playing a musical instrument or it's pointless.' Gill stood up and slipped into her reefer jacket which she wore over a short skirt and high, shiny boots.

'Craig's passion is football. He has a real feeling for it.'

'He's lucky to have you,' said Cherry. 'I wish you were my mother.'

Swallowing a lump in her throat, Gill buttoned her jacket. 'That's because you only see me once a week,' she said, blinking back the tears. 'If you saw me all the time and I had to nag you about keeping your room tidy and washing behind your ears, you'd soon get sick of me.'

'I bet I wouldn't.'

'Well, that's something we'll never know,' said Gill, feeling suddenly quite emotional, 'so let's just enjoy being friends, shall we?'

'Okay,' Cherry agreed.

Noticing that she seemed set to stay at the piano, Gill said, 'Give yourself a break from the exam pieces over the next few days. Play something just for pleasure. Something from that book of pop tunes I gave you.'

'All right, miss,' she said, 'but I just want to go through this once more.'

Such dedication. This girl has what it takes to go far as a musician, Gill thought, as she left the building and made her way along the gravel drive to the main gates. It was a dull, chilly March day with a sharp breeze swinging through ancient oaks and plane trees burgeoning with new leaves. The trees creaked in the wind and there was a smell of rain in the air as dark clouds rolled across the mottled grey skies.

Outside in the street the noise buffeted Gill after the quiet of St Theresa's grounds, bringing her back to reality and the weight of her problems. Teaching was her escape. Because it was so absorbing her thoughts couldn't drift on to the parlous state of her marriage or the fact that things couldn't go on as they were between herself and Arnie.

He was hardly ever home these days. Since he'd been made manager of the Fulham branch, he worked later at the shop in the evening. He even went in on Sundays for a while, supposedly to catch up on paperwork but she suspected he went to escape the tension of being with her. If he wasn't at the shop he was in a pub somewhere.

About the only thing he came home for was to eat and sleep, and to see his beloved son. He certainly didn't come home to see Gill. His attitude towards her led her to believe that he had finally grown to hate her. Naturally she wondered from time to time if he was seeing another woman, but she never gave this any serious thought because she believed their problems stemmed from something far more sinister and complicated.

She was worried about the effect the bad atmosphere between them must be having on Craig. Although they tried not to argue in front of him, surely he couldn't help but be aware of the coldness between his parents.

Deciding to walk to her mother's rather than wait for the bus, she strode out towards Maisie Road, the wind smarting her face with spots of rain. But she was glad of the fresh air to clear her head. Passing through Fulham Broadway, she glanced towards Bex Sports. Her heart had once leapt at the possibility of seeing Arnie; now her stomach knotted with dread at the thought, because they could no longer communicate.

North End Road market was in full Saturday flow as she headed for her mother's. The rowdy clamour hammered painfully into Gill's head and grated on her overstretched nerves: the shout of spielers, the uneven chant of people talking, the traffic roaring and Roger Miller's 'King of the Road' blaring out at full volume from the record stall.

Gill saw several people she knew and exchanged a few friendly words, but she felt isolated and alone as long as the worry of her failing marriage hung over her. She stopped along the way to buy fruit, some sweets for Craig and a bag of her mother's favourite toffees.

Somewhere between the market and Maisie Road, with a sinking heart, she made a decision. She was going to bring things with Arnie to a head – tonight.

She had to wait until after Craig was in bed before broaching the subject, at which point Arnie departed to the pub. When he got back he settled into an armchair and stared gloomily at the television.

Inwardly quaking, Gill went over to the set and turned it off.

'What's going on?' he asked, scowling at her.

'We have to talk, Arnie.'

'Oh no,' he groaned.

'Oh yes. You know as well as I do that we can't go on as we are.'

He got up in an agitated manner and glared at her. 'Don't you ever stop nagging?' he said, knowing he was being unreasonable but unable to stem the flow of words. Powerless to change anything, he felt compelled to strike out and hurt her.

'It's difficult not to nag given the situation,' she said.

'I've got a job now; I'm paying my share in the house. What more do you want?' he said, evading the issue.

'I want my husband back.'

'I'm here, aren't I?' he said, deliberately misunderstanding her.

'Your physical presence is occasionally here,' she told him, managing against all the odds to stay calm. 'But you haven't been here with me in your heart for a long time.'

'For God's sake, stop going on at me,' he snapped, 'or I'll go out again. I'm not gonna put up with all this bloody hassle. Nag, nag, nag, every time I set foot inside the door.'

As he marched towards the door, Gill went after him and dragged him back with a strength she hadn't known she had. 'Oh, no, Arnie, you're not running away from me this time.'

133

He stared at her, waiting.

'This time we're going to sort things out once and for all,' she said, her voice ragged with emotion, her body trembling all over as she let go of him and moved back. 'It isn't going to get any better by pretending there's nothing wrong. It isn't good for us and it isn't good for Craig.'

'All right. Say what you have to say,' he said, his voice shaking too.

'I'm not prepared to live like this any longer,' she said, struggling to remain strong. 'Your never being here and us bickering if we're together for more than a few minutes, I mean. I've had enough of your moods and your bad temper. I'm sick of making excuses for you.'

'Oh, so that's what all this is about,' he said, dodging the issue again. 'Just because I like to go out—'

'*No, no, no*! That isn't what this is about and you know it,' she said, her voice rising. 'It's the reason you stay out that's bothering me.'

'Why do you think I stay out?'

'Presumably because you can't bear to stay at home with me, because all we do is quarrel, and no matter what I do to stop it it still happens,' she said. 'I no longer have a husband so much as a sparring partner.'

His eyes were dark with emotion, his skin pale and suffused with a fine layer of sweat. 'All right. You want the truth, so I'll give you the truth,' he said, his voice quivering. 'You're right – I do stay out because I don't want to come home. And I don't want to come home because I can't cope with the way I feel and I don't know what to do about it.' He put his hand to his chest. 'There's so much pain inside here, and you are a constant reminder of how I've screwed things up and let you down.'

'In what way?'

'In every way,' he said. 'The accident, your not being able to have any more children – all of it. I'm sick of carrying a burden which I can't forget as long as I'm with you.'

'I've never blamed you for any of those things,' she said.

'Maybe not, but we both know it was my fault.' He put his hands to his head. 'I can't get away from the past when I'm with you, and I'm tired of it. You've become an albatross around my neck.'

The pain was so intense, she couldn't move or utter a word. Part of her wanted to throw herself at his feet and beg him to work with her to make their marriage work, to give it one more try. But she had tried everything she knew over a long period. She'd persuaded and coaxed and made allowances for him until she was weary of trying, and it had made not a scrap of difference. When she looked back on the punishing complexities of their life together these last few years, she knew she couldn't take any more. It seemed so long since they'd been happy.

'In that case I suggest you move out,' she said in a small voice, hardly able to bear the agony of uttering the words. 'The last thing I want to do is be a burden to you.'

He slumped into an armchair with his head in his hands, his body trembling, shoulders heaving. Knowing he was crying, she wanted to hold him and soothe away his pain. But it was too late for that. That would only delay the inevitable.

After a while he looked up and spoke, his words seeming unreal to Gill, echoing in her head as though she was dreaming. 'Yeah. I think you're right. It'll probably be best if I move out,' he said thickly.

'Oh.'

'As you say, we can't go on like this any longer,' he said. 'Apart from anything else it isn't fair to the nipper.'

'No.'

'I'll go tonight and stay in a hotel or something. I don't wanna turn up at Mum's place out of the blue at this time of night,' he said. 'I don't feel like answering questions yet anyway.'

'There's no need for you to leave right away,' she said.

'If I stay until the morning I'll only put it off . . .'

'Yes.'

'Right, then . . .'

'Craig will be sorry not to have seen you,' she said through dry lips.

'Tell him I'll come and see him in a few days' time, and I'll arrange to see him regularly after that,' he said.

'All that sort of thing will have to be worked out in due course.'

'Yeah, sometime – but not now,' he said.

'No, not now,' she agreed, knowing that neither of them could face the agonising practicalities of a broken marriage just yet.

'Just tell him I love him and I'll see him soon.'

'Sure,' she said, biting back the tears.

He went upstairs to pack a case while Gill sat rigid in the armchair by the living-room fire, hardly able to believe this was happening.

'I'll be off then,' he said, poking his head round the door.

'Right.'

'I'll come back for the rest of my stuff in a day or two.'

'Okay.'

'See you then,' he said, as though she was one of his mates.

'Cheerio,' she said numbly.

And he was gone. Just like that. They had parted like strangers. It didn't seem possible.

She went to the window and peered through the curtains into the murky night as he opened the door of his Ford Zephyr. The rain that had been threatening earlier had settled into a steady drizzle and a mist clouded the glow from the street lights.

He stood there in the rain, looking towards the house, a sad, wet figure oblivious to the weather. Gill's heart pounded as she stupidly hoped he would come back to her. But after a few moments he turned and got into the car.

Putting the curtains back into place with trembling fingers, she stood

135

with her back to the fireplace, staring at nothing, too tense to sit down or shed a tear. Although the break was a shock now that it had actually happened, she knew that her marriage had been over for a long time.

Looking back on it, she could see that it had begun to head for the rocks when Arnie had got his big chance in football. Everything had changed then. The bad times had heavily outweighed the good ones if she was brutally honest. So what had happened tonight was all for the best.

But even though she knew that she and Arnie were no longer compatible, she still loved him and felt utterly bereft now that it was over.

Mulling it over as he drove into Central London to look for an hotel for the night, Arnie told himself he'd done the right thing in leaving. For Gill's sake as well as his own, he'd needed to be free from his marriage for a long time, but had been too much of a coward to bring it to an end. The constant bickering had been destroying them all.

He'd never wanted any other woman but Gill, and still didn't. And he loved his son. But what should have been a winning combination just didn't work for them.

The wipers beat a path across the rainsoaked windscreen with their plodding rhythm, the tyres fizzing on the greasy roads. His thoughts drifted back to the beginning, to the good times he and Gill had had. They had been so right together once – before life had become grim and disappointing, before love and passion had turned to resentment and pain.

Even though marriage had been forced upon him before he'd been ready, he'd never felt trapped because Gill was all he had wanted in life. Not until after the accident had he felt the constant need to escape from the limitations that had been heaped upon him. Marriage had seemed like a prison then, because he'd been so hemmed in by his own sense of failure.

What had happened tonight was inevitable, and was the best thing for them all. Once you stopped being able to make a woman happy, it was time to get out of her life and leave the way clear for her to make a new start.

But if it was so right for them all, why was his heart breaking?

Chapter Eleven

'I guessed all wasn't well with those two,' said Winnie gravely a few days later. The Millers were having their evening meal, and the break-up of Gill and Arnie's marriage was now common knowledge. 'But I didn't think it would come to this.'

'Is it definitely all over between them?' asked Hal, cutting into a lamb chop.

'Sounds like it to me,' said Winnie, mashing some potato into her gravy. 'There didn't seem to be any doubt in Gill's mind when she said there's no chance of their making it up. Things have been really bad between them for ages, apparently.'

'It's a damned shame,' said Hal.

'There's been a terrible atmosphere between them for a long time,' said Winnie. 'I've felt uncomfortable in their company.'

'We all have.'

'Bearing that in mind, I suppose what Gill's going through now can't be much worse than living with all that bad feeling for so long.' Winnie sympathised strongly with her eldest daughter, who she knew was broken-hearted despite her brave attempts not to show it.

'It's the best thing that could have happened in my opinion,' said Carol sharply.

'That's a bit hard, dear,' said her soft-hearted father.

'I don't see why,' she said briskly. 'If they're not happy, why stay together?'

'They've had a bad patch.' Hal liked Arnie, and was disappointed to lose him as a member of the family.

'Come off it, Dad,' Carol said in a mocking tone. 'It was a lot more than just a bad patch. It was like a war zone at their place when they were both at home.'

'You're wrong when you say it's the best thing that could have happened, Carol,' Winnie intervened. 'The best thing would be for them to work through their differences and stay together . . . for the sake of Craig, if nothing else.'

'That's a very old-fashioned attitude,' declared Carol.

'I am old fashioned, and I've never pretended otherwise,' announced Winnie. 'I was old fashioned about Gill being pregnant before she got married too, and I was proved right. This is what happens when people get married before they're ready.'

'Not necessarily.' Carol was finding both her parents irritating in the extreme. Apart from their suffocating homeliness, they were so out of touch with the modern world.

'They were just a couple of kids with no experience of life when they got married,' Winnie said.

'We don't know that's the reason for their breaking up, love,' said Hal, who always tried to be fair. 'It could have happened anyway. Marriage doesn't work for everyone.'

'People change and want different things, that's why,' said Carol.

'People don't work at it, more like.' Winnie was uncompromising because this was something she felt strongly about. 'Marriage is for life in my opinion.'

'That's what we think, dear, but attitudes towards marriage aren't the same as they were,' Hal pointed out evenly. 'Some people don't even bother to get married at all nowadays.'

'Unheard of in our day, all this living together nonsense,' said Winnie.

'Mm,' Hal murmured.

'And what about young Craig?' Winnie said, her mind racing with the far-reaching consequences of her daughter's failed marriage. 'What's life gonna be like for him now? That little boy thinks the world of his dad.'

'He was always a good father,' said Hal, 'I'll say that much for Arnie.'

'And he still will be,' said Carol with seething impatience. 'He isn't leaving the country, for heaven's sake.'

'No, but it won't be the same for the child.' Winnie ignored her daughter's rudeness because she was used to it.

'Of course not. How can it be?' Carol said through clenched teeth. 'But if Gill and Arnie aren't getting on, they shouldn't stay together just because of Craig.'

'Plenty of parents do,' said Winnie, throwing her daughter a dark look. 'Many a marriage has survived because of the children.'

'It might have been like that in your day—' Carol began.

'And it still is today in a lot of cases,' said Winnie. 'All right, so you have the mini-skirt and the pill and free love and all the rest of it. But a lot of young people still believe in marriage. Even that bloke from the Beatles, Ringo Starr or whatever his name is, got married the other day. I saw it in the paper.'

'I know that. All I'm saying is that divorce isn't frowned upon these days,' Carol insisted. 'People do it all the time.'

'Hey, hang on,' Hal said with a deeply furrowed brow. 'Who said anything about divorce?'

'Well, I just assumed . . . I mean, that's what people do when they split up, isn't it? They get divorced. There's no point in their staying legally married if they're not together any more.'

'I suppose not,' Winnie agreed with reluctance.

'Frankly, I think their breaking up was inevitable.' Carol pushed her plate away.

'Oh, you do, do you?' Hal evidently didn't like his daughter's attitude.

'Yes I do,' she confirmed heartlessly. 'You can tell they've stopped loving each other. That's been obvious for ages.'

'I wouldn't go so far as to say they've stopped loving each other,' said Hal.

'Why are they always at each other's throats then?' Carol asked.

'Things have been difficult for them since Arnie's accident,' he replied.

'Because they fell out of love, that's why,' Carol stated.

'It isn't alway as cut and dried as that, love,' said Winnie knowingly. 'Marriage can be a very complicated business . . .'

'And I wouldn't know anything about that, of course,' said Carol acidly.

'Well . . . you can't speak from experience, can you, dear?' Winnie gave her daughter a shrewd look. 'Some things you have to experience personally to know what they're like. Marriage is all about everyday living as well as love.'

'Obviously,' Carol sneered.

'There's no call to get lippy,' Winnie rebuked.

'Oh God!'

'Don't you "Oh God" me.'

'Oh, for goodness sake—'

'I'll thank you to watch your manners, my girl,' Winnie retorted. 'You're impossible to live with these days . . .'

'Perhaps I should move out of here then,' Carol threatened.

'You know where the door is,' said Winnie, but she knew that the only way Carol would move out of the family home would be by getting married. She was far too fond of her personal comfort to strike out on her own, with all the extra expense and responsibility that would entail. As much as Winnie loved her daughter, she wished she would get a place of her own. Her moodiness made life unbearable for them all at times. Since that dreadful business with Dougie she'd been more difficult than ever.

'I'll get out of your hair,' she said. 'Don't you worry about that. It might not be tomorrow, but I'll go, oh yes.'

Down went Winnie's knife and fork, and she gave an expressive sigh. 'Oh, do stop being so difficult, dear,' she said wearily. 'I've quite enough to worry about at the moment with your sister.'

There was a brief hiatus while Carol reviewed the situation. When she spoke again her manner had changed completely. She knew she could only push people so far, even her pliable parents.

'Don't worry about Gill, Mum,' she said, forcing herself to be pleasant. 'She'll be fine. She's still young; she'll soon meet someone else.'

Winnie gave her a sharp look. 'Oh my Lord, I should think finding another man is about the last thing on her mind at the moment,' she said.

'Eventually, I mean,' said Carol.

'Oh, yes, I suppose she will eventually,' Winnie agreed. 'They both will in time.'

'Definitely,' said Carol. 'It's only natural that they should do.'

Carol's parents would have been very shocked had they known how delighted she was about the break-up of her sister's marriage.

Carol hadn't had such good news in ages.

When the bell rang one Saturday evening in September Craig rushed to the front door because he knew it would be his father. The boy spent most Sundays with Arnie, who sometimes collected him after work on Saturday so that they could spend Saturday evening together too.

'Hello, Arnie,' said Gill, following her son to the door.

'Hi. How are you?'

'Fine thanks,' she said. 'You?'

'Mustn't grumble.'

She looked at Craig, whose face was wreathed in smiles. The way his whole being seemed to light up when he saw his father brought a lump to her throat. 'Have you got everything you need, Craig?' she asked.

'Yeah,' he said excitedly, clutching his overnight bag.

'Here, let me take that for you, son,' Arnie offered, reaching for the bag.

'It's okay, Dad,' he said with boyish eagerness to impress his father. 'I can manage.'

Arnie smiled knowingly, then looked at Gill. 'I'll have him back by about five thirty tomorrow, okay?' he said.

'That'll be fine,' she said amiably. 'No later than that, though. He has to be up early for school on Monday morning.'

'Sure.'

They fell silent. The atmosphere had become suddenly highly charged. She could feel the insistent pull of chemistry drawing them together and she sensed that he could feel it too.

The spell was broken by Craig. 'Are we going then, Dad?' he asked.

'Yep,' said Arnie, looking at him.

'Come on then,' he said eagerly.

'We'll be off then,' Arnie said to Gill.

'Okay.'

'Do you wanna come with us, Mum?' asked Craig as an innocent afterthought.

Gill felt his words like a blow. How could an eight-year-old be

140

expected to understand the complicated nature of what went on between adults?

'I've things to do, love,' she said. 'You go off with Daddy and have a good time.'

'Okay.'

Sounding only mildly disappointed, he kissed his mother and trotted down the short path to wait for his father at his car.

'He's a bit too young to understand,' said Arnie sadly.

'Yeah. He seems to have accepted the fact that you don't live here any more,' she told him, 'but not the other things, like why you can't stay for supper and that sort of thing.'

'He'll get used to it eventually.'

'Course he will.'

'See you tomorrow, then.'

'Yeah.'

She closed the door and leant against it. She was trembling. It was six months since Arnie had left, and she was coping. Apart from whenever she saw him . . .

Her initial instinct after he'd gone had been to move away and start afresh somewhere else. But she had stayed because Craig was happy in Danny Gardens and had his friends here. And of course she had her teaching practice. Besides, she loved the house she and Arnie had chosen together, where they had been happy until their love had turned sour. The very walls were permeated with their life together – the fun as well as the fights – and she couldn't bear to lose that.

They were being very modern and civilised about their separation. The practicalities had been dealt with in a surprisingly amicable manner. He had insisted on continuing to pay the mortgage and the rates, so she had been equally as insistent about refusing maintenance payments from him because she thought that was only fair. She was determined to manage on the money she earned from teaching to keep herself and Craig.

For Craig's sake she gave Arnie unlimited access to their son on the understanding that their getting together didn't interfere with his schooling or any arrangements she had for him.

Now that the break had come the animosity had lessened, and they were getting on better than they had in ages. The worst had happened, so the situation was defused. Arnie had got a transfer to the Hammersmith shop and taken a flat nearby, so Gill was spared the fear of running into him every time she left the house.

Although the ending of her marriage was a lacerating heartache, it was also a relief to be free from the tension that had torn her apart day after day. Life was much quieter now, and more on an even keel. But it was also emptier. Whenever she saw Arnie she wanted him back with such ferocity that she could hardly keep her hands off him, even though she knew that a reconciliation would be a disaster for them all.

Being more or less self-supporting, money was an important factor in Gill's life again, and she had taken on more pupils to boost her income. She even did occasional playing jobs – accompanying a local soprano and playing for a dance class – for which she received modest fees. Peter Attwood had been helpful in this respect, and recommended her whenever anyone came into the shop looking for a good pianist.

The extra hours she spent teaching meant she had less time for her charitable work at St Theresa's, but still she was determined to continue. Cherry was her star pupil and was streets ahead of everyone else, including Gill's paying pupils. The girl's inception at the grammar school, with all its extra work and new interests, hadn't diminished her love of the piano. Gill had high hopes for her.

Gill wandered into the living room, weighed down with melancholy. Saturday nights were hard to take when Craig wasn't here. She went into the music room and started playing the first movement of Beethoven's *Moonlight* sonata, a piece she adored. Music was her personal bolt-hole, and she was always immediately soothed by it.

She was deeply immersed when the doorbell startled her.

'I've come to keep you company,' announced Carol, sweeping in clutching a bottle of wine. 'Mum told me that Craig was going to Arnie's so I guessed you'd be lonely.'

'Oh.'

Carol shot her a look. 'Well, don't look so pleased to see me,' she said sarcastically.

'Sorry, I wasn't expecting to see you, that's all . . .'

'I'll go if you like,' she said, offended.

'Don't be so sensitive.'

'I thought you'd be glad of the company.' Carol's eyes flashed with the beginnings of a tantrum, barely visible through the copious mascara which she wore to contrast with her fashionably pale make-up.

'And I am,' said Gill dutifully, though the last person in the world she wanted to see this evening was Carol, who could be exhausting if you were feeling a bit low.

'Good,' Carol handed over the wine and took off her coat to reveal a clingy white sweater and black tapered trousers. 'So, get the corkscrew out and we'll have a girls' night in.'

Gill opened the wine and the two women settled in the living room, chatting pleasantly about this and that.

'So, how was Arnie when he came to collect Craig?' Carol enquired casually.

'He seemed fine. Why?'

'No particular reason. I was just making conversation.'

'Oh.'

'Has he started seeing anyone else yet?' she asked.

'Not as far as I know.'

'And you would get to know, wouldn't you – if he did have a girlfriend?'

'Oh, yes. If he didn't mention it to me himself, someone else soon would. Mary or Phoebe would put me in the picture. They'd be sure to get to know if there was somebody, especially now that Phoebe works with Arnie.'

'Of course, his mother works at the Hammersmith branch of Bex Sports now, doesn't she?'

'That's right,' said Gill, 'and she thinks it's great.'

'Good for her.' Carol paused thoughtfully. 'So what does Arnie find to do in his spare time now he's on his own?'

'Apparently he does a lot of voluntary work for the supporters' club of Borough FC.'

'How very public-spirited of him!'

'Yes.'

'His having a new woman in his life is something you're going to have to face up to sooner or later, though, isn't it?' Carol's cheeks were beginning to flush from the effect of the alcohol.

'I suppose so.'

'I mean, he isn't likely to be on his own for ever,' she persisted. 'Not a man like Arnie.'

'No,' said Gill. 'But what he does isn't my business any more.'

'You have to get on with your own life,' said Carol authoritatively.

'Yes, and I am doing.'

'I mean, you should find a new man.'

'That's the last thing I feel like doing at the moment,' Gill said emphatically.

'You used to tell me I had to go out and find someone else after Dougie dumped me.'

'Yes, but it's rather different in my case. I'm a married woman with a child.'

'Not married in the usual sense of the word, not any more,' Carol was keen to remind her.

'No, but I'm still the mother of a young child. My main priority is Craig. Not having a partner isn't important to me.'

'It is definitely over between you and Arnie, isn't it?'

'Yes, I've told you . . .'

'Well then, put your marriage behind you and find someone else.'

'I'm all right as I am, thank you.' Gill was beginning to feel edgy.

'All right, there's no need to snap.'

'I don't need you to tell me how to run my life, Carol.'

'You've done plenty of that to me.'

'You seemed to need it.'

'I was only trying to help.'

'I can do without it.'

'Okay, I'll shut up.'

'Good.'

Carol, in this mood, would inevitably put Gill's nerves on edge. Since Gill's marriage had broken up her sister had seen fit to appoint herself as her personal counsellor, her unsolicited advice never going beyond suggestions that Gill should find a replacement for Arnie. Having always needed reassurance in spades, Carol now seemed to have drawn strength from Gill's misfortune and had become annoyingly overbearing, while somehow not quite losing that air of vulnerability that made you afraid to upset her. Gill didn't know which was worse – Carol being desperately insecure and pathetic or Carol being infuriatingly strident.

'Are you absolutely sure it's over between you and Arnie?' Carol ventured again.

Gill threw a cushion at her.

'Just teasing,' said Carol, and poured them each another glass of wine.

One afternoon a few weeks later, Phoebe went into Len and Mary's office with a tray of tea and cream buns. Setting the tray down on the filing cabinet, she unloaded the contents on to the desks, though Len wasn't at his.

'It's my birthday,' she explained, 'so it's cream cakes all round.'

'That's very kind of you, Phoebe,' said Mary, smiling. She patted her middle and made a face. 'I shouldn't really indulge as I'm so overweight, but I'll start the diet tomorrow.'

'Plenty of time for that,' said Phoebe, laughing because Mary's diet was a standing joke. 'You wouldn't be Mary if you were skinny.'

'I'll never be thin because I'm not built that way,' she said. 'But I do need to shed some weight. I've let things get out of hand lately and it's making me feel tired and puffed out.'

Phoebe glanced across at Len's desk. 'I didn't realise Len wasn't here or I wouldn't have poured him a cuppa tea,' she said.

'He went over to the Fulham shop a few minutes ago,' said Mary.

'I was out at the baker's getting the cakes. Must have missed him.'

'Have you poured yourself some tea in the staff room?'

'Not yet.'

'Why not have the one you poured for Len and take your break in here with me?' offered Mary pleasantly. 'Have his bun and replace it later.'

'I'd like that,' said Phoebe in a friendly but polite manner. Even though she and Mary had become firm friends since she'd been working at the shop, Phoebe always respected the fact that Mary was her employer and never overstepped the fine line between friendliness and familiarity.

The two women were of a similar age, had the same sort of outlook on life, and had shared interests – not least the fact that they were the only females working for Bex Sports. They had both been very upset by the break-up of Gill and Arnie's marriage.

'Arnie's still like a fish out of water without Gill, somehow, despite his keeping a cheerful front here at the shop,' Mary remarked, finishing her cream bun and licking the cream off her fingers.

'Mm.' Phoebe nodded.

'So is Gill without him, come to that,' continued Mary. 'After all the misery they'd been going through together, you'd think it would be a relief to be apart. But they both seem lost.'

'Some couples can't be happy together or apart,' said Phoebe.

'That's true.'

'They were lovely together once, before the rot set in.' Phoebe became misty-eyed. 'Love's young dream, you might say – even though they were very different. Arnie was noisy and sociable, a bit of a tearaway when they first started going out. Gill was quieter, with a touch of class about her. But you could literally watch them come to life when they were together.'

'It's a pity it's ended so unhappily.'

'He's filling his life with work at the moment,' said Phoebe.

'So I've noticed,' said Mary. 'He's always here after everyone else has gone in the evening, checking stock, working out ideas for sales promotions and catching up on paperwork. We've never had such a diligent manager on our staff.'

'And when he isn't busy here he's working for the Supporters' Club,' said Phoebe. 'All that staying out and pubbing he did when he and Gill were together – which couldn't have helped matters – he doesn't bother with it now he's free to do so. He just works or stays at home, unless he's got Craig with him, of course.'

'He's using work as a crutch to get him through this bad time,' said Mary.

'Oh yes,' Phoebe agreed. 'He might think he's fooling us all into thinking he's happy, but anyone can see it's an act.'

'Gill's always just that bit too bright and cheerful for it to ring true too,' said Mary.

'I've noticed.'

'I suppose they'll each meet someone else eventually.'

'I hope they do, for their sakes,' said Phoebe. 'Even though it'll break my heart for them to be with other partners. I love Gill like a daughter, and that won't change when Arnie finds someone new.'

'There's no sense in either of them being lonely, though,' said Mary, sipping her tea. 'They've too many years ahead of them.'

'No sense in anyone being lonely if they don't have to be,' declared Phoebe. 'I'm an expert on loneliness after so many years on my own, and I don't recommend it.'

'I'm surprised you haven't married again, actually, a bright spark like you,' Mary looked at her friend thoughtfully. 'I can't believe you haven't had any offers.'

'Plenty when I was younger, but not necessarily of marriage.' Phoebe laughed, wiping her sticky fingers with a handkerchief.

'Oh, Phoebe, you are a case.'

'It's true,' she said lightly. 'The men I met weren't prepared to take on someone else's kids for life just because they wanted to get their mother into bed for the night.'

'Oh dear . . .'

'My boys always came first with me anyway,' said Phoebe. 'Blokes don't like that. They like to be number one.'

'What about later on, when the boys got older?' Mary asked.

'I got older too and the propositions got less,' said Phoebe.

'You're still a very attractive woman, though.'

Phoebe shrugged. 'I make the best of myself for my own satisfaction,' she said. 'But it would take a very special man to make me consider marriage after all this time. I'm set in my ways now, happy with my life the way it is. I've got my friend from the flat upstairs to go to bingo or the pictures with.'

'You're very sociable.'

'I've always enjoyed being with people. My husband was just the same. After he died I had to get out for the sake of my sanity. People thought I was terrible 'cause I didn't sit about moping. Even if I'd wanted to I couldn't afford to – I had to get earning. Best thing for us all that I did, an' all. I'd have gone crazy indoors all day. The kids would have suffered then.'

'You still have John at home now.'

'Yeah – but not for much longer, I shouldn't think. He'll be flying the nest soon, and when he's ready to go I won't shed any tears. It's the natural way of things, innit? As long as he comes to see me now and then, that's all I ask.'

Mary nodded.

'You and Len never had any kids then?'

'No. We wanted a family when we were young, but it didn't happen so we got used to the idea and drew closer together.'

'Sometimes it works the other way and drives couples apart.'

'I'm sure it does, but it hasn't been like that for us.'

'Len's a good 'un.'

'One of the best.'

Phoebe finished her tea. 'Well, I'd better get back into the shop or I'll have the manager after me,' she said. 'Just because he's my son doesn't mean I get any special privileges.'

'I should hope not,' said Mary, 'but I would say that, wouldn't I?'

Phoebe stood up and loaded the crockery on to the tray. 'See you later then.'

'I'll open the door for you.' Mary rose and headed for the door.

'Thanks, dear.'

Phoebe halted at the door with the tray. Mary hadn't opened it. Turning, Phoebe immediately saw that she wasn't able to.

'Mary . . . What's the matter, love? Oh my Lord!'

The tray crashed to the floor as Phoebe reached out for Mary, who was flushed, gasping for breath and swaying as though about to pass out.

By the time Phoebe had got her back to her chair, she seemed to be recovering. 'I'm so sorry,' she said in a whisper.

'Don't apologise . . .'

'I came over all hot and breathless,' she explained weakly, mopping her brow with a handkerchief. 'I'm all right now, though.'

'Are you sure?' To Phoebe, Mary looked very shaken. She was visibly trembling, the colour having drained from her face.

'Yes, really . . .'

'I'll ring the doctor.'

'No!' Mary was adamant. 'It was only a funny little turn . . . nothing to worry about.'

'I'll get Arnie to take you down to casualty in the car as Len isn't here,' Phoebe suggested.

'There's no need for that,' Mary insisted. 'I'm fine now.'

Phoebe was still doubtful. 'I think you should see a doctor just to be on the safe side.'

'No, really, there's no need to make a fuss,' she said. 'It was just a passing thing.'

'You've had this sort of thing before, haven't you?' said Phoebe.

'Yes, now and again this last few months,' admitted Mary. 'But it's nothing that the loss of a few pounds of flab won't cure, and it never lasts longer than a few minutes.'

'It isn't very nice for you, though, is it?' said Phoebe with concern.

'No, it isn't.'

'Have you seen a doctor about it?'

'Good Lord, no,' Mary said. 'I'm at a funny age . . . it's obviously got something to do with that. They say weird things happen to menopausal women, don't they?'

'It might be an idea to get it checked out, though,' advised Phoebe. 'It's probably nothing to worry about, but at least a check-up would put your mind at rest.'

'If the turns continue and begin to bother me, I'll go and see a doctor – but there's certainly no cause for that at the moment.'

'Shall I get on the phone to the Fulham shop to ask Len to come back?' Phoebe persisted, because Mary still didn't look at all well.

'Definitely not,' said Mary firmly. 'I don't want Len to know anything about this.'

'Surely he ought to—'

'No,' Mary insisted.

'Why?'

'I don't want him worried when it isn't necessary,' she said.

'He'd want to be told.'

'He'll only get into a panic when there's no need. He's a terrible fusspot when it comes to me.' She gave Phoebe a long, hard look. 'I mean it, Phoebe. I don't want Len to know anything about what happened today, and I shall be very cross indeed if you tell him. And that means not telling anyone in case they pass it on.'

'But—'

'Look . . .' Mary seemed suddenly stronger and more forceful than Pheobe had ever seen her. 'It's *my* health and *my* business. If and when I think Len should know, I shall tell him. Until then I must insist that you say nothing.'

'Okay, dear, don't upset yourself,' Phoebe agreed with reluctance. 'I'll clear up the mess on the floor.'

'Thank you.'

'No trouble at all.' Phoebe got down on her hands and knees to collect the broken pieces of china, her hands trembling. Mary had felt a lot worse than she'd admitted, if Phoebe was any judge, and she thought it was wrong for her to keep it from her husband.

Oh, well, it's none of my business, and I must respect her wishes, she thought, collecting as much of the smashed crockery as she could by hand and putting it on the tray before going to the staff room for the dustpan and brush to finish the job.

Despite Mary's casual attitude towards the incident, Phoebe felt thoroughly unnerved by it.

Chapter Twelve

A crowd of teenagers was clustered excitedly around the record counter in the music shop when Gill called there after her teaching session at St Theresa's one Saturday morning in November.

'Don't tell me,' she said, grinning at Peter, who had appeared from the office to serve her, leaving Wendy to deal with the customers in her own peer group. 'There's been a new Beatles release.'

'It's the latest Rolling Stones record that's causing all the excitement, actually,' Peter said.

' "Get Off Of My Cloud"?'

'That's the one,' he said. 'The kids are still going mad for it.'

'Beatlemania doesn't seem to have abated because of the Stones' rising popularity, though, does it?'

'No, not at all. I expect the Beatles will top the charts at Christmas.'

'I saw in the paper that they got the MBE,' remarked Gill.

'Yes, I saw that too.'

'There was practically mass hysteria among the fans outside Buckingham Palace when they drove through the gates in a Rolls-Royce to receive their gongs, apparently.'

'It was chaotic, from what I've heard,' Peter said. 'They had to draft in hundreds of extra police to control the excitement. Crowds of teenage girls, screaming, shouting, waving banners . . .'

'We used to drool over Elvis when I was a teenager,' said Gill.

'That can't be long ago.'

'Long enough,' she said with a grin. 'I'm twenty-six.'

'You poor old thing,' Peter said jokingly.

She laughed.

'Elvis is still regularly in the charts,' said Peter.

'So I gather.'

'Anyway, what can I do for you?'

'Do you have the music for the Grade Two piano exam . . . the London College Examining Board, please?' she asked. 'One of my December candidates has had his copy chewed to ribbons by his dog and I don't seem to have any spares.'

'Sure.'

Peter found the music she wanted and put it into a bag. 'So, how's life?' he enquired casually.

'Busy,' she said. 'I've more pupils than I can comfortably

manage and I still have a long waiting list.'

'I meant, how's life as a single lady?' Peter had been given brief details of her separation when she'd asked him to recommend her for playing jobs.

'Not too bad . . . I'm surviving.'

'It gets easier with time.'

'Is that the voice of experience?' she enquired lightly.

'It is,' he confirmed. 'I've been divorced for a couple of years.'

'Oh, really?' she said, the knowledge making her feel less alone somehow.

'Yes, it's a miserable business,' Peter said, shaking his head sagely. 'No matter how bad things get when the marriage is in existence, it still hurts when it's over.'

'You don't have to tell me.' Gill took the bag and handed him the money. 'Do you have any children?'

'Two.'

'See them often?'

'About once a month.'

'My son sees his father most weekends.'

'That often?'

'Yes. I don't mind. In fact I encourage it,' she explained. 'Because Craig adores his dad and I don't want him to lose that bond.'

'Sounds to me as though you're being very fair about things.'

She nodded, taking her change and putting it into her purse. 'I find weekends difficult, though, with Craig being with his father on Sundays,' she said chattily.

'The weekends are difficult for most people who find themselves in that situation, I should imagine,' Peter said.

'This week it'll be even worse because my son is going to his father's tonight and staying over until tomorrow afternoon. There's something especially lonely, somehow, about being on your own on a Saturday evening.'

'You don't have to be alone tonight,' he said.

'I don't?'

'No. You could come out for a meal with me. I've nothing planned.'

'Oh, dear,' Gill said, embarrassed. 'I was just idly chatting. I wasn't angling for an invitation out.'

'I know you weren't,' he heartily assured her. 'But as we're both at a loose end, it makes sense to team up for a meal.'

'No, I couldn't, really,' she protested, feeling trapped into something she hadn't expected and wasn't sure she wanted. 'My sister will probably come over to my place anyway. She usually does if she knows I'm going to be on my own.'

'I was only suggesting we eat together to keep the loneliness at bay,' he said pointedly. 'I wasn't planning on anything more than that.'

'Now I really am embarrassed.'

'Don't be,' Peter said. 'It was only a spur-of-the-moment suggestion.' Unoffended, he was smiling at her, his eyes exuding warmth.

'It's just that I'm not ready for . . .'

'A new relationship.'

'Exactly.'

'I'm not sure I am either,' he said, 'so it would just be a meal – if you fancy it.'

'Okay,' she said, smiling at him. 'But only on the condition that we go dutch.'

'If that's what you want, that's how it'll be,' he said casually.

'I'll look forward to it then,' she said, realising how much she needed some fresh adult company.

One evening a few weeks later, Carol Miller was standing in the doorway of a shoe shop near Hammersmith Broadway with her eyes fixed on Bex Sports opposite. It was closed for the night, but she knew that Arnie was still inside, in the manager's office at the back of the shop, because she could see the light shining through the window. She had also taken the precaution of checking to make sure that his car was parked in a nearby side street.

She was not here by accident, nor as the result of a sudden whim. She had been planning this for months, and had done her homework beforehand. She had not deemed it wise to make a move too soon after Arnie's separation from Gill, in case it created bad feeling with her sister and their parents. But she had waited long enough; she daren't leave it any longer for fear he'd find someone else.

By artfully extracting information from Gill, and by making it her business to 'bump into' Arnie's mother in the street and interrogate her while supposedly having a neighbourly chat, she'd been able to keep up to date with his daily routine, which had allowed her to work out her strategy.

She knew that he never left the shop in the evening until long after everyone else, and more importantly she knew that he hadn't yet embarked upon another relationship with a woman.

It was a wet night with a penetrating chill, and she'd been standing here for nearly an hour. The cold and damp were seeping into her bones, something that wasn't helped by the fact that she wore her skirt mini length. Even though she was sheltered from the rain in the doorway it was cold and draughty, and every so often a blast of spray was blown into her face by the wind. Her feet, inside her long, black patent boots, were aching with the cold, her toes turning numb. She stamped her feet and pulled up the collar on her red wet-look raincoat.

She had lied to her mother. She'd told Winnie she wouldn't be home for tea because she was going to the cinema with a friend after work.

151

She had actually come straight here so as not to miss him. That was one of the drawbacks of living at home: although it was cheap and convenient, with meals and laundry service included, it was also very restrictive because you were expected to account for your movements. This was annoying at the best of times and infuriating when you didn't want your parents to know what you were up to. Carol comforted herself with the thought that, if things went according to plan, she wouldn't be there for much longer.

But now things were happening across the street. The light in the office had gone out, which meant Arnie was on his way. Up went her umbrella and she sallied forth into the rain, crossing the road and positioning herself a short distance away from the entrance to the sports shop, ready to spring into action.

As Arnie emerged and turned back to lock the door, she marched in his direction as though she'd been walking for ages and was on her way somewhere, her eyes pointed towards the ground until she was parallel with him.

'Arnie,' she said, turning to look at him with feigned surprise. 'You're working late tonight.'

He peered at her in the pale glow from the street-light.

'Carol?'

'Yeah.'

'I thought I recognised your dulcet tones . . . What are you doin' around here?'

'I'm on my way to the bus stop to get the bus home,' she lied without compunction.

'Oh.'

'I went to a friend's place straight from work,' she said. 'We were supposed to be having something to eat there and going to the pictures together, but her boyfriend turned up so she went out with him instead.'

'And left you high and dry?'

'That's right.'

'Not nice.'

'Not nice at all.'

'Never mind,' he said with genuine sympathy – Arnie had always perceived Carol to be a sad sort of person who needed lots of encouragement. 'Better luck next time.'

'I hope so.' She gave a violent shiver, hugging herself. 'Cor, dear, it isn't half parky tonight.'

'Too cold to be hanging about at the bus stop.' He finished locking the door. 'Forget the bus. I'll run you home.'

'Oh, would you?' she said in a sweet, girlish voice. 'I'd be ever so grateful.'

'No trouble at all. It's the least I can do for my favourite sister-in-law.'

152

'I'm your *only* sister-in-law – and I'm not even that any more.'

'You are unless Gill and I get divorced,' he was quick to point out as they walked around the corner to the car together, the uneven plod of his limp and the sharp click of her stiletto heels resounding into the quiet of the side street. Thinking it would please her, Arnie added, 'You'll always be Gill's kid sister to me anyway.'

Not if I've got anything to do with it, Carol thought. She intended to alter his perception of her with all possible speed. But for now she just said, 'That's nice.'

'Well, there's no reason for the families not to stay friends just because Gill and I are no longer together, is there?' he remarked as they got into the car.

'None at all,' agreed Carol.

'So, what have you been doing with yourself lately?' he enquired casually, keeping his eyes on the road ahead as the rain beat against the steamy windows, the wipers plodding to and fro.

'Nothing very exciting,' she said. 'The same old things . . .'

'Sounds to me as though there isn't a new man in your life yet.'

'There's been no one special since Dougie,' she told him.

'What's the matter with all the young blokes around here?' Arnie felt sorry for Carol, and was saying these things to be kind. 'They must want their brains tested.'

The compliment heartened her more then he could have realised. 'I've been out with a few, but nothing that lasted,' she said.

'You'll find the right one soon,' Arnie said reassuringly.

I found him a long time ago, but he's only just become available, she thought. She said, 'Yeah, course I will. And in the mean time I'm enjoying the freedom.'

'That's the spirit.'

'How about you? Are you enjoying being single again?'

'Not really.'

'Oh dear.' She sounded suitably sympathetic. 'Seems to me as though you're the one who needs to find someone.'

'No, not me.'

'Gill's seeing someone else . . .'

'What?' Arnie sounded devastated. 'Who is he?'

'The chap from the music shop,' Carol informed him with relish. 'She's been out with him quite a few times.'

'I didn't know that.'

'I'm not sure if it's serious between them . . .' Carol spoke with a falsely casual air. 'But I do know they've been out together quite regularly.'

There was a silence while Arnie digested this upsetting news.

'It's none of my business what Gill does any more,' he said at last.
'No.'

'I still can't get used to the idea that it isn't, though,' he added.

'I know the feeling,' she said chummily. 'I was just the same when I heard that Dougie had got engaged to someone else recently. I was hurt, even after all this time.'

'I'm sorry to hear that.'

'Don't be, I'm over it now,' she said. 'I think my pride was hurt more than anything.'

'That's only natural.'

Carol murmured in agreement. Then, choosing her moment, she said, 'Oh dear, I'm sinking with hunger.'

'Are you?'

'Yeah. I didn't get anything to eat at all in the end, and Mum won't have kept me anything 'cause I told her I was eating at my friend's . . .'

'Mm.' Arnie considered the matter for a few moments. 'I have to eat too, and I don't feel like cooking myself anything – so why don't we have a bite together somewhere?'

'You've no plans for this evening then?' she said, feeling triumphant.

'None at all.'

'Thanks very much, then,' she said, hardly able to believe how easy it had been. 'I'd like that.'

They went to a small place in Chelsea with pine walls, potted plants and scarlet tablecloths. The atmosphere was homely, the food delicious. Carol didn't often eat out, so it was a special treat for her. Arnie ordered steak, she had chilli con carne.

Hoping to please him, she got him talking about his charity work for Borough FC Supporters' Club. 'What do you do exactly?' she asked.

'Among other things, I organise the transport for the fans to go to the away matches,' he said, looking casually smart in a black polo-necked sweater over pale grey slacks. 'We've just managed to buy a coach for the disabled supporters, actually.'

'That must have cost a bomb.'

'It did.'

'How did you get enough money to pay for it?' she enquired with feigned interest, hoping to impress him.

'We raised it over a long period through various fund-raising social events, donations from businesses, collecting boxes on shop and pub counters and raffles,' he explained. 'If you want something bad enough, you get very persistent.'

Which is exactly what she intended to do.

'I admire you for giving so much of your time to charity work,' she said, though she would prefer he devoted his time to her.

'I'm not being holier than thou,' he said, forking a chip, 'I enjoy it.'

'It must be nice to do stuff for other people,' Carol said insincerely. 'I wonder if Gill gets a kick from teaching for free at St Theresa's.'

'I'm sure she does,' Arnie said, filled with regret for not taking more interest in Gill's work. He'd always been too full of himself to give her the support she'd deserved, he could see that now. Not a day had passed since they'd parted when he didn't remember something that made him sorry. 'She's a very charitable person.'

Carol instantly regretted bringing Gill into the conversation and would avoid it whenever possible in the future, because she couldn't bear the soft look that came into Arnie's eyes whenever her sister's name was mentioned.

She didn't see any reason to feel guilty about making a serious play for him. It wasn't as though she had ever tried to come between him and Gill when they were together, or tried to step into Gill's shoes while she was trying to adjust to the separation and still feeling wretched. She'd waited for a decent interval to elapse, giving Gill time to get him back if that was what she wanted. But no such moves had been made.

So she didn't have to feel bad.

Anyway, she had no intention of drawing back now, whatever Gill felt about it. The girlish hero-worship Carol had once felt for Arnie had developed into an all-consuming passion. She wanted him with a compulsion that exceeded anything she'd felt for a man before. And she was going to have him, whatever the obstacles! It was as much as she could do to keep her hands off him now, but she was determined not to show it too soon.

Although she'd never admitted it to anyone, she knew that her tendency to make her feelings too obvious frightened men away. She wasn't going to risk having that happen with Arnie.

'From what I've heard Craig has inherited your sporting talents rather than Gill's musical ones,' she said, because she knew it would please him to talk about his son.

'Yeah, that does seem to be the case at the moment . . .'

Carol was fired with jealousy at the tenderness in his voice when he spoke of Craig. My God, she was up against strong opposition for his affections! She tried to get the conversation on to a more general plane by asking him if he'd seen the recently opened Post Office Tower, Britain's tallest building.

'I took Craig to see it the other weekend,' he informed her brightly. 'We went up in the lift to the public viewing gallery and had something to eat in the revolving restuarant. He thought it was great fun.'

Every road led back to Gill or Craig, she thought with annoyance, but smiled sweetly and said, 'Ah, bless him . . .'

While Arnie smoked a cigarette over coffee, Carol was working out how she could get him to agree to another meeting.

'I've really enjoyed myself this evening, Arnie,' she said, meeting his eyes. 'You've cheered me up no end.'

'Good.' He looked at her, seeing a young woman with nice eyes buried behind copious mascara. 'I've enjoyed it too.'

'Really?'

'Don't sound so surprised,' he said. 'Why wouldn't I enjoy having a meal out with an attractive young woman?'

She looked suitably coy. 'I do believe you're chatting me up, Arnie Briscoe,' she said.

'Leave it out, Carol,' he admonished firmly – because such a thing had never occurred to him, 'I wouldn't do a thing like that to my ex-wife's kid sister.'

'Hardly a kid, Arnie . . . I'm twenty-three,' she pointed out.

'Yeah, I suppose you would be about that now,' he said casually. 'But it isn't a question of years. You'll always be Gill's little sister to me, and you're certainly not too old for me to tell you that you're wearing too much mascara.'

'Honestly,' she said, tutting.

'Are you tryin' to look like Dusty Springfield or somethin'?'

'Of course not. It's the fashion to look like this,' she said evenly. Although this light-hearted banter wasn't what she was after in the long term, at least his brotherly affection for her was something to build on.

'I've always put you right about things like that,' he said in a friendly manner. 'Remember when you were a teenager?'

'Will I ever forget?' she said, raising her eyes in mock disdain. 'It's a wonder I had the confidence to go out at all after you two had finished taking the mickey.'

'It was all very well intentioned. We had your interests at heart.' Arnie smiled, looking wistfully into the distance. 'Gill and I probably did give you a hard time, looking back on it. But only because we cared about you.'

'I'm sure.'

'We had some good times, didn't we? When I was one of the family.'

'Not half,' she agreed. 'I've missed your being around.'

'I've missed being around,' he told her. 'That's the sad thing when a marriage ends: other things you care about end too. People you counted as family aren't related any more.'

'It's a shame,' Carol said, seeing an opportunity to move things forward. 'But you and I could get together again sometime if you like.' She knew it would not occur to him to ask her out because he didn't think of her in those sort of terms. She was going to have to break with tradition and take all the initiative if she wanted him – in the early stages anyway – because it was obvious he wasn't going to come to her of his own volition. 'I mean, we're both on our own, we might as well keep each other company.'

'Good idea.'

'When?'

'Oh, I dunno, sometime soon,' Arnie said vaguely, already thinking of other things.

'How about this time next week?' she persisted, trying not to sound too eager but anxious to pin him down. 'I could meet you at the shop after work if you like, about the same time as I did tonight. We could go for a meal, or just a drink if you'd rather . . . just for the sake of old times.'

Arnie looked at her. He'd always been fond of Carol in a brotherly sort of way. She'd always been a lonely soul, never seemed to have many friends or much luck with men. He remembered how worried they'd all been about her after Dougie had let her down so cruelly. Her family had thought she was heading for a breakdown then. But even as a youngster she'd been a loner. He recalled how she used to hang around with him and Gill when all they wanted was to be alone.

She'd changed a bit since then, though, he thought, becoming aware of the fact that she was an attractive woman with the sort of figure for which the mini skirt and tight sweaters had been invented. But for all that, Carol still seemed to need protecting. He recalled how protective Gill had been of her when she was younger.

Frankly, it didn't matter to Arnie one way or the other whether he spent an evening with her next week or not. The idea was not repugnant to him; neither was it important. But she seemed so lonely, he didn't want to hurt her feelings. It was almost as though in hurting her he would hurt Gill, who had always been so fond of her sister.

'Okay, Carol, let's make it the same time next week,' he heard himself say.

'Great, Arnie,' she said, reaching over and resting her hand on his on the table. 'I'll look forward to it.'

'You and Arnie!' Gill exclaimed in disbelief. It was a few weeks later, and Carol had called at the house unexpectedly. '*You* have been out with *Arnie!*'

'I've been out with him a few times, actually,' Carol blurted out.

'Oh, Carol . . .'

They were having coffee in the living room. Carol was cradling her mug in both hands and observing her sister with caution. 'There's no need to be quite so shocked,' she said, on the defensive as usual.

'Of course I am—'

'There's no reason why I shouldn't go out with him, is there?' Carol cut in sharply. 'He's free to go out with anyone he likes, the same as you are. Anyway, you're going out with Peter.'

'We're just friends.'

'And so are Arnie and I,' Carol said. 'For the moment anyway.'

Gill felt buffeted by this unexpected news, even though she knew she had no right to object. 'You're saying that you'll be more than just friends if you have your way, then?' she enquired.

'Yeah, sure. Why not?' Carol bit her lip. 'I've always liked Arnie . . . well, fancied him rotten, actually.'

'Does he know what you have in mind?'

'Of course not. I'm not that stupid,' she said. 'It'll take a bit of time for us to get to know each other properly.'

'You know what you want, I'll say that much for you,' said Gill.

'Look, Gill, it isn't as though I'm taking him away from you or anything, is it?' said Carol crossly.

'Not much!'

'But it's over between you; you've said so many times. You've been separated for the best part of a year now. So why shouldn't Arnie and I get together? He's single and so am I. We've always got on well . . .'

'Everything you say is true,' said Gill. 'But it still hurts. This isn't about logic, Carol, it's about feelings.'

'Yeah, I suppose so.' Carol at least had the grace to look sheepish.

'Imagine how you would have felt if I'd started seeing Dougie after you split up with him.'

'That was different,' said Carol hotly. 'Dougie ditched me in the cruellest way possible. You and Arnie have split up by mutual agreement because it was over between you. Anyway, you've had plenty of time to change your mind and you've shown no interest in wanting him back.'

'Because it wouldn't work out, not because I don't still feel something for him.'

'You don't want him but you don't want anyone else to have him, is that it?' demanded Carol.

'That isn't how it is,' Gill denied. 'Of course he'll find someone new eventually. But my own sister . . .'

'Why shouldn't I be happy for a change?' she said. 'You've had your chance . . .' Her voice tailed off and there was an explosive silence as their eyes met. They both knew they were on the verge of a serious disagreement which could lead to a parting of the ways that neither of them wanted.

'Look, Gill,' Carol continued, feeling worse about this than she'd expected. 'I don't want to hurt you, but I really do like Arnie . . . Well, actually it's more than that. I'm in love with him.'

'Are you sure it isn't just love you want and Arnie just happens to be available to provide it if he's guided in the right direction?'

'That was a rotten thing to say.'

'Yes it was.' Gill had a sudden urge to grab Carol by the hair and shake her till she begged for mercy. 'I'm sorry. It isn't any of my business what Arnie does or who he sees.'

'No it isn't. I'm sorry if my seeing him upsets you,' said Carol. 'But I can't give him up now, Gill . . . I really can't.'

'I shall just have to learn to live with it then, won't I?'

* * *

158

Gill sat opposite Peter at a table in a small Italian restaurant in Fulham and poured her heart out to him over spaghetti bolognese.

'How could she do that? My own sister,' she said, gulping her Chianti in despair. 'Apart from the pain of seeing them together, can you imagine the hideous complications that will arise from this? My ex-husband and the father of my child would become my brother-in-law.'

'Hey, hang on, Gill. She's been out with him a few times, that's all,' Peter reminded her, twirling spaghetti around his fork. 'It probably won't go any further than that.'

'She seems very determined.'

'It takes two,' he said.

'Yes, there is that,' replied Gill, making a half-hearted effort to eat her meal. 'And I mustn't interfere.'

'No, you really mustn't do that,' he said emphatically.

'No?' she said, looking up quickly at his tone of voice.

'You're separated from Arnie,' he pointed out firmly. 'His love-life isn't your business any longer. Arnie and Carol are both single adults with minds of their own. They're entitled to give it a chance.'

She threw him a sharp look. 'And how would you feel if your ex-wife married your brother?'

'I don't have a brother, but I don't honestly think I would mind.'

'It's easy to say that when you know it can't happen.'

'I agree with you. It is easy to say it, but I do happen to believe it to be true,' he said. 'It's over between my wife and I. Whatever we once had is long gone, so it's immaterial to me who she is with now. She is getting married to someone I know, actually, and I don't mind a bit.'

'Oh. I'm sorry,' Gill said. 'You've never said much about your past.'

'Because it isn't important to me now,' he said. 'It's water under the bridge.'

'So is mine, I suppose.'

'Yes. But the difference between you and me is that you're still in love with your ex and I'm not in love with mine.'

'I didn't say I was still in love with Arnie,' she said.

'Why are you so upset about him seeing your sister then?'

She put her wine glass down slowly and leant her elbows on the table, resting her chin on her linked fingers. 'I do still feel something for Arnie, it's true,' she said.

'Tell me something I don't already know.'

'I must be completely bonkers after the life he led me. But I can't help it. He's just . . . always with me, somehow.'

'Is it worth giving your marriage another try, then?' Peter enquired. 'Before your sister gets too deeply involved with him?'

'Definitely not,' she said without hesitation. 'We were incompatible for years before we actually split up. I couldn't go through that again and I should think it's the last thing Arnie wants. All those terrible arguments and the bad atmosphere in the house . . . It was hell.'

'Sounds to me as though you'd come to the end of the line.'

'We had.'

'There you are, then . . .'

'But when you've been with someone a long time, you can't just feel nothing for them.'

'No, but you still have to move on, whatever you're feeling,' he said. 'It's no good hanging on to the past.'

Gill looked into his comforting grey eyes, the undulating candlelight gleaming on his face, which was too thin and angular to be handsome but was pleasant with smooth skin and a well-shaped mouth. Casually dressed as ever, Peter was wearing a black shirt and jeans, his long hair shining with cleanliness but chaotic in a way that suited his bohemian image.

They had been out together quite a few times now, and she looked on him as a true friend. Their most common interest was music. Peter was an accomplished guitarist and gave lessons after hours in the room at the back of the shop.

He had a very gentle nature and she could talk to him about anything. As there was no question of sex to complicate matters, he was very easy to be with. He'd seemed to accept what she'd said at the beginning – that she wasn't ready for a relationship and was happy just to be her friend.

'By that you mean I should stand back from Arnie and Carol,' she said, 'and let it happen if it's going to.'

'It's the only thing you can do, isn't it?' he said in a definite tone. 'After all, you no longer have any claim on Arnie.'

'You certainly tell it like it is, don't you?' she said.

'For your own sake.'

'Really?'

'Yes. Because you don't only have to let go of the past for Arnie and Carol's sake,' he said. 'You have to do it for yourself too. It's over between you and Arnie, so stop hankering for him and let yourself move on.'

'Easier said than done.'

'You have to do it though, Gill,' he advised with sincerity. 'You can't spend the rest of your life clinging to an old love and getting all bitter and twisted if he and your sister make a go of it. You're still young, you have a lot of life ahead of you. Don't let it pass you by.'

She knew he was right. 'That was quite a speech.'

'I can manage to string a few words together when I put my mind to it,' he grinned.

'It's strange how I can take it from you,' she said. 'But I get angry if anyone else suggests the same thing.'

'Maybe that's because we're both in a similar situation,' he suggested.

She put her fork down and reached across the table for his hand. 'You've been a good friend to me,' she said, realising at that moment how much difference he had made to her life. 'It's so good having someone to talk to, someone to go out with.'

'It isn't all one-sided, you know,' he said. 'I enjoy it too.'

'Good.'

As she drew her hand away, he raised his glass to her. 'And long may it continue.'

'Yes.'

She lifted her glass and chinked it with his, their eyes meeting. She wasn't naive enough to think their friendship would continue in this undemanding and platonic way for ever. But for the moment it was just what she needed.

Carol wasn't finding it as easy to move her friendship with Arnie on to another stage as she'd hoped. He was friendly enough to her and seemed to enjoy being with her, but he was often vague and preoccupied and she had difficulty getting him to commit himself to another meeting.

'I'll see you soon,' he'd say, or, 'I'll give you a bell in a few days.'

She was far too desperate to worry about seeming too presumptuous, so when he didn't call her she telephoned him and suggested a meeting. Once reminded of her existence, he usually agreed to take her out for a meal or a drink.

Anxious to keep the conversation away from the family and Gill, Carol encouraged him to talk about his work. That was always a safe bet. She even made a token suggestion that she could help him with his charity work. He replied casually that he'd take her up on her offer one of these days.

But still there was no hint of romance. The most promising sign she'd had in that direction was a friendly kiss on the cheek when they parted. She suspected that anything else just hadn't occurred to him.

But she simply couldn't accept that he wouldn't fancy her once he stopped seeing her as Gill's sister.

So far she'd managed to keep the extent of her feelings from him, but how much longer she could keep it quiet she didn't know – because she wanted him with ever-increasing ferocity.

Drastic action was going to be called for if she didn't make progress soon. But timing was crucial. She'd know when the moment was right, and she'd move in with all guns blazing.

Arnie Briscoe would be hers, one way or another!

161

Chapter Thirteen

'Well, how do I look?' Mary asked, sweeping into the lounge of the Bexes' home in Putney with an uncharacteristic flourish and giving her husband a twirl, the blue taffeta folds of her evening dress rustling around her ankles.

'Beautiful . . . really beautiful.' Len was looking very smart himself, in a tuxedo with a crisp white shirt, his grey hair giving him a distinguished air.

'You don't look so bad yourself,' Mary commented, her face specially made up for the occasion, hair freshly done at the hairdressers that afternoon.

It was the beginning of another year, and they were going to a hotel in the West End to a charity dinner in aid of an association for disabled sportsmen, of which Len was the president.

'It's worth making the effort for a special do like the one tonight,' he said.

'Not half,' she agreed. 'There'll be some smart frocks there tonight, I bet. If you can afford the price of a ticket, you can afford something a bit special to wear.'

'The tickets are a bit pricey, I know,' remarked Len. 'But people with dough to spend are only too happy to splash out to help a good cause if they know they're gonna have a good time in the process.'

'That's understandable.'

'Yeah.' He looked at his watch. 'Are you ready, love? The taxi will be here in a minute.'

'I'll be two minutes,' she said. 'I just have to pop upstairs to get my coat and handbag.'

In a spontaneous action, he swept her into his arms with a growling sound. 'You're very glamorous tonight,' he whispered into her hair. 'You'll upstage all the competition.'

'Leave it out, Len,' she laughed. 'I was never competitive in that way when I was young, let alone now.'

'You're not even fifty yet.'

'I'm not twenty either.' She drew away, smiling at him. 'And snogging is off the menu because it'll ruin my make-up and hair.'

She left him grinning and departed for the bedroom. This, their sanctuary, was lavishly appointed with all the trappings that years of hard work had enabled them to afford – endless fitted wardrobes, gilt-

163

edged mirrors, deep-pile carpet . . . Slipping into her white fur evening jacket, Mary picked up her dainty sequinned bag from the dressing-table and checked its contents before heading for the door.

In the centre of the room she stopped, rooted to the spot as the symptoms that were becoming all too familiar engulfed her. Her body was on fire, and she couldn't breathe. It was as though a heavy weight had smashed into her chest in a painful blast.

Trying not to panic, she fought against the faintness but the room was spinning horribly. Drenched in perspiration and gasping for breath, she finally felt her legs buckle and she sank to the floor.

For how long she sat there on the carpet she didn't know, but eventually she became distantly aware of Len calling her from downstairs.

'Mary! What the devil are you doing up there?' he was shouting. 'The taxi's here and the meter's running.'

Mercifully the abnormal sensations began to subside, and with a supreme effort she managed to struggle to her feet. Relieved to find her strength returning, she retouched her make-up, tidied her hair and made her way downstairs, hoping she didn't look as shaky as she felt.

'Ah, there you are at last.' Len gave her a close look, frowning. 'Are you all right, love? You've gone a bit pale.'

She hesitated, wondering if she ought to tell him about the funny turns she'd been having lately. But he was such a worrier when it came to her – which was understandable, since they only had each other. Anyway, these uncomfortable spells didn't last long; they were probably menopausal and would, therefore, stop troubling her in due course. She would seek medical advice if they got any worse, and talk to Len about it then. In the mean time, there was no point in bothering him if she didn't have to.

'I'm fine,' she assured him brightly. 'So let's go out and paint the town red.'

Arnie let himself into his flat, the echoing silence of its emptiness hitting him as soon as he set foot inside the door. At one time he'd had so much to come home to: a wife and son he adored, a comfortable house throbbing with family life – a piano playing in one room, the telly blaring in another, the smell of something cooking in the kitchen . . . Now he returned from work to an empty flat and something on a tray in front of the television, if he hadn't stopped off for a pie and a pint in the pub on the way home.

His present abysmal circumstances were entirely of his own making; he fully accepted that. He'd been vain and selfish in the glory days, self-pitying and guilt-ridden later, all his resentment aimed at Gill. God, how he had made that woman suffer! He wondered if he was a wicked man. He'd been weak and self-obsessed, certainly. In retrospect, it was as though he hadn't been in control of his own actions for a while.

Knowing that he was to blame for the failure of his marriage didn't make the regrets any easier to bear. Fortunately, he had a job that interested him and took his mind off things during the day. He had Gill to thank for that – and he'd been arrogant enough to object to her approaching Len on his behalf. His behaviour didn't bear thinking about.

Now that he lived alone he put far more into his work than was expected of him, just to help fill the lonely hours. But no matter how fulfilling the job, it couldn't possibly make up for the loss of the woman he loved.

Still, at least the flat is reasonably comfortable, he told himself, even if it did feel like a butcher's cold-room after being empty all day. He switched on the underfloor heating and wandered into the living room, turning on the television which was transmitting an episode of *Coronation Street*. This immediately made him think of Gill – it was one of her favourites.

His flat was in a modern block not far from the river at Hammersmith. It was adequately furnished but noticeably lacking in imagination. When he'd moved in he hadn't had the heart to do more than install the basics. It was a roof over his head rather than a home.

He sank into an armchair, keeping his coat on until the place warmed up, and stared blankly at the TV screen, wondering if there was anything edible in the kitchen. At best there would be the ingredients for cheese on toast.

Further investigation revealed some dodgy-smelling ham, a knob of cheese with a hairy green forest growing on it, and half a loaf of bread that was so hard you could break ice with it. Oh, well, it'll have to be fish and chips again tonight, he thought, cheering himself with the idea of stopping off at the pub on the way for a pint and a spot of company. He didn't go to pubs much these days, compared to the amount of time he'd spent in them in the dying days of his marriage.

His marriage ... He must have been crazy to let something so precious slip through his fingers. Oh well. No point in fretting. It was too late to do anything about it now.

He was on his way to the front door when the telephone rang in the hall.

'Hi, Arnie, it's Carol.'

'Hi, Carol,' he said, glad to hear a friendly voice. 'How are you?'

'Fine.'

'Good.'

'I just wondered if you were doin' anything this evening,' she said.

'Nothing that you could call anything,' he told her. 'I'm just on my way out to the chippy to get my supper, as a matter of fact.'

'Oh.' There was a short silence. 'In that case why don't I come over to your place and bring fish and chips for us both, save you going out?' she suggested.

Although he was tempted to agree, his sense of decency forced him to say, 'It's a nice thought, Carol, but I don't wanna drag you over to Hammersmith on a cold night like this.'

'I can easily hop on to a bus,' she said, though she had already done so and was in the phone box at the end of his road.

'I wouldn't want to put you to all that trouble just for a fish and chip supper.'

'I'd like to,' she said. 'I've nothing else to do and it would be company for me.'

'You've not eaten either, then?'

'No. I didn't fancy what Mum had cooked so I left most of mine,' she said. 'Fish and chips would be just the job.'

'Well, if you're sure . . .'

'I am.'

'You got enough money?'

'Yeah.'

'I'll pay you back when you get here.'

'Okay. See you soon.'

As he replaced the receiver, Arnie felt considerably brighter. Having known Carol for such a long time he found her easy to be with; and at least the evening no longer loomed miserably ahead with only the television for company.

He said as much to Carol later, after they had washed the dishes and were relaxing with a cup of coffee. 'You've really cheered me up tonight,' he told her. 'I was properly down in the dumps before you phoned.'

'You should have contacted me if you fancied some company,' she said.

'I didn't think of it,' he said, a little too truthfully for Carol's liking.

'Out of sight, out of mind, eh?' she said, keeping her tone light.

'Sorry. I didn't mean it to sound like that.' He made a face.

'S'all right.'

'Anyway, you can't get on the blower to someone every time you're feeling a bit lonely, can you?'

'I'm not just someone, Arnie,' she said, looking at him with a serious expression. 'We go back a long way, you and me. You can turn to me for company any time you like.'

'Thanks. But a young, unattached woman like yourself should be out enjoying yourself,' he told her, 'not cheering up your miserable old sod of a brother-in-law.'

'You're not a miserable old sod,' she said firmly. 'And as I've told you before, you're not my brother-in-law now.'

'Legally I am.'

'It's just a technicality.'

'I suppose so,' he said, but he didn't sound convinced.

'I don't think of you as Gill's husband,' she told him, leaning back in the chair and looking at him through somnolent eyes, her heavy lids lowered slightly.

'No?'

'No. When I look at you I just see a very attractive man.'

Warning bells rang in his head, but Arnie wasn't in the mood to listen. He was drowning in self-loathing and regret for hurting Gill and wrecking their marriage. Flattery from an attractive female was just what he needed to help boost his confidence.

'It's nice of you to say so,' he said, meeting her eyes and feeling obliged to respond with a similar compliment. 'I must admit that I see Gill's sister when I look at you, but I also see a good-looking woman.'

'Thank you,' she said, smiling contentedly and snuggling deeper into the chair, in a way that made Arnie uneasy. She was beginning to look so settled.

He looked meaningfully at his watch. 'Anyway, enough of all that. It's time I took you home,' he told her, suddenly aware that things could easily get out of control. 'We both have to be up early for work in the morning.'

'I don't have to go home,' she said. 'I'm quite willing to stay the night.'

'No, Carol!'

'But surely you don't want to go out in the cold to drive me home?'

'I don't mind,' he said, rising.

'I'd like to stay . . .'

'I'll get your coat.'

'Please Arnie,' she said, unashamedly coaxing him now. 'I'd really like to stay.'

'And I want you to go.'

'You don't mean that,' she said determinedly. 'You're just saying it because you think you ought to be a gentleman.'

In reply he marched into the hall and got her coat from the hook. 'Here, put this on,' he said, holding it out for her.

'Why can't I stay?'

'Because I can do without those sort of complications,' he said firmly. 'Now put on your coat and let's be on our way . . . please!'

With great reluctance she did as he asked, and they drove through the cold winter streets in silence.

'I'm sorry to have upset you, Arnie,' she said as they turned into Maisie Road, afraid that she had ruined her chances altogether by being too eager.

'Don't apologise,' he said. 'It's my fault for being so naive. There's obviously been some sort of a misunderstanding.'

Carol was disappointed, but not deterred. 'Will I see you again?' she asked.

'Yeah, course you will, kid,' he said, making his tone casual.

'Don't call me kid.'

'I'll remember that in future.'

'So, when will I see you?'

'I'll give you a bell sometime.'

Which meant he had no intention of doing any such thing – but Carol wasn't prepared to give up. She'd grovel if she had to.

'Don't be cold towards me, please, Arnie,' she said, injecting a sob into her voice. 'I didn't mean any harm. I only wanted to be there for you 'cause I know you're lonely.'

He drew up outside her house and turned to her, his heart turning over to see how forlorn she looked sitting there with her hands in her lap, her head lowered.

'Hey, come on, there's nothing to cry about,' he said, slipping a friendly arm around her shoulders. 'It's no big deal.'

'You must know that I've always thought a lot of you,' she said, turning to him so that even in the dim glow of the street-lights he could see tears glistening in her eyes.

'And I like you too,' he said, choosing his words carefully.

'But you don't fancy me?'

'It isn't a question of that,' he assured her, curbing his impatience because of her sensitive nature. He knew he must be gentle with her.

'Why didn't you want me to stay then?' she sniffed.

'I've told you . . . because it'll complicate everything,' he said, moving away from her. 'I'd prefer things to stay as they are between us. I like it the way it is with us being mates.'

'Oh,' she said, making a show of her disappointment to try to win him over. 'God, I feel so humiliated.'

'There's no need.' He leaned towards her again in a gesture of kindness. 'This is me – Arnie, who you've known for ever. You don't have to feel that way because of me.'

'Don't I?' she mumbled, sounding pathetic but quietly working out her next move.

'Of course you don't. Because we're good friends, Carol. But let's just leave it at that, shall we?'

She had no intention whatsoever of settling for friendship, but she said in a compliant manner, 'Okay, if that's what you want . . .'

He took a handkerchief from his pocket and gently dabbed her eyes. 'That's better,' he said softly.

'Thanks.'

'Thanks for coming over tonight,' he said. 'I enjoyed your company.'

She reached for the door handle. 'I'll see you soon then, yeah?' she said hopefully.

'Yeah.'

It would be soon, too, because she was going to make an absolute point of it. She would do anything to get him, *anything* at all.

'Night, then.'

'Night, Carol.'

Driving back to Hammersmith, Arnie regretted the fact that things had got complicated with Carol. It would be all too easy to have a fling with her. He was lonely, and she was willing. But he would never forgive himself if he took advantage of Gill's sister, who had already been driven to the brink of a nervous breakdown because of a love affair. Hurting Carol would be like betraying Gill's trust, and he'd done quite enough of that already.

He would have to tread carefully with Carol in future, though. He didn't want to hurt her, but neither did he want to have an affair with her. The sensible thing would be not to see her at all. But he had a horrible suspicion that it wasn't going to be as simple as that.

Ah well, another day tomorrow, he thought, letting himself into his flat and feeling its stillness close around him for the second time that day. It was even more depressing this time, too, after the recent warmth of company.

Mary Bex called on Gill at home one morning unexpectedly.

'I was practically passing the end of your road on my way back from the accountant's office, so I thought I'd come and scrounge a cup of coffee.'

'I'm glad you did,' said Gill, filling the kettle and plugging it in while Mary sat down at the kitchen table. 'It's nice to see you, and it'll give me an excuse to take a break. I'm catching up on my paperwork . . . piles of the stuff.'

'Even piano teachers have to do that, then?' asked Mary.

'Of course,' said Gill, spooning coffee into the mugs. 'As well as keeping my books up to date for the Inland Revenue, there's all the administration for the exam entries and pupils who are entering for competitions to be dealt with too.'

'It's obvious that you would have office-work to do, the same as anyone else in business,' Mary said, 'but for some reason I never associate musicians with anything as mundane as paperwork.'

'If I only had a few pupils I might not have to bother, but as I run it as a business I have to keep things in order.'

'Mm.'

'I enjoy having a busy schedule, though – which is just as well as it pays our keep.'

'How's Craig?'

'Full of beans,' said Gill. 'And still football mad.'

169

'Yes, so Arnie was saying in the shop the other day. He's really tickled about it, isn't he?'

Gill nodded. 'I think he's hoping to relive his glory days through his son,' she said, putting a plate of biscuits and two mugs of coffee on the table before sitting down opposite her friend.

Something about her tone of voice made Mary say, 'You haven't changed your mind about Craig becoming a footballer, then?'

'Definitely not.'

'I can see you and Arnie fighting that one out,' said Mary.

'So what's new about us two fighting?' Gill grinned.

Mary laughed. She had made it plain at the time of the separation that she wouldn't take sides, since she was a good friend of Gill's as well as a colleague of Arnie's. 'If there wasn't an issue, you two would find one to argue about.'

'We're getting on better now we're not together, though.'

'Really?'

'Yes.'

'But how are things developing with the man from the music shop?'

'They're not,' Gill said. 'Not in the way you mean, anyway.'

'No romance yet then?'

'Sorry to disappoint you, but we're just friends.'

'I'm your friend, but I don't take you out for candlelit meals of an evening,' Mary said with a wicked grin.

'Neither does he.' Gill thought about this. 'Well, there are candles on the tables at an Italian place we go to sometimes, but it's purely coincidental. Anyway, I always insist on paying my share.'

'So that there's no misunderstanding, eh?' said Mary.

'Something like that.' Gill paused. 'I've grown to like Peter a lot, though, and I enjoy his company. I'd miss him if he disappeared off the scene now. He's such a dear and very easy to talk to. He's certainly easier to be with than Arnie ever was, and we have more in common.'

'Music?'

'Mainly that,' she said, 'then of course there's the fact that we're both victims of a broken marriage.'

'You and Arnie have that in common too,' teased Mary.

'Oh, very droll.' Gill laughed.

'Well, I still think it's a heck of a shame about you two,' said Mary. 'You were so right for each other, somehow.'

'So much so that we couldn't say a civil word to each other when we were together.'

'I know.' Mary sighed.

They moved on to other things, touching briefly on the new random roadside breathalyser test that was soon to be introduced for drivers.

'It isn't a bad thing,' said Mary. 'Though I doubt if Len will agree. He'll say it's an infringement of liberty.'

'That would probably be Arnie's response to it too,' said Gill.

'Typical male reaction,' Mary said. 'And only because they don't want to have to watch how much they have, when they pop into the pub for a "quick one" and want to drive home afterwards.' She paused. 'And talking of driving, it's time I was off.'

'Are you going back to the shop?' Gill asked at the front door.

'Yes. Better do a bit to earn my keep.' Mary looked at her watch. 'Gosh, is that the time? Len will be wondering where I've got to.'

'Shall I ring him to let him know you're on your way?'

'There's no need . . . it won't take me long to get there in the car.'

'Well, thanks for calling in,' said Gill, giving her friend a hug. 'It's always nice to see you.'

'You too. We'll have to go out for a meal together one of these nights,' Mary suggested casually. 'When Len's out on one of his men-only dos, we could have a girls' night out.'

'That would be smashing.'

'But in the mean time, it's back to the grind for us both . . .'

Gill stood at the front door waiting for Mary to walk through the doorway. But nothing happened. Gill turned to her, instantly realising that her friend was ill. Her face was feverishly bright and beaded with perspiration. Even as Gill watched, her skin became ashen.

'Mary? What's the matter?'

'I've come over a bit queer all of a sudden,' she said in a whisper, eyes rolling, body swaying.

'Come back inside and sit down,' Gill suggested, feeling some concern.

'It's nothing, just one of my funny turns . . . I do get them from time to time, but . . . Oh, I think I'm gonna pass out . . .' Her body crumpled and she slumped against Gill, who eased her gently to the floor.

On her knees, Gill leant over her, speaking in a soothing voice. 'It's all right,' she said softly, smoothing her hand over Mary's damp brow. 'I'll get a doctor, you'll be fine.'

'There's no need. I'll be all right in a minute,' Mary said weakly.

'Okay. Whatever you want . . . but don't upset yourself.'

'Len . . .' Mary said feebly.

'I'll give him a ring.'

'Please get him,' she said, just before her body went limp and she closed her eyes.

Terrified but still managing to stay in control, Gill realised that this was more serious than just a fainting fit. With great relief, she found a pulse.

Mary's eyelids began to flicker and she opened her eyes. 'Len,' she said again.

'Don't worry,' said Gill, 'I'll ring him right away.'

171

'Thanks.' Mary's lids flickered then closed again as she sank into unconsciousness.

'Oh my God,' gasped Gill. She rushed to the telephone and rang for an ambulance, her heart beating so fast she thought it would explode.

Len and Arnie were talking business in the shop with the sales rep from a sports-shoe company when the telephone rang. As the manager of the shop, Arnie had authority to order stock from any of the reps without referring to Len or Mary. But if Len was around and not too busy when one of them called, he usually took part in the discussion, especially if it was a new company coming into the market and he wanted to know more about them.

'I'll answer it,' said Phoebe, who was at the counter but not actually serving anyone at that moment.

'Thanks, Mum,' said Arnie.

She went into Arnie's small glass-fronted office at the back of the shop to take the call. When she emerged a few minutes later, pale and trembling, she walked over to Len on legs of jelly.

'Can you tell whoever it is that I'll ring them back later, please, dear?' Len said. 'I'm tied up at the moment—'

'It was Gill,' Phoebe sounded dazed. 'She's at the hospital.'

'Gill's at the hospital?' Arnie gasped in an immediate panic. 'What's happened to her? Has she had an accident? Oh my God . . .'

Phoebe put a steadying hand on his arm. 'Calm down, now, son,' she said firmly. 'It isn't Gill.'

'It isn't . . .' Arnie's voice was suddenly light with relief. 'So, who . . . ?'

Phoebe looked gravely at Len. 'It's Mary,' she said. 'I'm afraid she's been taken ill.'

Len's face was brightly suffused for a moment, then became bloodless. Phoebe thought he was going to pass out cold. But he said in a breathless voice, 'Which hospital?'

'Hammersmith.'

Even as she said the word he was already hurrying to the shop door.

'You'd better go with him, Mum,' Arnie suggested wisely. 'He needs someone and I have to look after things here.'

Without even stopping to get her coat she tore after him, catching him up at his Jaguar, which was parked in his regular place in a side street. Len didn't argue about her going with him to the hospital, he just opened the passenger door for her to get into the car. He was about to drive away when Arnie came tearing towards them, carrying their coats.

'You'll freeze to death without these in this weather,' he said. 'We don't want you in hospital an' all.'

'Thanks, son,' Phoebe said, taking the coats from him. 'That was thoughtful of you.'

172

'I feel terrible about this, but I'll have to go in a minute,' Gill said to Phoebe that afternoon. 'As much as I'd like to stay, I have to collect Craig from school.'

Phoebe nodded.

'I would ring my mum and ask her to collect him, but she's gone to Essex to see her sister for the day.'

'You go, love,' Phoebe urged her. 'I'll stay with Len.'

They were still at the hospital, in the waiting area outside the ward where Mary lay in a coma having suffered a massive heart attack. The doctors said her condition was critical. Len was with her now – Gill and Phoebe had left him to be alone with his wife. They were both in a state of shock.

'I feel awful about leaving while Mary's so ill,' Gill said.

'You have to look after your child,' Phoebe sensibly pointed out. 'Mary would hate to think you were neglecting your duties because of her. And I'll keep you informed about what's happening here. I'll get on the blower to you soon as there's any news.'

'Okay.' Gill paused and looked at the other woman with tears in her eyes. 'Oh, Phoebe, it's so terrible. Why Mary, of all people?'

'I dunno, love,' she said with a sad shake of the head. 'I really don't.'

'She was fine this morning,' Gill said. 'Then, bang, this happens, right out of the blue. No warning, nothing!'

'There, there,' said Phoebe, giving Gill a comforting hug. 'I'm not so sure that this was right out of the blue. I don't think she's been feeling herself for a long time, even though she wouldn't admit it.'

'Poor Mary.'

'Poor Len an' all,' said Phoebe worriedly. 'He's in a hell of a state.' She drew back. 'But off you go, love, or young Craig will be hanging about waiting for you at the school gate.'

Soon after Gill had left, Len emerged unsteadily from the ward with a nurse holding his arm. Phoebe could tell by the stricken look on his face that the worst had happened. The nurse took Phoebe to one side and confirmed this, asking if she was a member of Mr Bex's family. Len stood silently by, looking stunned and showing no curiosity as to what they were talking about. The poor man seemed to be in a world of his own.

'I'm a friend of the family,' Phoebe explained to the nurse.

'Mr Bex is in a bad way. We had to drag him away from his wife after she'd slipped away,' she explained sadly.

'How sad.'

'He's in shock.'

'The poor dear.'

'He says there are no children to be with him at this sad time.'

'No.'

The nurse looked worried. 'It isn't a good idea for him to be on his own at the moment,' she said.

'Don't worry, nurse, I'll look after him,' said Phoebe.

'Thank you,' said the nurse, with obvious relief. 'I'll go and see if I can get you both some tea.'

Phoebe turned to Len, saw the pain in his eyes. His face was almost the same colour as his hair, his eyes bloodshot and vacant. Her own aching grief for Mary had to take second place to her concern for him.

'Come on, Len,' she said softly, taking his arm. 'Let's go and find somewhere comfortable to sit while the nurse gets us some tea.'

Normally a man of robust self-confidence, always in control and at the centre of things, now he allowed her to lead him away like a mother leading her child.

Chapter Fourteen

The crowd that came to pay their last respects to Mary was a testimony to her popularity. Their numbers spread far and wide in the cemetery on that bitter cold February day, as a piercing wind howled through the gravestones beneath angry grey skies that threatened snow.

Standing near to the graveside, the ground hard and slippery underfoot, it occurred to Gill that she had never heard anyone say a bad word about Mary in all the time she'd known her. Quite an achievement for someone involved in business and likely, therefore, to make enemies.

Glancing across at Len, standing between Phoebe and Arnie, Gill couldn't get over how much he had changed in such a short time. Usually so vigorous and sure of himself, he looked now like an emaciated old man, faltering both in speech and movement. It was heartbreaking to see him like this.

Afterwards, when the mourners were gathered at Len's house in Putney, Gill, Phoebe and Arnie hosted the party, as Len was too frail and tearful to take charge of the occasion. Gill and Phoebe had prepared a light buffet, and Arnie was in charge of the drinks.

'God knows how he's going to manage without her,' Gill remarked to Arnie in a quiet moment when the guests were all attended to.

'I've been thinking about that too.'

'Len was always the one with all the front, but I got the idea that Mary was the source of his strength in her quiet, homely way.'

'I shouldn't be at all surprised,' Arnie said.

'He just seems to have fallen apart.'

'Yeah. Poor bloke.' Arnie sighed and shook his head. 'He doesn't even have any kids to turn to for comfort.'

'He doesn't seem to have any close relatives either.'

'No. I reckon he and Mary were so complete in themselves, they didn't need anyone else.' Arnie looked across the room at Len who was standing by the window with a glass of whisky in his hand, puffing on a cigarette. Phoebe was trying to coax him into taking a sandwich from the plate she was offering but he was shaking his head. He'd eaten practically nothing this past week.

'And I suppose they drifted away from relatives over the years because of that,' Gill said.

'Now, when he needs someone, there's no family to turn to.'

175

She nodded sadly. 'Your mother's been wonderful to him, though,' she said.

'Yeah,' he agreed. 'I don't know what he'd have done without her to be perfectly honest.'

'I don't either.'

He threw Gill a look. 'But how are you coping with it?' he asked. 'Her death must have come as a blow to you. I know what good friends you were.'

'I'm still numb,' she confessed. 'I don't think it's really sunk in yet.'

'It's shaken me up an' all.'

'Something like this certainly puts things into perspective, doesn't it?' she said. 'Makes you realise that life's too short to waste time worrying about trivialities.'

'I'll say.' Arnie sighed. 'We'll all still do it, though, won't we – when the shock of her death has worn off?'

'Very probably,' she agreed chattily. 'We'll soon forget how frighteningly aware we were made of our own mortality.'

'I've had no end of funny pains since it happened.'

'Me too,' she said, smiling. 'The most harmless of twinges have been heart attacks in the making this past few days.'

He laughed. Drawn together by adversity, the atmosphere between them was warm. Neither Peter nor Carol was mentioned.

'So, what's happening in the office without Mary?' asked Gill.

'I've had to get a temp in, someone who can do a bit of everything,' he said. 'Mum's doing what she can to help but she isn't trained for office-work.'

'She's very quick on the uptake, though. She'd soon pick it up,' Gill said.

'Yes, she would – especially as there's hardly any typing to do.' Arnie paused. 'But we need someone who's familiar with the PAYE system because of the staff wages.'

'You'll get someone permanent to replace Mary once the dust settles, will you?'

'I suppose we'll have to, but that will be Len's decision. And he has no interest in the shops whatsoever at the moment. He's told me to do whatever I think best and not bother him about business.'

'So everything's been left to you?'

'That's right. And because the overall administration is done in the office above our shop, the responsibility for all the branches seems to have fallen into my lap,' he told her. 'Not that I mind. I'm only too happy to do what I can to help. But at the end of the day it is Len's business – and I don't want to do anything he might not approve of later, when he's feeling better.'

'It's a big responsibility.'

'Not half.'

'But now the funeral's over he'll gradually begin to take an interest again, I should think,' Gill said encouragingly. 'It might take a bit of time, though.'

'It isn't gonna happen overnight, that's for sure.' Arnie stared into space, an impressive figure in a dark suit and black tie. He looked exhausted though, tension pulling tight around his eyes. 'Poor old Len. He's been knocked sideways. I only wish there was something I could do to make him feel better.'

'All any of us can do is be there for him,' Gill said.

'Yeah.'

Suddenly the atmosphere between them became highly charged. Their eyes met and they both looked away quickly. Arnie glanced at his watch in hope of restoring normality. 'Time certainly goes on, doesn't it?' he said unneccessarily.

'It sure does.'

'Would you like me to collect Craig from school today?' he offered. 'If you want to hang on here for a while?'

'Thanks, but I've already made arrangements,' she said. 'My mum's collecting him today because I wasn't sure what time I would be back. I shall stay on here to help Phoebe clear up.'

'Are you teaching?'

'No, I cancelled everything for today,' she told him.

He fell silent. Gill's heart raced as she thought he was going to suggest that he come over to the house later on, so that they could be together at this sad time. She viewed the idea with a certain trepidation because, as much as she wanted to be with him, she knew it would be a bad idea. There was no point inflaming old passions just because they were both at a low ebb in the aftermath of Mary's death – it would be too painful later.

'It was probably the best idea,' Arnie said to stop the conversation from flagging. 'I shall have to go back to work soon, though. It isn't fair to leave the staff on their own for too long.'

For all her common sense, Gill ached with disappointment that he hadn't suggested they get together later. Today she needed him more than ever before. 'You're quite the dedicated businessman these days,' she said lightly.

'I have to be,' he said. 'If I don't apply myself to the job I won't last long as manager.'

'No.'

'But I like the work anyway, so it isn't a problem.'

'Good.'

Feeling dangerously emotional, Gill knew she must distance herself from him before instinct took over and she suggested something she would later regret. 'Well, I'd better take the sandwiches around again,' she said. 'Or we'll end up giving them to the birds.'

'See you, then.'

'Yes.'

For some reason the light tone of their conversation seemed to put a seal on the end of their marriage. It was as though they had now reached the stage where they could converse in the detached way of strangers at a party, and part with an equal lack of feeling.

The latter was just an illusion, though. There was no lack of feeling – not on Gill's part, anyway.

When she got to her mother's to collect Craig that evening, having helped Phoebe clear up at Len's place and left her to keep him company, Gill was imbued with sadness. For the first time since it had happened, the implications of Mary's death really came home to her. Now that the horror of her passing was over, Gill had to face the dull reality of her friend not being around any more. She missed her already.

'Are you staying to eat with us?' asked Winnie, who was seated at the table with Hal, Carol and Craig when Gill arrived. 'You'll have to wait for Craig to finish anyway.'

'Just a cup of tea for me, thanks, Mum.' Gill sat down and poured herself a cup from the large pot on the table. 'I've been eating bits and pieces all afternoon at Len's place.'

'How is the poor man?'

'In a bad way.'

'Shame,' said Hal.

'He might start to pick up now that the funeral is over,' said Winnie. 'Once he gets back to work.'

'That's what I'm hoping,' said Gill.

'Awful for him,' said Hal. 'Especially having no family.'

'Phoebe is being very good to him, though,' said Gill.

I'll bet she is, Winnie couldn't help thinking. If she gets her claws into him and all his money she'll be set up for life. But she kept her uncharitable thoughts to herself to avoid a storm of protest from Hal and Gill.

'Who's actually running the business with Mary gone and Len in a state of shock?' Hal asked, forking a piece of meat pie.

'Arnie's in charge at the moment,' said Gill. 'The whole thing seems to have fallen on to his shoulders.'

'It's a lot of responsibility for him,' remarked Hal.

'That's what I said.'

'He doesn't mind, does he?' said Winnie.

'Oh no, he doesn't mind in the least,' said Gill proudly. 'But it's a lot of extra work and worry, with Len being out of the picture altogether.'

'Mm,' said her father.

'He couldn't even stay long at the funeral because of the pressure of work,' Gill continued. 'He went back to the shop quite early on and God knows what time he'll get home tonight.'

'He'll be worn out,' said Winnie.

'He certainly will,' said Gill. 'And, of course, he's quite cut up about Mary's death too. They did work together, after all.'

'Poor old Arnie,' said Carol, joining in the conversation with feigned compassion. It was as much as she could do not to show her delight, because the opportunity she had been waiting for had just presented itself – and she was going after it with everything she'd got.

Gill had a long soak in the bath after she'd put Craig to bed that night. Her muscles ached with the tension of the last week. As she began to unwind she felt hot, salty tears running down her wet cheeks: tears for the loss of a true friend, a woman who had still had so much to give. She lay there for a long time letting the sadness come, her tears mingling with the steamy bath water.

She had just dried herself and slipped into her dressing gown when the front doorbell rang.

'I hope it isn't someone enquiring about piano lessons at this hour,' she muttered to herself as she hurried downstairs. She wasn't expecting anyone but Peter sometimes called round unexpectedly.

'Peter,' she said looking pleased. 'How nice to see you! Come on in.'

'I thought you might need cheering up after what must have been a lousy day,' he said, handing her a bottle of wine. He glanced at her apparel. 'I hope you weren't just going to bed, though.'

'No, not this early,' she explained. 'I've just got out of the bath.'

'So, how was the funeral?'

'I'm very glad it's over.'

'I can imagine.'

She handed the wine back to him. 'Thanks for this,' she said. 'You go and do the honours while I slip upstairs and get dressed. You know where everything is.'

'Will do.'

Upstairs she put on a pair of jeans and a sweater. On the way back down she popped into Craig's room and pulled the covers up over his shoulders.

'Who's downstairs?' he asked, stirring.

'Uncle Peter.'

'What's he come for?'

'To keep me company.'

'Oh.' He sounded satisfied. He'd met Peter several times and seemed to get along with him. His eyes closed. 'Night, Mum.'

'Night, love.'

Downstairs, Peter had poured the wine and put some crisps into a dish.

'Oh, Peter, this is the first time I've felt remotely human since before

179

Mary died,' Gill said with a sigh of relief, sinking into an armchair by the fire opposite him. 'It was so thoughtful of you to come over.'

'I wanted to,' he said, looking at her over the rim of his wineglass. 'I want to be there for you whenever you need me.'

'Yes, I know,' she said softly, realising the extent of her affection for him. 'And I really appreciate it.'

'My pleasure.'

They chatted about things other than Mary's death; Gill had had enough morbidity for one day. Peter suggested that they take Cherry Betts to a concert sometime soon.

'What a lovely idea,' she said.

'I'll look out for something that won't be too heavy for her and get some tickets.'

'Thank you. She'll be thrilled,' Gill said, warming to him even more. 'We'll have to keep an eye out to see what's on.'

The evening passed quickly and all too soon Peter said he had to be going.

'Already?' she said, depressed at the thought of being alone. 'I could sit here talking to you for ever.'

'Me too,' he said, 'but I have to be up early for work tomorrow.'

She got his coat from the hall and held it out for him. He slipped into it and turned to her.

'Gill . . .' he began uncertainly. 'This probably isn't the time . . .'

'Probably not, but go on.'

'You must know how I feel about you,' he said hoarsely.

'I think I can guess,' she said with great tenderness.

Her need to be loved at that moment was overwhelming. The grief of losing a dear friend combined with the realisation that her marriage really was over culminated in a feeling of indescribable loneliness. She needed so much to be held, to be reminded that she was alive and not repulsive to the opposite sex.

She responded to his embrace instinctively. This was the first time she'd felt like a woman for a long time – far too long. Because of this she welcomed his arms around her and revelled in the throb of physical contact.

Vaguely aware of passing through an important turning point in her relationship with Peter that she had resisted for so long, she realised that somehow she didn't mind now.

Arnie was feeling like death when he finally got home from work on the night of Mary's funeral. He hadn't been as close to her as he was to Len, but he'd known her well enough to feel shock and sorrow at her passing. Mostly, though, his grief was for Len, who was a broken man.

That night Arnie's thoughts were also with Gill. He was aware of having let her down today in his attempt to behave honourably. Knowing she was feeling awful about her friend's death, he'd wanted to hold her in his arms and soothe away her pain. Instead he'd made small talk, because to follow his heart would be to hurt her even more in the long run. If he'd given in to his feelings he would have put them both on a roller-coaster back to hell.

Heartsick and tormented, he mooched into the kitchen and put the kettle on for coffee, then checked out the food situation. Baked beans on toast, he decided in the absence of a choice.

He'd just put some bread under the grill when the doorbell rang.

'Carol!'

'Hi, Arnie.'

'What are you doing here?'

'Don't go overboard with the welcome,' she said with mild sarcasm.

'Sorry.'

'And so you should be.'

'I wasn't expecting you,' he said, 'and I'm absolutely shattered.'

'Aren't you going to ask me in?'

He hesitated, chewing his lip anxiously. 'Actually, I'm not in the mood for company,' he said, knowing he was being bad-mannered but sensing danger in letting her over the threshold on this particular occasion. 'It's been one hell of a rotten day.'

'Yes, I know. That's why I'm here,' she explained.

'It's very nice of you to bother to come over, Carol,' he said patiently, 'but I'm really not feeling sociable. I'm gonna have something to eat and go straight to bed.'

'You shouldn't be on your own, not tonight,' she said.

'I think I ought to be the judge of that, don't you?'

'Look. There's no point in your trying to send me away,' she declared with an air of ruthless determination he hadn't seen in her before, 'because I simply won't go.'

'But—'

'You shut the door on me and I'll ring the doorbell again and again . . . I'll keep on doing it until you do let me in.'

'Why?'

'Because you need someone.'

'I don't, but come in anyway,' he said with an exasperated sigh, moving back so that she could step inside.

'Thank you.'

Taking off her coat, she hung it on the hook in the hall to reveal a tight black sweater worn with a mini skirt.

She sniffed. 'Something's burning,' she said.

'The toast,' he said, rushing to the kitchen to retrieve it.

She followed him into the kitchen and stood behind him while he scraped the blackened toast over the sink.

'I keep meaning to get a pop-up toaster,' he said in an effort to head

181

off the situation he suspected was about to develop.

'Do you?'

'Yes. Burnt toast has become the bane of my life since I've been living on my own.'

'You need someone to look after you, that's your trouble.'

'No I don't,' he protested. 'I manage well enough.'

Having decided that subtlety was not an option she could afford to consider in this instance, she slipped her arms around him from behind and pressed her face against his back, breathing deeply, her eyes closing with pleasure. She could feel the throb of his heartbeat through his sweater. God, how she wanted him.

'Leave the toast,' she said.

'I have to eat.'

'I know that, but—'

'Please stop playing games, Carol,' Arnie cut in irritably, trying to extricate himself from her by pulling away.

'This is no game.'

'I'm hungry and I want to have my supper,' he said as an excuse.

'You need me more than you need food at this precise moment,' she said blatantly.

'So you know more about what I need than I do?' he said.

'No. You know it too,' she said. 'So forget about your supper and I'll get us both something to eat later on.'

'But, Carol . . .' he said, his tone still admonishing but slightly less firm now.

'Don't pretend you don't need someone tonight, Arnie,' she said.

'I'm not pretending anything—'

'I think you are.'

'What makes you think that?'

'Because it's obvious after the sort of day you've had.'

'He didn't reply, but she could feel the resonance of his body as nature took over from his intellect.

'You're feeling rotten . . . you're as lonely as hell,' she continued.

As he turned slowly round to face her, the toast slipped from his trembling fingers into the washing-up bowl. 'Sure I'm lonely,' he said, struggling to stay in control.

'Well then . . .'

'But I'm not in the habit of using my friends just because I'm feeling a bit low,' he said. 'I'm not that degenerate.'

'Don't be so silly,' she said in a soothing whisper, stroking his face with her hands. 'That's what friends are for. That's what this friend is for anyway.'

'Carol . . . stop it,' he said. 'This has gone quite far enough.'

'I want to be with you, Arnie, to make you feel better,' she said softly, urgently. 'I want to make love to you.'

'No—'

'There'll be no strings attached,' she lied, 'I promise you.'

'For God's sake, Carol, this is madness,' he muttered thickly.

'If you're thinking about Gill you can forget her, because she's got someone else.'

'That makes no difference . . . This isn't right, not you and me,' he protested.

'It feels right enough to me,' she said in a strong voice tinged with jubilance. 'Very right indeed.'

And his biology couldn't argue with that. She felt warm and welcoming against him and it was so good and natural to have a woman close to him again after so long.

'Oh God,' he muttered.

The toast turned soggy in the bowl and the baked beans remained in the unopened can as he finally gave up the fight against Carol's relentless persistence.

Chapter Fifteen

'Oh, it's you,' said Len in a bellicose manner.

Arnie had called at his employer's house on a matter of business, having used his own lunch hour for the visit. 'Can I come in, mate?' he asked when it became clear that Len wasn't going to offer.

'Yeah, I s'pose you'd better,' was Len's gruff reply.

Arnie followed him into the lounge, the expensive furnishings barely noticeable beneath the muddle.

'Blimey!' Arnie exclaimed, almost choking on the smell of stale booze and cigarette smoke. Thick layers of dust covered everything, and were made more obvious by the shafts of sunlight beaming through the mucky windows. The room was littered with overflowing ashtrays, used teacups and crumpled newspapers.

'Is your cleaner on strike or something?'

'No.' Len's tone was contemptuous.

'But . . .' Arnie cast an indicative glance around the room.

'I've told her not to clean in here.' Len also looked grubby and unkempt. 'I don't want some strange woman coming in here and invading my privacy.'

The problem would be far more expediently solved if Len was out of the house during the day looking after his business instead of sitting about indoors feeling sorry for himself, Arnie thought, but he said, 'Oh, I see. It's a bit of tip though, innit, mate?'

Len shrugged as though he couldn't care less.

'Mary must be turning in her grave,' remarked Arnie.

The other man threw him a piercingly critical look, cheeks sunken in his lean face, eyes bloodshot and lacklustre. 'I've always thought that was a ridiculous saying,' he snapped. 'I mean, how the hell can someone disapprove of anything if they've passed on?'

'It's just a figure of speech,' said Arnie, trying to be tactful. 'To remind us of the sort of person they were.'

'I know exactly what it means, thank you very much,' Len barked. 'And I don't want to hear you saying it again.'

'Okay, boss,' Arnie sat down and opened his briefcase. 'No offence meant.'

'That's all right then,' Len growled.

'I've just come over with the wages cheque for you to sign and one or two queries I need to discuss with you.'

185

'Do you wanna drink?' offered Len.

'Yes, please. I'll have a small beer if you've got one,' said Arnie, taking the papers relating to the staff wages from his briefcase.

'I don't have any beer.' Len picked his way over to a drinks cabinet. 'Will whisky do?'

'Not for me, thanks,' said Arnie. 'I've a lot to do this afternoon and whisky will send me to sleep.' He looked at his watch. 'I don't really have time for a drink, anyway.' He got up and handed some papers to Len. 'So if you could just check the figures and sign the cheque . . .'

Len signed the cheque but didn't bother to check the figures on the wages sheet. He finished his drink, immediately poured another, and settled back in his armchair.

'Everyone at the firm is wondering when you'll be coming back to work,' said Arnie pointedly. 'It's four months since—'

'I know how long it's been, and I'll come back when I'm ready.'

'Fair enough.' Arnie put the papers back into the briefcase and took out a wholesaler's catalogue of sportsgear, which he handed to Len.

'What do you want me to do with this?' Len asked in a disgruntled manner.

'We've been offered a special deal on cricket gear by this firm,' Arnie explained. 'I thought you might like to have a look through it to see what they have to offer.'

'I'm not bothered.'

'Oh!' Arnie paused, silently counting to ten. 'Well, they're offering us such good rates, I was thinking of putting some stuff on sale at reduced prices.'

'This early in the season?' said Len scathingly. 'You must be joking!'

'It isn't early in terms of trade though, is it?' Arnie was worried by Len's reaction to his suggestion; to him it illustrated just how out of touch with the business he had become. 'Most of the clubs already have everything they need for this year.'

'Yeah, yeah,' said Len, losing interest. 'You do whatever you think best.'

'Okay.'

'So is that it, then?' Len asked, keen to be alone again with his grief.

'There's just one other thing I'd like to discuss with you,' Arnie ventured.

'What is it?' Len enquired with rising impatience.

'My mother has been helping out in the office, and she seems to be getting the hang of things really well under the guidance of the temp we're using from the agency. She even seems to have come to grips with the PAYE system, which means she could cope with the staff wages if necessary . . .'

'So?'

'I was wondering if it might be a good idea to move her into the office permanently when the temp has trained her up properly,' said Arnie. 'Mum's only a two-finger typist but there's hardly any typing to do anyway.'

'Who'll cover for your mother in the shop?' Len asked in a perfunctory manner.

'We'd have to get someone to replace her, of course. But I thought . . . rather than have a stranger working with you in the office when you come back to work, you might prefer someone you already know.'

Len couldn't even bear to think about the office without his darling Mary in it. 'If you think that's the best thing then go ahead and do it,' he said sharply. 'Don't bother me with every little detail.'

Hardly a little detail, Arnie thought. 'There's no need to bite my head off, mate. I'm doing my best.'

'Yeah, yeah, I know,' Len said, with a glimmer of remorse. 'You're managing okay, though, aren't you?'

'Yes, I'm managing.' Indeed, Arnie had amazed himself by coping with the responsibility for the entire Bex chain in Len's absence. A few years ago he wouldn't have believed himself capable.

Len looked at him through narrowed eyes, as though seeing him through mist. 'Well carry on doing it then,' he said miserably, 'and leave me alone.'

'Fair enough, boss.' Arnie gathered the rest of his papers and put them into the briefcase. 'I'd better be getting back to work. Don't come to the door, I'll see myself out.'

'Cheers,' said Len absently, sinking back into his own personal sorrow without noticing how worried Arnie had looked when he left.

'The man has become completely impossible,' Arnie complained to Gill one Sunday evening a few weeks later; he had just brought Craig back from a trip to Chessington Zoo. 'I've never known anyone change so much as Len has. He's like a stranger . . . and so damned aggressive.'

'That's what grief does to people,' Gill said with a sad shake of the head. 'His life, as it used to be, has been completely demolished, and he just can't cope with it.'

'I'm worried sick about him.'

Arnie had sat down at the kitchen table while they'd been talking. Gill looked at him. 'Fancy a cup of tea?'

'Please,' he said in a preoccupied manner because he was still thinking about Len.

She put the kettle on and went to the larder for the tea-caddy. It constantly surprised her to find how well she and Arnie got along these days. She'd thought that now they were both seeing someone else there'd have been awkwardness. But it seemed to have eased the tension between them even more. It was strange!

'He's lost in a world of his own,' Arnie continued. 'He doesn't seem to give a damn about anyone or anything. And he's lost interest in his business altogether.'

'That isn't like Len.'

'It isn't,' he agreed. 'I'm beginning to think that Mary really was the driving force behind it all. As you said – she was quiet and homely, and he appeared to be the stronger of the two, but he must have been heavily reliant on her.'

Gill nodded. 'So, what does he do all day if he doesn't go to work?' she asked.

'Sits at home chain-smoking and boozing, from what I can gather.'

'While you're rushed off your feet running his business?'

'I honestly don't mind that,' said Arnie emphatically. 'I want to do whatever I can to help.' He shook his head gravely. 'But Len means a lot to me, and I don't know what's gonna become of him. I mean, he isn't going to come to terms with Mary's death and rebuild his life this way, is he? He'll just get more and more miserable and out of touch with things.'

'Mm.' Gill brought the teapot to the table. 'Len has always struck me as a man who needs to be at the centre of things, not stuck at home alone.'

'Exactly. And the only way he's ever going to get back on his feet again is to come back to work. But if I so much as hint at that he hits the roof.'

Gill pondered the problem as she poured tea. 'Well, Arnie, I think you are just going to have to give Len a dose of his own medicine.'

'What do you mean?'

'Do you remember when you resigned from the job – when you found out I'd been to see Len – and he got tough with you?'

Arnie nodded.

'Well, it worked for you, didn't it?' Gill said. 'You went back to work.'

'Hmmm.' Arnie was thoughtful. 'You're forgetting one important detail, though . . .'

'I am?'

'Yeah – he's the boss,' he reminded her. 'If I start getting stroppy with him I could find myself out of work.'

'You do have a point,' she said, putting a mug of tea down in front of him and sitting down. 'But there are times in life when you have to take a personal risk for the benefit of someone else. I believe that this is one of those times.'

'And what do I do if he fires me?' Arnie asked with a wry grin.

'Get another job.'

'Just like that?'

'Yes. You're an experienced retail manager now,' she reminded him.

'You shouldn't have too much trouble finding something suitable.'

'I suppose not.'

'But I don't think it'll come to that, anyway.'

'I'll be round here with murder in mind if it does,' he joked. 'I like working for Len and I don't want to change my job.'

'I've got Craig to protect me,' she said with a giggle.

And suddenly they were both laughing at the sheer idiocy of the conversation, as they had done in their halcyon days. It felt so wonderfully exhilarating to have a rapport with Arnie again.

Wondering what was causing the hilarity, Craig appeared from the other room. 'What are you two laughing at?' he asked with a half smile.

'Nothing that you would find funny, son,' said Arnie.

'Just your dad being daft,' Gill said, exchanging a glance with Arnie.

If only we could have got on like this when we were together, she thought wistfully.

Smoking a cigarette in his armchair, Len glowered at Arnie. He didn't appreciate having home truths frankly spelled out to him. 'You've got a nerve, coming round here telling me what I ought to be doing!' he roared. '*You* work for *me*, remember, not the other way around.'

Arnie could have pointed out to him that he was currently doing the job of a managing director on the salary of a branch manager, but he didn't want to kick a man when he was down. 'I'm well aware of that, Len,' he replied. 'But that doesn't mean I don't worry about what happens to you.'

'Staff don't worry about the boss . . . that isn't the way it works,' Len said. 'Anyway, I'm quite capable of looking after myself.'

'It doesn't look that way from where I'm sitting.' Arnie cast a disapproving eye over Len's scruffy appearance before letting it wander over the untidy room.

'Meaning?'

'You're a bloody mess,' Arnie declared, determined to stand his ground for Len's sake no matter how angry the man became. 'And you have been ever since Mary died. It's high time you pulled yourself together and came back to work.'

'Shut it!'

'Sorry if the truth hurts, mate,' Arnie replied, undaunted, 'but someone needs to give it to you straight now that Mary isn't here to do it.'

Seeing the other man wince, Arnie was filled with compassion. But if Len was to come through this trauma and take up his life again, certain things had to be said. Arnie would be as brutal as he considered necessary.

'I've told you not to mention Mary's death,' Len said crossly.

'It happened, Len. Mary died several months ago and now life goes on, however much you want it to be otherwise. I realise that you're missing her something awful, but you have to get out there and face up to things without her now. Shutting yourself away from the world isn't going to solve anything.'

'I haven't shut myself away.'

'That's what it seems like to me.'

'I go out . . .'

'Yeah, to the pub and the off-licence to get your fags and booze,' Arnie said harshly. 'But I can count the times you've been into the office since Mary died on one hand. And on the odd occasion that you have shown your face you couldn't get away quick enough.' He paused. 'Don't get me wrong, boss, I'm quite happy to run things for you and to come out here to your house to get cheques signed and queries answered for as long as you want me to. But when it comes to the crunch, it's your business and not mine. You're the guvnor, and you need to be there in the thick of it, to keep abreast with what's going on.'

'I'm glad you've remembered that I'm the guvnor . . .' Len puffed at a cigarette. 'Because you're fired.'

'What!'

'You heard,' Len said, erupting into a fit of coughing.

'Isn't that a bit unfair?' suggested Arnie, brows raised.

Len ignored the question. 'I don't know what makes you think you have the right to come round here telling me how to run my life,' he said. 'But I'm not gonna to put up with it, so I'm sacking you and putting an end to it. You're finished with this company as from this minute.'

Although Arnie had known he was putting his job at risk by speaking out, this was still a blow. He enjoyed working at Bex Sports, thought the world of Len, and didn't want to work anywhere else. No doubt if he apologised and grovelled a bit Len would eventually reconsider. But that would be tantamount to condoning his behaviour, and Arnie wasn't prepared to do that. He'd sooner look for another job.

'If that's how you feel, then fair enough.' Arnie decided not to press the fact that a week's notice on either side was clearly stated in the terms of his employment. If he had to leave, the sooner he went the better. 'I'll go back to the shop and clear my stuff out.'

'Yeah, you do that,' said Len.

The house felt achingly quiet after Arnie had left. Shaky from the reaction of the argument – because he was fond of Arnie and had thought of him as a mate until now – Len lit another cigarette and sunk back in his chair, deep in thought.

Arnie had got too big for his boots. Who did he think he was – coming round here throwing his weight about? He'd do well to remember that he'd been unemployed and wallowing in self-pity himself when Len had first met him. Len recalled a time when he'd had to be heavy with the truth to him. And here he was telling the guvnor what to do, the cheeky bugger.

Just because he'd done well in the job and become an asset to the firm, he'd got above himself. Well, Bex Sports was well rid of someone who thought they were God's gift just because they'd been running the show for a while.

Running the show! Arnie had been running the whole damned shooting match!

For the first time since Mary's death, the fog in Len's mind cleared sufficiently for him to realise the position Arnie had been in these last few months. He'd been in sole control of a high-turnover business, looking after the needs of all the other managers as well as running his own branch. The man must have been working all hours to keep on top of things . . . and all for no extra money!

A lesser man might have used the situation for his own ends – to go on the fiddle without the beady eye of the guvnor about – but all Arnie seemed to want was Len back at work.

Smarting with his conscience, Len cast a wary eye around the room, forcing himself to see the dust and smell the foul air. He got up and flung open all the windows, noticing the garden bathed in sunshine and wanting to cry because Mary wasn't here to share it with him.

Moving away from the window, he caught sight of himself in the mirror above the fireplace. Blimey, what a sight! Arnie was right – he was a mess.

He went into the hall to the telephone and phoned the office.

'Hello, Phoebe,' he said.

'Wotcha, Len,' she replied, sounding pleased to hear his voice. 'How are you?'

'Not so dusty.'

'I'm pleased to hear that.'

'Look . . . er, Arnie is on his way back to the shop.' He cleared his throat. 'We've had a few cross words to tell you the truth. But can you tell him not to go anywhere until I get there?'

'You're coming into the office?' she said, sounding even more delighted.

'Yeah.'

'That *is* good news,' she enthused. 'Everyone here will be so pleased to see you.'

Moved by her warmth, tears burned beneath Len's eyelids. 'I'll be there soon,' he said, adding silently, just as soon as I've cleaned myself up.

'So he sacked you and reinstated you, all on the same day?' said Gill. It

191

was the following evening, and Arnie had come to collect Craig to take him to see a midweek, out-of-season football match.

'All within a couple of hours, actually,' said Arnie.

'Even better.'

'And that isn't all . . .'

'No?'

'He's made me a partner in the business.'

'Oh, Arnie, that's wonderful!' Gill gave him a beaming smile. 'Fancy it coming out of the blue like that.'

'Len said that my looking after things while he was away has made him realise how valuable I am to the firm,' he explained.

'That *really* is something,' she said. 'Congratulations!'

'Thanks.'

They had been chatting in the kitchen, but now they wandered into the living room where Carol was ensconced on the sofa looking through a women's magazine, having come to spend the evening with Gill.

'Arnie's been made a partner in Bex Sports, Carol.' She paused thoughtfully. 'But I expect you already know about it.'

'No, I didn't know,' she said, scowling.

'Oh,' said Gill, feeling suddenly awkward.

'It only happened yesterday,' Arnie said rather sheepishly, as though he needed to justify himself to Carol for not telling her first.

'Well, anyway, it's terrific news, isn't it?' said Gill.

'Yeah, great,' Carol said flatly.

'It's good about Len going back to work too,' said Gill, looking at Arnie.

'And all thanks to you,' said Arnie with a warm smile.

'Me?'

'It was you who suggested I take a hard line with him,' he said.

'So I did,' she said, adding jokingly, 'I'll have my fee in hard cash, please.'

They were both laughing when Craig entered the room dressed in a replica strip of Arnie's old football club.

'All set, son?' Arnie asked.

'Yes, Dad.'

'Right. Let's be on our way then or we'll miss the kick off.' He looked at Carol. 'See you soon. I'll give you a bell.'

'Okay,' said Carol moodily, turning her attention back to her magazine.

Gill went out to the car with Arnie and Craig. It was a fine summer's evening, the scent of garden flowers faintly perceptible above the urban dust and traffic fumes that drifted from the busy main roads and lingered in this quiet street of traditional houses, their tiny front gardens fringed in places with privet hedges.

'Have a good time then, fellas,' said Gill. 'And don't get too rowdy.'

'As if we would,' said Arnie with irony, ruffling Craig's hair affectionately and exchanging a conspiratorial look with him.

The boy grinned knowingly at his father who opened the car door for
him.

'Just as well I'm not coming with you, for your sakes,' said Gill,
remembering a time when the three of them had done things together as
a family. 'I'd make you behave.'

Arnie gave her a slow grin, as though he was sharing her thoughts.
'See you later,' he said through the car window as he turned the key.
'Shan't be late back.'

'Okay.'

Gill stood at the gate waving until they had turned the corner out of
sight. Overcome by a current of bitter-sweet emotion, she composed
herself before going inside to face Carol.

Watching this happy family scene from the window, Carol was aflame
with jealousy. Gill and Arnie shared something that she could never
be a part of – their child. They were also getting to be very chummy
lately, she'd noticed. Could it be that Arnie was still in love with Gill
after all that had happened? The thought struck fear into her heart.
The way Arnie looked at her sister often made Carol feel quite ill
with worry.

Although Carol was seeing Arnie on a regular basis, he was very
casual about their meetings and the initiative was still almost entirely
hers. He seemed to have taken her literally when she'd told him there
would be no strings attached. She'd hoped to have extracted some sort
of commitment from him by now. In fact, she had expected him to ask
her to move in with him. She'd thought there would be talk of his
getting a divorce from Gill so that he could marry her.

But even though she and Arnie got on well together and were now
lovers, she was conscious of a definite holding back on his part.
Although she didn't often allow herself to admit the depressing truth,
she knew in her heart that he didn't feel the same about her as she felt
about him. In fact, if she was brutally honest, she knew that their
relationship would never have gone beyond friendship if she hadn't
seduced him into it when he was at a low ebb.

Even now she always made the first move in that direction. But,
determined as she was to have him, she didn't see these things as a
deterrent, and was still convinced that he would grow to love her in
time if she persisted.

Then he would be truly happy, because she loved him deeply and
wanted nothing more than to devote her life to him. One thing she did
know for certain, she wasn't going to give up. She would be his wife
one day or die in the attempt.

Meanwhile, the frustration of not making headway as quickly as she'd hoped was beginning to take its toll on her.

So, if a nudge was what Arnie needed to guide him in the right direction, then that was what he would get. The sooner the better, too. As long as she chose her time carefully.

As it happened, the perfect moment for Carol to try to alter the course of her relationship with Arnie came the following Sunday afternoon when they were strolling through Hyde Park in the sunshine.

Carol had been delighted when he'd agreed to a trip up West with her, even though she knew he had only done so because Craig had gone out to a birthday party this Sunday, leaving his father at a loose end.

'The way some blokes dress these days you'd think they were pansies,' Arnie remarked as they passed a long-haired hippie dressed in an Eastern-style kaftan and beads. He had his arm around an extremely attractive young woman with long blonde hair. 'But they don't seem to have any problem getting good-looking women, do they?'

'It's just the fashion for some men to dress like that,' said Carol, who was very up to date in the ubiquitous mini-dress, her shoulder-length hair worn loose. 'You should try it. After all, I wear all the latest gear.'

'Me, go about in a dress?' he said predictably. 'Not bloomin' likely.'

'They're not dresses,' she corrected. 'They're kaftans. They can be worn by women or men.'

'They look like frocks to me, and the blokes who wear 'em look like ponces,' Arnie said.

'You should be more trendy . . .'

'If that's being trendy I want no part of it,' he said, appalled at the idea. 'Anyway, I'm a bit past faddy dressing.'

'Rubbish. You're only twenty-eight,' she reminded him.

'I wouldn't wear that sort o' gear if I was seventeen.'

'You wore teddy boy clothes when you were a teenager, and that was even more in for a dig,' she said in teasing admonition. 'I remember Mum and Dad going on about it when you and Gill started going out together.'

'I'll have you know I was wearing an army uniform when I was eighteen, young lady,' he said lightly.

'Well, things have changed since then. National service has finished.'

'Just as well,' he laughed. 'It would kill the hippies.'

'There you go again, being old fashioned and talking like an old man,' she teased, enjoying the happy atmosphere between them. 'You're beginning to sound like my dad.'

'You don't have to wear dresses to be in fashion, you know,' he said playfully, twirling around to show off the slim-line trousers he wore with a striped shirt with a white collar. 'Some of the pop stars are dressing like this.'

'You'll do,' she said, linking arms with him and smiling up at him adoringly.

They walked on towards the Serpentine, which was crowded with boats and gleaming in the sunshine on this fine afternoon, gulls soaring and swooping across the lightly rippling waters. They couldn't find any unoccupied deck-chairs so they sat down on the grass under a tree, away from the main crowds gathered around the lake.

'It's almost like being at the seaside,' remarked Carol.

'Yeah, it's lovely,' he replied, leaning back on his hands with his legs stretched out in front of him. 'So, what do you fancy doing later on?'

She laughed saucily.

'Apart from that, you sexpot,' he grinned.

'What did you have in mind?'

'We could have tea somewhere and then see a film at the Marble Arch Odeon, if you like.'

At moments like this Carol felt as though Arnie was hers and she had the power to make him do anything she wanted. Nibbling the end of a blade of grass, she said, 'I honestly don't mind what we do. As long as I'm with you I'm happy.'

He looked away quickly and she thought she'd upset him by being too affectionate. But he turned back to her and smiled.

'I should hate to think I make you miserable,' he said.

'Far from it. Actually, Arnie . . .' she began, emboldened by the warmth of the atmosphere between them. 'I've been thinking lately that it might be a good idea if I were to move in with you.'

His mood took a dive. He'd been dreading something like this. Carol had been hounding him for months and he didn't know how to put an end to her unwanted attention. He'd been trying to find the courage to tell her he wanted to stop seeing her for ages. But somehow he never could. She had a way of evoking pity, and at the back of his mind lay the fear that she would become seriously depressed again if he told her it was over, as she had after Dougie had let her down.

Anyone else would have got the message long ago from the deliberate casualness of his behaviour. Every one of their meetings was at Carol's instigation; surely that must speak for itself. But the truth had obviously not dawned on the girl, who seemed so fixated with him that he was beginning to feel suffocated. These past few months he had begun to understand why Dougie hadn't been able to go through with the wedding, or break off their engagement any earlier than the actual day.

It wasn't that Arnie wasn't fond of Carol, because he was. And this made it even more difficult. The last thing in the world he wanted to do was hurt her. But he wasn't in love with her and never would be. He was angry with himself, for allowing her to manipulate him into this position.

He would have to nip this latest idea of hers in the bud, or heaven only knows where it would end.

'I don't think that's a good idea,' he forced himself to say, feeling like a brute as her soulful eyes rested on him.

'Why not?'

'For one thing, it would upset your family,' he said.

'It isn't unheard of for a couple to live together these days.'

'No—'

'Well then . . .'

'But your parents are old fashioned, and I am still married to Gill.'

'But it'll take ages for your divorce to come through,' she said, pouting. 'We can't wait until then to live together.'

'Divorce?' He sounded shocked.

'Surely you're going to start proceedings eventually,' she said.

'Gill and I have never discussed it,' he said.

'Oh.' A surge of anger scorched through her, similar to a feeling she had been prone to as a child, when she couldn't get her own way about something. Then she used to throw a tantrum and keep it going until she finally wore her mother down. But this needed more careful handling. She knew she risked losing him altogether if she got careless and showed her hand too clearly. She'd managed to become his lover by blatant means, but the long-term situation called for a more delicate touch.

'It's just one of those things we haven't got around to yet,' Arnie said, adding pointedly, 'As neither of us is planning to get married again it hasn't seemed important.'

'I see,' Carol said, biting back her fury and smiling sweetly at him. 'But even so, I still think it would be a good idea for me to move in with you. It would be much more convenient for us both.'

'Why don't we just leave things as they are for the moment and see how it goes?' he said. He was trying to be gentle.

With a supreme effort Carol managed to restrain herself from physically attacking him in her frustration. 'Okay, Arnie, if that's the way you want it, then that's fine with me,' she said with a calmness she didn't feel.

'Good.'

'I just thought it would have been easier for us both, and nice for you to have someone there when you get home from work to cook you a meal and so on,' she said in one last attempt to persuade him. 'But, as you say, it's probably best to leave it and see how things go.'

With the pressure off, Arnie felt more charitable towards her again. 'I'm sure that's the right thing,' he said, smiling at her.

Behind Carol's returned smile a plan was forming. If he wouldn't do what she wanted of his own volition, she would have to resort to devious means. There's more than one way to get a man to the altar!

'Shall we go and get some tea then?' she suggested, getting up and brushing grass from her dress.

'Yes, let's do that,' he said, and they strolled towards Marble Arch together.

Chapter Sixteen

While Carol and Arnie were going for tea, Gill, Peter and Cherry Betts were among the crowds pouring out of the Royal Festival Hall on the south bank of the Thames. There were hordes of people about on this lovely afternoon, ambling along in groups eating ice creams and chatting, watching the boats on the river, filling the paths and benches.

Having first got permission from the nuns, Gill and Peter had taken Cherry to a concert given by a youth orchestra featuring performances by young soloists. The highlight of the afternoon had been a piano recital by a woman of eighteen who obviously had a future as a concert pianist.

'So, what did you think of the concert, Cherry?' Gill asked as they strolled beside water splintered with sunlight, formations of swans riding its gentle waves with a proprietary air, oblivious to the attention of the camera-waving tourists.

'It was smashing, miss.' Cherry was now a developing twelve-year-old with the beginnings of a new shape filling out her summer dress. 'I wish I was as good at playing the piano as that gel who played on the stage.'

'One day you will be, if you keep at it,' said Gill.

'Do you really think so, miss?'

'I certainly do. As long as you continue to come for your lessons and practise regularly.'

'That gel goes to music college, though, don't she?' said Cherry enviously. 'It said so on the programme.'

'Yes, I read that too,' said Peter, exchanging a look with Gill.

'I suppose you've gotta go to college to study music proper if you wanna be a concert pianist,' said Cherry.

'It does help,' said Gill.

'I'd love to do that.'

'Then maybe you will when you're old enough,' said Peter.

'Nah, not me. It'll cost too much. The nuns won't be able to afford it.'

'There might be a way of getting over that,' Peter said.

'Really?' Cherry's face lit with hope.

'I'm not absolutely certain, but I've an idea there are sometimes grants and scholarships available for students who show real potential but don't have the means to go to college,' he explained.

'But you've a long time to go before you even need to think about anything like that,' said Gill cautiously. She didn't want to raise the girl's hopes only to have them dashed later on, since Cherry had no relatives to support her through any sort of further education. 'You concentrate on your schoolwork for the moment.'

'And the piano,' Cherry said quickly, as though needing reassurance.

'Of course,' Gill replied. 'That goes without saying.'

'I'll never give the piano up, no matter what job I do when I leave school,' Cherry said ardently. 'Even if I have to work in a factory all day to keep myself, I won't give up the piano. I'll save up and buy myself a second-hand one when I leave Terry's.'

'Good for you,' said Gill.

They stayed for a while by the river, eating ice creams and idly chatting, until Peter suggested they have tea out somewhere.

'Ooh, smashing!' Cherry enthused.

They got into Peter's car and headed for a place he knew of in the King's Road, Chelsea.

'Cor, the King's Road!' said Cherry, whose knowledge of the world outside St Theresa's came mostly from hearsay. 'Isn't that where all the trendy people go?'

'It's supposed to be one of the places they gravitate towards, yes,' said Gill.

'Some of the older girls at school come here to get their clothes,' Cherry said excitedly as they passed Mary Quant's boutique and various other well known emporiums, all closed on this Sunday afternoon. 'I've heard 'em talking about it in the playground. My mates at Terry's'll be green with envy when I tell 'em I've actually *been* here.'

Peter parked the car and they went into a café with wooden tables and pine walls liberally sprinkled with contemporary art and hand-written poetry. They tucked into a pile of sandwiches, a huge plate of home-made cakes and a pot of tea. Most of the other people were arty types: long-haired men with beards, women in loose tops and tight trousers.

'How come you know this place?' Gill asked when the owner addressed Peter by his name.

'I used to play my guitar in here at one time,' he explained. 'They sometimes have live music in the evenings.'

'How fab!' said Cherry.

Looking at her glowing little face, the darting eyes devouring everything she saw with relish, Gill shared a smile with Peter. Giving Cherry a treat had brought its own rewards; the girl was living proof that giving can be better than receiving.

Later that evening, when Craig was safely tucked up in bed, Gill and Peter were relaxing downstairs with a glass of wine.

'Thanks for getting the tickets for the concert,' Gill said. 'It was thoughtful of you to organise an outing for Cherry.'

'My pleasure,' Peter said graciously. 'It was nice to meet her at last. I've heard so much about her.'

'I think she loved every moment.'

'Yes, she did seem to, didn't she?' he said. 'I enjoyed it too.'

'So did I,' Gill said. 'But then you and I usually manage to enjoy ourselves wherever we go, don't we?'

'We do.' He lapsed into a thoughtful silence. 'Actually, Gill, I think it's about time we had a talk, and now seems as good a time as any.'

'What about?'

'Us.'

'Oh dear,' she said, making a face. 'That has the ring of gravity about it. Am I about to get the elbow?'

'Quite the opposite.'

'Oh?'

'The fact is, I'd like to know where I stand . . . to know where our relationship is going,' he said solemnly. 'What is all of this leading to?'

'Well it can't go much further, since I'm still married to Arnie.'

'I want more, Gill,' Peter said, giving her a penetrating look. 'I want us to be together properly – to get married, when you are free to. Until then . . .' His voice tailed off.

'You want us to move in together?'

'Yes. Don't you think it would be a good idea?' he said. 'I mean, I spend so much time here anyway, it would be far more convenient for us both. And Craig and I get along well enough. I would suggest that you both move in with me, but I don't think you'd fancy living in a flat.'

'Oh, no. I don't want to move away from this house,' she said at once. 'I wouldn't want to uproot Craig. Anyway, my teaching practice is established here.'

'So, I'll move in with you then . . .'

She had known that it would only be a matter of time for this question to arise, but she had chosen to put it out of her mind. Now she could avoid it no longer. She drank a sip of wine to give her courage. 'Please don't take this the wrong way . . .' she began.

'But you'd rather I didn't move in with you,' he cut in sharply.

She sighed. 'I'm quite happy to carry on as we are,' she explained.

'Oh.' He sounded downhearted.

'Everything's fine as it is. Why complicate matters?'

'You don't want to make a commitment to me, do you?'

'Let's just say I don't feel ready to make *that* sort of commitment at the moment,' she told him.

'You might never . . . ?'

'You're right,' she agreed with candour. 'I might never feel ready. So if you'd rather stop seeing me, knowing that, I'll understand.' She looked at him over the rim of her wine glass. 'I wouldn't half miss you, though.'

'There's no question of my not seeing you,' he said.

'Oh, Peter, I am glad,' she said. 'I really value our time together.'

'I'm an incurable optimist,' he told her, smiling. But she knew he was bitterly disappointed by her answer.

'Actually, Peter,' she said with some hesitance, 'now that you've put things between us on to a more serious plane, even though we're going to carry on as we are for the moment . . . er, there's something about me I think you should know.'

'I don't like the sound of that,' he said with forced levity.

'I can't have any more children,' she said, the pain rising in her voice even after all this time. 'I have some permanent damage as a result of a miscarriage a few years ago.'

'Oh, that's a shame . . . I'm very sorry, for your sake,' he said with genuine compassion, sensing her regret. 'But it doesn't make any difference to the way I feel about you. I still want to share my life with you.'

'Don't you want a family?'

'It doesn't bother me unduly,' he said. 'It isn't as though I don't have one already from my first marriage.'

'There is that . . .'

'It obviously bothers you quite a lot, though,' he commented.

'I must admit I did want to have more children,' she confessed. 'I'd have loved to have a daughter, and I was devastated when I first knew I couldn't have any more. But I've accepted it now, and most of the time I'm okay about it. Sometimes it hits me and I feel terrible. I'm still only twenty-seven . . . it's young to know your child-bearing days are over.'

He nodded.

'But I'm luckier than a lot of women because I have Craig.'

'Yes.'

They lapsed into a comfortable silence, both immersed in their own thoughts. That was the good thing about Peter's company, Gill thought, there were never any of those exhausting silences that happened with some people.

A dark shadow had fallen over her mood, though. In wanting more than she felt able to give, Peter had forced her to face up to her own feelings. She didn't want to make a life-long commitment to Peter, because she was still in love with Arnie. No matter how wrong he was for her, he still made every other man pale in comparison.

But she couldn't continue to live in the past for ever, clinging to something that could never be. And she didn't want to lose Peter. At some point in the future he was going to force the issue. Perhaps then she would find the courage to let go of the past and allow herself to move on to the next stage in her life.

Arnie poked his head into the office. 'Can you give us a hand in the shop, please, Mum?' he asked. 'The place is packed to the doors and I'm short-staffed.'

'Course I can, son,' Phoebe said good-naturedly, putting her pen down and getting up from her desk where she had been working on some figures. 'I'll be glad of a break from the paperwork.'

'Thank God for that,' Arnie said, and made a hasty exit.

'What it is to be needed, eh?' remarked Len, who was busy at his desk, studying the turnover for each of the shops as at Friday night's close of business, a regular Saturday-afternoon ritual.

'I thrive on it,' she told him. 'As much as I enjoy working in the office, I like to get out there among the punters every so often.' She hurried across to the door. 'See you later.'

And she was gone like a whirlwind, leaving the office with a feeling of emptiness. Her boundless energy seemed to make any room she was in throb with vitality. Whereas Mary had been quiet and gentle of manner, Phoebe was like a gale-force wind in comparison. This was an observation rather than a critisism; Len liked Phoebe, and considered her to be valuable to the business, being popular with staff and customers alike. He could see from where the Briscoe brothers got their personality. Mother and sons had all proved to be an asset to him. Even young John, who had got off to such a bad start, had knuckled down once his problem had been solved, and was doing well at the Fulham branch. As for Phoebe – well, nothing was too much trouble for her.

Giving the matter some thought, Len supposed that this job was something of a promotion for her after working on the counter in Woolworth's. Here at Bex Sports she ran the office, helped out in the shop and made an intelligent contribution to the general running of the business. She also did all sorts of personal errands for Len, like taking his suits to the cleaners and doing his shopping. As he had to have someone other than Mary working in the office, he was glad it was Phoebe.

Half an hour or so later she came bursting back in. 'Cor blimey! It was like Wembley Stadium on cup final day out there for a while,' she told him. 'Talk about busy.'

'It's music to my ears,' he replied lightly, 'to know that punters are keen to offload their money in our direction.'

'Not half.' Phoebe sat back down and looked at her watch. 'Soon be time to knock off. I'll just have time to finish this.'

They were both silent for a while, each concentrating on the job in hand.

'Saturday night again, eh, Len?' Phoebe said after a while. She had got to the end of what she was doing and was tidying her desk. 'How the week flies past.'

'Yeah.'

'Are you going out anywhere tonight?' she enquired chattily.

'No.'

'Do you fancy coming down the Rose and Thistle with me?' she asked casually. 'They have live entertainment there on a Saturday night. Some good turns an' all.'

'No thanks,' he said. 'I'm not in the mood for pubbing.'

'Oh, go on,' she urged, 'be a devil. Let yourself go for a couple of hours.'

'No, honestly . . .'

'It'll do you good to get out, and you'd be doing me a favour 'cause I'd like to go and I can't very well go on my own.'

'What about that friend o' yours – the one you go to bingo with?'

'She's doing something else tonight.'

'Oh.'

'That only leaves my John, and I can't see him agreeing to go out with his mother on a Saturday night, can you?'

'Not really,' Len said. 'He'll be off to some disco or other, I expect.'

Phoebe's expression became serious. 'Thanks to you, Len, he's free to go out and enjoy himself,' she said. 'If he'd carried on hanging out with Harris and his mates he'd most probably be banged up by now.'

'Yeah, well, that's all in the past, isn't it?' said Len. 'I'm glad he's a bit more choosy about his friends now.'

'Me an' all.' Phoebe grinned. 'Kids, eh . . . who'd have 'em?'

'I wouldn't have minded . . .'

'It was a shame you didn't,' she said, keeping her tone light so as not to depress him. 'But it just wasn't to be.'

He tidied the papers in front of him with an air of finality.

'Well, Len, that's enough work for one week,' she said looking at her watch again. 'It's time we weren't here.'

'I'll be here for a while longer, just to go over things with Arnie when he's cashed up,' he said. 'But you get off home, ducks.'

'I will if you don't mind,' she said. 'I have to call in at the fish and chop shop on my way home. I don't cook on a Saturday night. It's one of my house rules.'

'I don't blame you.'

She took her coat from the stand and slipped into it. 'See you Monday then,' she said.

'Yeah.'

'Have a nice weekend.'

Len nodded, but he knew there wasn't much chance of that. Weekends for him were simply long expanses of loneliness that had to be endured.

'And you.'

'I will . . . Don't worry,' she said, 'I'll find someone to go down the Rose and Thistle with.'

204

As she reached the door a sudden impulse made him call her name. She turned to look at him and smiled.

'I was wondering . . .' he began hesitantly. 'Can I change my mind about coming with you?'

'Course you can,' she beamed.

'What time shall I pick you up then?'

'Oh, about eight o'clock will be fine,' she said delightedly.

There's nothing quite like a sentimental ballad to make the hairs on the back of your neck stand on end, Phoebe thought that evening, especially when you'd had a few gins and were in the mood to enjoy yourself. She and Len were sitting at a table in the crowded functions room of the Rose and Thistle with their eyes glued to the stage, where a broad-chested man with a black shirt open almost to the waist was belting out the Tom Jones hit 'The Green Green Grass of Home'.

'Good, wasn't he?' she said as the singer concluded the first half of the entertainment to loud clapping and whistling.

'Not half.'

'Some of these singers who work the pubs are every bit as good as those we see on the telly, I reckon.'

Len nodded. 'The comedian was pretty pathetic though, wasn't he?' he remarked, smiling and puffing heavily on his cigar.

'Oh, yeah, wasn't he awful?' Phoebe giggled at the memory. 'I felt quite sorry for him when all of his jokes died the death.'

'Poor bugger,' said Len, 'at least he was having a go.'

'They say comedy is the hardest thing of them all to do, don't they?'

'I have heard that.' He finished his drink and gave her an enquiring look. 'What are you having?'

'A gin and tonic, please.'

'Coming up, right away,' he said jovially, leaving the table and pushing his way through the crowds to the bar.

Phoebe looked around the large room, at the heavy red and gold wallpaper, the maroon curtains and the stage, on which stood the equipment of the three-piece band and a microphone in the centre. Small tables, squashed together to provide maximum seating, covered the whole area. Opposite the stage was a bar around which people were swarming to get their drinks before the second half of the show. The atmosphere was warm and friendly, a boisterous roar of conversation and laughter filling the air. Looking through a pall of cigarette smoke, Phoebe saw Len idly chatting to the man standing next to him as he waited to get served. She thought he was magnificent. A king among men, tall and distinguished with his mane of thick white hair and large features, which might be ugly to some but were attractive to her.

He was still slimmer than he'd been before he lost Mary, but now that the awful emaciated look had gone the weight-loss suited him, and his jacket sat well on his broad shoulders. Even from this distance she could recognise his charisma.

He was everything Phoebe had ever wanted in a man. The fact that he was comfortably off had nothing to do with it. He was strong, but not invulnerable – as his reaction to Mary's death had proved; he was kind-hearted without being weak; and when he was on form he had a terrific sense of humour, which made him an entertaining companion. He was also in very good physical shape for a man in his fifties.

She was well aware of the fact that women of a certain age weren't supposed to have sexual desires. They were encouraged to believe that the only sort of feelings they had to look forward to were hot flushes and the mild palpitations of a modest win at bingo. But Len had made her realise that there was more to maturity than that.

He wasn't interested in her as a woman, she knew that. He was far too busy worshipping Mary's memory to open his mind to the possibility of a new relationship with someone else. At the moment he just saw Phoebe as someone useful to have around in the office, someone who didn't mind helping out with personal errands too.

But as time passed, his grief would inevitably begin to lessen. And when that happened, Phoebe would be on hand to help him see her in a different light. And if that didn't happen, she would still be there for him simply because she wanted to be.

But now she was jolted out of her reverie by Len returning to the table with their drinks.

'I thought I'd never get served. It's like a ruddy battleground at the bar,' he said.

'I noticed.'

'They must be making a fortune.'

'A lot of the pubs around here have stopped having live entertainment and make do with the juke box,' she said. 'That's why people flock to this one on a Saturday night.'

'I see.'

'The landlord probably gets back what he pays the acts in extra business.'

'Trebles his money, I should think.'

'Could be.' She raised her glass. 'Thanks, Len . . . Cheers.'

'Cheers,' he said warmly. 'I haven't had a night out since before Mary died.' He made a face. 'And I'm ashamed to say I'm enjoying myself.'

'There's no need to be ashamed.'

'No?'

'Course not!' she exclaimed. 'It's been more than eight months. You're not expected to go about with a long face for ever. That's the last thing Mary would have wanted.'

'You're right.' Len paused, his eyes filling with tears. 'I'm so lost without her, Phoebe.'

'Now don't upset yourself,' she said, patting his hand companionably.

'I didn't know that such pain existed until she was taken from me,' he said.

She nodded sympathetically.

'I haven't wanted to go out anywhere – except perhaps to my local, but that was only to anaesthetise myself,' he said.

'Getting back to work must have helped, though,' she said.

'It's helped, yes, but it's still been an effort to talk to people outside of that,' he said. 'The last thing I want to do when I get home is go out socialising.'

Sipping her drink, Phoebe looked at him with tenderness in her eyes. 'It is hard when you lose your partner,' she said. 'But we all react differently and cope in our own way. After my husband died I felt the need to go out and be with people . . . to take my mind off the pain, I suppose. I was a lot younger too. But I didn't get much chance to get out of an evening with two young boys to look after. Whenever I did manage it, it made me feel human and part of the world again. You feel so cut off from other people, don't you? So isolated, somehow, because you're feeling so awful and they aren't. And no one can really help because it's all locked inside.'

'Yeah, that just about sums it up,' Len said.

'It does get easier eventually, though,' she told him. 'And I can say that with the benefit of experience.'

'I don't think I'll ever stop missing Mary,' he said sadly.

'I don't suppose you will either, but time does make a difference,' she said with conviction. 'It's nature's way.'

'I'm not sure I want to stop missing her,' he said.

'I remember feeling like that about my husband,' she said. 'But although it's a very gradual process you do get over it.'

'I'll never, *ever* get married again,' he stated categorically.

'It's still early days . . .'

'Yes, but I mean what I say.' He said it with such emphasis that she wondered if he was making his position clear should she be harbouring any romantic notions about him. 'Mary was the only woman I ever wanted to be married to, and I shan't be doing it again.' He gave her a questioning look. 'You never have?'

'No.'

'You've never felt the need to share your life with anyone?'

Not until I met you, she thought. But she said, 'I've often wished I had someone. But there was always the boys to consider . . .'

'Yes, of course. I bet you've been glad of them, though.'

'Not half,' she said. 'They were my life . . . They still are.'

'It must have been hard bringing them up on your own.'

207

'Yeah, but it was rewarding too,' she said. 'And now that they're grown up it means I never feel really alone.'

'Whereas I—'

'You've got lots of friends who care a lot about you,' Phoebe said quickly.

'I know, I'm lucky.'

'Luck doesn't come into it,' she said in a definite tone. 'You get back from people what you give to them.'

'You reckon?'

'Yes, I do. You look after your staff and treat them as people with a right to consideration and respect, unlike some of the employers I've worked for. There isn't a person on the staff in any of your shops who doesn't like and respect you.'

'Here, give over, Pheeb . . . You'll have me blushing in a minute,' he said lightly to cover his embarrassment.

The awkward moment soon passed, however, as the compère returned to the stage and called for silence so that the entertainment could continue.

The comedian came on for his second slot, and sadly showed no sign of improvement. He was followed by a hilariously incompetent magician and a female singer who did a reasonable impersonation of Dusty Springfield. Then came the finale: the black-shirted male singer with a heart-stopping version of 'Danny Boy'.

'Not a bad show, was it?' said Phoebe as they sat chatting and finishing their drinks.

'I thought it was excellent.'

'So, now that you've had a night out and managed to enjoy yourself, I hope you'll do it again,' she said casually.

'Well, actually, it's set me thinking,' he said warily.

'Oh?'

'Well, as you know I'm involved with various organisations for business and charitable reasons . . .' he said.

'Yes, I do know that.'

'Which means I'm expected to attend certain social functions.'

'Mm. I remember Mary talking about all the dinners she used to go to with you.'

'I haven't been to anything like that since she died,' he confessed. 'I've always managed to make up some excuse.'

'I'm sure the people concerned understand,' she said.

'I'm sure they do, but I ought to start supporting these things again.'

'Perhaps you'll feel more like it now you've taken that first step and been out for a social evening,' she said.

'Yes. The thing is . . .' He cleared his throat nervously. 'I really need a partner to go with, a lady to accompany me on these occasions . . .'

'I suppose you would do,' she said, wondering where all this was leading.

'And . . . actually, I wondered if you might be willing to help me out. Purely as a friend, you understand. There would be no funny business, I promise you.'

Phoebe was more flattered than he could possibly have imagined. 'I'd love to do this for you Len,' she said, her enthusiasm fading with a realistic thought. 'But . . . er, I can't.'

'Oh? Why not?'

'Because I don't have anything posh enough to wear to the sort of do you're talking about,' she said, looking down at her sequined sweater which she wore with an ordinary black skirt. 'This is about the dressiest thing I've got.'

'That's no problem,' he said. 'I'll stand the cost of any clothes you need.'

'Really?'

'Well, I can hardly expect you to pay for them out of the wages I pay you, can I?'

'In that case I'd love to do it for you,' she said, smiling.

'Smashing,' he said. 'I'll find out when the next one is and you can get yourself kitted out ready.'

'I can't wait,' Phoebe said, hardly able to believe her luck. This was the most exciting thing that had happened to her in years.

Chapter Seventeen

Towards the end of the year an unexpected new dimension was added to Gill's work: an influx of adult pupils. It began with a genteel little man called Horace, who found himself with time on his hands after retiring.

'Every house in the street had a piano in the front room when I was a boy,' he explained mistily. 'I didn't have the patience to learn how to play then, and I didn't have the time when I grew up and had a living to earn. Now my time's my own, I fancy giving it a try.'

'Good for you.'

'My wife says she'll take lessons as well if I get on all right with it,' he said, adding jokily, 'We'll be able to play duets together.'

His wife became a pupil soon afterwards, and other retired people followed as word got around. Inspired by the amount of adult interest – and the fact that she could fit them in, because the majority could come in the daytime rather than after school hours when she was fully booked with children – Gill put a card in the music-shop window advertising the fact that people of all ages were welcome.

The response was good – and wasn't limited to the retired. An aspiring young pop-star with shoulder-length hair and an embroidered shirt billowing over his skin-tight jeans joined her band of learners. He was a guitarist in a rock band, and hoped that being able to play the piano would be an advantage to him in his career. He looked a bit wild and threatening, but was actually very charming. She liked him at once.

As well as receiving fulfilment from the extra work, the increase in pupils meant a boost to Gill's income. At last she could afford her own transport, and she bought a second-hand Triumph Herald early in 1967.

The time seemed to fly past, and Gill found it hard to believe that Craig would be ten years old that summer. It was a different world now to the one he had been born into. Who could have predicted then the extent of the social revolution just a decade later, the changes to people's attitudes towards class and sex?

Although the hippies and the flower-power cult movement were outside Gill's personal experience, she noticed an increase in the hippie style of dress on the streets. Some young people were turning their backs on conventional living altogether in favour of a less materialistic way of life.

But grim reality was piped into the homes of the majority as the horrors of the Vietnam War filled their television screens. The reports made Gill's blood run cold.

Things remained much the same between her and Peter, and she continued to have an amicable relationship with Arnie. He was still seeing Carol on a regular basis, but Gill perceived a definite reluctance on his part when he and Carol were together. It seemed incredible that Carol couldn't see it too. Gill guessed it was a case of there being none so blind as those who didn't want to see.

She feared it would all end in tears, but if she so much as hinted this to her sister it was seen as jealousy and she was aggressively reminded that it was none of her business. Sadly, Gill accepted the fact that the time had long passed when Carol would listen to the advice of her elder sister.

Their mother wasn't happy about Carol and Arnie's relationship either.

'It's all wrong, a woman and her sister's ex-husband,' she was often heard to say. 'There used to be a law against that kind of thing.'

Just lately, however, someone else had been setting the tongues wagging in Maisie Road . . .

'That Phoebe Briscoe's doing all right for herself,' Winnie said to Gill, who had called round one afternoon when Hal and Carol were at work. 'The poor bloke won't stand a chance once she gets her claws into him.'

'That isn't how it is, Mum.' Gill had heard all about Phoebe's exciting new social life from the woman herself, whom she still saw regularly despite her separation from Arnie. 'Phoebe's only going out with him because he needs a partner at certain functions and he hasn't got a wife to go with him now.'

'Humph.'

'It's purely an arrangement of convenience.'

'And I'm Jean Shrimpton,' snorted Winnie.

'Mu-m.'

'Whatever the truth, she's having a high old time with him.'

'Good for her.'

'He's even buying her clothes to go in an' all,' said Winnie. 'And I know that's true 'cause Carol told me and she heard it from Arnie.'

'Yes, it is true,' Gill confirmed. 'And it's only right that he should pay for the clothes. Phoebe can't afford to buy the classy gear she needs to go in, not out of her salary. It's all part of the deal they have. Honestly, Mum, they're just friends and she's helping him out.'

'Helping herself, more like.'

'Personally, I think it's about time Phoebe had some pleasure,' Gill said. 'She hasn't had an easy life.'

'All right, I know I'm being bitchy,' Winnie admitted with a surge of conscience.

'Yes, you are.' Gill paused. 'I wouldn't mind someone buying me nice clothes and taking me to posh places, no strings attached. You must admit, it's very exciting for her.'

'Oh, it's exciting for her all right,' said Winnie. 'But that woman always seems to come up smelling of roses.'

'I don't know how you can say that,' said Gill with strong disapproval. 'She lost her husband when she was still young and had two kids to bring up on her own. The poor woman had to work hard to put food on the table. Getting that job at Bex Sports was the first chance she'd ever had to show what she was really capable of, and she's practically running the business with Len now. If anyone deserves a bit of pleasure it's Phoebe.'

'Yes, yes, I know all that,' said Winnie. 'And what I meant by her always coming up smelling of roses is that, no matter how many knocks she takes, Phoebe Briscoe always picks herself up and carries on as though she owns Selfridge's.'

'That's what comes of being on her own for all those years,' said Gill. 'You have to be bold with no one to fight your battles for you – I can vouch for that.'

'Confidence is what she has more than her share of.' Winnie felt a stab of envy at the way Phoebe sailed merrily through life with all its hardships. 'Because she has so much of it, if she were to fall into a sewer she'd behave as though she smelled of Chanel when she came out.'

Gill smiled reflectively. 'Yes, I know what you mean,' she said. 'She's become an expert in putting on a brave face, I think.'

'She really has fallen on her feet this time, though,' said Winnie. 'If she manages to get Len Bex to the altar she'll want for nothing.'

'It isn't like that between them, though, Mum,' Gill told her again. 'Len doesn't want to get married again. He's made that very clear to Phoebe.'

'Time will tell . . .' said Winnie insistently. 'Time will tell.'

One bitterly cold February evening Arnie came out of the factory of a sportsgear manufacturer on the Fulham–Chelsea borders. He'd been there at the invitation of the management for a tour of their works, and had taken advantage of the occasion to negotiate a special price on boy's football strips on orders above a certain amount. He'd done good business, and was feeling pleased with himself.

The area was practically deserted after working hours along this industrial stretch of the river, and his footsteps echoed eerily as he walked towards his car, parked on derelict ground not far from the British Railways freight depot. The tall chimney stacks of Fulham electricity power station dominated the landscape above abundant dumps of wrecked cars, gas works, and large expanses of industrial wasteland, shadowy and sinister in the pale glow of the street lighting. The floodlights of Stamford Bridge Football Stadium were visible behind the looming gas-holders.

There had been a lot of talk in the local press about plans to smarten up this scruffy bank of the Thames, by replacing old-fashioned factories with modern office blocks and building stylish residential accommodation. Arnie didn't know if the plans would actually come to fruition, but he wouldn't be surprised, because the tide of gentrification had already begun in Fulham where it met the Chelsea borders.

But as the penetrating cold cut deep into his bones and a far more pressing personal matter came into his mind, Arnie couldn't bring himself to care one way or the other about it.

Carol! What am I going to do about her? he asked himself, shivering violently as he got into his car. There was only one decent thing to do, and he'd been trying to do it for months. He must come right out and tell her that he didn't want to continue with their relationship any longer. Things certainly couldn't go on as they were.

Her determination to take over his life was crushing him. If she wasn't waiting for him outside the shop when he finished work, she was at his flat when he got home, having persuaded him to give her a key. She insisted on cooking his meals and tidying the place, even though he begged her not to. When he'd got in the other night she was even doing his ironing, and had turned on the tears when he'd been none too pleased.

Once she'd been fun to be with and he'd enjoyed her company. Now all he wanted to do was put distance between them. He'd hinted at how he felt a million times, but she simply didn't hear what he was trying to say. So he was going to have to spell it out for her loud and clear. His heart lurched at the thought, because she would be very hurt and he was still fond of her.

He leaned his arms on the steering wheel for a moment, his thoughts lingering on Gill's sister. She had seemed different lately, happier and annoyingly ebullient, as though something had happened to please her, though she hadn't mentioned anything in particular.

That would all change when he'd said what he had to say. But he must do it, the very next time he saw her, which would probably be tonight because she rarely left him in peace of an evening.

'It's very good of you to go to all this trouble for me, Carol,' he said when he got home to find the table laid for supper and Carol bustling around in a pinafore, having prepared them a meal of spaghetti bolognese. 'But I've told you before, I'd rather you didn't.'

'It's no trouble at all,' she said, beaming at him as she put the plates on the table. 'I enjoy doing it.' She patted the chair with cloying sweetness that made his skin crawl. 'So come and sit down before the food gets cold.'

'The thing is, Carol . . .' he began.

'The wine!' she said, ignoring him. 'I almost forgot.'

'Wine . . . on a Wednesday?'

'Yeah. I thought I'd treat us . . . It's in the kitchen,' she smiled. 'I'll leave you to do the honours.'

'Carol, I've something to tell you . . .'

'In a minute,' she said, sitting down at the table. 'Go and open the wine first.'

He did as she said, returning and pouring them both a glass. She looked flushed and happy and he felt like a heel. He didn't know how he was going to swallow so much as a morsel of food. But when he'd said his piece Carol wouldn't want anything to eat either. If he hesitated now he'd be lost, as had happened on every other occasion when he'd tried to tell her. She had the knack of stopping him in his tracks.

'The thing is, Carol . . .' he began again.

She raised her glass. 'I'm not actually going to drink any of this, you know,' she said mysteriously.

'No?'

She shook her head.

'Why go to the trouble of buying it then?' he asked.

'To keep you company in a celebration,' she said with a giggle.

He gave her a questioning look, a dull ache beginning to nag in the pit of his stomach as he realised he was being deliberately deterred from saying his piece – almost as though she knew what it was about. 'Celebration?' he said.

'I'm pregnant,' she announced excitedly. 'I found out for sure today. Isn't it *wonderful*? I'm going to have our baby!'

The words buffeted him. The thought of becoming a father again barely registered against the dramatic implications of this development.

'What . . .' he managed at last.

Her face crumpled into a pout. 'You don't sound very pleased,' she said.

'Don't I?' he muttered, hardly knowing what he was saying.

'No.'

'It's so . . . unexpected.'

'I don't see why it should be,' she said pointedly.

'You told me you were on the pill,' he said, remembering how keen she'd been to take care of that side of things, how she had insisted most adamantly that the contraceptive pill would be the safest method.

'And so I was, but I must have forgotten to take it on the odd occasion,' she lied. She'd come off the pill months ago, conception firmly in mind.

He was far too traumatised to pretend to be pleased, because he knew there could be no escape from Carol now. He was completely trapped.

215

He rested his elbows on the table and put his head on his hands. 'Bloody hell, Carol,' he said involuntarily. 'What a mess!'

'Is that all you can say?' she said with a sob in her voice.

'I'm still trying to get used to the idea,' he replied dully.

'The least you can do is show a bit of enthusiasm.'

'I'm sorry, Carol. But I hadn't reckoned on anything like this . . . which is why I wanted to take precautions against it,' he said. 'I mean, ours isn't a having-a-family sort of relationship, is it?'

'It is now, mate,' she said, and the triumph in her voice told him the reason for her recent cheerful mood. She'd used the oldest trick in the book to get what she wanted.

'You planned this, didn't you?' he said, his eyes narrowed with suspicion. 'You stopped taking the pill on purpose.'

Huge tears began to roll down her cheeks, forming black rivers of mascara. 'I thought you'd be pleased,' she sobbed pathetically, 'and all you can do is accuse me of getting pregnant on purpose.'

She looked so vulnerable sitting there with her make-up smudged, shoulders drooping, Arnie didn't have the heart to continue with the accusation. 'It's come as a bit of a shock,' he told her. 'And it's certainly gonna complicate matters . . .'

'It'll bring things to a head, if that's what you mean.'

'Yeah.'

'You'll have to get a divorce from Gill now,' she said. 'So that you can marry me.'

'Mm. I suppose I will,' he said with a worried look.

'There's no "suppose" about it,' she said in a voice thick with tears but strong with determination. 'I'm not having my baby brought up as a bastard.'

'All right, Carol,' he sighed. 'You've made your point.'

'No one except the two families and our close friends need know we're not married, because we'll be living as man and wife when the baby is born,' she informed him in a manner that didn't invite argument. 'Then, as soon as your divorce comes through, we'll slip off quietly to the register office and make it legal.'

'You've got it all worked out.'

'You can't leave things to chance when there's a child involved.'

'No.'

Carol wiped her eyes with her handkerchief, leaving black smears on her cheeks. 'It's going to be wonderful, Arnie,' she said, brightening considerably. She knew there was no way out for a man like Arnie, whose conscience wouldn't allow him to leave her in the lurch. 'The three of us – you, me and our baby – will have a good life. We'll be a proper family.'

'Course we will.'

She fiddled with her handkerchief, affecting nervousness to evoke

216

his pity. 'You won't leave me, will you?' she said, tear-rinsed eyes beseeching him. 'You will stand by me through this?'

What else could he do? He knew that she had set him up. But he wasn't going to make an issue about it. Carol was a very insecure and complicated person who found it difficult to sustain relationships with men. She had known he would never marry her of his own accord, and had been determined to get him by whatever means it took.

He couldn't help feeling angry and tricked. But he had done the deed – so now he must pay the price. Carol was carrying his child and was therefore his responsibility. There simply wasn't a choice.

For the first time he thought of the child as an actual human being and experienced a leap of pleasure. 'No, I won't leave you,' he said, standing up and opening his arms to her.

'Not ever?' she queried, wanting reassurance as usual.

'Not ever,' he repeated dutifully, slipping his arms around her and holding her gently against him. 'You can rely on me. I'll look after you and the baby. Everything will be all right.'

'Oh, Arnie,' she sighed, looking up at him lovingly.

'Can you do me one favour, though?'

'Depends what it is.'

'Will you let me tell Gill before you tell anyone else at all?' he requested. 'I'd rather she heard it from me.'

'Sure,' she agreed, for she now had nothing further to gain. 'If that's what you want.'

Gill stared at Arnie in a state of shock. He'd called at the house to see her during his lunch hour, and they were having a sandwich at her kitchen table.

'A divorce,' she said through dry lips, her heart pounding. 'You want a divorce . . .'

'Yes.' He had to force the words out. 'That's right.'

'Well, I suppose it is time we did something definite about our situation,' she said, though the idea depressed her more than she could possibly have imagined. 'We've been separated long enough now. It will tidy things up.'

'That isn't the reason,' he said, his voice ragged with emotion.

'No?'

He shook his head.

'What's happened?'

He took a deep breath.

'Carol's pregnant.'

'Oh!' His words felt like a fist in Gill's face. 'Oh, I see . . .'

'So I need to get divorce proceedings under way right now,' he explained, his heart breaking as he saw his own pain mirrored in Gill's eyes, 'so that I can marry Carol as soon as possible.'

'Yes, of course.'

'Obviously we won't make it in time for the baby's birth, but the sooner things get started the better for the child's sake.'

'Mm.'

'I'll pay all the legal fees. Carol being pregnant will be proof of adultery even though that isn't why the marriage broke up.' He spoke rapidly, as though he wanted to get the discussion over. 'The solicitors might find the information useful to speed things up.'

'Yes, they might,' Gill said dully, her voice barely audible.

'It's all just a question of getting it to go through as soon as possible because of the circumstamces,' he said, scratching his head in agitation.

She nodded. 'When's the baby due?'

'July.'

'Oh, another July baby, the same as Craig,' she remarked, forcing a light note, though this only added to her pain somehow. 'There'll be exactly ten years between them.'

'I wonder how he'll feel about having a new half-sister or -brother.'

'I don't know,' she said. 'How about you? Are you pleased?'

'I'm thrilled about the baby . . .'

'And the rest?' she asked.

'I wasn't planning on getting married again,' he said.

'I thought not.'

'But now this has happened. So I'm going to do everything I possibly can to make a go of it,' he told her. 'I messed it up with you. Now I want to get it right with Carol – which is something I know will please you, given how protective you've always been of your sister.'

Protectiveness was the last thing she was feeling now. At that precise moment she wanted to slit Carol's throat. 'I suppose she will move into your flat,' she said.

'To begin with, yeah. But I suppose we'll have to start looking for a house with the idea of moving in before the baby's born,' he said thoughtfully. 'A fourth-floor flat won't be very convenient with a baby.'

'No.'

'Strange, isn't it?' Arnie said, looking at her in a curious way. 'How much different divorce seems to separation.'

'I'm still recovering from the shock of hearing you say it, actually,' she said. 'Which is quite ridiculous since we've been apart for nearly two years and our marriage was in trouble for a long time before that. But I won't lie to you, Arnie: the thought of a divorce really hurts.'

'It hurts me too,' he confessed, looking at her with anguish in his eyes. 'It's so final.'

'Yes.'

'In my heart I'd always hoped we might give it another try sometime,' he told her. 'No chance of that now . . .'

'None at all.' She paused. 'What's really tearing me apart is that

Carol is having your baby,' she said, her voice quivering slightly. 'I know I'm being selfish, but I do find that hard to take. I wanted another child – your child – so much.'

'Oh, Gill,' he said in a broken voice, coming towards her, 'I'm so sorry.'

'Arnie . . .'

And she was in his arms, feeling his lips on hers, firm and sweet and thrilling after such a long absence, their tears mingling. How could they have been so stupid as to let something as precious as this slip from their grasp?

'I love you, Gill.'

'Don't,' she said, drawing back. 'You mustn't say things like that.'

'I know I shouldn't, but it's true,' he said, his face wet with tears. 'I've never stopped loving you. Through all the bad times, all the grief and heartache I gave you, I always loved you . . . I always will.'

'I feel the same, but there's no future for us now.'

'No, there isn't,' he agreed, his voice becoming hard. 'I have to fully commit myself to Carol from now on.'

'We shall have to be very firm with ourselves about it,' she said miserably. 'No more lapses of control like this one.'

'No.'

'It's bizarre,' she said with a disbelieving shake of the head. 'I mean, we won't even be able to avoid seeing each other as we're still going to be related to each other.'

'When I screw things up, I really do it in grand style.'

'You certainly do.'

'I can't believe what a fool I've been,' he said. 'How can anyone be that stupid?'

'It wasn't all your fault, Arnie,' she said, looking into his eyes. 'I made mistakes too. I let resentment linger when I shouldn't have. I couldn't forgive you.'

'I shouldn't have done all that stuff in the first place.'

'It's all water under the bridge now,' she said, managing a brave smile. 'I think the only way we're going to cope with this new situation is to put our feelings for each other behind us.'

'We can't do that.'

'Not literally, no,' she said, 'but we can behave as though they don't exist. And we must. It's the only chance you and Carol have of happiness, and the best chance for any of us to move forward to the way our lives must be from now on.'

'It'll be difficult . . .'

'But we have to do it.'

'I know,' Arnie said with a deep sigh of resignation.

They embraced briefly and she showed him to the door, watching as he walked to his car. She'd be seeing him all the time. When he came to collect Craig, at family occasions . . . He would be her *brother-in-law*. Although she had known for a long time that a reconciliation wasn't possible, now that the last shred of hope had gone, the pain was unbearable.

That evening Gill telephoned her sister and asked her to meet her for lunch the next day.

'Congratulations, Carol,' she said when they met in a coffee bar near to where her sister worked. 'Arnie's told me your news.'

'Thanks, sis,' said Carol, far too immersed in her own success to worry about how Gill might be feeling. 'I can hardly believe it's happened at last. It's what I've always wanted.'

'Arnie, you mean?'

'Yeah. Marriage, babies – the whole thing. I won't have to slave my guts out at a desk any more. Arnie says I can give up work as soon as I like. With him being a partner in the business, we can afford for me not to have to go out to work.'

'You do love him, though, don't you?' said Gill, studying the hand-written menu.

'Course I do,' Carol said. 'What on earth made you ask that?'

'You seem to be more interested in marriage and babies than the man himself.'

The waitress came to take their order, which was chilli con carne for them both.

'Trust you to come out with a snide remark like that,' snapped Carol. 'Just because you're as jealous as hell . . .'

'I'm a human being, not some kind of a saint,' said Gill. 'Of course I'm jealous, because you're having his baby.'

'You and Peter might . . .'

'You know I can't have any more children,' Gill reminded her sharply.

At least Carol had the decency to look a little shamefaced. 'Sorry, sis,' she said, her manner becoming contrite. 'That slipped my mind for a moment. I really am sorry for you.'

'Don't make me feel worse by giving me your pity,' said Gill. 'That really would be twisting the knife.'

'I was only trying to be civil.'

The silence was fraught with tension.

'I was surprised to hear that you're pregnant, actually,' Gill said eventually.

'These things happen,' said Carol, adding meaningfully, 'as you very well know.'

'Yes, but there wasn't a contraceptive pill available when it happened to me,' said Gill. 'And you've made no secret of the fact that you're one of the pill's biggest fans.'

Carol grinned and shrugged her shoulders nonchalantly. 'I am, but I forgot to take it,' she said. 'So what?'

Gill threw her a shrewd look. 'You stopped taking it with the deliberate intention of trapping Arnie into marriage, didn't you?' she said.

'So what if I did?' There was no mistaking the smugness in Carol's tone.

'Carol, how could you?'

'Well . . . if I'd waited for Arnie to ask me to marry him I'd have been too old to have babies.' She gave her sister a warning look. 'And if you tell him I've admitted it, I shall deny it.'

'I shan't say a word,' Gill said. 'There would be no point.'

'Good.'

'You must have been desperate to get him to resort to something like that.'

'I was desperate,' admitted Carol. 'I love him so much, and I just couldn't get him to make a commitment to me.'

'But this way . . . ?'

'He's had his fun,' Carol cut in. 'Now he has to face up to his responsibilities.'

'It isn't much of a basis for marriage, though, is it?' said Gill.

'You're in no position to judge me, considering you were already in the club when you married him.'

'I didn't trick him into it, though.'

'You didn't manage to hang on to him either, did you?'

'True.'

'So stop criticising.'

'Believe it or not, I care about you both,' Gill said truthfully. 'I admit I wanted to scratch your eyes out when Arnie told me you were pregnant. But now that I've calmed down and accepted the fact that I can't have him, I want it to work out for the two of you.'

'And it will.'

'I hope so.'

'Why shouldn't it? I'm in love with Arnie and I'm planning on being a good wife to him. Okay, so he needed a shove in the right direction, and I gave him one. There's nothing too terrible about that. It happens to an awful lot of people and they go on to have happy marriages.'

The conversation was interrupted by the waitress with their meal.

'Look, Gill,' Carol said, twisting a huge wooden pepper-mill over her food, 'I've never had much luck with men. Now, at last, I have the chance to be happy, and I'm grabbing it with both hands. We shall all have to forget that you were once married to Arnie, or things could be very awkward.'

'Don't worry,' said Gill, 'Arnie and me are past history. I won't do anything to make things difficult for you.'

221

'Thanks, sis.'

'That's okay.'

'Do you think you and Peter will get married when the divorce comes through?'

'I don't know,' Gill said. 'I'm still uncertain about that.'

'Perhaps Arnie and I getting together properly might help you to make up your mind about him,' suggested Carol.

'Maybe.'

'I hope you get your life sorted out.'

'I will, don't worry . . . And I'm glad you're happy.' Gill reached across the table and touched her sister's hand. She was besieged by a mixture of emotions. She was sad to have lost Arnie for ever, and envious of her sister, who was starting a new life with him . . . but by some strange mechanism of thought – presumably born of blood ties and sisterly affection – she also found herself hoping ardently that Carol would find the contentment that had eluded her for so long.

This was a watershed in all their lives. Carol and Arnie were about to become a family. Gill had to look to the future now too, and decide what to do about Peter.

She was recalled to the present by Carol, who was saying, 'I'm going to tell Mum and Dad tonight. I don't know quite how they'll take it.'

Gill had a pretty good idea, but she kept her thoughts on the subject to herself.

'Getting one of my daughters into trouble was bad enough, Arnie Briscoe,' said Winnie the following day, after she'd marched into the shop and demanded to see him in private, 'but doing it to them both is a damned disgrace.'

'I know how you must be feeling—'

'No woman is safe with you,' she ranted.

He didn't reply.

'You ought to get treatment.'

'Oh, that's a bit strong!' he blurted out. 'Carol is a full-grown adult; no one forced her into anything.'

Quite the opposite, Arnie thought. If anyone was the victim in this affair it was him. It occurred to him how shocked Winnie would be if she knew of her younger daughter's deviousness and astonishing sexual prowess, and how she used it as a means of getting what she wanted.

'That doesn't alter the principle of the thing,' Winnie reproved.

Wanting to be courteous, Arnie waited in silence for her to continue.

'Surely you can see that getting both sisters pregnant is beyond the pale.'

He certainly could – and, yes, he was ashamed of himself, more for causing Gill such pain over the years than for getting Carol pregnant,

222

since that was so obviously what the woman wanted. She was positively radiant.

Winnie's hair was almost white now. Her grey eyes burned with indignation as she glared at the man who had violated the daughter she saw as a wronged woman. But despite all her abrasiveness Arnie knew she was a good sort, and he had no intention of shattering her rosy maternal illusions by telling her the truth. Winnie was a devoted mother who was obeying her primal instinct to protect her young. The fact that both her daughters were grown women made no difference, apparently.

'Yeah, of course I can see that,' he said, 'I'm not a complete moron.'

'I'm glad to hear it!'

'I didn't want this to happen any more than you do, you know.'

'You should have had more sense.'

'I know that.'

'When it happened to Gill it was excusable because you were just a boy,' she continued, 'but you're going on for thirty now. It's high time you knew better.'

'You're right,' Arnie agreed wholeheartedly. 'You are absolutely right.'

'Really?' She seemed deflated by his ready agreement.

'You seem surprised to hear me agree with you,' he said.

'Yes. I was expecting to have a real barney with you.'

'How can I argue with you when everything you say is true?' he said. 'I know only too well that I'm old enough to know better. I know I've made a mess of Gill's life . . . and my own.'

'I'm glad to hear you admit it.'

'How can I deny it when it's true?'

'I felt I had to come and talk to you without Carol being around,' she said, feeling more inclined to explain since he was being so decent. 'Without any of them around.'

'I understand.'

'You've given Gill enough heartache over the years—'

'And you're here to tell me that if I do the same to your other daughter, you'll have my guts for garters.'

'Something along those lines, yeah,' she said. 'And I mean it.'

'You've nothing to worry about as far as Carol is concerned.'

'I hope not.'

Winnie was so genuine in her concern for her daughter, Arnie decided that she deserved the part of the truth that couldn't hurt her.

'I'd like to be really honest with you,' he said, looking her straight in the eyes.

'Go on.'

'I wasn't planning on sharing my life with Carol, and I wasn't pleased when she told me she was pregnant,' he said.

'I never saw the two of you making a go of it, I must admit,' she said.

'But I'm used to the idea now, and I intend to do everything I can to

223

make sure that Carol and our child have a happy life. So you can rest easy in your bed at night.'

'You'd better mean it an' all, Arnie Briscoe,' she said, but all the threat had gone from her voice now, because she believed him.

'I do.'

'Carol isn't the easiest of people to get on with,' she said, thawing slightly now that he had reassured her of his intentions. 'As much as I love her, even I have to admit that.'

'We've spent enough time together for me to know that,' he said.

'She was always a difficult child, you know,' Winnie confessed.

'I can imagine.'

'She'd throw herself into the most awful tantrum if she couldn't get her own way over even the smallest thing.' She paused. 'I used to give into her more than I should have, perhaps.'

He thought she was probably right, but felt it wise not to say so.

'You'll have to be firm with her.'

'Yes.'

'She's a strange girl,' Winnie continued.

'Always seems so insecure,' he said.

'God knows why, because she had a stable enough upbringing . . .'

'It's more to do with adult love, I think,' he said.

'Yes. She seems to need more love and attention than the rest of us.'

'Perhaps,' he said. He didn't add that he was only too painfully aware of Carol's constant need for love and reassurance, which was already exhausting him. 'But you can stop worrying about her from now on. Because I shall be a good husband to her, I promise you.'

'I believe you.'

'Now, how about a cup of coffee to warm you up before you go?' he suggested pleasantly.

'That's very nice of you,' Winnie said, thinking that perhaps she might enjoy having him back in the family again after all. And she knew for certain that her husband would.

'Two sugars, isn't it?'

'That's right,' she said, surprised and warmed by the fact that he had remembered.

Chapter Eighteen

It was the evening of Donna Briscoe's third birthday, a fine Sunday in the summer of 1970. There had been a kiddies' tea-party that afternoon at Carol and Arnie's Chiswick home, and the family members had stayed on afterwards. Taking advantage of the nice weather, they were in the garden.

Carol was making so secret of the fact that she couldn't wait to see the back of them. The last thing she wanted was the bother of entertaining visitors after coping with an invasion of hell-raising three-year-olds all afternoon. But Arnie had been keen to make a night of it and had, for once, put his foot down.

Because Arnie was such a considerate husband and Carol got her own way about almost everything, when he did make a stand she found it hard to take. Not being blessed with the patience to hide her feelings for the sake of others, her displeasure was being made obvious to their guests as she stamped thunderously about offering savoury nibbles and uttering the odd disinterested comment.

'Your sister's in a right old mood tonight,' remarked Peter quietly to Gill as they sat on the patio watching the dying sun slip behind the suburban rooftops in a glorious blaze of orange. 'She looks as though she could cheerfully murder the lot of us.'

'She didn't want to have an adult do after the kids' party,' whispered Gill, who was wearing a floral mini-dress, her dark hair shoulder-length and casual. 'She wanted us all to leave at the same time as the children so that she could relax and put her feet up.'

'Why are we here then?'

'Arnie insisted that the family stay on into the evening for a few drinks, apparently,' she said. 'He's a great one for family get-togethers.'

'The poor devil's probably glad of some company, the terrible life Carol gives him,' said Peter, who was casually dressed in jeans and a white open-necked shirt. 'I don't know how Arnie puts up with her, I really don't. The woman gets away with murder from what I've seen.'

Gill couldn't argue with that. Arnie's determination not to repeat past mistakes with this marriage had made him rather too eager to please, and Carol capitalised on this to the enth degree. She was sulky and demanding, and thought nothing of nagging him in public. Frankly, Gill thought he was a saint to stand for it. He certainly wouldn't have let her get away with that sort of behaviour when she'd been married to him. A contributory factor to his submissive behaviour, in her opinion, was the fact that he'd not been a good husband to her. With a weird kind of logic, he was trying to make up for that by being good to Carol. Whatever the reason, he certainly was an exemplary husband. But watching Arnie being so attentive to Carol had been harder to take than she could possibly have imagined – even though, perversely, she knew she would have quarrelled with him if he hadn't treated her sister right.

'Does she have to make it so obvious that she wants us all to leave?' Peter continued. 'I feel most uncomfortable.'

'I don't think she can help it.'

'Rubbish!'

'Carol never has been able to hide her feelings,' said Gill, instinctively defensive towards her sibling. 'If she's in a bad temper, the world knows about it.'

'She should make more of an effort, for all our sakes.'

'Yes, all right, Peter,' said Gill, sighing. 'Don't go on about it.' She paused, watching her sister storm towards the house carrying a tray of used crockery. 'I'd better go and give her a hand before she ruins the party completely by driving everybody out.'

'Don't do that.'

'Why not?'

'Because you do more than enough for your sister already,' he said, putting a restraining hand on her arm. 'You're always running around after her, helping her to look after Donna and baby-sitting for her. Arnie's done most of the entertaining here today, anyway. He seems to have done all the work.'

'But—'

'Let them get on with it,' he persisted. 'It's their party, not yours. You've been here all afternoon helping with the children . . . you've done more than your share. So why not just relax and enjoy yourself – as far as that's possible with old Sour-Chops about? You are supposed to be a guest, after all.'

He was right. She did do too much for her sister. But it was more for Donna than for Carol. Gill had been smitten with her niece from the moment she'd first set eyes on her, and welcomed the chance to look after her on the frequent occasions when Carol wanted to off-load her. Carol had a very low threshold to the demands of small children.

'I am family, though,' she said now, 'which isn't quite the same thing as being just a guest.'

'And don't I know it,' said Peter sharply. Gill had unintentionally hit a sore spot.

'Oh, Peter,' she said, looking into his troubled eyes with a sinking heart. 'You know I didn't mean anything by that. I meant that if you're family you always get roped in to help.'

'I do know what family is all about, you know,' he hissed. 'Just because you won't let me be a part of yours doesn't mean I don't know what being family feels like.'

'This isn't the time, Peter,' she said in gentle admonition.

'I know.' He sighed. 'Sorry.'

'We will talk about it, though,' she said, 'I promise.'

Peter had moved in with Gill soon after Carol had moved in with Arnie. Gill had known that she either had to commit herself to Peter or end their relationship altogether, and she couldn't face that. Gill and Peter were never going to have the love affair of the century, but they got on well enough. At least, they had done at first. But when Gill's divorce from Arnie had been made absolute and Arnie and Carol had quietly made their union legal, Peter had wanted to do the same with Gill. And she couldn't bring herself to agree.

What was the difference? she constantly asked herself. She shared her life with Peter anyway, so why not go ahead and get that vital piece of paper? But for all that it made sense she didn't want to do it, and this upset Peter who saw her reluctance as a personal slight.

But now someone was nudging her knee and she looked down to see a pretty little thing in a blue party frock, light brown curly hair tumbling over her forehead, cheeks flushed from running around.

'Donna, my special birthday girl . . .' Gill swept her adored niece up on to her lap and smothered her with kisses. 'You're up late tonight, precious.'

'Mummy says I can stay up late 'cause it's my birthday,' she said, yawning widely. 'No bed, no bed, no bed.'

'All right, sweetheart, don't panic.' Gill smiled. 'But you must go to bed without a fuss when Mummy says it's time.'

'I want you to put me to bed tonight, Auntie Gill.'

'All right, but only if Mummy says I can,' she said, ever careful not to undermine Carol's authority. Even though Carol was usually delighted to hand her exuberant daughter over to Gill if she happened to be around at Donna's bedtime, if you took anything for granted and Carol was in the mood to take umbrage she would fly into a rage. Carol had never been an easy person, but she'd been more difficult than ever since she'd been with Arnie.

'Will you read me a story at bedtime, Auntie Gill?'

'Yes, course I will, darling.'

But Donna's childish mind had already moved to other things.

'Craig. Where's Craig?' she asked.

'He's around somewhere, love.'

'We were playing at hidin' and I don't know where he's gone.'

At that moment Craig, now a lanky thirteen-year-old who got more like his father every day, sauntered into view.

'Ah, there you are,' he said, smiling affectionately at Donna, on whom he doted. Unusually for someone entering adolescence, with its tendency

227

towards self-centredness, he had endless patience with his half-sister. 'You were supposed to come looking for me. I got fed up of waiting.'

'I don't think she's quite old enough to play hide and seek properly,' Gill said to her son. 'Ring a ring a roses is more up her street.'

This struck an instant chord with Donna. 'Me want roses, Auntie Gill, me want roses,' she chanted.

'Come on, then,' Gill set her down on the ground and took hold of her hand. 'Let's go on to the lawn.' She grinned at Peter. 'Come on. Come and join us.'

'No thanks,' he told her, miffed because he had lost her attention.

'See you in a minute then,' she said, turning a blind eye to his disapproval because she didn't want Donna's birthday to be spoiled by adult disagreements.

Dragging Craig on to the grass, the three of them joined hands, Donna squealing with delight at the traditional repetition of the nursery rhyme.

'Come and join in, you lazy lot,' Gill called to her parents and Phoebe and Len, who were sitting on the patio with John Briscoe.

'We'll leave that one to you,' said Winnie, smiling. 'We're all still recovering from this afternoon's shindig.'

Arnie, who appeared from the house with a tray of drinks, handed them out and joined Gill and the others on the lawn.

'Okay then, Donna,' he said, smiling at his daughter and taking her hand and Craig's on the other side, 'let's show them how this should be done.'

Donna was in her element as the four of them moved round in a circle, laughing breathlessly when they got to the bit where they 'all fall down'.

'I'm too exhausted to get up,' Gill said to Arnie, who was sitting beside her on the grass. 'Your daughter has run the legs off me today.'

'You and me both,' he said, helping her up. 'She's tireless.'

In the kitchen, fixing herself yet another gin and tonic, Carol turned to the window just at the moment when Arnie was helping Gill to her feet, the two of them laughing with Craig and Donna.

Carol spent most of her life in a state of jealousy, forever tormenting herself with thoughts of Gill and Arnie having an affair. Now the green-eyed monster consumed her completely, rooting her to the spot, glass in hand, as this happy family scene tore at her heart. Arnie and Gill, happy together, laughing and talking, probably planning some assignation . . . Craig and Donna barely registered. The only thing Carol could see was her husband and her sister enjoying themselves together.

'I'll soon put a stop to that,' she muttered to herself.

Making short work of her drink, she marched purposefully out into the garden and on to the lawn.

'I know what you two are up to, so don't think you can pull the wool over my eyes,' she said with loud belligerence, bringing the hubbub of conversation to an abrubt halt. 'I know you're having an affair.'

'Carol!' gasped Arnie, his eyes glinting with anger. 'Don't be so ridiculous.'

'Don't try and fob me off,' she said, her voice rising, the guests on the patio listening in shocked silence. 'I'm not a fool; I know what's going on.'

'Nothing's going on,' said Gill.

'I won't have it. Do you understand me?' she rasped as though Gill hadn't spoken, her voice harsh and resonant in the evening air. 'I won't let you make a fool of me!'

Frightened by this sudden hostility, Donna started to cry. Before her despair had time to take root, Craig picked her up and carried her over to the swing, talking to her loudly enough to drown out the sound of her mother's voice.

'Calm down, Carol,' Arnie ordered in a low voice. 'You're upsetting Donna.'

'Don't patronise me!' she screamed. 'I'm not a child.'

'Stop behaving like one, then, and pull yourself together,' he said in a quiet but firm voice. 'You're upsetting Donna and embarrassing our guests.'

'That's all you care about – your daughter, your son and your bloody ex-wife!' she shrieked, completely out of control.

'Carol, that's enough,' said Gill, taking her by the arm.

'Don't touch me, you slut,' Carol said through gritted teeth, pushing Gill away. 'You've never been able to accept the fact that Arnie isn't yours any more. Well, it's time you did. You just keep your hands off him!'

Arnie exchanged a glance with Gill. This wasn't the first time they had had to suffer a scene like this one; Carol was prone to slanging matches, especially when she'd had a few drinks. But this was the first time she'd done it in public.

'Okay, Carol, that's it,' Arnie said, taking her arm in a firm grip. 'That's quite enough from you for one party.' And he propelled her, protesting loudly, into the house.

When Winnie went to go after them, Gill said, 'Leave them alone to sort it out, Mum. Carol doesn't know what she's saying. She's had too much to drink, that's all.'

Gill was feeling very shaky herself as she went over to the swing and began to push it for Donna.

'Higher, Auntie Gill,' shouted her niece. 'I want to go higher.'

'Okay, darling,' said Gill, glad that Carol's ranting didn't seem to have had any lasting effect on her daughter. The poor little thing must have got used to it.

* * *

'Carol wants her backside smacking,' Winnie said to Hal in a low voice so that she couldn't be overheard by the others 'Carrying on like that in public . . . I've never been so embarrassed.'

'God knows what happened to the manners we taught her,' said Hal.

'That's what comes of marrying a man who's already been married to your sister,' said Winnie sagely. 'It's bound to lead to trouble.'

'Fancy accusing Gill of something like that, though,' said Hal.

'And in front of Peter too,' Winnie said, glancing towards Peter who was talking to Phoebe and Len near the French doors.

'It is definitely all over between Gill and Arnie, isn't it?' said Hal.

'Course it is,' she said. 'Carol doesn't know when she's well off. Arnie's a husband in a million to her . . . a damned sight better than he ever was to Gill.'

'That's true,' said Hal.

They stopped speaking abruptly as Gill came towards them, leaving Craig in charge of Donna on the swing.

'Don't worry about it, Mum,' Gill said. She knew her mother would be upset by what had happened. 'You know what Carol's like when she's in one of her moods. She'll have forgotten all about it tomorrow.'

'She might have, but I certainly won't,' snorted Winnie. 'Showing us all up like that . . . It was a damned disgrace.'

'I don't know why people bother to get married. All they seem to do is fight with each other.' John Briscoe was sitting with his mother and Len Bex, Peter having wandered off to talk to Gill. 'It puts me right off, I can tell you.'

'It isn't like that for everyone,' Phoebe pointed out.

'Course it isn't,' agreed Len.

'Doesn't seem like a barrel-load of laughs between those two from what I've seen of it,' John persisted. 'Carol always seems to be having a go at Arnie about something.'

'Take no notice of that, son,' said Len, who had become like one of the Briscoe family over the last few years. 'While we're all sitting here worrying about them, those two will be all lovey-dovey. It's all part of the fun.'

'Fun? Shoving sharp needles up your nose would be more fun than that.' John was now twenty-four, enjoying a bachelor life in a modern flat in Hammersmith. He was smart and trendy, with long hair and a light jacket worn over slim-fitting trousers. 'Give me the single life any day, where you can come and go as you please with no one to answer to.'

'You'll change your mind when the right one comes along,' said Len.

John sipped at a glass of beer, looking at Len thoughtfully. 'You don't seem in any hurry to try it again, though, do you?' he said

230

tactlessly. 'And you've been going out with Mum for yonks.'

'John!' Phoebe said, smarting with embarrassment.

'I'm only saying—'

'Well don't,' Phoebe rebuked.

'What's the fuss?' said John casually. 'It's no big deal, I was only making a comment.'

'I'd rather you didn't.'

'Let him speak,' said Len, putting a steadying hand on her arm. 'He has every right to be concerned about his mother.' He looked at John. 'Your mother and I are very good friends and we're happy to carry on as we are. It doesn't suit us to get married.' He turned to Phoebe. 'Ain't that right, Pheeb?'

Wrong, thought Phoebe, but she nodded and said, 'That's right.'

'Oh well, whatever lights your candle,' said John breezily.

For a while Phoebe had been Len's partner only every few months at the social occasions he was obliged to attend. But they had got on so well together he'd begun to suggest other outings too, and they had gradually become established companions.

Being together all day at work brought them even closer. But Len still made it plain that he had no intention of remarrying or of them moving in together. It was all to do with his lingering devotion for Mary, Phoebe guessed. But although she wanted that final commitment from him, she knew she must either accept him on his own terms or end their relationship altogether. And as that was the last thing she wanted, she carried on regardless and enjoyed having him as a close friend with the occasional bit of something else to spice things up.

'There you are, what did I tell you?' Len said as Carol and Arnie reappeared together and mingled with their guests as though nothing untoward had happened. 'They've made it up. They're all over each other now.'

'Don't you believe it,' said Phoebe, noticing Carol's bloodshot eyes despite the extra make-up she'd piled on to hide the fact that she'd been crying. 'That's all show, put on for our benefit and instigated by Arnie.'

'Perhaps you're right,' said Len. 'The poor bloke must have wanted the floor to open up and swallow him.'

'He's got his hands full with Carol all right,' she said with motherly concern. 'Those two are not right for each other and they both know it.'

'Oh well, I'm gonna go and ask Arnie for another drink,' said John, getting up. 'Either of you want one?'

They both shook their heads.

'Gill has always been the only girl for Arnie, despite all their troubles,' Phoebe said to Len after John had wandered off.

'Do you think Carol knows that and that's why she's so jealous?'

'Probably. And if today's performance is anything to go by she's getting paranoid about it,' declared Phoebe. 'I'm amazed Arnie puts up with her tantrums.'

'He does seem exceptionally patient, I must say,' said Len.

'Guilt,' declared Phoebe. 'He's letting her get away with murder to make up for the fact that he isn't in love with her. Arnie's trouble is, he doesn't know a good thing when he has it.'

'Gill?'

'The worst thing he ever did was letting her go,' Phoebe said, shaking her head sadly. 'And I bet he knows it now that it's too late.'

It is easy to see how the British got their reputation for stoicism, Gill thought, observing the way everyone carried on regardless in the aftermath of Carol's blistering performance. Carol and Arnie continued to host the party as though everything was normal, though not without the presence of simmering undertones.

Gill couldn't bring herself to be civil to her sister until she had received an apology. This came, albeit grudgingly, after Donna was in bed, having been bathed and read to by Gill. Apart from Peter, who was downstairs talking to Arnie, everyone else had gone, and the two women found themselves alone together on the landing on the way downstairs.

'Look, I'm sorry, okay?' Carol said in a perfunctory manner.

'And so you damned well ought to be,' rasped Gill, keeping her voice down so that she couldn't be heard in Donna's bedroom. 'You were right out of order.'

'Maybe I was, but I still say that you and Arnie fancy the pants off each other,' she said, her eyes narrow with accusation. 'And don't bother to deny it.'

Gill emitted a sigh. 'How many more times must I tell you? There is nothing going on between us,' she said. 'And there never will be.'

'There had better not be either,' Carol said vehemently. 'I'll kill the pair of you if I ever find out that there is.'

'Don't you ever give up, Carol?' Gill said in frustration. 'The only thing that is going on between Arnie and me is inside your head.'

'Oh, so I'm some sort of a loony now, am I?' she snarled.

'You will be if you don't calm down and stop imagining things.'

'Bloody cheek!' Carol exclaimed. 'How dare you suggest I'm not right in the head!'

'I'm just trying to get through to you . . .'

'Don't try and get out of it by making out I'm mental.'

'I've nothing to get out of,' said Gill, clinging to her rapidly diminishing patience. 'And I am sick to death of all these ridiculous accusations. The best thing I can do is stay away from you and Arnie altogether.'

Carol's attitude changed instantly – it wasn't in her interests for Gill

232

not to be around when she needed her. 'You can't do that,' she said. 'It would break Donna's heart.'

'Yes, it would.' Gill's heart turned over at the thought of not seeing her niece on a regular basis. She knew Carol would miss her too, because she was useful to her as a companion as well as baby-sitter.

'So you can't stay away.'

'Mum will probably help out with Donna instead of me.'

'It wouldn't be the same,' said Carol, fear in her eyes because she was reliant on her sister in so many ways. 'Donna dotes on you. She loves coming over to your place.'

'I would never stop her from coming over, you know that, but I don't want to be in the firing line of your nasty accusations any more,' said Gill. 'So I think it'll be best if I collect and deliver Donna but don't stay around to listen to your rotten insults.'

'I won't do it again, Gill, I promise.' As well as Gill's usefulness to Carol, it had also occurred to her that she would incur Arnie's anger if she caused a family rift. 'Just don't give up on me, please.'

'Well . . .'

'Don't stay away from us . . .'

Gill sighed, knowing she couldn't refuse her. Carol was weak and selfish, but the sisterly bond remained as strong as ever. Gill was actually rather sorry for Carol. It must be dreadful to feel so insecure that you lashed out with accusations without the slightest justification.

'All right.'

'Oh, thanks, Gill.' Carol hugged her. 'You're a pal.'

'You don't seem to appreciate what a gem of a husband you have in Arnie,' Gill said in a warning tone.

'I do.'

'You don't seem to,' Gill repeated. 'And if you carry on as you have been you'll drive him away. Not in my direction, but he'll go – and no one will blame him.'

Carol gasped, clutching her throat in a theatrical overreaction. 'Don't say that, Gill!' she said, her eyes half-closed as though the mere thought of losing Arnie caused her physical pain. 'I couldn't bear to lose him.'

'Stop behaving like a sulky teenager then, and work at hanging on to him. You're a wife and mother now. It's time you grew up.'

'I don't know what happens to me,' Carol said. 'I get so terrified of losing him that my thoughts run wild and I lose control. That's why I say these things.'

'Calm down and give him some space and there won't be any question of your losing him,' said Gill. 'Arnie's a good man – better than he's ever been now. He's improved a lot with maturity. You treat him right and he'll be with you for ever.'

'I'll try,' she said.

* * *

'I'm really sorry about what happened earlier, babe,' Carol said to Arnie later that same evening. Gill and Peter had just left, and Carol had gone into their living room to find Arnie watching the ten o'clock news.

'S'alright,' Arnie mumbled. He was sitting in an armchair near the open window, his eyes glued to the TV. The news was dominated by the recently elected Conservative Prime Minister, Edward Heath, who had declared a state of emergency as the dockers staged their first national strike since 1926. Attractively appointed in the contemporary style and decorated in a variety of blue tones, the room was cool and comfortable. It was situated at the front of the house, overlooking a pleasant suburban street.

'I promise you it won't happen again,' Carol said ardently.

'Yeah, yeah, okay,' Arnie said, still looking at the screen as the sports news came on.

'You don't believe me, do you?' she persisted.

'Hang on a minute, Carol,' he said without looking at her. 'I want to see what the scores were at Wimbledon.'

Rage scorched through her because she couldn't get his immediate attention. How dare he ignore her! She had to restrain herself physically from rushing over to the television and turning it off, because she knew that would make things even worse. She sat down in an armchair opposite him and managed, with great difficulty, to stay silent until he'd heard what he wanted to.

'I don't know what gets into me,' she said the instant she saw the opportunity to capture his attention.

'Forget it,' said Arnie. He was so tired by now of her temper tantrums and endless chatter, he could hardly bear to look at her.

'I mean, it isn't as though anything would be going on between you.' She paused, then added, 'Is it?'

'Oh not again, Carol,' Arnie sighed, looking at her now even though he was exhausted by her insane jealousy. 'Please don't start on about that again.'

'I just want to make sure, then I'll never mention it again.'

'There is nothing going on, nor is there ever likely to be, between myself and Gill,' he said through clenched teeth. 'Now give us a break and let the subject drop.'

'Okay, Arnie,' she said meekly.

She knew she had pushed him as far as she dared – today. Oh God, if only the suspicions that plagued her during her every waking moment would go away and leave her in peace!

Gill was glad to get home that night. 'Phew! I don't want another evening like that for a long time,' she said to Peter after Craig had gone to bed and they were relaxing with some music on the record player.

'Me neither,' said Peter.

234

'Surely Carol doesn't really believe there's anything going on between Arnie and me, does she?' she remarked idly.

'I don't know if she does or not,' he said in an odd tone.

'Peter?' she said, looking at him sharply. 'What's the matter?'

'Nothing.'

'There is, I can tell.'

He sighed. 'Well, I can sympathise with Carol in a way,' he said.

'Surely you're not suggesting—'

'I'm not suggesting anything,' he cut in. 'But I am saying that there is *something* between you and Arnie . . .'

'I swear there's nothing going on.'

'You're not having an affair with him, I know that,' he went on. 'But there's still something going on between you, whether you intend it or not. It's like electricity in the air. I can feel it when you're together, and Carol obviously can too . . . That's why she gets these awful fits of jealousy.'

'I *was* married to the man,' said Gill, strongly defensive now. 'There's bound to be some sort of a bond; we have a son, for goodness sake.'

'I'm not criticising you,' Peter pointed out. 'I'm just telling you the way it is between you and Arnie, how it must be for Carol.'

'It isn't intentional . . .'

'I know that.'

'Look, Peter,' Gill said, feeling a surge of tenderness for him; she thought she must inadvertently have hurt him. Perhaps it wasn't fair to him to leave things the way they were between them. 'I think it's time we talked . . . about us.'

'Oh?'

'About putting things on to a more permanent footing.'

'Getting married, you mean?'

'Yes.'

'This isn't the time,' he said quietly, surprising her with his lack of interest.

'You usually want to talk about it.'

'Yes, I do – but you're only suggesting it because you're feeling guilty about what I've just said.'

'Of course I'm feeling guilty. I don't want to hurt you . . .'

'Forget it.'

'I really think we should talk.'

'Not now, Gill,' he said wearily.

'But, Peter . . .'

'It's been a hell of an evening,' he said. 'So let's just leave it and relax.'

'Okay, if that's what you really want,' she agreed, but she felt very troubled. Peter seemed strange, different towards her suddenly. It was so unlike him to be off-hand about setting a date for their wedding. He'd been pestering her about it for months.

Something was wrong, she could feel it in the atmosphere. And she had a horrible suspicion that it was serious.

Chapter Nineteen

A few weeks later Gill went to see the mother superior in her office. She perched on a chair facing the nun, who was sitting behind her desk regarding her visitor quizzically. On the wall behind her a wooden crucifix hung next to some glass-fronted bookshelves, upon which stood a white plaster statuette of the Virgin Mary wearing a blue robe.

'So, how can I help you?' the nun asked in the soft, breathless way she had of speaking. 'You said on the telephone that it was a matter of some urgency.'

'Yes, it is rather urgent,' Gill confirmed.

The nun looked troubled. 'I do hope you're not having problems with any of our girls.'

'Nothing like that,' Gill quickly assured her. 'All the girls from here are a joy to teach. Cherry Betts in particular.'

'Ah, yes. What a difference music has made to that child's personality.' The mother superior gave a small smile. 'She used to be such a naughty girl, before she discovered her musical talent.'

'So I understand.' Gill paused. 'Actually, Cherry is the reason I've come to see you.'

'Oh?'

'Yes. She is exceptionally talented and has worked very hard at her music. She's passed all her exams with flying colours, as you know . . .'

'Indeed I do,' said the nun expectantly, wondering what Gill was leading up to. 'We're all very proud of her here at St Theresa's.'

'With the right training, I think she could have a career in music,' Gill continued.

'And . . . ?' The nun clasped her large hands together on the desk, waiting for Gill to come to the point.

'I've heard of a piano competition I think she should enter.'

'And you want my permission to put her name forward?' The mother superior looked puzzled. Cherry regularly competed in musical events, and permission was normally dealt with by Sister Maud. 'It goes without saying that you can go ahead and enter her. We always encourage our girls to compete. That sort of thing helps to build the character of a child.'

'This competition is rather different, though,' Gill started warily.

'Some kind of special event?' speculated the other woman.

'Very special indeed,' said Gill. 'So special, in fact, that the winner

237

will be given the opportunity to study music at college as a full-time student, all expenses paid by the competition sponsors.'

'Oh, now wouldn't that be wonderful for Cherry?' said the nun, blue eyes sparkling for a moment before becoming serious. 'But nothing that good comes easily. She has to win the competition first.'

'Winning the competition is the least of our problems,' said Gill.

'Really?'

Gill nodded. 'The event is an international one. It's being staged in Boston . . . in America,' she explained. 'Cherry would have to find the money for her fare and enough to cover her expenses while she's in the States.'

'Oh, dear.' The nun brushed her brow with her hand worriedly. 'We help our girls as much as we can from our special fund, particularly if they have a genuine talent. But I don't think we could run to sending one of them to America. I wouldn't feel justified in spending so much money on one girl when we have so many to consider.'

'If she were to win the competition she would be able to study music at the famous Alder College in Boston.' Gill was desperate to emphasise the magnitude of the opportunity. 'It would be the chance of a lifetime for her.'

'I understand that, and we would be prepared to contribute to the cost – but we couldn't possibly manage it all.' She shook her head. 'And we couldn't allow her to go alone, so that would mean double the expense.'

'If we were somehow able to raise the money, would one of the nuns be able to go with her?' Gill asked. 'I'd go with her myself, but I have too many commitments here.'

'I'm sure we could spare one of the sisters to accompany her,' said the nun. 'That isn't a problem. Finding the money is.'

'Yes, I thought you might say something along these lines – which is why I haven't said anything to Cherry about it.' Gill paused. 'The trouble is, and the reason I said it was urgent . . . the entries have to be in quite soon in time for the closing date, though the competition isn't until December.'

The mother superior stroked her chin, staring meditatively into space. 'I would so much like her to have this opportunity,' she said sadly, 'but we just don't have that kind of money.'

'What if I were able to raise *some* of the money?' said Gill, desperate that Cherry shouldn't miss this opportunity.

'That would put a different light on the matter altogether. As I've said, we could make a contribution.'

'Good.'

'But if this was to be a serious possibility we'd need to work out the exact cost, so we'd know what sort of sum we're talking about.'

'I've already done that,' said Gill. What had been a vague idea was now becoming a definite challenge. 'Because I *will* come up with the cash we need.'

'You have that sort of money yourself?' queried the nun.

'Oh no,' Gill said with a wry grin. 'But Cherry is going to have her chance, even if I have to go out begging in the streets for the money.' She gave the nun a wicked smile. 'Fortunately that won't be necessary, because I have a much better idea . . .'

Gill was so excited about her plan that she couldn't wait until the evening to tell Peter about it. She stopped off at the music shop on the way home.

'He isn't here,' explained Wendy, sitting on a stool behind the record counter filing her nails.

'Will he be long?'

'Shouldn't think so,' she said casually, 'he's only gone to the bank.'

'I'll wait for him then.'

'Sure.'

Gill stood aside while Wendy went off to sell a woman a metronome and man a music stand. The long-haired youth who had been drooling over an electric guitar departed, leaving the shop without customers.

'God, I hate weekdays when the shop's as quiet as this,' said Wendy, yawning.

'Some people would welcome the chance of not having much to do,' Gill remarked, just to be sociable.

'Not me. The time drags too much when the place is like a morgue,' Wendy said. 'Give me a busy Saturday when the place is packed out anytime. The time just whizzes by then.'

'Yes, I suppose it would do,' said Gill, looking at her watch.

'He should be back any minute,' said Wendy.

'If he isn't back soon I'll leave it and see him tonight.'

'He'll have met someone in the street and got chatting, I expect.' Gill nodded.

'The good thing about Peter is that he's very easygoing about things like that,' said Wendy. 'He lets me pop out to the shops during working hours and doesn't tell me off if I'm a few minutes late in the morning.'

'I can imagine him being easy to work with,' said Gill.

'I shan't half miss him.'

'Miss him?'

'Yeah. God knows what the new bloke will be like.'

'New bloke?'

'The new manager taking over from Peter,' Wendy explained.

'Someone else is taking over?'

'When Peter leaves, yeah.' Wendy was beginning to sound bored.

Gill was astounded. 'Peter's leaving the shop?'

'Yeah, that's right.' Wendy studied her nails before resuming work with the file. 'He's got himself a job up north somewhere.' She looked at Gill thoughtfully. 'But surely you know about it . . . I just assumed you'd be going with him.'

'I suppose he hasn't got around to telling me about it yet,' Gill said lamely.

'He's leaving it a bit late,' Wendy said. 'He finishes here a week Saturday.'

Gill was too stunned to speak.

'Ooh, blimey!' Wendy made a face. 'I hope I haven't dropped him in it.'

'Tell him I'll see him tonight,' said Gill, and she hurried from the shop.

Gill waited until Craig had gone out to football training that evening and she and Peter were sitting down in the living room before she confronted him with what she'd heard.

'Oh dear,' he said, looking shamefaced at her across the hearth. 'I'm sorry you had to hear about it from someone else. I was waiting for an opportunity to tell you.'

She couldn't believe it. All afternoon she'd been telling herself it must be a mistake, that Wendy had got hold of the wrong end of the stick. She'd barely been able to concentrate on her teaching for thinking about it.

'I take it by that that I'm not included in your plans,' she said, deeply hurt.

He scratched his head, then looked her straight in the eyes. 'No, I'm afraid not,' he said. 'I want to make a new start in the north.'

'The north,' Gill repeated dumbly.

'I've a cousin in Leeds. I'll doss down with him until I find a place of my own.'

'Oh, Peter . . .' Gill's voice was leaden with disappointment. 'I can't believe you'd be so devious. To do something like this without telling me . . . You and I have always been so honest with each other.'

'Yes, well, it hasn't been an easy decision to make,' he told her soberly. 'I wanted everything in place before I said anything to you . . . so that I wouldn't change my mind. I don't want to hurt you, but this is how it has to be.'

'But why?' she asked, her voice rising. 'Why are you doing this?'

'Because you and I don't have a future together,' he stated.

'But I told you we'd set a date to get married.'

He shook his head. 'Getting married isn't going to change anything,' he said. 'It's taken me long enough to realise it, but I've finally accepted it.'

'What are you talking about?' she asked, shaking her head in despair.

'I thought that us getting married was the answer, that it would bring us together, would make you love me.' He looked at her unwaveringly, his mouth set in a grim line. 'But I know now that it wouldn't make any difference.'

She combed her hair from her brow with her fingers, feeling distraught and let down. 'And may I ask what's brought you to this sudden conclusion?' she asked coldly.

'It isn't sudden, not really,' he said. 'I think I've always known it but wasn't man enough to face up to the root of the trouble – the reason why you aren't able to give me the sort of commitment that I want from you.'

'And the reason is . . . ?'

'You're still in love with Arnie,' he replied with a sigh of resignation. 'And that's something I can't compete with.'

Gill was assailed by a variety of emotions – guilt, sadness, anger at having been betrayed by Peter . . . She couldn't deny that he was right about her feelings for Arnie, but that didn't mean she couldn't care for him too. She had done her best to make him happy while they'd been together. Whatever her true feelings, she had shared her life with him. Surely she deserved better than to have him end their relationship without so much as a word to her about it. It was deeply wounding!

'As I've told you before, it's only natural that I should still feel something special for Arnie,' she said. 'I was married to the man for a long time; there's bound to be a bond between us. I've never denied that.'

'When you and I first started seeing each other it was quite soon after your separation from Arnie,' he said. 'I thought you'd get over him eventually. But now I don't believe anyone else stands a chance against him. It's no wonder Carol gets so worked up about it.'

'Ah, so that's at the bottom of all this,' she said with sudden realisation. 'My sister's performance at Donna's party.'

'That's what set me thinking seriously about it, yes,' he admitted. 'But it was there at the back of my mind anyway.'

'Why take notice of Carol when we all know she's paranoid about Arnie?'

'She has the whole thing out of proportion,' he admitted. 'But I see you and Arnie with the same eye as she does when you're together. I know what it feels like to be on the outside of something as rock solid as that.'

'But Arnie and I don't do anything out of place,' she said.

'You don't have to do anything for your feelings to be obvious,' he said. 'To me, anyway – and to Carol, apparently.'

'Oh?'

'Something happens to you when the two of you are together,' Peter said. 'You come to life in a way that you never do when you're with me.'

241

'Not intentionally.'

'Which makes it even worse from my point of view. Because it's inside you and not within your control. There's nothing that you or I or anyone else can do about it. It's just there, like the air we breathe.'

'I care a lot about you, Peter,' Gill said, and it was the truth.

'But not in the way that I want.'

'It was enough once.'

'Yes. I thought I could cope with being just "good old Peter",' he said. 'But it isn't enough for me now, Gill, I want a woman who lights up for me like you do for Arnie.'

'I can't force something that isn't there,' she admitted. 'But I've been so happy with you. I don't want us to split up.'

'I'm sorry, Gill,' he said, 'but my mind is made up.'

'I'm sorry too. Really sorry. I'm going to miss you.'

He stood up purposefully. 'I think it'll probably be best if I move out of here right away,' he said. 'I can stay with a mate until I've worked out my notice at the music shop.'

'If that's what you want,' Gill said, because she could tell his decision was final.

'I'll go and pack my things then.'

'Okay.'

Sitting in the chair by the fire, listening to him moving about upstairs, Gill was smarting with rejection, desperately sad at the thought of not having him around. But she felt no impulse to fight for him, no urge to persuade him to change his mind. Because deep in her heart she knew that what he was doing was the right thing for them both.

Peter hadn't been the only one to delude himself while they had been together. She had done her share of that too, trying to convince herself that what she felt for him was sufficient to choose him as her partner for life, when it wasn't.

God, what a mess!

The following Sunday, when the family was gathered at her parents' house for lunch, Gill made her announcement.

'I've two things to tell you all,' she said. 'The first is that Peter and I have split up.'

Her mother gasped and her father stopped carving the joint, standing with the knife poised in mid-air while a shocked silence fell over the room.

'Don't worry, I'm all right,' she said, looking at her parents and then at Carol – but not allowing her eyes to linger on Arnie because Peter's comments had made her afraid even to cast a glance in his direction. 'It's all for the best. We were never really right for each other.'

'Perhaps you'll patch things up,' Winnie suggested hopefully.

'No, it isn't the sort of thing you can patch up,' explained Gill. 'We didn't have a quarrel as such. It was more a mutual facing up to things. Peter's going to live in Leeds.'

'Oh, I *am* sorry, love,' said her mother.

Knowing that the last thing Gill would want was pity, Arnie made a hasty intervention.

'So, what was the other thing you had to tell us?' he asked.

'That's much more cheerful,' she said, brightening. 'I'm going to put on a concert to raise money.' She explained why she needed to do this. 'And I'm going to need your help.'

'She's already got me down as general dogsbody,' said Craig.

'Me wannabe a dogbody,' chanted Donna, causing a roar of laughter.

'Who's going to be taking part in this concert?' Hal enquired with interest, slicing the beef while Winnie served them all with Yorkshire pudding.

'My pupils,' she said, 'with Cherry as top of the bill.'

'What a smashing idea!' said Arnie, no stranger to fund raising. 'We'll do whatever we can to help.' He looked at Carol, careful as always to ensure she wasn't excluded. 'Won't we, love?'

'Yeah, course we will,' she said in a casual manner that belied the fact that she was in a state of high agitation. Her mind was still reeling with her sister's first piece of news. The fact that Gill had been in a settled relationship had been Carol's safeguard against Arnie's committing adultery. To her fevered imagination the presence of Peter in Gill's life was the only thing that prevented her and Arnie from having an affair. Carol didn't credit either of them with so much as a crumb of decency. Now that Gill had returned to the single state, she felt more seriously threatened than ever and would have to keep an even closer eye on them. But she daren't be too obvious about it. She didn't want to put them on their guard. 'Anything at all we can do to help,' she said evenly, 'just let us know.'

'You'll probably live to regret having said that.' Gill grinned. 'By the time I've got the show organised you'll all be worn out.'

The main hall at St Theresa's was transformed into a perfect auditorium for the November concert, the mother superior having been delighted to allow Gill the use of it for the evening. The stage from which morning assembly was normally taken was now colourfully banked by flowers and graced with a grand piano, the former donated by an acquaintance of Len's who owned a flower shop, the latter on loan from the music shop, courtesy of the new manager.

The show was drawing to a close and Gill was waiting at the side of the stage to deliver her speech of thanks, listening as Cherry finished a technically brilliant and moving performance of Mozart's Sonata in C.

Every seat was taken. Gill was touched by the practical help and support she had received in putting the concert on. Arnie had been an absolute godsend, turning his hand to anything from organising sponsorship to persuading the shopkeepers of West London to sell tickets. He had even set to and painted the walls of the hall in honour of the occasion, assisted by John and Craig. Phoebe, Winnie and Carol had worked together to provide the light refreshments that had been on sale in the interval, and Len and Hal had been selling programmes and raffle tickets at the door.

As the applause rose for Cherry, who stood up and bowed graciously to the audience, Gill prepared herself for a moment, then stepped on to the stage, elegantly attired for the occasion in a white satin evening blouse and a long black skirt.

'Thank you for coming to our concert tonight,' she said when the applause had finally died away and Cherry had left the stage. 'I'm thrilled to be able to tell you that, thanks to your support, we have reached our target.' She paused for a moment as the buzz of excitement grew. 'Which means that the star of our show, Cherry Betts, will be able to go to America to take part in the piano competition that could change her life.'

Cheers rose to the rafters and Gill beckoned to Cherry, who was sitting with the other young performers in the front row. The girl's eyes were brimming with tears as she came back on stage and stood beside Gill, who was herself feeling very emotional.

'I'd like to thank everybody who helped make our concert possible,' Gill managed, albeit with a wobble in her voice. 'Especially my family and friends who gave so generously of their time to make this evening an occasion to remember.'

Another burst of applause.

'And last, but by no means least, my final thanks go to our young performers who have given us such a treat this evening, and who I would like to welcome back on stage.'

And with her heart so full she thought it would burst, Gill watched her talented charges file back on to the stage to join her and Cherry, their faces flushed with pleasure. She was completely overwhelmed when Donna, looking adorable in a red velvet dress with a white lacy collar and accompanied by her mother, trailed on to the stage carrying a bouquet of flowers which she handed to her aunt. This was almost too much for Gill, who took her final bow through a blur of tears, after which Cherry went over to the piano to end the show with the national anthem.

The warmth of spirit in that hall on that cold November evening was something Gill knew she would never forget.

'What a night!' she said later, when family and friends had gathered at her house for an informal supper. 'I won't forget that in a hurry.'

'Neither will anyone else,' said Winnie, as everyone helped

themselves to the buffet meal laid out on Gill's kitchen table. 'And it's all down to you, Gill. You put the whole thing together.'

'Hear, hear!' said her father.

'You were great,' said Winnie.

'Terrific,' added Carol.

'I couldn't have done it without your help, all of you,' Gill was quick to point out.

'We didn't have much choice with you bullying us into it,' joked Phoebe.

'The bouquet at the end was a lovely surprise.' Gill looked at her sister, who had just put the sleeping Donna into the spare bed. 'How on earth did you manage to keep Donna awake so late?'

'She had a long sleep this afternoon,' explained Carol. 'She's fast asleep now, though.'

'You can leave her here for the night if you like,' Gill suggested in her usual helpful manner. 'To save disturbing her when you go. I'll bring her home in the morning.'

'Thanks,' said Carol, taking Gill's accommodating nature for granted as usual.

'And thanks for the flowers,' said Gill warmly, though she couldn't help being puzzled by her sister's sudden burst of good nature.

'I'm glad you were pleased.' Carol had come up with the idea of organising a bouquet for her sister. For her it was a way of hiding her savage jealousy, which grew and festered with every passing day, filling her with hatred for her sister. Try as she might to put the torturous suspicions out of her mind, they just wouldn't go away. Gill and Arnie – Arnie and Gill . . . Thoughts of them together absorbed her so completely, she could hardly think of anything else. The run-up to the concert had been agonising, as Arnie had immersed himself in helping Gill with the organisation. Carol had only got involved herself in an effort to prevent them being alone together.

'Young Cherry was a smash hit,' said Phoebe, helping herself to a slice of pork pie and pickles. 'What a talent!'

'She certainly deserves a chance to show what she can do in America,' said Len, forking some ham on to his plate.

'I thought all the kids were good.' Arnie almost added something complimentary about Gill's part in their success, but thought better of it because of the effect such a remark would have on Carol. Even the most casual compliment would be seen by his wife as evidence of his love for Gill and further fuel for Carol's obsession.

'It says something for your teaching, Gill,' said Carol, forcing a smile to hide what she was really feeling.

'It's very satisfying, seeing the children perform so well,' Gill said.

'It's a good experience for them an' all,' said Winnie.

'Not to mention the proud parents,' chuckled Phoebe. 'Someone

245

could have done a good trade in paper hankies tonight.'

'That's what Mum and Dad will be like when I play in my first cup final.' Craig looked at his mother and added saucily, 'You'll go all soppy then, won't you, Mum?'

'You know my feelings about that,' she said, smiling so as not to spoil the party but feeling a shadow dampen her mood.

'We'll all be in tears on that day,' said Hal happily.

'Not half,' agreed Arnie.

Although the mood was light and the remarks made in a jokey manner, the fact that Craig spoke with increasing frequency about a career in football was seriously beginning to worry Gill. When everyone began to drift into the other room with their supper, she took the opportunity of a few words with Arnie on the subject as he limped out of the kitchen behind Carol.

'I think Craig really believes he can become a professional footballer, you know,' she said, waylaying Arnie by the door.

'I'm sure he does, and I agree with him,' he said, moving back into the kitchen and perching on a stool by the worktop – he still needed to rest his leg at night if he'd had a busy day.

'You really think he's good enough, then?' Gill said, standing opposite him with a plate in her hand.

'No question about it,' he said. 'With the right training he could be a really good player.'

'I don't want this idea encouraged,' she said anxiously.

'Why not?'

'Because I think it would be better for him to concentrate on getting some qualifications so that he can get a steady job.'

'But if football is what he wants to do for a career—'

'He doesn't know what's best for him at the moment,' she said.

'I'm not so sure about that.'

'It's up to us as responsible parents to give him the right guidance,' she said emphatically. 'Being a footballer is every working-class boy's dream. But how many of them make it?'

'I did.'

'You were one of the few. And look what it did to you – it changed you and almost wrecked your life. I don't want that to happen to him.'

'It's a sin to waste talent, Gill,' Arnie pointed out gravely. 'You of all people should know that, given that you spend your life nurturing talent and have spent so much time and effort to give young Cherry Betts a chance.'

'That's a different thing altogether,' insisted Gill.

'Different subject, same principle,' Arnie said in a firm tone. 'A life in music is not a secure one by any means. How many of the people who want a performing career actually make a full-time living at it?'

'Only a small percentage,' Gill was forced to admit, 'but that isn't

246

the point. I don't think it would be right to encourage Craig to think of football as a career.'

'It's early days yet, anyway,' Arnie said in an effort to defuse the situation; Gill was getting heated, and this was neither the time nor the place for an argument. 'Let's just wait and see what happens when he gets a bit older, shall we?'

'Just as long as you know where I stand on this one,' she said ardently. 'I really feel strongly about it.'

'Okay. Point taken.'

'Good.'

'So, having established that you don't want another footballer in the family, let's go and join the others.'

'Yes, let's do that,' she said, smiling to indicate that there were no hard feelings.

At this moment, there was an unexpected interruption.

'Oh, *very cosy*,' Carol's voice was clipped with rage.

'Carol . . .' Arnie said in a warning tone.

'So, you don't even bother to be discreet about what you're up to now.'

Gill's tolerance on this subject was becoming threadbare. 'For heaven's sake—'

'It's a wonder I don't actually catch you at it—'

'We were only talking about Craig,' Gill cut in, her stomach knotting with tension.

'Oh yeah?' Carol sneered.

'Yes, we were.'

'Give it a rest, Carol,' said Arnie.

'Don't you speak to me like that, you two-timing git.'

Gill stepped forward and took her sister by both arms, staring into her face. 'Look . . . Arnie and I were doing no harm. We were simply having a conversation about our son, whose welfare is something we share whether you like it or not.'

'Talking about Craig, my foot,' Carol said, pulling away.

'You're being ridiculous.'

'And you're a slut.'

'Just listen to yourself, Carol—'

'Shut up!'

'You made a damned good job of ruining Donna's birthday celebrations, but you're not going to spoil the party here tonight.' Gill looked at her sister, forbidding her to argue. 'So either behave in a normal, civilised manner or go home. But don't subject us all to your idiotic notions yet again.'

'We'll both go,' said Arnie. 'That'll be the best thing for everyone.'

'Surely there's no need for that,' said Gill, disappointed to have the evening spoiled so unnecessarily.

'There's no point in us staying with Carol in this mood,' Arnie said, looking sharply at his wife, who seemed to have retreated into a sulky silence. 'I'll only be on edge, wondering what she's gonna come out with next.'

'Don't talk about me as though I'm not here,' Carol objected.

'Don't behave so disgracefully that we're driven to, then,' said Gill.

Arnie walked towards the door. 'Come on, Carol,' he said resignedly, 'I'll get our coats.'

As he left the room and Carol went to follow, Gill put a restraining hand on her sister's arm. 'You won't be happy until you've wrecked all our lives, will you?' she said, and without waiting for a reply she turned away and went to join the others in the living room, her light-hearted mood shattered.

Chapter Twenty

Although Arnie was an expert at putting on a front, he couldn't fool his mother.

'What's up, son?' she asked, one Saturday afternoon the following January. Arnie had come into the office with a query, and Phoebe was alone because Len was at one of the other branches.

'Nothin'.'

'Come on, Arnie, this is your mum you're talking to,' she said. 'I know there's something wrong, no matter how much you pretend otherwise.'

'Leave it, Mum.'

But Phoebe wasn't easily deterred when someone she cared about was unhappy. 'Carol's giving you a hard time again, isn't she?' she said, having witnessed his wife's neurotic behaviour on too many occasions.

The understatement of the decade, Arnie thought gloomily. Marriage to Carol had become so unbearable that he dreaded going home. Hardly a day passed when she didn't pick an argument with him about his supposed adultery with Gill.

Her neurosis ran to a pattern: she would assail him with accusations until he finally managed to convince her that her suspicions were groundless, when she would calm down; but a day or so later the whole process would begin again. He was reaching the end of his tether.

Normally he would not discuss the subject with anyone, out of loyalty to his wife, but the need to share his problem was suddenly overwhelming.

He sat down opposite his mother. 'She's driving me crazy.'

'Oh, son . . .'

'And the worst part is, I don't think she can help it.'

'That's awful.'

'I just don't know what to do about it, Mum,' he confessed. 'She's making her own life a misery as well as mine. And who knows what sort of effect all this is having on Donna?'

'Kids are very resilient, you know,' she said. She could see how distressed he was and was anxious to reassure him.

'But Carol is so wound up all the time. She's obsessed with her suspicions about me and Gill, and it's making her bad tempered with Donna.'

'I think Carol should see a doctor,' said Phoebe, 'to get something to calm her down.'

'I think so too, but if I suggest it to her she flies off the handle,' he said. 'And I can't force her to go.'

'Course you can't.'

'One mention of medical help and she says I'm trying to cover my own tracks by pretending that she's mental.'

'Oh dear.' Phoebe was worried sick.

'She's even accused me of wanting her to go on tranquillisers to dull her senses so that she won't notice what's going on.'

'Sounds to me as though she really does need help.' Phoebe tutted.

'I wouldn't mind if I was getting up to mischief,' he said. 'But I'm not, I swear it.'

'I believe you.'

'I'll admit I wouldn't have married Carol if I'd had any choice. But knowing I had to, I went into the marriage determined to make a go of it.' Arnie felt on the verge of tears finally, after keeping his feelings to himself for so long. 'And I'm still doing my damnedest. But Carol isn't making it easy.'

'She must be feeling very insecure about you,' said Phoebe.

'That's the problem,' he said, shaking his head in despair. 'But how can I convince her that she's got nothing to worry about when she just won't accept it?'

'I wish I knew the answers,' said Phoebe, leaning towards him with her forearms on the desk.

'I try to give her a good life,' Arnie said. 'She wants for nothing.'

'No one would argue with that.' Phoebe was thoughtful. 'Why don't you take her away for a weekend? Just the two of you. Go to a posh hotel somewhere and spoil her rotten,' she suggested. 'It'll do you both good to get away, and it's time you had a Saturday off from work.'

'At this time of the year?'

'Yeah, why not?' Phoebe said with rising enthusiasm. 'Somewhere in the country would be nice. It's a bit bleak for the seaside in winter.'

'What about Donna?'

'Gill would probably be willing to look after her for a weekend,' she said. 'I'd have her myself but I'm at the shop all day on a Saturday.'

'Mm.'

'And there's always Winnie if Gill can't do it for some reason,' said Phoebe, hoping to remove all the obstacles. 'But Gill is nuts about Donna so I can't see her refusing the chance of having her to herself for a weekend.'

'There is that,' Arnie said, smiling at the thought of his adored daughter.

'Donna is the daughter Gill will never have,' Phoebe remarked. 'And for all Carol's bad feeling about her sister, she always seems pleased enough to use her as a baby-sitter if she wants to go off somewhere.'

'It's a thought,' said Arnie. 'But I don't know if Carol will agree to it. She can be so damned awkward these days.'

'Get it all organised before you say anything to her, then give her a surprise,' Phoebe suggested. 'That way she'll be far too thrilled that you've gone to all that trouble on her behalf to make any objections.'

'You reckon?'

'I think it's worth a try.'

But he had his doubts about Carol's reaction to the idea. She could twist the most well-meant intention into a plan of evil intent. 'I'm not sure, Mum,' he sighed.

'The first thing you need to do is arrange for Gill to look after Donna.' Phoebe persisted in the thought that anything was worth doing if there was the slightest chance of it improving the appalling state of her son's marriage. 'Once that's settled you can go ahead and book a hotel – one of those places you see advertised in the paper with log fires and a cosy bar would be nice . . .' But Phoebe could see he still wasn't convinced. 'It's only a suggestion, son, but it's well worth considering.'

'Yeah, I'll give it some thought.'

It was on Arnie's mind for the rest of the afternoon. He was still mulling it over as he drove home through the darkened streets, a nocturnal frost already beginning to form on garden walls and rooftops, the street-lights blurred by a gathering mist.

As a partner in a thriving business he could afford to take his wife somewhere special. Surely even Carol's warped mind couldn't misconstrue his motives for a weekend away for the two of them.

Thinking ahead to the reality of two days alone with Carol, without Donna's entertaining company as a diversion, he wasn't sure if he could cope with it. Even apart from his wife's recent behaviour, they had little in common. But if it would help to make her feel more secure, it was worth making the effort. Yes, he would do it, and the sooner he got it arranged the better.

With his mother's advice in mind about his first move, he turned off the main Chiswick road and headed back to Fulham to ask Gill to look after Donna for a weekend.

Carol looked at the kitchen clock, her temper rising. Arnie was late home from work. Admittedly only by about fifteen minutes, but it was annoying just the same. On weekdays he could never be sure exactly what time he would be home because he often had things to do after the shop closed; but on Saturdays she insisted he be home by six o'clock. It was the weekend, for heaven's sake! The meal was ready and keeping warm in the oven; the least he could do was make sure she wasn't kept waiting.

Donna had gone to Winnie and Hal's for the afternoon and they hadn't brought her back yet, so Carol didn't even have her daughter to take her mind off Arnie's non appearance. Fraught with tension, she stamped across to the living-room window and peered through the curtains into the street, the lights in the houses opposite obscured by the mist. No sign of Arnie. She marched angrily to the telephone in the hall and dialled the number of the shop. No reply! Becoming more furious with every second that passed, she dialled his mother's number.

'Hello, Phoebe, it's Carol. Is Arnie there?' she asked.

'Well, no,' said Phoebe, surprised at the question.

'Oh. He isn't home yet and I couldn't think where else he might be,' Carol explained. 'I've rung the shop and there's no reply.'

'There wouldn't be. He left at the same time as Len and me,' said Phoebe. 'You know Arnie, he never hangs about on a Saturday.'

'Did he say he was stopping off anywhere on the way home?'

'No.'

'Oh.'

'It's quite foggy,' Phoebe pointed out, 'so he wouldn't have been able to put his foot down like he usually does.'

'It doesn't look all that foggy outside to me,' said Carol.

'It's patchy,' said Phoebe, 'and very deceiving. He's probably having to drive at a crawl.'

'That must be what it is then,' said Carol, not believing it at all.

'He'll be in in a minute, love,' said Phoebe confidently. 'Don't worry.'

'Okay. See you.'

Replacing the receiver, Carol paced about the house, her temper getting more explosive by the second. 'Held up by the fog, my Aunt Fanny,' she muttered to herself, looking out of the window again. 'It's hardly more than a mist.'

Arnie wasn't yet even half an hour later than usual, but to Carol it was more than long enough. Her rage at being kept waiting turned to icy fear as a terrible suspicion came into her mind. The bugger had gone to Gill's. That's where he was – *with her*! The thought buffeted her, causing her to rush to the bathroom to be sick.

Emerging in a cold sweat and beyond reasonable thought, she tore to the telephone in the hall and feverishly began to dial Gill's number. But when she got to the last digit she stopped and slammed down the receiver. What would a telephone call achieve? Arnie wouldn't answer someone else's phone, and Gill was hardly likely to admit to Carol that he was there with her.

She ran a trembling hand over her clammy brow. She *had* to know for sure if he was there, and the only way to find out was to go to Gill's to see for herself. If she didn't know for certain it would torment her for days. If she was wrong – and please God that she was – she could rest easy.

Damp with nervous perspiration, her heart thundering in her ears, she threw on her coat and rushed from the house, the meal in the oven forgotten, as well as the imminent return of her daughter.

Phoebe was right, Carol thought in the car. The mist really was denser than it had seemed from the window, and the roads were icy. Normally Carol would have been too afraid to drive her car in these conditions, but her unstable frame of mind obliterated all fear and trepidation. All that mattered was knowing the truth, and she was aware of nothing but this as she roared towards Fulham.

As she drew up outside Gill's house her heart turned over. Arnie's car was parked outside! So now she really did know the truth. But she wished she didn't.

She put her head in her hands in despair.

'Blimey, is that the time?' Arnie looked at the clock on the mantelpiece in Gill's living room. 'Carol will murder me. She goes berserk if I'm late home from work on a Saturday. Six o'clock on the dot or I'm a dead man.'

'It isn't long past six,' said Gill. 'You've hardly been here any time at all.'

'I'll still be late, though.'

'In Carol's interests . . .' Gill reminded him.

'She doesn't know that,' he said. 'And it'll spoil the surprise if we tell her.'

'Perhaps you'd better ring her and tell her you're on your way, if she's that particular.'

'She's bound to ask where I'm calling from and I'll have to lie or give the game away,' he said. 'I don't wanna tell porkies.'

'It shows how little time you've been here,' she remarked, glancing at the biscuit-coloured suede coat he was wearing. 'You haven't even stayed long enough to take your coat off.'

'True.' He walked across the room to the door, Gill following him. 'Just long enough to get you to agree to have Donna for a weekend.'

'It'll be a pleasure,' said Gill. 'I shall look forward to it.'

'Thanks, Gill.'

She paused, remembering something. 'Oh, by the way, I had a letter from Cherry this morning.'

'Did you?' Arnie said with interest. 'How's she getting on?'

'She seems to be having a wonderful time,' she said. 'She's made friends at the music college and loves living in Boston.'

'All your efforts were worthwhile then,' he said.

'*Our* efforts . . . all of us.'

'Well, whatever,' he said lightly. 'But is she doing wild teenage things now that she's out of sight of the nuns?'

'No chance,' Gill said with a wry grin. 'She's staying at a local convent. The nuns at St Theresa's arranged for her to have a room there. They're all of the same order, apparently.'

'No wild parties for Cherry then.'

'Not for the moment, anyway.'

They were startled by a continuous ringing at the doorbell.

'That'll be Craig back from football, I expect,' said Gill, crossing to the front door. 'He must have forgotten his key.'

'Good. It'll give me a chance to say hello to him,' said Arnie.

Gill opened the door. 'Carol, hi!' she said with surprise and instinctive trepidation. 'I wasn't expecting to see you tonight.'

'Obviously not,' rasped Carol, pushing past her sister into the hall where Arnie was standing, her eyes wild with jealousy. 'Now, what have the pair of you got to say for yourselves?'

'What are you doing here, Carol?' asked Arnie, his eyes dark with dread.

'You were late home,' she said. 'I guessed you'd be here.'

'You drove here on a foggy night like this just because I was a few minutes late?'

'No, I drove here because I suspected you'd be with *her* and I had to know for sure,' she corrected, her voice rising hysterically. 'And I certainly know the truth now, don't I?'

'Where's Donna?' Arnie asked.

She stared at him blankly, in such a state of confusion that she could hardly remember where her daughter was. 'With my parents,' she said at last.

'Thank God for that,' he said, his voice dropping with relief. 'For a minute I thought she was in the car . . . that you'd driven the car with her in it, while you're in this state, and in this weather.'

'You're not talking your way out of this one by making out that I'm in some sort of a state,' Carol said, looking from Arnie to Gill with unveiled hatred. 'The cat really is out of the bag now.'

'Oh, don't be so bloody daft,' Arnie said with impatience. 'I called in to see Gill about—'

'About what, Arnie?' Carol said accusingly. 'Come on, let's see how creative you can be this time with your story.'

'Carol, please stop this,' Gill put in.

'Don't you talk to me, you cow.' Carol swung round on Gill and punched her hard in the face before clawing her cheek with her fingernails, drawing blood.

'Hey, now, calm down!' Arnie stepped forward and dragged her away from Gill. 'This has gone quite far enough, Carol.'

'What you two have been doing has gone too far for my liking,' Carol said, her face crumpling and voice breaking as she collapsed into tears. 'Well I've come to the end; I've had enough of it, do you understand? From now on you're welcome to each other.' Her voice was distorted with anguish. 'You've betrayed me and I want nothing more to do with either of you.'

'Carol, it isn't what you think,' said Arnie, recognising the depth of his wife's distress and softening towards her.

'Nothing's happened between us, I promise you,' said Gill, holding a handkerchief to her cheek to wipe away the blood. She was shocked by her sister's sudden display of raw despair. This had not been evident before. For the first time since all this began Gill perceived real pain, rather than just the tiresome ramblings of a neurotic woman seeking attention from her husband.

'Don't make things worse by insulting my intelligence,' Carol said, though the words were barely audible because she was sobbing so much. 'I'm not a fool.'

'What Gill says is true,' Arnie said emphatically, knowing now that he must tell the truth about why he was here. 'I only came here tonight to organise a surprise for you.'

'Oh, do me a favour,' Carol sobbed cynically. 'Which film did you pinch that from?'

'Please believe him,' Gill urged, her cheek smarting from the nail-wound and her head throbbing from the blow.

'Oh, shut up the pair of you!' Carol spat.

'You're torturing yourself for nothing, believe me' said Gill.

'I won't believe anything you say ever again,' Carol said.

'Please, Carol . . .'

'I never want to see either of you again.'

Crying loudly, she ran out of the front door with Arnie in hot pursuit.

He caught up with her at her car and put a restraining hand on her arm. 'Carol, you're wrong—'

'Don't touch me!' she cut in, her voice deep and guttural.

'But . . .'

In reply she brought her foot up and kicked him sharply on the shin. As he recoiled in agony she gave him a violent shove which sent him crashing to the frosty ground.

While her sister was helping him to his feet, Carol got into the car and roared off into the mist.

'I'll go after her,' Arnie said, scrambling to his feet.

'Yes, I think you'd better,' Gill agreed, feeling shaken.

'God knows what she'll do if she's at home on her own.'

In a state of shock and bewilderment, Gill stood in the freezing street watching Arnie's car disappear around the corner.

With the combined effects of tears, the patchy fog and an icy wind-screen, Carol's vision was seriously impaired as she headed for home, despite having got out of the car to scrape off ice that had quickly reformed. Peering ahead, her eyes narrowed in concentration, she drove towards the main road in a state of high anxiety.

Images of Gill and Arnie filled her mind, her venom towards them all-consuming. As for that story about him going to Gill's to arrange a surprise for her . . . Oh, really. Did they take her for a complete idiot?

If only it could be true, though. The thought was so pleasant, Carol lingered on the possibility of it being genuine. After all, it was still only early evening – an odd time of day for a romantic liaison, especially when he knew he had to get home to his wife.

Something else occurred to her too. Arnie had been wearing his outdoor coat, and had seemed about to leave. So he couldn't have been there long, because the shop didn't close until half past five, after which time he still had to cash up.

Don't be so naive, she told herself as she approached the main road – Arnie was there because he is in love with Gill and always will be.

The truth stayed in her mind with throbbing intensity. This was the first time she had accepted this as an actual fact rather than just a tormenting suspicion.

Whether or not they had actually been having an affair became irrelevant, as Carol finally accepted the painful fact that Arnie would never love her in the same way as he loved Gill, and there was nothing on God's earth she could do about it.

What a fool she had been to try. What a prize idiot she'd been to trap him into marriage in the first place. She'd been driving herself crazy with worry about them being together, when it would have made no difference to his feelings for Gill whether he was with Carol or not. Because he didn't just fancy Gill. He *loved* her. It was Gill he wanted to be with. Even though they hadn't been able to live together in harmony, they still wanted each other.

Tears rushed down her cheeks as the truth took root. But with this acceptance came a new feeling of peace, too, as she hit rock bottom, all hope of Arnie's love gone. She would be better off without him; she knew that now. But she didn't have the courage to try to manage on her own with a child to raise. God, what a mess she had created for herself – for all of them!

Engrossed in thought as she came to the junction with the main road, she gave a cursory glance to the right and saw only a bank of fog. In her preoccupied state she pulled out too swiftly . . .

The noise was deafening. The vehicle travelling from the right crashed into the side of hers with such force that both cars were shunted several yards from the point of impact.

The pain was so excruciating, Carol couldn't identify where she was hurting. She couldn't even cry out. Relief came only when she passed out, slumped over the steering wheel.

The noise of the impact of metal on metal had been muffled in the foggy night air. A line of cars soon began to form, stretching away from the crash site. Unaware of the cause, Arnie sat in the tailback, cursing the traffic.

Chapter Twenty-One

The medical team at Hammersmith Hospital was doing everything they possibly could for Carol, but she had sustained serious injuries, and the family had been told to prepare themselves for the worst.

'This is all my fault,' Gill said to Arnie in the early hours of the next morning, when they emerged from the side-ward to allow Winnie and Hal a few moments alone with their daughter, even though she was still unconscious.

Phoebe was at Arnie's place looking after Donna. Craig had come to the hospital with Gill but had now gone off in search of coffee for them all, needing a break from the tension, she suspected.

'What on earth makes you think that?' Arnie asked, sinking wearily on to a seat in the corridor, grey with worry, his eyes red and shadowed.

'I should have been more patient with her, tried harder to convince her that she was wrong to doubt us,' she said, sitting beside him, her mind still racing though she was physically exhausted.

'If I'd managed to do that she wouldn't have gone rushing off in a rage – and in no fit state to be driving in such dangerous weather conditions.'

Arnie shook his head. 'You've nothing to reproach yourself for,' he said firmly.

'She shouldn't have been at the wheel of a car, and she *wouldn't* have been if it hadn't been for her suspicions about us.'

'I'm to blame for the accident, Gill, not you,' said Arnie.

'But you had no more chance of calming her down than I did.'

'I'm not talking about what happened last night,' he said grimly. 'The cause of the trouble goes back further than that.'

She waited for him to continue.

'I should never have got involved with Carol in the first place, when I knew that affection was the most I could ever feel for her,' he explained. 'I think she's always known in her heart that it was you I wanted and not her. That's the cause of the obsession that drove her to the brink of insanity, and caused her to go out in her car on such a terrible night. If she and I had never got together, she wouldn't be at death's door now.'

'Oh, Arnie, you mustn't think like that,' Gill said with feeling. 'Carol was determined to have you at any price . . . and you've given her so

259

much. You've been a wonderful husband and a marvellous father to Donna. No man could have done more.'

'It wasn't enough to make up for the one thing I could never give her, though, was it?'

'You can't blame yourself for Carol's confused state of mind.'

'I can, because I caused it,' he said. 'I'm responsible for what happened to her last night, and nothing anyone says will make me believe otherwise.'

The conversation was interrupted by Gill's father, with the news that Carol had regained consciousness and was asking to see them.

Weak with nerves and hardly able to swallow because her throat was so dry and constricted, Gill followed Arnie to Carol's bed. She was barely recognisable. Her head was swathed in bandages, lips grotesquely cracked and swollen, cheeks grazed and blotched purple with bruising.

Winnie was sitting by the bed holding her daughter's hand. She got up and moved back so that Arnie could get near to his wife.

'Hi,' he said, gently taking her hand in both of his.

She opened her mouth as though to speak but was unable to. Visibly distressed by this, she shifted her head slightly, tears glistening.

'Don't try to talk, love,' Arnie said with infinite tenderness.

'Gill,' she managed to say after a great deal of effort.

'Gill's here.' He beckoned to Gill, who sat beside him, staying within her sister's range of vision which was limited because of her restricted head movement.

'You and Gill,' muttered Carol.

'Nothing's going on between us,' said Gill. 'I promise you.'

'I swear to you on my mother's life that I really did go to Gill's to ask her to help me in a surprise I'm planning for you,' Arnie said. 'She's agreed to look after Donna while I take you away for a weekend, just the two of us.' In a bizarre attempt to sound positive in a hopeless situation, he added, 'As soon as you get out of here we'll be off, just the two of us, for a weekend of self-indulgence.'

Carol managed a smile, more evident in her eyes than her mouth which was too sore to move more than a fraction. 'You and Gill,' she said again.

'There's nothing going on,' he told her again.

Clearly upset, she moved her head from side to side as far as she was able, to indicate that he had misunderstood her. 'I know now that I can never make you love me . . . because you're still in love with Gill,' she managed with a great deal of effort, her voice scratchy and barely audible.

'Oh, Carol, please don't,' Arnie said, huge tears rolling down his cheeks. The fact that he wasn't in love with her didn't stop him aching with sorrow. There was more than one way to love someone.

'You don't understand. I want you to be together now,' Carol said in a whisper, her lips hardly moving. 'It's the way it should be. And Donna will be happy with the two of you. I trust you to take good care of her for me.'

My God, she knows she's going to die, thought Gill, her blood running cold. She wants to bow out with good grace. She bit back the tears, hardly able to bear the pain. She couldn't move or speak, so she just sat there, frozen in the horror of the moment.

When she was able to function again a few moments later, Gill put her lips to Carol's brow just seconds before she slipped back into oblivion.

They were all with her when she died peacefully an hour or so later – all except Craig, who was overcome by youthful fear of death at such close range and retreated to the corridor.

Leaving the ward with the others in a stunned silence, Gill felt buffeted and broken inside. But she knew she must stay in control for the sake of her parents, whose suffering must surely be greater than her own; no parent expects to outlive their offspring. And, seeing Arnie so obviously tormented, she wondered how he was going to cope with the guilt of believing that he was responsible.

The shock-waves of Carol's death reverberated throughout the neighbourhood. She had only been twenty-nine years old.

The fact that it need never have happened made the pain even more intense for Gill. Carol hadn't been the most endearing person, especially lately, but she had been a part of Gill's life and her death left a void. She concentrated on comforting her parents to try to make herself feel better.

Surprisingly, her mother proved to be the soul of fortitide while her father shocked everyone by falling apart. The poor man was inconsolable. Even when the trauma of the funeral was over he couldn't contain his grief, and had to take time off work because of a tendency to weep on duty.

It was Arnie who worried Gill most of all, though. Deeply depressed, he seemed locked in a world of his own. Neither he nor Gill mentioned her sister's dying wish. Even apart from the fact that it didn't seem appropriate so soon after the death, Arnie's cool restraint towards her made it obvious that he wasn't interested in Gill other than as an aunt to his daughter, whom Gill looked after while he was at work, assisted by Winnie who helped out when she was teaching.

Gill was imbued with pity for Arnie. Carol's death alone was punishment enough, but to castigate himself for causing it must be living hell. She wanted desperately to help him, but he had created a barrier between them.

Despite her efforts to stifle a nagging feeling of resentment – that Arnie wasn't there for her when she needed him so badly – Gill couldn't help feeling let down. She didn't mention it to him until about two months after the funeral. The subject arose one day when he called at her house to collect Donna after work.

'I wanna stay here with Auntie Gill and Craig,' the little girl announced in recalcitrant mood, her saucer eyes resting on her father in a challenge.

'But you have to go home with Daddy now, sweetheart,' said Gill.

'Why?'

'Because it's where you live, darling, where all your things are . . . your toys and everything.'

'Don't wanna go,' Donna said, her mouth set determinedly. 'I like it here with you and Craig.'

'But Daddy will be lonely if he doesn't have his little girl at home with him,' said Gill persuasively.

'Won't.'

'He will,' said Gill.

'Don't care. I wanna stay here.'

'Put your coat on now, Donna,' Arnie intervened firmly, holding out the garment for her to put her arms in.

'No,' she said stubbornly.

'You'll do as you're told,' he said with noticeable impatience.

Giving him a reproving look, Gill said to Donna, 'Will you be a good girl and go into the living room with Craig for a few minutes – while Daddy and I have a little talk?'

The child scampered off and Gill led Arnie into the kitchen and closed the door behind them.

'There's no point in getting angry because your daughter wants to be with me instead of you,' she said, sitting down at the table and indicating for him to do the same.

'It's annoying when she won't do as she's told, that's all,' Arnie said.

'She's a little girl who's lost her mother and is with me all day while you're at work,' Gill said. 'It's natural she wants to stay because she feels secure here. And if you're no more cheerful at home than you are outside of it, then she's better off staying here.'

'I'm doing my best,' he said, staring at his clasped hands on the table.

'If losing your temper with her as soon as she shows the slightest resistance to what you want her to do is your best, then I don't think you're trying hard enough.'

'You're probably right,' Arnie said in a defeated way that twisted Gill's heart. 'I'm failing her like I did her mother.'

'You didn't fail Carol, and you're not failing Donna,' she told him. 'If you're failing anyone, it's me.'

He looked up sharply, his eyes resting on her questioningly.

'By pretending there's nothing between us,' she explained.

'Oh, that,' he said dully.

'Yes, *that*. It was painful enough staying apart when you were married to Carol. Don't let's punish ourselves by doing the same thing now that she isn't around,' she said. 'All right, so our marriage didn't work out. But neither did the divorce. It didn't kill what we had between us.'

'It was what we had that killed Carol . . .'

'It was her insane jealousy that killed her,' Gill said, having given the matter a great deal of thought over the last couple of months, and having come to the conclusion that neither of them was to blame for what Carol had brought on herself. 'She would have been paranoid about you even if there had never been anything between us. She was that sort of a person. She needed so much love . . . too much. The man hasn't been born who could satisfy Carol.'

'I'm better off without a woman in my life anyway,' Arnie said grumpily. 'This way I can't ruin things for anyone else.'

'What about Carol's last wish?'

'She was seriously ill. She didn't know what she was saying.'

'I believe she did.'

'That's something we'll never know,' he said, shrugging his shoulders.

Gill studied her nails, wondering where to go next with this conversation. 'Has Carol's death changed your feelings towards me?' she asked.

'Having her death on my conscience dominates me to such an extent, I hardly know what I feel any more,' he confessed, his skin tinged with a terrible pallor even now. 'The guilt is already bad enough. It would be a thousand times worse if you and I were to get back together.'

'Carol's dead, Arnie,' she said. 'You can't hurt her now.'

'Guilt about Carol isn't the only thing I have to contend with.'

'You mean you're afraid to commit yourself to anyone again?'

'It scares the hell out of me,' he readily admitted. 'No relationship, no complications.'

'That's no way to live.'

'I'll only screw up like I did before and you'll get hurt,' he said. 'This way will be safer for us both.'

'You're going to spend the rest of your life running away, then?'

He looked at her broodingly. 'If you like,' he said. 'But I'd sooner do it than wreck your life.'

'And I have no say in the matter?'

'Look, Gill, there's a little girl in the other room who doesn't have a mother because of me,' he said, his voice quivering with emotion. 'My son was brought up without his father in the family home because I ruined our marriage. I'm a walking disaster and I've done enough damage. I don't want to do any more.'

'What about me?' she enquired. 'Don't my feelings count for anything?'

'They count for everything,' he said hoarsely. 'I want to be with you more than anything else in the world. To be a family with you and

263

Donna and Craig is all I could ever want from life. But it would be the wrong thing to do.'

'I can see why you feel this way,' she said compassionately, 'but I don't think you're right.'

'It's time I stopped acting on instinct, doing what I want to do regardless of the consequences,' he told her gravely. 'It's time I did what I know is right.'

'Oh.' Gill couldn't help feeling dejected as it became more obvious that he was immovable on the subject.

'I'm sorry if I've been off-hand with you lately,' he said with genuine contrition.

'You're sorry, but you're still going to hurt me?' she said.

'I have to, Gill,' he said from the heart. 'I've needed you *so much*, and I knew you needed me – but I also knew that I would hurt you more in the long run if I didn't keep my distance.'

'None of us have been thinking straight after the shock of Carol's death,' she said. 'But I do know that you and I should be together, Arnie. It's what Carol wanted at the end.'

'It wouldn't work.'

Although she was deeply hurt and didn't agree with his logic, she knew it would be wrong to try to persuade him to act against his principles. This was something he obviously felt strongly about and must work out for himself. 'All right, Arnie, if that's the way you really want it, then that's how it will be,' she said, standing up with an air of finality and changing the subject. 'Now, about Donna – would it be a good idea to let her stay overnight here on the evenings that you're going to be late back from work? It's so late for her by the time you get her home and into bed.'

'I'd miss her.'

'You could always call in and see her on your way home if she's still awake,' Gill said. 'At least she wouldn't have to be dragged out in all weathers when she's tired.'

He still looked doubtful.

'It would probably be the best thing for her,' she pointed out.

'Yeah, I suppose so,' Arnie said with a sigh of resignation. 'Shall I let her stay tonight as she really wants to, or would that be giving in to her?'

'Let her stay,' Gill advised. 'By the time you get her home she'll be thoroughly overtired.'

'It's very good of you to look after her for me. I do appreciate it,' he said. 'It can't always be easy, what with teaching and everything.'

'My mum's a great help,' she said. 'And I enjoy having Donna. It's lovely having a little girl around the house.' She paused and gave him a small grin. 'I've managed to get her to do something I was never able to get Craig to do.'

'Really?'

'Yes. She's let me teach her a little tune on the piano,' she said. 'Only a very easy one, but it's a start.'

'Oh, you must be really chuffed,' Arnie said, brightening. 'Craig was always a non-starter in that direction.'

'He's never had any time for anything except football,' she said. 'But Donna really seems to like it. She's been pestering the life out of me to teach her some more.'

'That's Donna,' he laughed. 'She knows what she wants and goes all out to get it.'

Just like her mother, thought Gill. But she said, 'I'll say she does.'

'Thanks anyway, Gill, for looking after her,' he said.

'I'm glad to be in a position to do so,' she said. 'It's what Carol would have wanted.'

'Yes.'

There was an awkward silence as they both remembered Carol's last words.

'Let's go and tell Donna she can stay here tonight, then, shall we?' Gill said, stifling the need to cry at the sheer sadness of everything.

'Yeah, let's do that.'

They went into the other room, both feeling emotionally exhausted after such a highly charged interlude.

One day in April, when Winnie was shopping in Hammersmith, she was struck with a sudden unexpected longing for a chat with Phoebe Briscoe.

Not normally an impulsive woman, today she found herself inside the shop before she'd had time to think about it.

'I hope I'm not imposing,' she said, having been taken to the office where Phoebe and Len were working at their desks. 'But I just . . .' Her voice tailed off. She could hardly believe she had been so hasty in coming, and now she wasn't at all sure why she was here. 'Er . . . I felt like a chat, but it doesn't matter. I can see that you're busy. Silly of me to call to see you at work . . .'

'Don't be daft, love,' said Phoebe warmly. 'We're pleased to see you.'

She exchanged a glance with Len, who immediately caught on. 'Course we are,' he said, standing up. 'I've got something I need to do in the shop anyway . . .' He paused, looking at Winnie whom he had last seen at Carol's funeral. 'How are you now, ducks?'

'Oh, bearing up, you know,' she said, embarrassed to have burst in on them like this and painfully aware that Len was about to make himself scarce for her benefit. She couldn't imagine what had possessed her to come in off the street to talk to a woman she had never even liked.

'Cuppa tea?' Phoebe offered, smiling that warm smile of hers.

Winnie opened her mouth to reply and collapsed in tears instead, sobbing loudly and uncontrollably.

Phoebe put her arms around her and held her. 'There, there. Let go and let it all out, love,' she soothed.

'Oh dear,' Winnie said when she was able to get a word out, mopping her face with her handkerchief and drawing back from Phoebe. 'I really don't know what's got into me today. This isn't like me at all. I'm ever so sorry.'

'Don't apologise,' said Phoebe. 'I expect you've been bottling up your feelings ever since Carol died. You had to let go sometime.'

'You're probably right,' Winnie agreed, blowing her nose. 'I got this sudden urge to talk to someone, and you must have come to mind because I was near the shop. Sorry to burden you . . .'

'You're not burdening me.' Phoebe was emphatic about this. 'I'm only too pleased to help. You should have come to see me before. We live in the same street; you only had to pop over . . .'

'I never thought . . .'

'It sometimes helps to talk to someone outside of your immediate family.'

'It just never entered my head,' Winnie said. 'I can't talk to Hal or Gill about how I *really* feel because I don't want to upset them any more than they are already.'

'You've been so busy being strong for everyone else, you've neglected your own feelings.'

'I suppose I must have,' she agreed. 'I've been worried sick about Hal. He's taken Carol's death so badly.'

'So I've heard.'

'Being the strong one has helped me to cope somehow.'

'But today you need someone to lean on,' said Phoebe.

'Yes, today I do,' she said.

'And the family isn't always the answer at a time like this, 'cause you're all hurting too much,' Phoebe said kindly. 'I mean, I was devastated by Carol's death, of course, but it isn't quite the same as losing my own child.' She shook her head. 'I can't even begin to imagine what it would be like to lose Arnie or John.'

'And I couldn't begin to describe it,' said Winnie. 'I don't think I'll ever get over it.'

'I don't suppose you will, dear,' said Phoebe thoughtfully. 'But the pain will lessen in time, I expect. It's nature's way, isn't it? And if it helps to talk about it, come and see me. You're welcome any time.'

'I've been feeling so queer, sort of tight inside,' said Winnie, 'and I couldn't seem to shed a tear.'

'Thank God you've managed it now,' said Phoebe, adding with a grin, 'That's what I do to people. One look at me and they burst into tears.'

'Oh, Phoebe,' said Winnie, laughing and crying simultaneously, 'you are a case.'

'At least I've brought a smile to your face,' she said. 'Now I'll pop out to the kitchen and make some tea.'

When she returned, Winnie said, 'I'll go as soon as I've had this. You'll be wanting to get on with your work . . .'

'Relax and have your tea,' said Phoebe. 'I'll catch up later.'

Glad of the drink to moisten her parched mouth, Winnie sipped thirstily.

'Arnie's taken Carol's death very hard,' remarked Phoebe. 'He's gone right into himself. He's like a different man now . . . so quiet and withdrawn.'

'Yet they weren't the happiest of couples, were they?' said Winnie. 'No.'

'It was always Arnie and Gill, even though they were divorced,' said Winnie. 'Carol just couldn't cope with that.'

'Actually, I thought Arnie and Gill would turn to each other for comfort, but they don't seem to have done it yet.'

'Perhaps they think it's too soon after her death to get back together,' suggested Winnie.

'I think it might be more than that,' said Phoebe, her brow creasing into a frown. 'He hasn't said much about it to me, but I get the impression that Arnie blames himself for Carol's death. I reckon that's what's keeping them apart.'

'That's terrible.' Winnie frowned. 'He shouldn't punish himself that way.'

'I agree with you, but we daren't interfere,' said Phoebe.

'No.'

'This is something he and Gill have to work out for themselves.'

'Yes,' agreed Winnie, pausing for a moment as she remembered her youngest daughter's dying wish. 'I'm afraid you're right.'

She left the shop shortly afterwards feeling better than she had in ages, warmed by the knowledge that she could call on Phoebe at any time and receive a genuine welcome. After all these years, the woman she had always disapproved of had become her friend. It was a wonderful feeling.

One evening the following week, Phoebe and Len were drinking coffee at Phoebe's place, having been to the cinema to see *The French Connection*.

'I enjoyed the car chase,' said Phoebe. 'That was the best part of the film for me. How about you?'

'Er . . . yeah. It was quite entertaining,' Len said in a preoccupied manner.

'What's up?' Phoebe asked, noticing that he wasn't nearly as chatty as usual. 'You've been a bit quiet all evening. Things on your mind?'

'Mm.'

'Oh dear,' she said, immediately concerned. 'Well, you know what they say about a trouble shared . . .'

'It isn't really a trouble,' he said, stroking his chin ponderously. 'More a decision I am trying to come to.'

'Same thing applies,' she said, her blue eyes bright with friendliness, bleached hair dramatically corn-coloured in the electric light. 'But if you'd rather not talk about it . . .'

That's Phoebe, Len thought affectionately – ever respectful of his privacy and careful not to intrude upon his space. In all the years they had been going out together, she had never once ventured beyond a certain point in her attitude towards him, because he had made it clear at the beginning that that was what he wanted.

But just lately Len had not been happy with the present arrangement. He had found himself wishing she was with him all the time, rather than just going out together and staying at each other's places occasionally. He often found he wanted to share a passing thought with her, or a joke. The other night he'd actually started to say something to her about something he was watching on the television, before realising that she wasn't there.

She'd become important to him so gradually that he hadn't noticed it happening. But she was an independent lady used to managing her own affairs, having brought up her sons single-handedly. Admittedly he had made the rules at the beginning, but she seemed quite content with the way things were. Maybe she wouldn't welcome a change.

'Oh, I want to talk about it all right,' he said now, looking worried.

'What's stopping you then?'

'I'm not quite sure what your reaction will be.'

'Oh Gawd, Len,' she said anxiously, 'I don't like the sound of that. I hope you're not gonna give me notice at the shop.'

'That's the last thing—'

'Thank God for that, 'cause I love my job.' She threw him a sharp look. 'But if it isn't that, what is it?'

He took a deep breath. 'I was wondering what you'd think about us . . . er, getting married,' he said.

'Well, it's taken you long enough to get round to asking me,' she said, grinning even though there were tears in her eyes.

'It has?'

'I'll say it has,' she said, her voice cracked with emotion. 'If you'd left it much longer I'd have been too old to get myself all glammed up for the wedding.'

'Not you, Phoebe. You'll never be too old to be the star of the show,' he said, adding hesitantly, 'But is that a yes?'

'You bet it's a yes,' she said, standing up with her arms open to him, her face wreathed in smiles. 'Come here, you daft bugger, and I'll show you just how much of a yes it is!'

Chapter Twenty-Two

'What's wrong, love?' Winnie enquired. Gill had called in to see her mother after shopping in North End Road market. Donna was at nursery school and Gill's father was out at work, so the two women were alone.

'Nothing.'

'Oh, come off it . . .'

'I've come to see how *you* are, not to burden you with *my* problems.'

'Don't worry about me,' said Winnie, 'I'm all right.'

'Yes, you're looking a lot better,' Gill remarked, noticing that her mother was much less emaciated than she'd been in the period immediately following Carol's death. There was colour in her cheeks again too. 'Being pally with Phoebe seems to agree with you.'

'It does.'

'What a pity she's moved to Len's place now that they're married. Just when you and she had made friends.'

'Still, she's only a bus-ride away,' Winnie said. 'And just knowing she's on the end of a telephone has made a lot of difference to me.'

'It's odd, the two of you becoming friends now that she's moved out of Maisie Road,' remarked Gill, 'after living in the same street for all those years and never much liking each other.'

'Yeah, it's funny how things work out,' agreed Winnie. 'I was a bit overawed by her until recently. She always seemed too full of herself for my liking. I was probably jealous of her if the truth is known, her being so sociable and popular, but I get on really well with her now that I've got to know her better.'

'I'm glad.'

'She's the first close woman friend I've had since before I was married,' Winnie went on. 'I was always too wrapped up with the family to bother about making friends. But it's nice having a female of my own age to talk to.'

'It must be.'

Outside it was cold and grey, with rolling clouds and rain in the air; inside they were cosily ensconced in armchairs either side of Winnie's living-room fire with coffee and biscuits.

'But don't change the subject,' said Winnie, fixing her daughter with a penetrating look. 'I asked you what was up.'

'What makes you so sure that anything's the matter?'

'I'm your mother,' she said, as though that was sufficient explanation.

271

'Oh, well, you'll get to know soon enough anyway, I suppose,' sighed Gill, cradling her coffee mug in her hands and regarding her mother thoughtfully. 'But don't say anything to Phoebe in case Arnie hasn't mentioned it to her yet . . .'

'About what?'

'He's moving away from London.'

'*Never in a million years!*' Winnie exclaimed, eyes wide with shock.

'It's surprising, I know, but it's true.'

'But Arnie would be like a fish out of water anywhere else.'

'That's what I think, but he seems determined to go,' said Gill. 'He wants to make a fresh start somewhere else with Donna.'

'Oh, that poor child,' Winnie said, shaking her head and tutting loudly. 'First she loses her mother, now she's going to lose you . . . and me, on a daily basis anyway.'

'I'm worried to death about her,' Gill confessed. 'Well, about them both really. I'm sure he's making a big mistake.'

'I'm certain of it.' Winnie sipped her coffee. 'Where's he going?'

'He doesn't know yet,' said Gill. 'He's still looking for a job in the trade journals. He doesn't seem to care where he goes, as long as it's away from London and all the bad memories. And, more importantly, away from me.'

'You?'

'That's right . . . He thinks his feelings for me caused Carol's death.'

'That's plain stupid.'

'He's got it into his head that it would be wrong for us to get back together, and it will be easier if he isn't around.'

'And you?'

'I've never stopped loving him.'

'I know that,' said Winnie, 'but will his going away make it easier for you?'

'I shouldn't think so. While he's around there's always a chance,' she said, 'once he's gone we'll drift even further apart.'

'Mm.'

'But my main concern in all this is Donna.'

'Poor little mite.'

'The trouble is, he really believes that his leaving London is the right thing for all of us,' Gill said, her dark eyes full of sorrow. 'He's making a sacrifice that he thinks will stop me being hurt, but he's hurting us all by doing it, not least himself.'

'There must be something you can do to make him change his mind.'

Gill gave a slow shake of the head, emitting a lengthy sigh. 'I've already tried,' she said. 'But there's nothing anyone can do. He's made up his mind and that's all there is to it.'

We'll see about that, thought Winnie. 'That man is his own worst enemy,' she said.

'You can say that again,' agreed Gill.

That same evening, Winnie took the tube to Chiswick Park station and walked to Arnie's house in the rain. Not wanting to worry Hal with the problem in the hope of solving it herself, she had told him she was popping over to Gill's for an hour or so. She didn't telephone Arnie to say she was coming in case he tried to put her off; and had guessed he would be at home because of Donna, who only stayed overnight at Gill's sometimes.

He seemed surprised to see her, but greeted her warmly. 'You're out of luck if you've come to see your granddaughter because she's fast asleep,' he told her, taking her raincoat and hanging it up in the cupboard.

'It's you I've come to see,' Winnie told him, sitting in an armchair in the living room. 'And I'll come straight to the point.'

'Cuppa tea?'

'In a minute, when we've had a talk.'

'Oh,' he said, sitting down opposite her.

She could see how tormented he was by the tension around his eyes and the grim set of his mouth.

'I've heard you're thinking of moving away,' she said.

'That's right.'

'You want your brains testing.'

'With respect, I think that's for me to decide,' he told her.

'If you were the only one affected, that would be quite true. But you're not, which is why I feel justified in interfering,' she said. 'You're going to hurt a lot of people by doing this, Arnie, particularly my daughter and my granddaughter. Donna needs people she loves around her at the moment. It would be cruel to take her away.'

'She's young enough to adjust, which is why I think I should do it now rather than later,' he said.

'Why do it at all?'

'I can't stay around here, Winnie,' he said forcefully. 'So the sooner we go the better – before Donna starts school, when a disruption really would be upsetting for her.'

'And all this because you blame yourself for Carol's death?'

'Mainly, yes,' he said, too distressed to wonder how she knew.

'But you can't take a thing like that on your shoulders, son,' she said in a kindly tone.

Looking up sharply, Arnie said, 'I should have thought you would jump at the chance to blame me. You never wanted me as a son-in-law.'

'I admit that at one time I didn't think you were good enough for either of my daughters,' she said. 'You were a right tearaway when you were young and you've made plenty of mistakes over the years, including breaking Gill's heart . . .'

273

'Exactly.'

'But this last few years you've changed and I've seen you in a new light.'

His brows rose in surprise.

'You were a damned fine husband to Carol,' she continued. 'You did everything you possibly could to give her and Donna a good life.'

'It was my duty.'

'I saw the patient way you dealt with Carol's tantrums and her demanding nature,' Winnie continued. 'You never put a foot wrong when you had every provocation, especially as it was Gill you really wanted.'

'That obvious, eh?'

'To people who know you, yeah.'

'Unfortunately Carol knew it too – and that's why she died,' he said.

'That simply isn't true, Arnie,' Winnie said emphatically.

'She shouldn't have been out driving—'

'She was a full-grown adult with a mind of her own,' Winnie interrupted with feeling. 'You couldn't have stopped her going out in the fog that night any more than I could. You know as well as I do that Carol always did exactly what she wanted and no one on earth could make her do otherwise if she'd set her mind on a thing. As much as I loved my daughter, I wasn't blind to her faults. I brought her up, remember. I know just how difficult she could be.'

'Even so—'

'From what I can make out she was torturing herself unnecessarily about something that wasn't happening.'

'You're right about that.'

'So your conscience should be clear.'

'It isn't as simple as that.'

Winnie sighed. 'Don't break Gill's heart a second time, please, Arnie,' she entreated.

'That's what I'm trying to avoid.'

'You won't avoid it by going away,' she said. 'She wants you to be together. Don't let her down by turning your back on her. It's what Carol wanted at the end – the two of you together with the children.'

His brows rose questioningly.

'I was in the room . . . I heard her last words,' Winnie explained.

'She was very sick at the time.'

'She meant what she said, though. I'd stake my life on it.'

Arnie leant forward with his elbows on his knees, hands clasped. 'I can't explain how I feel,' he said. 'There's something deep inside of me that says it's wrong for Gill and me to be happy together. As you said, I've made enough mistakes. I don't want to make another. I have to do what I believe to be right.'

'You feel you have to be made to suffer for Carol's death?'

'Yes, I suppose that's about the size of it,' he said.

'And Gill and Donna and Craig have to be punished too?'

'Donna won't suffer, I'll make sure of that. And Craig's almost grown up now, he has a life of his own. Anyway, he's old enough to come and visit us on his own.'

'It won't be the same, though,' Winnie said. 'You've always lived near enough to have a close relationship with him. Don't throw it away.'

'Look, I know you mean well, Winnie, but I have to work this thing out for myself,' he said, standing up suddenly in an obvious state of anxiety. 'I'll make us some tea.'

'Not for me, thanks,' she said sadly, knowing there was nothing more she could say to persuade him. A change of heart had to come from within him. 'I'd better be getting off home. I've said my piece. That's all I came for.'

'I'll run you back,' he offered. 'It's a terrible night.'

'I'd rather make me own way, thanks,' she said. 'I need to be on my own for a while.'

'As you wish,' Arnie said, and showed her to the door, his limp noticeable as it always was at the end of the day.

Gales of laughter and the sound of a tinkling piano drifted from inside the house in Danny Gardens. Arnie rung the doorbell and waited on the doorstep in the smoky autumn dusk for someone to let him in to collect his daughter. He'd left the shop earlier than usual today, with the intention of spending more time with Donna before he put her to bed.

He wanted to get into the habit of doing this. When they moved away from London Donna would have someone other than Gill or Winnie looking after her while he was at work. Then it would be vital to spend as much time as he possibly could with his daughter.

His heart lurched at the thought of Donna in the care of a stranger. Soon she would be starting full-time school, but he still needed someone to collect her and look after her until he got home from work, and to be on hand in the holidays. A nanny cum housekeeper would be his best bet.

Winnie's visit last week had really set him thinking. Although he still couldn't agree with her about his staying in London, he had thought of little else but making sure Donna had a happy and secure future.

'Hi, Dad,' Craig said, opening the door and standing back for his father to enter, a smile lingering on his face as though he was still amused by some recent happening.

'Wotcha, son,' Arnie said. 'What's so funny?'

'Donna,' said Craig affectionately. 'You're just in time to hear her doing her stuff at the piano. Mum finished with her pupils early, so the two of them are having some fun.'

'I didn't think it sounded like an ordinary lesson,' remarked Arnie.

'Mum says Donna has a lot of potential, but I don't think she's gonna be entering any competitions just yet awhile.'

'She's much too little for anything like that,' said Arnie fondly.

'Yeah.' Craig glanced towards the closed door of the music room, from where the first few notes of 'Twinkle Twinkle Little Star' could be vaguely distinguished. 'You'd better go on in. I don't think Mum heard the doorbell.'

'She wasn't expecting me to be here this early,' he explained.

'I must get on, Dad,' Craig was already heading for the stairs. 'I have to get my gear ready for football training.'

'Okay, son.'

Arnie opened the music-room door and was instantly overwhelmed by an atmosphere of affection, so strong and sweet it brought a lump to his throat. Gill and Donna were seated side-by-side at the piano with their backs to the door, far too engrossed in what they were doing to have heard him come in.

He stood in the doorway, soothed and softened by the special essence of this room. It was not a tidy chamber by any means. Sheet music and primers were piled around the room in varying degrees of disorder; Gill's desk was littered with paperwork – she had always been a more dedicated musician than she was office worker.

Donna's small body was rigid with concentration as Gill showed her which notes to play. She hit a wrong key and giggles erupted before Gill gently corrected her, leaning over and kissing Donna's head in a natural action. More concentration, more laughter . . .

Arnie tried to curb the flow of tears. But he was so unbearably moved by their unity, the rightness of their being together, that he couldn't hold back. How could he have even thought of taking Donna away? She needed Gill and Craig. And Arnie needed them all. Carol had known and accepted this before she died.

Suddenly a future with Gill didn't seem wrong and selfish but the only right thing to do.

His thoughts were interrupted by Craig's exuberant tones booming from upstairs. 'Mu-m! Where are my football shorts?' he called urgently. 'They were in my sports bag and they've disappeared.'

Gill turned around to shout back to him and saw Arnie standing in the doorway. 'Arnie! I didn't realise you were here,' she said in surprise.

'Daddy!' Donna whooped, slipping off her chair and tearing towards him, throwing her arms around his legs and clutching him.

'Hello sweetheart,' he said thickly, sweeping her into his arms and kissing her.

'I'm playing toons,' she said proudly.

'I've been listening,' he said. 'You're doing very well.'

Donna peered into his face. 'Why are your eyes watering, Daddy?' she asked.

'Because I'm happy,' he said.

276

Craig's voice bellowed down the stairs again. 'Mu-m . . .'

'They're washed and ironed and in the airing cupboard!' she shouted.

'Oh!' he called back. 'I didn't realise they were dirty.'

'Dirty!' she screeched in amusement. 'I've seen less mud on the Thames riverbed at low tide.'

'They weren't that bad . . .'

'Give me strength,' said Gill, tutting affectionately. 'That boy wouldn't notice mud if I filled his bed with it.'

Donna struggled out of her father's arms and bounded up the stairs to Craig.

'Gill,' Arnie said, moving into the room and looking at her solemnly.

'What is it, Arnie?' she asked, frowning. 'You look worried.'

'Can you ever forgive me?'

Her heart fluttered, but she was afraid to raise her hopes. 'It depends which particular sin you are referring to,' she said, teasing him.

'For everything I've done to hurt you over the years, and especially for not being there for you since Carol died,' he said.

'Oh, Arnie,' she breathed.

'I've been confused and I'm so very sorry for everything,' he said softly. 'Please let me put things right.'

'I might consider it,' she said, slipping her arms around him. 'But only if you're very good and you stop all this talk about moving away.'

'I don't know how I could have even considered it,' he said, kissing her. 'This is where I'm meant to be, with you and the children.'

One spring afternoon the following year, Gill and Arnie and their family and friends were gathered in a stand at Wembley Stadium to watch Craig play football in the National Schoolboys' Cup Final. Pale sunshine slanted across the green and hallowed Wembley turf. The stands were resonant with the exuberance of youth, the adult contingent mostly made up of relatives of the players and PE teachers. The atmosphere was warm and vibrant, the excitement rising as the game drew towards the end of the first half.

'Come on you whites!' yelled Arnie, cheering on his son's team.

'Come on whites,' echoed Donna who was sitting on her father's shoulders.

'Get in there, Craig!' shouted Arnie. 'Go on, shoot, boy! Go on . . . Yes! Nice one!'

'Well done, Craig!' Gill shouted proudly, jumping up and down and squealing with excitement as her son scored a goal, then throwing her arms around Arnie in jubilation.

Sitting on Gill's other side were Hal and Winnie, next to Phoebe and Len.

'Makes you wanna weep with pride for our grandson, doesn't it,

Win?' said Phoebe, shouting to make herself heard above the roar of the crowd.

'Not half!'

'Things worked out all right in the end for our two eldest,' said Phoebe.

'Yeah,' said Winnie, adding sadly, 'I'm still grieving for Carol, but at least Gill seems settled at last.'

Phoebe nodded. 'She and Arnie seem to be getting it right the second time around,' she said.

'They've had time to grow up since they got married the first time,' said Winnie.

'True.'

'Looks like you'll be having another wedding in the family before long,' said Winnie, peering beyond her friend to where John Briscoe was sitting with his arm around a pretty young woman with long blonde hair. 'He's had that same girlfriend for ages, hasn't he?'

'Yeah, they have been knocking about together for quite a while. I hope he settles down with her,' said Phoebe.

'She seems nice.'

'She's a lovely girl, and they get on well together. Of course it doesn't necessarily follow that they'll get married. People don't always bother these days.'

'It's all changed since we were young.'

'A different world.'

'You've never regretted marrying for the second time, have you, Phoebe?'

'I'll say I haven't,' she said. 'I've never been happier than I am with Len.'

A roar from the crowd drowned their chatter as a goal was almost scored. They turned their attention back to the game, comfortable with each other and glad to be friends.

At half-time the others went to stretch their legs, while Gill and Arnie stayed in their seats drinking Coca-cola and chatting. Donna went in search of ice cream with her two adoring grannies.

'Craig is so much like you were when you were young, on the football pitch, Arnie,' she said. 'It's almost uncanny.'

'Is he?'

'I'll say he is,' she said. 'It really takes me back.'

'Seeing him out there takes me back to my playing days an' all,' he said. 'He's achieved something I never managed and he's only fifteen.'

'What's that?'

'He's playing on Wembley turf,' he told her wistfully.

'Yes, of course,' she said, recalling a time when Arnie couldn't have spoken about the tragic end to his career without bitterness. 'It was tough luck your coming out of football the year before Borough FC got into the cup final.'

'Yeah, it was. Still, it's just the luck of the draw, innit?'

Gill remembered how trauamatised he'd been at the time. How long ago those dark days seemed now. And how good it was that he was now able to embrace the game again, albeit only as a spectator and ardent fan of his son.

'Maybe you'll achieve your cup final dream vicariously through Craig,' she said, with a smile in her voice that made him turn to her in surprise.

Craig had recently received an offer from Arnie's old football club to join them as an apprentice player when he left school. Their scouts had seen him play on several occasions and were eager to sign him up with the idea of developing his talent for a future as a professional player. Very few boys were offered such an opportunity, and he'd been thrilled.

His joy had been marred, however, by Gill's insistence that he should have a steady job. He'd been bitterly disappointed by her reaction. They all knew how much he wanted to accept the offer, but he said he would turn it down if it was going to upset his mother.

'You mean . . . ?' Arnie said now.

'I've been giving it a lot of thought,' she said ponderously.

'And . . . ?'

'And after seeing him play today, I've realised that I don't have the right to stand in his way,' she said.

'Oh, Gill, I'm really chuffed – and so will Craig be.'

'He's more than just good – he's brilliant. And a special talent like that must be developed,' she said. 'As Cherry was born to play the piano, so Craig was born to play football.'

'You've no need to worry about Craig,' said Arnie, 'he won't ruin his chances like I did, he's far too sensible.'

'I know now that he stands more chance of ruining his life in a steady job,' she said. 'Because his heart wouldn't be in it. He'd always be thinking of what he'd missed because of me.'

'I can't disagree with you about that,' Arnie said. 'My career as a footballer may have been short, but I wouldn't have missed it for anything.'

'As soon as the match is over I'm going to give him my blessing to go ahead and accept their offer,' she said.

'You'll make him the happiest lad on the planet,' he said, smiling at her and thanking God for this second chance with her.

'The teams are coming out for the second half,' Gill said, looking towards the pitch to see the youngsters resuming their positions.

The others returned to their seats, and Donna decided to sit on Winnie's lap as the second half got under way. Gill had only a distant view of her son from where they were in the stands, but she could see that he was in his element. Her heart swelled with pride as she watched him go into action, the personification of his father at a younger age.

As she was rummaging in her handbag for a handkerchief to dry her tears, Arnie took her hand. Together they watched their son capture the heart of the crowd, a golden future ahead of him.